Shifting, Swirling HERitage

Edited by D. J. Stevenson

Bluetrix
Books

Shifting, Swirling HERitage

Published by Bluetrix Books
www.BluetrixBooks.com

"The Mercury 13" © 2024 by Rigel Ailur
"A Winter's Day" © 2024 by Lorraine J. Anderson
"The Ghosts of Bhopal" © 2024 by Rasana Atreya
"History is Written by the Losers" © 2024 by Diana Dru Botsford
"The Harvest Moon" © 2024 by Deborah Daughetee
"Ostraka" © 2024 by Dana Fredsti
"The Shield Maidens" © 2024 by Carrie Harris
"'Victoria for President,' Says Nellie Bly" © 2024 by Rosemary Jones
"The Empire Builder's Wife" © 2024 by Shabana Kayum
"The Way of Water: Jeanne's Resurrection" © 2024 by Donna J. W. Munro
"Our Lady of the Gatling Gun" © 2024 by Marsheila Rockwell
"Playing the Long Game" © 2024 by Susan Shwartz
"The Phoenix Dynasty" © 2024 by Mariah Southworth
Introduction © 2024 by D. J. Stevenson
"The Woman Who Would Be Queen" © 2024 by Laura Ware
"J'ai Deux Amours" © 2024 by K. Ceres Wright

Cover art and design, interior art © 2024 by Kathleen Hardy

ISBN-13: 979-8-32527-153-3

Copyrighted material. All rights reserved. Please do not reproduce in part or in whole without the express prior written consent of the author.

All events in this work are fiction. All references to persons living or dead are fictionalized.

Shifting, Swirling
HERitage

Table of Contents

Introduction i
    by D. J. Stevenson
The Harvest Moon 1
    by Deborah Daughetee
"Victoria for President," Says Nellie Bly 21
    by Rosemary Jones
The Ghosts of Bhopal 41
    by Rasana Atreya
A Winter's Day 73
    by Lorraine J. Anderson
The Phoenix Dynasty 99
    by Mariah Southworth
The Empire Builder's Wife 129
    by Shabana Kayum
History is Written by the Losers 159
    by Diana Dru Botsford
The Mercury 13 193
    by Rigel Ailur
Ostraka 225
    by Dana Fredsti
The Woman Who Would Be Queen 239
    by Laura Ware
J'ai Deux Amours 269
    by K. Ceres Wright
Our Lady of the Gatling Gun 299
    by Marsheila Rockwell
Playing the Long Game 327
    by Susan Shwartz
The Shield Maidens 355
    by Carrie Harris
The Way of Water: Jeanne's Resurrection 373
    by Donna J. W. Munro
Tellers of the Time-Twisting Tales 401
    Author Biographies
Acknowledgements 407

Introduction
D. J. Stevenson

Welcome to *Shifting, Swirling HERitage*! I'd toyed with this concept for a long time. I love history, real history. I love alternate history. I love science fiction. I also *really* love stories that don't marginalize women by objectifying them or turning them into plot points or props instead of depicting them as vibrant characters with their own agency. I believe a person should write what they want to read, and these are the kinds of stories I love to read. Even better, I found a wonderful bunch of insanely talented writers who agreed with me.

The mission—and these fifteen women chose to accept it—to depict a change to a specific point in history so that the new outcome shows a marked and permanent improvement to women's cultural standing and the roles women play in society.

These stories came from that idea. The tales needed to be positive and optimistic and hopeful. Although they could be incredibly intense, no downers allowed; only uplifting. Our version of making right what once went wrong.

The setup created two particularly daunting challenges. The question wasn't *if* they prevailed, but rather, *how*? That stipulation potentially made creating suspense much more difficult. And more importantly, and perhaps the even more difficult question, what happened next? It's a common trope that stories resolve the conflict and end with a 'life goes on' feel to them, often with a tag along the lines of, 'just wait to see what happens next!' or 'who knows how far they'll go from here?' (For the record, I love those kinds of endings.) In this anthology, however, the stories' entire raison d'être was to *answer* that very question. What *was* the aftermath? The endings needed to show what *did* happen next. The authors dealt with that dilemma in various ingenious ways.

When I tossed out this concept for consideration, I set the bar super high. These stories blew past it. The very best thing—exceeding my already sky-high expectations—was the sheer variety of stories I got back. They spanned four continents. They covered over two millennia. Some humorous, some harrowing, they included wild action; behind-the-scenes machinations; all-out war, sometimes on the battlefield, sometimes in the press, sometimes in political chambers; and sometimes just sheer quiet stubbornness. The incredible diversity in tone, plot, historical era and geographic location astonished and delighted me. Every author brought a wonderfully unique voice and sensibility to her story.

The only thing connecting these stories is the theme; otherwise they are wholly independent of each other. So as not to imply a sequential link between them, the stories in the anthology are not in chronological order. They jump from era to era, location to location.

All of these stories stem from actual historical events. Most, but not all, use the names of the real-life people involved whenever possible. A few of them name-drop like crazy and base almost every named character on a real person.

As this collection shows, powerful rulers (as expected) made a difference. Plenty of leaders and fierce warriors happened to be women. Our anthology doesn't lack for Queens, Empresses and Presidents. But everyday people (wholly unexpected) also made a difference. Sometimes a tenacious pilot refused to give up her quest, or a relentless scientist wouldn't accept being silenced. A reporter continued to chase the story that power brokers wanted to suppress. Some women fought not just for ideals, but for their very families. Athletes prevailed, echoing battles from eons ago. Singers, actresses, and writers—and nuns—all proved their mettle.

Introduction

Every culture in history, every era, every location on Earth, has had women rulers, women warriors, and women leaders in every field. One must search the historical documentation to find them. Sometimes an ancient king erased all record of the queen who preceded him. Sometimes modern male scientists left their woman colleague's name off of the research she helped conduct. Male archeologists, upon learning a grave belonged to a woman, suddenly changed their evaluation of all the weapons it contained and decided that, no, the person buried there couldn't possibly have been an actual warrior after all. Bureaucrats barred the Mercury 13 from flying because 'it wasn't suitable for women' to do such a masculine job, although the women—all highly-skilled pilots—did in fact pass the same tests as the men.

Some men just burned women at the stake or hanged or stoned them.

I hope this volume brings hours of entertainment to all those who read it, but I also hope it does a whole lot more than just that—that it also enlightens and inspires. I'd love it to help provoke and accelerate the push toward equality that is gradually taking place all over the world.

In this current age of 'see it, be it', 'women hold up half the sky', and 'be the change you want to see'—*none* of which is actually a *new* philosophy—I believe that entertainment is among the most powerful tools of change, and of normalizing the idea that women's rights *are* human rights. Making things better for women makes things better for everyone. Most women have the exact same goals as most men.

Hopefully people will remember that when reading these stories, and find them as thought-provoking as they are fun.

One final note: As if the whole collection of wonderful tales weren't already fantastic, we had the extreme good fortune to include stunning artwork for each story. I was absolutely overjoyed with these magnificent drawings by the same artist who did our lovely cover.

D. J. Stevenson
May 2024

The Harvest Moon

Deborah Daughetee

SERENITY LED HER CLASS TO A SPECIAL PLACE IN THE FOREST WHERE cushioned benches and desks had been arranged in a half-circle in the oak grove. The trees were so large that it took a dozen people to encircle each one, arms outstretched. The Harvest moon would rise in an hour, and it was time to tell the story of Abigail Stone.

"You aren't going to need your tablets," said Serenity in English, knowing that her students knew they wouldn't need them. But with the festival looming, her teens were making plans with friends from other clans arriving soon, so their tablets seemed glued to their hands. "Nor any other electronic devices, so put them all away."

She waited silently, watching the students stow their electronics in their backpacks and settle on the benches. Then she took a deep breath and closed her eyes, centering herself and opening her mind to the Mother's inspiration.

A wind came, and the leaves around and above them began to laugh. The cries of a flock of Canadian geese flying over their heads joined the leaves. Serenity drank it all in, knowing they would soon retreat to the long houses with their clan. The forest had whispered that this winter would be long and bitter, meaning in-person communication between clans would be difficult.

The walls of each family's living area could be tuned to screens for Zoom calls. They could also be programed to display scenes of the forest in Summer. Or they could be great windows looking out on the snowscaped forest, which had its own beauty.

Serenity thought about Abigail Stone and felt her heart and soul expand, the energy of the trees filling her. She opened her eyes.

"It was at Harvest Moon when the Fathers of Salem decided to hang Abigail Stone's entire family for witchcraft. All over a piece of land along the coast that someone else wanted."

The students said in unison, "No one owns the land."

"No one owns the land," repeated Serenity. "But back then, men thought they could. They took it from the people who lived here and killed all who stood in their way," said Serenity, switching to Algonquian as her assistant began to beat the drum.

"Abigail's story starts long before her family is accused of witchcraft. It begins when she is in the forest picking blueberries."

The forest of Salem, draped in the shadows of oak and elm, whispered secrets as Abigail Stone wandered through its labyrinthine paths. Shafts of sunlight filtered through the dense canopy, casting dappled patterns on the forest floor. The air was heavy with the scent of earth, moss, and the sweet perfume of wildflowers that danced at the edges of the woodland. Overhead came the coo of a mourning dove and the caw of a crow.

Abigail loved the forest. She didn't understand the fear most in her community had for its quiet depths. For her, the forest was a place of peace and quiet contemplation.

Her footsteps were soft against the bed of fallen leaves, her senses attuned to the ancient rhythms of the forest. She was supposed to be picking blueberries for her mother's pie, but she dawdled, trailing her fingers along the rough bark of the trees, feeling their silent strength beneath her touch.

The Harvest Moon

The woods served as her sanctuary, a haven away from the oppressive strictures of Salem's rigid society where women were pieces of property like chickens or horses. Even now, Jeremiah Smith was visiting with her father to make a contract to take her as his wife. Jeremiah was considered a good match in Puritanical terms. He was a rich merchant and was a leader of the community, which would help her family's standing. But the real prize was the land that would come as part of her dowry, land Jeremiah had tried to buy from her father. But he would not sell. She and her father had discussed that land, and had decided to turn it over to the Indians living there. It had to remain deeded to her father, or someone like Jeremiah would swoop in and discover the small enclave of Indians living and hunting there, and chase them off at best. She shuddered to think what the worst would be.

She knew her father would not sell her to Jeremiah. John Stone loved his wife and children and didn't agree with the poor treatment that many of Salem's men heaped upon women in the name of God. This was enough to make him an outsider in Salem. But even more damaging was the fact that he felt we had much we could learn from the Indians of the area. He did not believe they were evil, as most of the colony did. He was taking a great risk by letting Indians remain on the land that, in all reality, was actually theirs.

Abigail's younger sister Marjorie, however, was all about image, and she begged her father to offer her as an alternate wife to Jeremiah. She would welcome a life of luxury and prominence in the community. Her father reluctantly agreed, but while he would give Marjorie an attractive dowry, he would not include the parcel of land that Jeremiah coveted.

As Abigail neared the blueberry patch, she heard grunting and the obvious sounds of something pushing through the bushes. Abigail made sure she was downwind, then crept forward, keeping out of sight, to spy on the black bear sitting on its rump scarfing down blueberries. The sight was comical, and Abigail almost laughed. She stifled the sound, a cold wash of fear squashing every desire to laugh, as the bear stopped and looked around. When it heard no further sounds, it went back to eating.

Abigail quietly crept away, daring to breathe freely only when she could no longer hear its grunting.

"Abigail Stone." A woman emerged from the verdant foliage, her presence commanding yet gentle, like a guardian of the forest itself. Her hair, streaked with silver, cascaded down her back in unruly waves, and her dark eyes held the wisdom of countless ages. The color of her skin was difficult to determine. It was luminous, a dark brown like the bark of a tree, or a deep dark green like the leaves of the deep forest, and sometimes it looked red and yellow like the leaves at harvest time.

"You have wandered far from the confines of your village." Her voice was a melodic whisper that seemed to echo through the trees like the rustle of leaves.

"I'm not afraid," said Abigail. "The forest calls to me. It is the only place where I feel truly free. I'm sorry, but I don't think I know you."

"You may call me Mother. Now come with me. We have much to do."

"Much to do?"

"To claim your birthright. The one that has been stolen from you."

"I don't understand," said Abigail.

"You will," said Mother. "Now come."

Abigail hesitated. She didn't know this woman and knew she shouldn't go with her. But there was something that called to Abigail like a spring of clear, cold water. There was something of the forest about her, something wild, yet accessible. So, in the end, she followed Mother deeper into the forest.

Serenity paused her storytelling. The drumming stopped. Serenity's teaching partner, Joy, came to take Serenity's place. She smiled at the students, then raised her arms and began to sing, her lilting voice floating up to dance with the leaves.

> *In the heart of the forest, where the moonlight gleams,*
> *Lived a woman of wisdom in the land of dreams.*
> *Mother, they called her, keeper of the earth,*
> *Guiding souls like Abigail to discover their true worth.*

The Harvest Moon

Oh, Mother of the forest, guardian of the green,
Teach us the magic that within us lies unseen.
On the Harvest Moon, we gather 'round the fire,
To honor your legacy, to lift our spirits higher.

She whispered of herbs that could heal the pain,
Of foods that nourish, of forests to sustain.
With reverence, she spoke of stewardship divine,
And how to embrace the magic in every woman's line.

Oh, Mother of the forest, keeper of the flame,
Your teachings echo softly, in Abigail's name.
On the Harvest Moon, we sing your ancient song,
For you helped us find our place, where we truly belong.

In the days of Salem, when fear gripped the land,
You stood with courage, extending your hand.
Together with Abigail, you forged a new way,
A society of peace, where all colors could sway.

Oh, Mother of the forest, we honor you this night,
For your wisdom and your guidance, shining ever bright.
On the Harvest Moon, beneath the starry sky,
We celebrate your legacy as the forest spirits fly.

Mother, we thank you, for the lessons bestowed,
For showing us the path where love and harmony flowed.
On this Harvest Moon, in your memory, we dance,
In unity and peace, beneath your gentle glance.

The clearing had more visitors who had come to hear Joy's song soar above the trees to meet the sky. These were not people but the creatures of the forest, drawn by the story of the Mother who taught Abigail Stone how to bring peace and magic where neither dwelled.

As the last echoes of Joy's voice faded away, Serenity continued her story. "Mother taught Abigail about the herbs for healing, and Abigail taught her mother. Her father was concerned, for the atmosphere in Salem was turning dangerous, and any excuse could cause someone to be the target of the clergy. And if you were denounced as acting in non-Christian ways, then life could get very difficult.

Mother had a small structure of branches and animal hides deep in the forest. Abigail followed the path her feet had made after so many times of passing. Mother had taught her how to find her way through the forest, read the signs of animals passing, a piece of fur here, a print there, claw marks on the bark of trees. She learned about plants and trees, how bark could be used as a tea to ease pain, and how mushrooms could either enhance a meal or kill.

She told Abigail that Salem cut too many trees, that trees take a long time to grow, and that the forest would be devastated long before their need for wood would subside. She told her the wolves and bears would be hunted until they were gone.

"These rich and powerful men are only powerful because you allow them to be," said Mother.

"That's not true," said Abigail, insulted. "These men use their money to buy what they want. And if they want us to hang, they will hang us."

"Money doesn't give them power. What gives them power is a silent agreement of all citizens to allow them to have power."

Abigail started to object, but Mother continued. "Their power is an illusion. Yes, men are stronger than women. And yes, they are more prone to aggression, which is beneficial for hunting and protection. Once, men and women were wonderful partners. Until men started to think that because they were stronger and more aggressive, they should be able to command women. They became jealous of women's magic, and their aggression turned toward the accumulation of power."

"My father isn't like that," said Abigail.

The Harvest Moon

"Many men are not like that. However, those men, even your father, do not use their power to stand up against these men."

Abigail wanted to argue, but she couldn't. She thought about her father refusing to sell Jeremiah the land. He stood up to the man. And yet Jeremiah was a community leader wielding power like a king ruling over his subjects, manipulating and controlling others for his own sinister ends.

She tried to figure out what made Jeremiah and men like him so powerful, and she could see that Mother was right. They only had power because the people let them have it. Fear of these men ruled the majority.

"How do women regain their power?" she asked. "How do I regain mine?"

Mother came to her and placed her hand on her abdomen. "This is your power center. This is where you hold the power of life and death."

Abigail started.

"Yes," said Mother. "You hold the power of both, for you cannot have one without the other. But these powers come with great responsibility."

Abigail suddenly felt dizzy, and then she was no longer herself but running with a wolf pack. A shiver of fear ran through her, afraid that at any moment, the pack might turn on her and tear her to pieces. But a thrill of joy and freedom ran through her as well.

She heard Mother's voice as if from far away. "A wolf hunts to eat. The wolves use their aggression for hunting, as your men once did. They do this to survive, and they will use it to protect the pack."

Abigail was sitting with Mother again. "They do not kill for sport. They do not kill for gain. Death is a sacred contract, and when that contract is broken, then the person breaking it is broken. Do you understand?"

"I think so. It's okay to kill for food and for protection?"

Mother looked at Abigail intently. "Men think it is their job to protect their society, but it is not. It is a woman's. A woman protects her children and the children of her sisters. A woman protects the sanctity of the hearth. A woman protects other women. But you need not kill to do it."

"But how?" asked Abigail, jumping up and pacing around. "How do you protect the village against hostile animals or Indians? Or even other villages?"

Mother stood to meet her. "What do you believe in, Abigail Stone?"

"I believe in God."

"Yes!" said Mother. "But men have taught you that God is a Father and a Son, but NOT a Mother or a Daughter. The truth is that God is both Mother and Father, Daughter and Son. And when you find that truth inside of you, you will find your magic as well. And when you find your magic, you will find the way to protect not only your people but the land, the trees, and the creatures of the forest."

Serenity left her place and walked in front of the first desk, where a girl of thirteen, for they were all thirteen, sat. She was looking down at her hands, and Serenity lifted her chin with one finger.

"What did Abigail learn that day?" Serenity asked.

"That God is both Mother and Father, Daughter and Son," answered the girl.

Serenity smiled, then walked to the next student, a boy. "What did Abigail learn that day?"

"God is both Mother and Father, Daughter and Son," he answered.

Serenity moved to each child in the half circle and asked the same question. Each child responded with the same phrase. Then Serenity returned to her place.

"Abigail felt that this kind of talk was blasphemy. But that night in bed, as she thought about it, it made more and more sense. The God her father taught them was not the God the Reverend taught in church. The Reverend's God was strict and vengeful, whereas her father's God was loving and kind. Abigail was on her way to discovering the truth.

"Then the day came," said Serenity gravely, "When the accusation of witchcraft was first levied."

Abigail stood with the rest of Salem as three women were led to the hanging tree. The first was Tituba, who had been brought in as a slave

The Harvest Moon

from Barbados in Samuel Parris's household. The second was Sarah Good, a beggar and social misfit, and the third was Sarah Osborn, a quarrelsome old woman who had not attended church in quite some time. Abigail's father warned his family that they must watch the hanging, not turn away. Fear in Salem was rampant, and any perceived empathy for the accused would not bode well for them.

The judge who had sentenced these women to hang was none other than Jeremiah Smith. When Abigail's father refused to give him her hand but offered him Marjorie's instead, at first, Jeremiah angrily refused. But a day later, he had returned, apologized for his bad behavior, and proposed to Marjorie. Now, Marjorie stood beside him as he read the pronouncement, her skin ashen and her once smiling face drawn and frowning.

Each woman was given a chance to confess so her soul would be clean when she stood before God in judgment. Sarah Osborn spit in the judge's face. Sacks were roughly pulled over their heads so their faces were hidden, and the chairs were knocked away so they fell the length of the rope and danced there like mad marionettes.

Marjorie fainted. Abigail wanted to go to her, but her father held her back, tears in his eyes. Jeremiah pulled Marjorie to her feet, but Marjorie could not stand alone. Jeremiah had his man carry Marjorie away.

Abigail watched. She watched the women's jerking stop. She watched her sister carried away from the hanging, and her anger surged. These women's only sin was that they were on the outside of Salem society, which made them vulnerable to Jeremiah's accusations. They were not witches any more than Abigail was. And yet the entire colony had watched them hang.

Abigail thought of what Mother had said about how men like Jeremiah had power. No one had stood up for these women. No one had challenged his sentencing them to death. Not even her. And shame swirled inside her along with anger.

A few days later, Abigail and her mother visited the Smith home to check on Marjorie. Her sister served them tea and spoke of how happy she was with Jeremiah, but she wouldn't look them in the eye, and her frowning face belied her words. Abigail wanted to press her into the truth, but Jeremiah entered and came to stand behind Marjorie, placing his hands on her shoulders. Marjorie flinched at his touch.

"Did you tell our dear sister and mother the good news," asked Jeremiah.

"I was just about to." Marjorie's voice was barely a whisper.

"Then allow me," said Jeremiah. "Marjorie is with child. I'm to have a son to carry on my name."

Abigail stared at Marjorie, wondering what would happen if she gave Jeremiah a girl.

"Congratulations," said Mother, truly delighted. "I have longed to be a grandmother. John will be so pleased."

"Yes," said Jeremiah. "However, because of Marjorie's weak constitution, the doctor has ordered her to rest, so we will not be accepting visitors until after the baby is born."

Abigail's mother looked stricken.

"But surely her mother can visit her. I have herbs that can help ease…"

Jeremiah's voice hardened. "No visitors at all. Doctor's orders. Be careful, Esther Stone, that you do not fall into the path of witchcraft with your herbs."

Abigail's mother shrank back, horrified at the admonition. But Abigail was angry, and she stood, looking Jeremiah in the eyes.

"You may keep me away from my sister, but you cannot keep her from our mother."

"Oh, but I can," said Jeremiah. "She is my property now, and I will treat her as I see fit."

Abigail saw Jeremiah's hands tighten on Marjorie's shoulder and heard her gasp in pain. She looked up at Abigail, her eyes pleading, and Abigail realized that Marjorie would pay for Abigail's actions. She swallowed her anger and her pride.

"I forget myself," she said. "Of course, that is your right. My concern for my sister overwhelmed me. Please forgive my outburst."

Jeremiah's hands relaxed. Tears ran down Marjorie's face.

"Now my wife is to bed. Thank you for your concern."

Marjorie kissed them both goodbye. When it was Abigail's turn, Marjorie slipped a note in her hand.

"Goodbye, sister," she said. "I often think of the game we played around the oak tree in our yard. This oak," she pointed out the door at a huge oak, "reminds me of those times."

The Harvest Moon

Abigail's mind raced. The game they played was hiding notes for each other in the tree.

"I remember those times well, sister."

Then Abigail and her mother left. Her mother's tears escaped down her face, but Abigail refused to cry. She was angry. But deeper than that was a dark despair. Women were possessions, and no one would interfere between a husband and wife. It would be that way when she married and when her daughter married. Women would never be more than chattel, for how could that be changed when it was so deeply engrained in their society?

And yet Marjorie had found a way to communicate with her sister. Perhaps she could find a way to take Marjorie away, and they could hide her somewhere deep in the forest.

This was crazy thinking, but Abigail felt desperate.

When they arrived home, Abigail went to the room she used to share with Marjorie and opened the note. It was written in the special language they had created as children. To anyone else, it would look like a bit of nonsense.

"He's a monster. He wants our father's land. He hates you for refusing. Be very careful."

The students leaned forward on their benches, caught up in the story of Abigail Stone.

"Mother taught Abigail many things about herb craft and the ways of the forest," said Serenity. "Abigail passed this knowledge on to her mother, who became a proficient healer. But more people were being accused of witchcraft. They were imprisoned, and their property confiscated. Abigail knew it was only a matter of time before Jeremiah came for her family.

Mother had a small hut deep in the forest. Deer and squirrels ate from her hand, and birds landed on her shoulder. But when it came time to teach Abigail, she shooed them away. The two women sat outside in the warm sun on the stumps of two old oak trees. Mother sat cross-legged, and Abigail came to imitate her.

"Close your eyes," said Mother.

Abigail obeyed.

"Now, I want you to take three deep breaths with me. Ready? Breathe in. Breathe Out. In. Out. In. And out. Now keep your eyes closed and listen to the sound of my voice, to the sounds of the leaves rustling on the wind, the branches creaking as they sway, the song of each new bird, and the scurrying of animals all around us."

Abigail did listen, and the more she listened, the more she heard. It was like there were layers of listening, and as she breathed and let Mother's voice caress her consciousness, she could penetrate those layers.

"Now, I want you to turn your awareness inward. Let any thoughts that come into your mind drift back out again without engaging with them. Let your worries drift away. Look inside with your mind's eye until you find your center."

"How will I know?" asked Abigail in a whisper that didn't break the spell.

"You will know," answered Mother.

Abigail sank deeper and deeper into herself. Thoughts whirled through her head: thoughts of the witch trials, Marjorie being hurt by her husband, her mother's healing, and her father's worry. At first, it was difficult to let them fly away, but as she practiced, it became easier. And then suddenly, there were no more thoughts. Abigail's mind quieted, and all her fears and worries were washed away, leaving only tranquility in their wake.

"Now," said Mother as if she knew that Abigail had found her center, "I want you to bring back one of your worries and imagine yourself navigating through it with grace and ease. Pluck the fear out of the worry and send it on its way. It is fear that controls us. Fear that binds us."

Abigail brought back the idea of her family being accused of witchcraft. The fear almost overwhelmed her.

"Fear controls and binds us," the Mother repeated.

Abigail took a deep breath, allowing herself to return to tranquility, and then let the thought come again. This time, she didn't let the fear

The Harvest Moon

ruin her tranquility. Instead, Abigail saw herself standing between her family and Jeremiah Smith and the other judges. Then she saw all the women standing with her, holding hands like a long string of paper doll cutouts. And suddenly, a bright light came from inside her being and filled her with power.

Abigail started and lost the power, the light, and the women. She opened her eyes.

"No! That is… unnatural."

"Why?"

"Because. It was like… like magic. I felt like I could do things."

"That, my daughter, was your natural state of being. It is the woman God intended."

"But it's witchcraft."

"Witchcraft is a made-up concept. It was meant to tie women's magic to evil. But when a woman finds the tranquility of her center, she finds the essence of God inside of her. And that is not evil. That is embracing God's grace."

Serenity smiled at her students. "What did Abigail learn?"

In unison, the class repeated. "We all carry the essence of God inside us."

"That's right. But Abigail had difficulty reconciling it with what she had been taught all her life. On one level, she thought that what she was doing was evil. But on the other hand, connecting to her center helped her through the days to come.

"Marjorie gave Jeremiah a son but Jeremiah kept Abigail and her mother from them. In a spark of rebellion, however, Marjorie continued to pass notes with the help of the oak tree.

"Marjorie wrote of the beatings and how Jeremiah conspired with other men to accuse people of witchcraft to gain their property. Maybe it was because of some perceived transgression. Marjorie was fearful that Jeremiah would come after her family in this way.

"The oak became a symbol for Marjorie; a symbol that she was still sister, daughter, mother, and woman—the very things that Jeremiah Smith attempted to kill in her."

Serenity stepped away, and twelve people, six men and six women, emerged from the trees as if they had stepped from the ethers. They were dressed in bright colors, the women wearing shawls that, when they put their arms out to their sides, looked like the wings of a bird. Four more drummers joined the drumming circle, and the beat quickened and was full of celebration.

The dancers encircled one of the giant oaks and began to stamp their feet and twirl while the drummers started to chant.

"We dance in gratitude for the oak. We dance in joy at the secrets it keeps." They chanted once in English, once in Algonquian, and finally in French.

The dancers circled the oak three times, their joy and gratitude radiating from them like the sun's corona.

Then they stopped and melted back into the trees.

Serenity resumed her place at the head of the class.

"The oak," she said, "played a role in saving the life of Abigail and her entire family."

Jeremiah is going to accuse you, Mother and Father, of witchcraft! You are to be hanged. Abigail sat staring at the words her sister had written. The shock and fear turned her blood cold and settled like a stone in her stomach.

Abigail put the note in a wooden box where she kept all of Marjorie's notes and went to the kitchen where herbs hung drying from the ceiling. It didn't help that she had expected it. She knew Jeremiah hated her for refusing him and hated Father for keeping the land Jeremiah coveted. Four other people had been hanged, and the powerful of the town had benefited. With her family dead, Jeremiah would inherit all their worldly goods.

The house was empty. Father was out in the fields, and mother was visiting a sick neighbor. Abigail grabbed her hat and gathering basket

The Harvest Moon

and headed into the forest to find Mother, but Mother was gone. Only the skeleton of the shelter remained, the hides and furs were gone. A great despair filled her. But as she turned away from the shack, she found the stumps of the great oaks. Her resolve hardened, and she went to the stump. She closed her eyes and took three deep breaths. Then she imagined following the great roots of the giant trees down into the ground. She pulled strength from the energies stored there and felt their groundedness, felt them anchor her presence to the earth. Then, she brought her awareness inward until she felt she could pluck out the fear that threatened to overwhelm her. With great difficulty, she snipped the threads that attached her fear to her thoughts, then threw that fear far from her. She imagined facing Jeremiah Smith. She found the light, the women, the power. And she knew what she must do.

Serenity fell silent for a moment. Her students didn't stir, anticipating the next words.

"When Abigail returned home, the men came for her and her family, and they were jailed. They were asked to confess, but none of them would. Let us pray for Abigail and her family."

Everyone stood and bowed their head. Serenity began.

"Our Mother and Father who art in heaven," she said.

The others joined in. "Hallowed be thy names, both seen and unseen. Thy kingdom come, thy will be done, in the vast expanse of the natural world, as it is in heaven. Give us this day our daily sustenance from the earth and forgive us our exploitation of nature as we seek forgiveness and strive to restore balance.

"Lead us not into heedless consumption but guide us towards harmony with all living beings. For thine is the kingdom, the power, and the beauty of creation, Forever and ever. Amen."

Serenity looked out over her students' serious faces.

"During her time in her cell, Abigail created that prayer. She combined her faith in God with her faith in the Mother. She thought of her mother and father and their affinity with the natural world. And when the prayer was finished, what happened?"

"She found her magic," the class said in unison.

"She found her magic," Serenity agreed.

Marjorie told Jeremiah that she could get Abigail to confess to witchcraft.

"But you must let me see her alone, husband," said Marjorie. "For she will never say such a thing in front of anyone else."

Jeremiah agreed, and on the day that Abigail was to be hanged, Marjorie went to her cell. She and Marjorie embraced, and when tears leaked down her sister's face, Abigail patted her on the back.

"Do not cry, sister, for no one will hang this day."

Marjorie pulled away from her to look her in the eyes. "Jeremiah will not be swayed."

"Jeremiah's power is illusory. Today, you will be free of him. I promise."

"How can that be?" asked Marjorie.

"Have you ever wondered what would happen if Jeremiah came across a real witch?"

Marjorie looked confused. "Of course not. I know of no such evil person."

"And what," said Abigail, "if the magic of women was not evil or from the devil. That men created this lie to keep women below men?"

"The magic of women?" said Marjorie.

Abigail smiled. "Do you trust me, sister?"

"With my life," said Marjorie.

Abigail put her hand on Marjorie's abdomen and said, "Awaken."

And Marjorie eyes lit up with the light of knowledge. At first fear contorted her face. Then it relaxed, and Abigail saw Marjorie embrace the magic that was surging inside her.

"How could we not have known?" whispered Marjorie, wonder coloring her voice.

Just then, the guards came to take Abigal to the hanging tree.

The Harvest Moon

As she and her parents had the noose placed around their necks, Abigail saw Marjorie moving to take her place beside Jeremiah. Jeremiah turned to talk to her, but whatever Marjorie said infuriated him.

"Abigail, William, and Esther Stone, you have been found guilty of witchcraft. Will you confess so that you may stand before your Maker with a soul cleansed of evil?"

"You should look to your own soul, Jeremiah Smith, as it is yours who has committed murder by hanging innocent people."

Jeremiah's face twisted with anger. "Hang them."

As the chairs were kicked away, the ropes dissolved, and all three fell, keeping their feet under them. The crowd gasped.

"What makes you think, Jeremiah Stone, that if you found a real witch, she would let you hang her?"

"You hear it from her own mouth and see what she has done. She is a witch!" cried Jeremiah.

"As are all women," said Abigail.

Marjorie left her place beside Jeremiah. When he grabbed for her, he found he could not touch her.

She went to stand beside her sister and they joined hands. They smiled at each other, then faced the bewildered crowd and shouted, "Awaken."

Serenity smiled, "And at that moment, all the women were awakened to their magic. Some rejected it, still believing it was the devil's work. They stayed shackled to the men forced to leave the colony. Many men, however, like Abigail's father, stayed and embraced the women and their newly found power.

"Abigail taught the women how to recognize and use their magic. Men and women worked as partners in Salem, each celebrating the strengths of the others. A council was formed of both men and women.

"Instead of vilifying the Native Americans, they made treaties with them. We learned Algonquian, and they learned English. We learned from each other. You learn from both European and Native American teachers; all languages are treated as equally important.

"England tried to take us, but we learned how to use our magic, the magic of the Indians, the strength and aggression of men, and the magic of the forest to protect our shores. And as we came into contact with other colonies, we awakened women's magic, and the clans were born. Our constitution comes from representatives from each clan and had the signatures of men, women, and all races in the area at the time, including those who, like Tibutu, had been enslaved.

"It was decided that each Harvest Moon, a clan would be chosen for the Give-Away to prevent the abuse of power through the acquisition of wealth. Today, it is the great honor of the Stone clan to gift our possessions to the different clans. Give with joy and a grateful heart, and watch the joy of those who receive. With the Give-Away, we learn the joys of both.

As Abigail approached the clearing where she had met Mother, she was overcome with great sadness. She wandered through the forest, each step heavy with grief. But as she walked, something miraculous began to unfold. The rustle of leaves in the breeze, the song of birds in the canopy above, the dance of sunlight filtering through the branches—every aspect of the forest seemed to echo Mother's spirit.

In the quietude of nature's embrace, Abigail felt a stirring deep within her soul. With each breath, she sensed Mother's essence intertwining with her own, filling her with a sense of peace and understanding. She realized that although Mother's physical form was gone, her spirit lived on in every blade of grass, every whispering breeze, and most of all, within Abigail herself.

With renewed clarity, Abigail looked up at the towering trees, their branches reaching toward the sky like outstretched arms. She felt a profound connection to the earth beneath her feet and the vast expanse of the heavens above. In that moment, she understood that Mother was

The Harvest Moon

not confined to a single place or time but transcended all boundaries, weaving her presence throughout the tapestry of creation.

As the realization washed over her, Abigail felt a sense of liberation and empowerment. She knew that she carried Mother's legacy within her, a spark of divine wisdom and love that would guide her on her journey forward. With a newfound sense of purpose, she followed the well-worn path home, embracing the boundless magic that surrounded her and knowing that Mother would always be with her in every beat of her heart and in every breath she took.

"Victoria for President,"
Says Nellie Bly

Rosemary Jones

Victoria Clafin Woodhull Blood Martin balled up another sheet of paper and pitched it toward the fireplace. She missed. Just as she failed to capture her thoughts in words that would set her audience alight.

"You need a real writer to help you," said Cornelius Vanderbilt from his seat by the window.

Victoria ignored the Commodore. Why he chose to haunt her, when her sister Tennie had been the object of his adoration, she didn't know. While the ghost's advice on stocks was still uncannily sound, she doubted his understanding of the political challenges of 1900. What she truly needed was an absolute rabble rouser of a speech, something to invoke the Victoria of nearly thirty years earlier when she'd made her first run for president.

"You can't stand in front of the crowd and drone on about scientific farming," continued Cornelius. "Or spiritualism."

"I have no intention of talking about either." Goaded into a response, Victoria faced the apparition in her sitting room. Cornelius smirked with a certain smug satisfaction which had been annoying when he was alive and was positively irksome now she couldn't throw anything at him.

Pens, wads of paper, and even the occasional vase had sailed through Cornelius to splat against the wall. Since chucking things in this sitting room certainly upset the staff of the Waldorf-Astoria, Victoria now restricted her displeasure to glares and the occasional request that the ghost keep his opinions to himself. Cornelius had never cared to keep his mouth shut, having plenty of opinions to share. He was even more disinclined to ignore suggestions for silence now that he was dead.

"I should never have come back to New York," Victoria declared. "This city hates me."

"That never stopped you or Tennie."

Well, Cornelius was right. Which was just one of the reasons that he was such an annoying spirit. But nothing had stopped them, not in those heady days of becoming the first female stockbrokers on Wall Street, launching their newspaper, testifying before Congress, fighting the press and police when they dared to speak about things that "nice women" didn't talk about, and being jailed. They did it all despite two simply terrible husbands for Victoria and a few unfortunate decisions by Tennie. Was it any wonder they had fled to London when Vanderbilt's horrible heirs offered to pay for their passage?

After all, they'd prospered in England. Tennie was now Lady Cook with a stately London home and a castle in Portugal. Victoria had had her romantic and happy marriage with John, the only one of her three husbands that she regretted losing. Further she'd inherited the houses and a share of Martin's Bank from the father-in-law who had never liked her but had died three days before his son. The irony of her inheritance even made Cornelius smile.

So why had she returned to New York? Why not just settle in the Martin family home at Bredon's Norton to play the lady bountiful like Tennie in her Portuguese castle?

"I hate the press," she grumbled to the ghost. "No woman has ever been hounded as I am hounded by them."

"So you've touched bottom with the press. Time to sail on the incoming tide," said the man once known as the Commodore because he'd been a sailor of fortune's tides and a ferry boat captain.

"Victoria for President," Says Nellie Bly

Victoria started. She remembered saying something very similar to Tennie once, when it seemed they had lost everything. It wasn't bad advice.

"Who do you think could write my speech?" she asked Cornelius.

"Nellie Bly," said the ghost.

Victoria blinked. "The one who traveled around the world?" She vaguely remembered the newspaper stories in London about how the New York reporter stopped off in Southampton or maybe when the woman met Jules Verne in France. One or the other. There was a children's game too, a board game where you threw dice and hopped along an ever spiraling trail to go around the world in 72 days. "How do you know about Nellie Bly? Weren't you dead by then?"

"I never stopped being interested in the news. Or daring women," Cornelius winked at her. Winked! He was an unrepentant flirt at times, something that she did not remember from when he was alive. At least not directed at her. His behavior around Tennie... Well, less said of that, the better. Being a ghost did seem to rejuvenate him even more.

"Go on, Vicky, admit I am right. You need a good press agent. And who would be better than Nellie Bly?" Cornelius couldn't stand to lose an argument.

Besides, she was beginning to see some merit in his idea. She had battled the press for all her life. It might be nice to have a woman reporter on her side.

"So which newspaper does she write for? This Nellie Bly?"

Cornelius shook his head. "She doesn't write any more. Runs a pots and pans factory for her husband. But it would cause quite a stir if Nellie Bly came back to writing because of you. Almost as good as an endorsement from Susan B. Anthony."

Victoria snorted. "Susan will burn in hell before she endorses any campaign of mine."

"Now, Vicky..."

"Don't call me Vicky. You know I'm right about Susan. Her group will keep marching, and compromising, and nibbling away at the issue like mice. But they would rather fill their ears with wax than hear what I have to say!"

Cornelius shut up, perhaps because he knew he could never reconcile the decades-old dispute between Victoria and the current leaders of the suffrage, especially Susan B. Anthony. The women wanted vague and respectful talk about liberty. Victoria talked loudly about sex and birth control. No one had been ready for her in the 1870s. She wasn't sure they wanted to hear her ideas in this new century.

But maybe this Nellie Bly could find a way.

"How do I find her? This pots and pans woman who went around the world?"

Cornelius raised his eyebrows. "Ask the hotel switchboard. She must have a telephone. At least her husband's company must have one." One of the reasons that Victoria elected to stay at the Waldorf-Astoria was their placement of a telephone in every room. Of all the conveniences of the new century, Victoria loved the phone, which allowed her to bypass letters and telegrams. What she and Tennie could have done with a phone in 1872! The press would have had a much harder time silencing them then.

"Do you happen to know the name of the factory?" Nellie asked Cornelius.

"Iron Clad Manufacturing."

"I don't understand how you can know all this."

"I was seized by an overwhelming gust of inspiration."

"Oh, don't quote me to me," grumbled Victoria. Then she called the switchboard to ask for a connection to the Iron Clad Manufacturing Company.

The woman who met Victoria for lunch at Delmonico's was small, round-faced, and nicely dressed. Her hat was not sophisticated enough to belong to one of the very wealthy matrons who patronized New York's finest milliners or shabbily made enough to mark her as working class. Just ordinary, thought Victoria with a sigh. She judged the former Nellie Bly to be in her thirties.

"Mrs. Martin?" asked the younger woman as she walked up to the table.

Victoria rose from her seat and held out her hand. "Mrs. Seaman, I presume?"

"These days," said her guest with a firm handshake. "But I think you are more interested in who I was than who I am?"

"Victoria for President," Says Nellie Bly

"You earned quite a reputation as Nellie Bly, crusader for justice and world traveler," said Victoria as they settled into their chairs. All around them, people ate and chatted but nobody paid them much attention. In her younger days, walking into a restaurant caused an uproar. Just because she and Tennie wanted to dine without a man at their table. Lorenzo Delmonico had sputtered and offered to escort them quietly out the door. As if Tennie and she ever went quietly anywhere! But they had maneuvered around Lorenzo's rules by having their coachman join them. Such a fuss to order a bowl of tomato soup!

Now, thirty years later, a richly dressed widow in her sixties could host a young matron without comment. Victoria sighed again, rather missing her former notoriety.

Once ordered, the food appeared quickly courtesy of the restaurant's famously efficient waiters. Victoria started with a bowl of soup for old time's sake. When the staff was out of earshot, she leaned forward. "So what is your opinion of the vote?"

"Given the current state of affairs, I doubt women will win the vote before 1920," said Mrs. Seaman. "We have a long way to go before we have the support needed. Some of the Western states allow local voting but nothing will be done nationally for years. Simply passing an amendment through the House could take at least two decades."

"What if I said that you could vote today for President?" replied Victoria.

"Your argument in 1871," said her guest, cutting her chicken into neat, ladylike bites and efficiently consuming everything on her plate.

This woman has known hunger, thought Victoria, and she's no fool. "So you know about my testimony before Congress?"

"It's not easy to find, but I have a few friends who kept copies of the articles about your appearance in Washington. I also spoke to a judge, a friend of my husband, who thinks your argument was legally sound and an interesting idea."

"So did the men who funded my first campaign. They abandoned me to my critics as soon as the press turned against us."

"You attempted to blackmail a number of people into supporting your campaign and preached about the value of free love, all at the urging of dead spirits. You terrified your opponents and the press into naming you Mrs. Satan." The former reporter looked at Victoria with approval. "I have been called names too. I rather liked yours." She finished her last bite of lunch. "Are we ordering a dessert?"

Victoria laughed. "Certainly. Do you prefer cake or pie?"

"Whatever costs the most on the menu."

The confection of whipped cream, chocolate, brandied cherries, and an unpronounceable French name accompanied tiny cups of strong coffee. The preliminaries settled in Victoria's mind, she asked her guest how she should run her campaign this time.

"Oh, call me Nellie," said her newest friend. "For I'll have to resurrect Nellie Bly and all her passion for crusading. I've missed her, I admit. Helping Robert with the factory is interesting, but this will be exciting."

"So how do I do this, Nellie?"

"Blackmail the important men into supporting you, of course, or at least make them afraid to denounce you. If they are going to pour buckets of ink over your campaign, make it tell the story you want to tell rather than blacken your character. Continue to attract the crowds with your talk of spirits inspiring you while displaying your Bible prominently. Be on the side of angels rather than the devil's wife. Make amends with Susan Anthony and her ladies. And positively don't give speeches about free love until you are elected."

"So you think I can win?"

"You can win popularity through the press. President McKinley will take the Republican nomination. If the Democrats run William Jennings Bryan this time too, the press will be hungry for something new. Otherwise it's simply the 1896 election and discussions of free silver all over again. You'll be the leading story, especially if your sister joins your campaign. Americans love English nobility. Have Lady Cook travel from Boston to San Francisco speaking about her position in high society these days, how far you sisters have come from your humble roots but how you will always remain American in your hearts. The reporters will adore it. Everyone enjoys a rags-to-riches story."

Victoria nodded. "Anything else?"

"Pick a politician for your running mate. Someone who can campaign for you."

"Victoria for President," Says Nellie Bly

"Who?"

"Have you heard of Teddy Roosevelt?" asked Nellie. "He supports corporal punishment for wife beaters and brought women into the New York City Police Department. He is ambitious, clever, and well-connected. A war hero too."

"Good choice," rumbled Cornelius in her ear so Victoria nodded again.

Nellie Bly reached into her handbag and pulled out a notebook. "Let's order more coffee. I need to ask you a few questions for my article."

The first article stirred some interest, if only for the byline of Nellie Bly linked with the formerly infamous Victoria Martin. The second brought a few reporters to the Waldorf-Astoria to meet with the woman that they now described as the "charming" and "still beautiful" Victoria. Which caused Victoria to rattle the newspaper pages and complain to Nellie. "Didn't we talk about the need for reform and a way forward for a new century? Why are they commenting on my dress and figure?"

"It will take more than a new century to stop a man from defining a woman by her face," said practical Nellie. "Be glad they see you as an appealing widow of a certain age. It makes you less of a threat and more of an amusing anecdote. Right now we want compliments and not condemnations, Mrs. Satan."

So Victoria did what she had always done. Smiled, flattered, and watched with eyes well-trained by a conniving father and two scoundrels for husbands as she cataloged any flaw or weakness which could be turned to her advantage.

A judicious application of money secured the fledgling campaign a hall and a crowd. Backstage, Victoria sat on a tall coil of rope connected to something needed for the raising of the curtain. On stage, various women and a few men thundered from the podium about the ills of the past century and the hope for the coming one. Nellie collected their initial speakers from those formerly associated with the National Association of Spiritualists, the International Workingmen's Association, and Victoria's first People's Party. All remembered those heady days in 1872 when anything seemed possible and they were willing to try to invoke the same excitement again. Representatives from the National American Woman Suffrage Association were noticeably absent, although invitations had been extended. Victoria blamed the old dispute with Susan B. Anthony for this. Nellie simply shrugged.

"We have enough to start the stories rolling across the country," Nellie said, viewing the giant scarlet banners proclaiming "Freedom" and "Victoria" in golden letters hanging from the hall's ceiling. The banners evoked the old campaign enough to create some comments, but the reporters who were coming knew the "freedom" proclaimed tonight would be centered on the legitimacy of women voting and not the legalization of prostitution. Nellie gauged exactly how close to dance up to the line of what was acceptable while dangling echoes of the more scandalous campaign speeches of the past.

Besides, nobody truly remembered the events of thirty years ago, Nellie told Victoria. "We can recast your history. Make you the victim, not the villain, a courageous martyr to the cause."

"Not too much of a victim, Nellie," said Victoria. "I like the title of winner more."

But the echoes of the old campaign also moved her. Would the crowd listen or would she be shouted down again for her licentious ways? The world was changing, but women were still being gagged by accusations of immorality. So once again, Victoria sat backstage and tried to guess the mood of the crowd from the clapping, cheers, and, of course, some cat calls. She should have waited in her dressing room, but too much energy coursed through her veins to allow her to be closed off from the audience that she longed to address.

"Thou were always impatient," said the ghost of Lucretia Mott watching by her side.

Victoria sighed. "Shouldn't you be haunting Elizabeth? Or one of the others? Keep Susan awake with your knocking."

"Lizzie has enough trials," Lucretia said.

Victoria snorted. She suspected Lucretia was still miffed at Elizabeth Cady Stanton for describing her as a fading tree in her final years.

The crowd roared approval as the next-to-last speaker stepped up to the podium. The energetic Theodore Roosevelt began his introduction of Victoria. Although he was nearly twenty years her junior, Victoria was surprised to feel such a kinship with the avid sportsman and New York

"Victoria for President," Says Nellie Bly

politician. His interest in women's rights seemed sincere and he confided in her that he felt he could make history quicker by joining the campaign. Certainly Roosevelt's jovial willingness to take second place behind a woman had come as a shock to the Republican establishment, who apparently had been considering him as a running mate for McKinley.

"I consent to take this position so that the door of hope—the door of opportunity—is open for all our citizens," shouted Teddy from the podium. "All men and all women have an equal right to vote!"

The roar became a tidal wave of sound as people rose from their seats clapping for Teddy.

"He does know how to give a speech," Victoria remarked to Lucretia. A glimmering invaded the shadows backstage. She sensed other ghosts drawing nearer. Victoria rather hoped Harriet Beecher Stowe would be among them. She took some joy in outliving her enemies, including the woman who called her a "brazen tramp" for daring to run for President the first time.

"Be thou humble, Victoria," said Lucretia, ever the Quaker and apparently able to read her thoughts. "Delight not in the downfall of thine enemies."

"Humility won me nothing. I lopped off my hair, pleaded with my audiences, and they still abandoned me," Victoria retorted. "I much prefer being rich to being poor. Being a comet blazing across the sky to a meteor sunk in the mire."

Victoria glared at the spirit. The ghost managed to look faintly abashed.

"I once told Lizzie that we must proceed slowly," said Lucretia. "To ask for suffrage too soon would make us ridiculous."

"And now?" asked Victoria.

Lucretia shook her lace-capped head. "I am dead. Patience gained us nothing. Virtue became the tool which our enemies used to shatter our alliance. Let us learn the value of pride, Victoria." In the wings, Lucretia was joined by the ghosts of Mary M'Clintock, Martha Coffin Wright, Jane Hunt, and the others who had rallied at Seneca Falls more than fifty years ago.

Victoria nodded and stood up. She strode across the stage as Teddy bellowed her name and took her place at the podium.

"Dear friends, rise! Our moment has come," Victoria began.

Luckily Nellie had already sent the speech to the newspapers. The cacophony of cheers from her followers and the shouts of anger from her detractors shook the hall and drowned out her next words. Victoria raised her head. She stared them all straight in the eye, drawing strength from the army of ghosts assembling behind her. The ghosts of the Woman's Rights Convention surrounded her with their passion, their heartbreak, and their willingness this time to win the White House. They may not have been seen, they may not have been heard by the audience. But Victoria knew they were there. Their power and her purpose fueled her speech.

"Let us lead this nation into a glorious new century!" Victoria shouted from the stage. According to all the witnesses, her shout rang from the rafters, making the banners dance above their heads.

Tennie sailed into New York on the Cunard Line's most luxurious steamer. By the time she arrived with a dozen trunks and a French maid, Victoria had a table full of newspapers in the center of a much larger suite in the Waldorf-Astoria. In fact, Victoria's new supporters and campaign workers had taken over the entire floor. The hotel had even assigned a special concierge to take requests from "Glorious Victoria" as the press and the hotel staff proudly called her.

"Well, sister, I like your Teddy," said Lady Cook, collapsing onto a sofa as she pulled off her gloves and feathered hat. "But I love your Nellie."

The young woman who once walked proudly down Wall Street in a man's jacket and shirt draped over a simple black skirt was now every inch the aristocrat bedecked in lace, velvet, and ribbons. But Victoria could see her younger sister's remarkable charisma and energy still shining through her conventionally fashionable ensemble. The whirlwind named Tennie was ready to blow through the mansions of the gilded rich from coast to coast. Nellie was right. The society reporters would love every minute of it.

"Everything went well at the dock?" Victoria asked, although she was already certain of Tennie's grand entrance as Lady Cook.

"Mr. Roosevelt was waiting to greet me with two dozen yellow roses." Yellow roses signified their support for women's suffrage. A

"Victoria for President," Says Nellie Bly

clever touch for the campaign even though the national organization had yet to acknowledge them. "Nellie Bly made sure that twice as many reporters questioned us. It will be in all the papers tonight."

"Perfect. Did you bring the book?"

Tennie's perfectly plucked eyebrows flew up. She patted the silver mesh purse hanging from her belt. "I kept it close through the crossing and under my skirts during the customs check. All of Alice's clients and a few others. But will anyone care? Won't many of them be dead?"

"The prostitutes may be dead, but those clients are respectable grandfathers these days who would prefer not to have their exploits published." This time, Victoria wouldn't denounce the hypocrites from the stage or the pages of her own newspaper. This time she planned to use Tennie's lists from the madams of New York's bordellos much more quietly and competently. Several talks with Cornelius had helped pinpoint the most susceptible to blackmail among New York's elite. Some of those elite had moved over the decades, now holding sway over high society in Boston, Chicago, and San Francisco. A few stops on Lady Cook's tour should prove properly motivating for certain politicians and their supporters.

"It's all about the electoral college," Victoria explained to her sister. "We can lose the popular vote and still win the White House. We simply need the majority of electoral votes."

A Harvard-trained running mate who enjoyed battling the political machine was proving to be quite advantageous this time. Teddy explained it all so very well to the rest of them.

"So how do we win the electoral college without the popular vote?" Tennie asked.

"Well, Teddy is asking the men to vote for us as a protest against the incumbent and his perpetual challenger. They may do it as a lark or a jest, but it counts for us and reduces the support for the other two. Still, our best bet is to overwhelm the polls with women. I'm calling on all women to exercise rights already granted. Nellie has planned a series of articles to be published across the country telling them why they can and should vote."

"Last time, your argument didn't work."

"We never should have bothered with those stuck-up politicians in Washington or let the press turn against us," said Victoria. "They'll debate our rights for decades. Let the women decide for themselves in November."

"But won't their votes just be thrown away? Won't the women be arrested?"

"In some places. But in others they will have the right to vote in local elections and there's nothing to stop them from writing in a presidential candidate. It's easy to arrest one Susan B. Anthony and fine her for casting one vote. But when all the women cast their votes on the same day, how do you stop them?"

"It will make for chaos on Election Day."

"Exactly," said Victoria with a smile so vicious that Tennie burst into laughter. "Millions of women invading the polls everywhere! Complete and utter chaos. Terrific doubt cast on who won the popular vote. So it all comes down to the electoral votes. With your book of names, pressure from the suffrage-minded wives and mothers, articles calling for Glorious Victoria to lead the nation into a new century, and a little spiritual guidance from Cornelius and friends, we should be able to sway enough electors to our cause."

"Winner takes all," said Tennie with some satisfaction. "Is it too early to order champagne? I'm parched from talking to everyone at the pier."

Victoria called for room service as Tennie shuffled through the newspapers on display.

"Oh, I like this one," she said, holding up the front page with the giant headline: "Victoria for President, Says Nellie Bly!"

The early press was glorious, but as Election Day loomed ever nearer, the Democrats and Republicans grew more shrill in their denouncements of "That Martin!" as they'd taken to calling Victoria. For a variety of reasons, some found in Tennie's book, neither side quite had the gumption to bring back Nash's label of Mrs. Satan, but the cartoons which did circulate were vicious enough.

"We'll need an exceptional turnout at the polls," said Teddy.

"The women must show up," said Nellie. "Susan B. Anthony must endorse us."

"Victoria for President," Says Nellie Bly

"Oh, damn," said Victoria as Tennie sighed. Even Cornelius seated in his usual chair by the window looked concerned. "I'll have to apologize to her. Help me write the letter, Nellie." Because this was Susan B. Anthony, and only a well-written appeal would do.

It took nearly a day to come up with a draft which met everyone's approval. It took more than a week for a response. But a date was set for a meeting at the Waldorf-Astoria.

Victoria waited alone in her suite. She'd sent everyone out, although she knew a number would be waiting in the halls to catch a glimpse of the famed Anthony. Nellie planned to bring her up the elevator from a private entrance, as arranged by the hotel staff to avoid the crowds packing the main lobby for news of Victoria and her campaign.

Cornelius appeared in his chair by the window.

"No company," snapped Victoria, betraying her nerves.

"A silent witness only," said Cornelius, laying a finger against his lips. "You're making history today." Lucretia shimmered in the other corner of the room. She said nothing.

Victoria huffed but felt a little better to have her ghosts there. She wished Tennie wasn't in Boston playing aristocratic guest of the New England bluebloods, but they needed those influential supporters.

The elevator doors opened with their usual clang, audible through the half-opened door and in the stillness on the floor. Then the whispers of her staff: "She's here."

There was only one she, the true leader of the national suffrage movement, indomitable Susan B. Anthony stumping into her parlor. Victoria sprang up from the sofa like an overanxious schoolgirl. Susan always impacted her, and everyone else, like the most stern of teachers.

"I'm here," said Susan. "What do you have to say for yourself?"

Behind her, Nellie quietly closed the door on the staff peeping in. She shrugged at Victoria, a sign that she couldn't gauge Susan's mood either. It all came down to this. If Susan gave her endorsement, they had more than a fighting chance to win. If she did not...but Victoria refused to accept defeat.

"I am sorry," said Victoria, stepping forward and grasping both of Susan's hands in her own. "The blackmail letters were a mistake. I should have listened to you."

Susan stared at her, all dour frown lines and disapproving eyes. And so old. When had their champion begun to look so ancient and tired? A quick calculation surprised Victoria into realizing Susan must be more than 80 years old. Then Susan's fingers curled around Victoria's. She clasped Victoria's hands lightly and then pulled away. From Susan, it was the equivalent of a kiss and a bear hug.

Stunned, Victoria stared at Susan, unsure what to say next.

"Elizabeth sent a telegram to me," said Susan. "Every time I listened to her, we went forward. Every time I didn't, we wandered in the wilderness. She reminded me of my own words. Once I wrote that you heralded the whole future of women."

Well, thought Victoria, may the heavens bless the philosopher of Seneca Falls and her memory. If Elizabeth Cady Stanton had written in her support and conjured up those early days, Susan might well turn favorable to their cause. Which meant the other women would follow. "I stirred Susan, and Susan stirred the world," Elizabeth had told her long ago.

"How is Elizabeth?" Victoria said out loud.

"Dying, discouraged, but not yet defeated. Much like the rest of us. Fifty years of fighting and still we fail to secure our rights, our very sovereignty," said Susan. "Elizabeth told me not to wait any longer. That she wants to be above ground when women march through Washington behind a president that they elected."

Nellie advanced into the room. "Can I quote you for our articles? Can I say you stand with us?"

"You can do more than that," said Susan. She pulled out a sheaf of closely written pages from her old-fashioned black bag. "You may publish our new manifesto stating that all women hold the right to vote, protected by the existing amendments to our Constitution and the laws of this great land. We will no longer cajole or plead for the right to be heard. We will shout our rights on every corner! The National American Woman Suffrage Association stands behind you. All will vote in November. Women, their rights, and nothing less. I have given my life and all I am to our cause. Now I want my last act to be the placement of a woman in the White House."

"Huzzah!" cried Victoria. She heard Cornelius cheer and a quiet "Well done, dear Susan" from Lucretia. The silenced voices of

"Victoria for President," Says Nellie Bly

thousands of women who fought and died before this day rang through the ether. Their time had come.

Nellie snatched the papers from Susan's hand and ran for the door, shouting for her staff to grab the phones. Tonight the switchboards across the country would be busy as the women spread the news. Tomorrow all the newspapers would proclaim: "Victoria for President, Says Susan B. Anthony."

As the days progressed, Susan came often to the campaign headquarters, bringing reports from the other leaders. "Carrie Nation says she'll apply her hatchet to any poll which tries to bar a woman from voting, as will her followers. Jane Addams plans to lead the immigrants of Chicago, women and men, to their voting stations. Let them try to stop her. Ida B. Wells will march with her brave sisters upon the polls of the South. In the West, women are gathering to demand their right to vote in national elections as well as local."

Through it all, Nellie wrote, Tennie charmed, and Victoria spoke. Until at last, the chaos of the election was done. Hundreds of thousands, nay millions of women overran the polls across the nation, according to the newspapers on November 7. The electors gathered behind closed doors and cast their votes. Some for the incumbent, some for his Democrat challenger, but enough, oh barely enough, for Glorious Victoria.

Lawsuits began the next day, and arguments rang through the courts, but the spirits whispered in the ears of the judges. As did their mothers, wives, sisters, and daughters. Still, by the slimmest of margins and with many learned dissents, Victoria's victory was confirmed.

On Monday, March 4, 1901, Victoria Clafin Woodhull Blood Martin became the President of the United States. With a sour face, Chief Justice Melville Fuller administered the oath of office. Equally discontented were the long faces of the members from the House of Representatives and the Senate gathered on the East Portico.

But Victoria didn't care. She looked past them to the sea of women who had marched down Pennsylvania Avenue carrying their yellow roses, hatchets, and banners. At Ida B. Wells proudly leading the delegations from across the country. At Elizabeth Cady Stanton surrounded by her daughters. At Susan B. Anthony almost smiling in approval.

She saw and heard quite clearly the ghost of Cornelius Vanderbilt shouting triumphantly with Lucretia Mott and the others who had not lived to see this day.

Victoria reached out her hand. She felt a hard squeeze from her sister Tennie, standing beside her as always.

"Go on, Victoria," whispered Tennie.

So the 26th President of the United States stepped up to the podium and began her speech. In her very first paragraph, she talked about the freedom to love as a choice, as a right, as essential as the vote. She spoke about equality, true equality of pay and distribution of wealth, not as an ideal but as a practical necessity to be protected by the laws of the land. Victoria called for the women to follow her into office, to make all branches of the government as balanced as they should be. Most importantly, she said, every citizen had the right to vote their heart and conscience, the right to be heard by their government.

She concluded, "Thus do I claim this administration will be the friend and the exponent of the most complete equality to which humanity can attain. We will create a land where there shall be no distinction among citizens on any grounds whatsoever. Let us strive for the broadest individual freedom compatible with the public good!"

The director of the Smithsonian enjoyed her early morning walk through the empty galleries. Later in the day there would be crowds and speeches, so many speeches, from those who had benefited from the last century of progress. And cake. A very large cake to celebrate the 100th anniversary of the inauguration of the first female President of the United States.

The exhibition looked grand. They'd borrowed from the Martin Presidential Library and private collections. Several significant loans had arrived safely from the British Museum to illustrate Lady Cook's impact on her adopted country.

"Victoria for President," Says Nellie Bly

The artifacts and mementos were all very well. But as she paused at the entrance to the centennial exhibition, the director was moved by the most important display as much as when she first read and understood what it meant as a very small schoolgirl in Virginia. The words of the 19th Amendment covered the wall. The greatest achievement of President Martin during her third term in office. The words spoken with husky emotion at President Martin's funeral by Judge Alice Paul: "Equality of rights under the law shall not be denied or abridged by the United States or by any state on account of sex."

FACT VERSUS FICTION

The preceding story is a work of fiction. The ghost of Cornelius Vanderbilt did not haunt Victoria Martin, although the living Cornelius set up Victoria and her younger sister Tennessee as the first female stock brokers on Wall Street.

In 1871, Victoria testified before the House Judiciary Committee that American women already possessed the right to vote under the 14th and 15th Amendments, thus eliminating the need for Congressional support and a state-by-state campaign for what would become the 19th Amendment. Congress declined to follow through on her suggestion that they pass legislation to clarify this.

Then Victoria ran for President in 1872, but the campaign collapsed in a bizarre series of events which spawned press condemnation and (worse) complete dropping of campaign coverage. It also led to great biographies by later historians, although the sisters were left out of the history of suffrage by Stanton and Anthony.

Victoria and Tennie eventually fled their scandals by sailing to England. The sisters' trip was probably financed by Vanderbilt's heirs, perhaps to keep them out of the lawsuits swirling around Vanderbilt's will after his death. After arriving in England, both married extremely well. Victoria wed John Martin and then inherited his father's wealth due to the old man dying three days before John. Tennessee married Lord Cook and also inherited a fortune in 1901 when her husband died.

Victoria tried a few political comebacks. But her divorces, her outspoken support of free love and birth control, and her work as a faith healer and medium always made her a target of the press. Her earlier blackmail scheme involving the leaders of the American suffrage movement, including Susan B. Anthony, didn't help. Their biographers vary greatly on what Victoria and Tennie did or didn't do in terms of blackmail, but quoted letters from Susan show that Susan was very angry with Victoria after indeed calling her first campaign the "future of women."

Following John's death, Victoria settled (sort of) into English country life and indulged her passion for automobiles. As Lady Cook, Tennie became a frequent speaker on women's rights in the United Kingdom and United States, including a meeting with President Theodore Roosevelt at the White House.

For those who would like to learn more about these complicated and fascinating sisters, I highly recommend *The Scarlet Sisters* by Myra MacPherson, *Notorious Victoria* by Mary Gabriel, and *Other Powers* by Barbara Goldsmith.

As far as I can determine, Victoria and Tennie never met Nellie Bly, who arrived in New York in 1887, a decade after the sisters sailed for London. Nellie, also known as Elizabeth Cochrane Seaman, led an equally adventurous life including her famed journey around the world. Nellie left journalism for a few years after she married the much older millionaire Robert Seaman. One of the pieces of Nellie Bly memorabilia that I own is an advertisement for their company's exhibition at the 1901 Pan-American Exposition. The card proudly proclaims that Nellie Bly was the only woman in the world personally managing "industries of such magnificence." She later returned to reporting as a widow.

In her article on the "Woman Suffrage Procession of 1913", Nellie predicted that women wouldn't win the vote until 1920. She was, of course, quite correct. Neither Susan B. Anthony (d. 1906) nor Elizabeth Cady Stanton (d.1902) lived to see the passage of the 19th Amendment. Victoria (d. 1927), Tennie (d. 1923), and Nellie (d. 1922) did.

The amendment quoted in this story is not the 19th Amendment as it exists in the Constitution. It is the Alice Paul Amendment, first introduced in 1923 and since known as the Equal Rights Amendment.

The Ghosts of Bhopal

Rasana Atreya

Prologue

On the night of December 2ND, 1984, a tour bus carrying a group of pilgrims cut through the streets of Bhopal. The night was eerily still, the streets bathed in the soft glow of streetlights. In the distance, the Union Carbide India Limited (UCIL) pesticide plant loomed, a sprawling behemoth against the starlit sky. As the clock ticked over from December 2nd to December 3rd, the bus halted for the night. It was 12:45 a.m. The pilgrims disembarked. Having skipped their tea break by consensus because they wanted to make it to their night halt by 12:30 a.m., the pilgrims sat on the wooden benches laid out next to the tea stall across from the private residence where they would spend the night.

On that bus was a couple, Shankar and Shobha. Having left their only child, eight-year-old Lakshmi, in the care of Shankar's parents, they were accompanying Shobha's parents on their pilgrimage. At the tea stall, Shankar and Shobha huddled together in the chill of the night, smiling at the thought of returning to their little Lakshmi, their hearts full of gratitude for this spiritual journey. A gentle breeze carried the faint scent of something chemical, acrid, but the city slumbered on, oblivious to the impending catastrophe.

Suddenly, screams pierced the night, followed by a choking, burning sensation in their throats and eyes. Shankar and Shobha watched, aghast, as some of the older pilgrims clawed at their chests, gasping for air. They were dead before they hit the ground. Terrified, the couple hustled Shobha's parents back into their bus. The tour bus operator checked for pulses—there were none—jumped into the bus and honked hard. All those still alive clambered on, and the bus tore out of Bhopal.

As the bus navigated the streets, Shankar and Shobha watched in horror as people stumbled out into the streets. The city had dissolved into chaos, bodies collapsing like puppets with their strings hacked off.

The catastrophic gas leak at the UCIL pesticide plant in the early hours of December 3rd, 1984, released a deadly cloud of methyl isocyanate gas. Thousands died agonising deaths, choking on the very air they breathed. Thousands more suffered devastating injuries—blindness, organ damage, neurological disorders. It was one of the worst industrial disasters in history. Over 500,000 people were affected.

The bus carrying the pilgrims travelled non-stop, with only quick halts for bathroom breaks and hasty meals. The journey was a blur of grief and fear, the survivors left to process the unimaginable horrors they had witnessed.

In the early hours of December 4th, the bus driver drove them to a hospital in Hyderabad. There he collapsed, never to wake again. Shobha's parents—maternal grandparents of Lakshmi—died that night. Shankar lived another two years, constantly in and out of hospitals. When he passed away, their family was destitute, and Shobha was pregnant with her second child, Mithila. There was no record of any of the pilgrims being in Bhopal on the night of the tragedy. Nor of the ones who made it out of Bhopal. Consequently, none received compensation.

From the ashes of this tragedy, a new India was born. An India that vowed "Never again." Strict regulations on corporate accountability and environmental safety were enacted. Sustainability became more than a buzzword—it was a mandate. Companies were held to the highest standards, with transparency and integrity non-negotiable. The spectre

The Ghosts of Bhopal

of Bhopal loomed large, a constant reminder of the cost when profits are prioritised over people and the planet.

But for little Lakshmi and her family, the scars ran deep. The gas that stole her grandparents and father would shape the course of her life, and that of her unborn sister, in ways she could never imagine. The ghosts of Bhopal would haunt them forever.

Chapter 1

December 3rd, 2017, thirty-three years to the day of the Bhopal Gas Tragedy, Renuka Prasad stepped off the office bus in Hyderabad, Telangana. It was her first day at her first job as an environmental engineer. Renuka, daughter of Lakshmi, stood across from the gleaming façade of EcoTech Solutions, the significance of the day weighing heavy on her.

Growing up in the shadow of the Bhopal disaster, Renuka had witnessed first-hand the devastating and long-lasting impact of corporate malfeasance. She had watched her maternal grandmother succumb to the lingering effects of the gas leak, her vibrant eyes more often than not dimmed by a haze of pain.

Even more heart-breaking was the story of her aunt, Mithila, born two years after the disaster. Though Mithila had never directly inhaled the toxic gas, the poisonous legacy was seeped into her very DNA. She battled a host of developmental issues and learning disabilities, her potential forever stunted by the sins of Union Carbide. The scars of Bhopal ran deep in Renuka's family.

As Renuka mentally prepared for her first day at EcoTech Solutions, she couldn't help but think of her aunt Mithila, whose life had been forever altered by the tragedy.

Earlier that morning, Renuka had paused outside her aunt Mithila's room, her hand resting on the doorknob. She took a deep breath, steeling herself, then stepped inside. The room was dimly lit, the air heavy with the mingled scents of incense and illness. Mithila lay on the bed, her frail form dwarfed by the white sheets, medical equipment blinking and beeping around her.

On the walls, photographs of a vibrant Mithila seemed to mock the present reality. There she was, forever childlike in her thirty-year-old body, flying a kite on a breezy day, her eyes sparkling with innocence and joy. Renuka blinked back tears as she approached the bed.

"Renu, my baby," Mithila rasped, her thin hand trembling as she reached out. Renuka clasped it gently, feeling the bird-like bones beneath papery skin.

"I like bobbatlu, Mithila said. "Renu, my baby, do you know I like them so… sweet?" She looked up expectantly at Renuka.

Renuka's throat tightened with emotion. "I know you do. Akka will make them for you." On the other side of the bed, Renuka's mother, Lakshmi—Akka to her younger sister—nodded.

Renuka leaned down and pressed a kiss to Mithila's forehead. "I have to go away now. You remember, I told you? I have a job in Hyderabad?"

Mithila's head bobbed. "Renu, my baby, will do big people work." Turning sideways to her sister, she said, "You'll make me bobbatlu?"

Lakshmi smiled gently. "You know I will."

With a final squeeze of Mithila's hand, Renuka left for the bus station on the pillion of her father's Maruti Suzuki scooter. Two hours later, she was in Hyderabad.

As Renuka stepped through the doorway of EcoTech Solutions, the weight of her family's history settled on her shoulders. She silently renewed her vow to honour her grandmother's memory and her aunt Mithila's daily struggles by fighting for a world where such tragedies could never happen again. In this gleaming building, she would work tirelessly to ensure that corporate accountability and environmental safety were more than just buzzwords—they would be the guiding principles of her work.

The atrium soared above her, a stunning fusion of modern architecture and traditional elements. Chrome and glass intertwined with intricately carved teakwood and vibrant Kanchi cotton tapestries, creating a perfect blend of the industrial and the ecological. A living wall of verdant plants, reminiscent of the lush Araku Valley, dominated the space. Recycled rainwater gurgled through a series of sculptural fountains, each one shaped like a majestic temple gopuram, paying homage to the iconic architecture of South India. The floor, a mesmerising mosaic of intricately patterned Athangudi tiles from Tamil Nadu—handmade and eco-friendly—added a touch of timeless elegance to the space.

Employees dressed in a mix of Western business attire and traditional Indian clothes bustled about, engaged in animated conversations. When Renuka looked at herself in the mirror earlier this morning, a polyester sari draping her slender frame, her long braid draped over a shoulder, she was excited about the next phase of her life. Now, as she eyed the snooty Fab India types, attired in their crisply starched cotton saris and kurtas, their hair professionally styled, her confidence was shaken.

She squared her shoulders. They would learn to accept her—respect her, even—because she was as intelligent as any of them. She had no choice; her parents were counting on her salary. Without it, they wouldn't be able to afford the education of her younger brother, who would be starting college in a few months. They had drained their savings to pay for Renuka's college, so she owed them this, at the very least.

You can do this! She took a deep breath, inhaling the comforting smell of jasmine incense. She walked to the reception to check in.

"You can wait there," the stern receptionist said in her posh English, pointing to a cluster of expensive sofas.

Renuka eyed the sofas. The people sitting there were too fancy-looking for her, so she pretended to be absorbed by the architecture. It was both innovative and sustainable, she had to admit. She felt an overwhelming sense of pride—and apprehension—to be part of a company that not only embraced the future but also celebrated the rich heritage of India.

"Welcome to EcoTech, Renuka!" Priya Reddy, head of the Water Treatment Division, greeted her warmly. "We're so thrilled to have you join the team."

As Priya led her through the state-of-the-art facility, happiness—tinged with anxiety—suffused Renuka's being. This was her company now—the place she worked! To be part of a company that understood the weight of the legacy left by Bhopal and was dedicated to forging a better path forward, and paid so well—what more could she expect?

When Priya introduced Renuka to the brilliant minds behind EcoTech's ground-breaking projects, Renuka felt a sense of rightness, of belonging. This was where she would use her training as an environmental engineer to help create real, meaningful change. As she shook hands with her new colleagues, Renuka hoped that she would find her place amongst this intimidatingly competent team of individuals committed to building a safer, more sustainable world.

Chapter 2

Renuka quickly fell into a rhythm at EcoTech. Her days were a whirlwind of training; college had taught her theory, but it did not prepare her for the real world. She was particularly grateful to be mentored by Siddharth, a brilliant engineer in his late twenties, and Neelima, their meticulous and driven project manager.

Siddharth had a lean, wiry build with sharp, observant eyes that missed nothing. His clothing of choice was raggedy t-shirts with logos of various companies that occupied the sustainability space. Neelima, on the other hand, had a polished, professional appearance, and a smile that never seemed to reach her eyes. Siddharth and Neelima tackled complex challenges, brainstorming late into the night over steaming cups of filter coffee and South Indian tiffins from the popular food stall conveniently located right across from their office building. Renuka eagerly soaked up all that knowledge.

Soon she began to work on small projects. The work was challenging but energising. Renuka marvelled at how Siddharth could seemingly pluck ground-breaking ideas out of thin air, his eyes sparkling with excitement as he scribbled furiously on the white board in their meeting room. Neelima, on the other hand, kept their tiny team grounded and on track, her colour-coded Gantt charts and meticulously organised Kanban boards ensuring that no detail was overlooked. Renuka found herself thriving in the innovative environment, her mind stretched in ways she had never imagined.

"What do you want to work on for your first independent project?" Siddharth asked.

According to the Central Ground Water Board, geogenic contamination was a major issue in their district. These contaminants—which included heavy metals like arsenic, lead, and mercury, as well as elements like fluoride and radon—originated from geological formations and processes, such as the weathering of rocks and minerals, and the leaching of elements from soil and bedrock. These contaminants often entered into drinking water sources, soil, and air, leading to potential health hazards for humans and ecosystems.

"The groundwater in our district has geogenic contamination issues. Do you think I should start with that?"

"You're not in college anymore," he said in gentle reprimand. "Be assertive. Make statements like—I want to look into that."

"Sorry," she whispered.

"Don't be sorry, either. We're colleagues. That means we're equals." He smiled to take the sting out of his words.

Renuka nodded. Efforts to mitigate geogenic contamination typically involved monitoring and assessing the levels of these substances in the environment, implementing appropriate remediation measures, and ensuring safe drinking water supplies through treatment technologies when necessary.

EcoTech's almost-ready-to-launch filtration system was state-of-the-art, providing safe drinking water to their district. She'd start here, and familiarise herself with this particular aspect of it. Then, who knew, maybe she could come up with a design improvement! Her favourite lady professor at college often said that to design improvements to a system, you had to thoroughly understand it first.

Renuka spent days—and more nights than she could count—working on gaining an understanding of their filtration system. She'd even skipped her last weekly video call with her parents back in Mahbubnagar just so she could write up what she had learnt. Seated in the cubicle she shared with Siddharth—their backs to each other—she raised her chin; she was finally finding her place here.

Late one evening, as they pored over design schematics armed with filter coffee and melt-in-your-mouth pongal, Siddharth turned to Renuka with a grin. "Your proposed modification to the filtration system design is good work, Renuka. You're on your way to a promotion, girl!"

Renuka felt a flush of pride at his words. For four years, she'd poured herself into her college studies, driven by the memory of her grandmother's rasping breaths and her aunt's broken body. At EcoTech, she was getting the chance to make an actual difference.

Long months on the project, and today was the day she would get feedback from Neelima. Hopefully, Neelima was impressed enough that she'd ask Renuka to present it to the upper management.

Renuka drummed her fingers on the keyboard tray. The calendar notification for the long-awaited meeting popped up on her screen, and she jumped to her feet.

"Time for that promotion." Siddharth teased. Since the two shared a cubicle, a casual friendship had developed between them.

Renuka blushed. Was she that transparent?

"Seriously, though. You've earned it."

Renuka flushed with pleasure. After all the hours she had put in, researching, refining, rethinking—she had earned the promotion.

"You're on schedule, too. Fourteen months is a little early for a promotion, but not by too much."

Giving him a brief smile of thanks, she exited the cubicle and walked towards her manager's office. She passed by the cubicle next to her, where

The Ghosts of Bhopal

a group of people her age was gathered. So many people of all ages occupied this floor, and her only friend was Siddharth. Probably because he shared his workspace with her. She had hoped that he'd introduce her to his friends, but he didn't seem to need the validation of his peers.

The group was laughing at something. Hopefully, not at her. She looked down at her cotton sari. She'd seen this in an ad for an upscale clothing store. She winced at how much she'd paid for it—money that would have been better used towards her brother's college fees. He was studying computer science at a private college now. The college was prestigious enough, but the fees—her stomach tightened at the thought. The next instalment would be due soon. She HAD to get this promotion.

Neelima's office was against the wall, along with those of the more senior engineers. Someday, she would be in one of them, Renuka promised herself. This promotion was only the first of many steps to Priya's office. Along the way, she'd pay off the loan for her brother's education, then start saving up so her parents could buy themselves their own flat. No more living in one-bedroom flats. No more being at the mercy of intractable landlords.

All of her parents' married life had been spent in service of Renuka's maternal grandmother and maternal aunt. Renuka had the deepest respect for her father for this reason. Which man, if not an honourable one, spent a lifetime in the care of the mother and sister of his wife?

Her grandmother had passed away three years ago, but her aunt still lived with them. Her parents continued to pay off Renuka's grandmother's hospital debts, even as new ones appeared each month for her aunt.

This promotion, and the extra addition to her salary that came with it—it would be a validation of her work. She thought of her parents' joy when she told them, and she glowed with happiness. Squaring her shoulders, she knocked at the door of her manager.

Neelima beckoned her in. "Close the door."

Renuka pulled the door shut and sat, her heart pounding in excitement.

"I want you to familiarise yourself with the real-time monitoring capabilities of our filtration system. It integrates advanced sensors and data analytics to enable continuous, real-time monitoring of water quality and system performance."

Renuka was taken aback at the abrupt way Neelima spoke. "What about the contaminant work I've been doing?"

"With the launch coming up," Neelima said. "I want you to focus on the monitoring."

"But—"

"Your idea is good enough—"

Good enough? Just three weeks ago, Neelima couldn't lavish enough compliments on her work. "But funds were allocated—"

"And now they've been unallocated because we're trying to make sure all eyes remain on the launch. Nothing can go wrong." Neelima pushed a file forward. "This is your performance evaluation."

Renuka opened it, and looked down at it, not able to understand what was happening. "Exemplary" for a project not worthy of being funded?

"I know I've been giving you work that an intern could do. But the launch is demanding all our attention. Thank you for your hard work," Neelima said. "I hope you are happy with the new salary." She got up and opened the door.

Renuka watched as Neelima strode away, her crisp cotton saree swishing around her ankles, her heels clicking on the polished marble floor. Renuka returned to her workstation in disbelief. She dropped into her chair in her cubicle.

"So?" Siddharth wheeled his chair around.

"My project was killed."

"What?" Siddharth looked at her in disbelief.

"Neelima said the funds have been unallocated." Tears flooded Renuka eyes without warning. She turned away, rapidly blinking back tears.

"Oh. I'm so sorry about the promotion."

"The strange thing is, I got both the promotion and the salary hike I was expecting."

He frowned. "That's odd."

It was odd. "But…" Her voice caught.

He gentled his voice. "I know you're disappointed. I also know how hard you worked on it. But innovation does have to meet budgetary expectations."

She turned around to face him, her shoulders slumped. At least she had the promotion. Her parents would be happy for her. Thankfully, her brother's fees would also be taken care of.

"And," he added, "there's the launch."

Right. The launch. "Has such a thing happened to you?" she asked. "Projects getting pulled from under you?"

"I've been here for four years now, and I've seen this happen more than once," he admitted. "But, unless you're able to fund your passions, you have to accept that there will always be someone else who pulls the strings."

"That's a pretty depressing way of looking at the world," she said.

"It's also reality." He looked at her, eyes softening. "Still, don't ever lose your convictions. Because, what are we without them?"

"Where do I go from here?"

"Home." Siddharth got to his feet and slung his backpack over a shoulder. "It's 8:30 pm." Waving goodbye, he strode towards the lifts.

Renuka shook her head. Home was Mahbubnagar, where her parents and aunt were. Her apartment in Hyderabad was a shared bedroom with two other girls. They lived over a tiffin centre that dished out cheap meals that she shared with her roommates. The thought depressed her.

She remembered the envy her classmates in environmental engineering had expressed when Renuka snagged this job. EcoTech's new filtration system was to be the best in the business. The Central government was touting this venture as their promise of continuing sustainability in the post-Bhopal world.

The disappointment Renuka felt was crushing.

Chapter 3

One month later, Renuka boarded an air-conditioned bus in Hyderabad. The bus, a modern and comfortable vehicle, offered a welcome respite from the sweltering heat outside. But her heart was heavy with sorrow. She was journeying to Mahbubnagar to bid a final farewell to her beloved aunt, who was not expected to live long enough to see the following morning's sunrise.

She gazed out of the window as the bus navigated its way out of the city. The urban landscape slowly gave way to the countryside. The rocky terrain of the Deccan Plateau, dotted with small towns and smaller villages, and the occasional hillock, stretched out before her. The bus cut through villages, past impromptu roadside temples and churches and mosques. She watched as people went about their day—farmers tending to their crops, children playing in the streets, women walking the streets with their pushcarts, hawking vegetables. A foreign SUV roared past, egged on by a muscular Mahindra Scorpio.

The kilometres flashed by. Renuka's thoughts turned to the inevitable goodbye that awaited her at the end of her journey. She tried to prepare herself emotionally for the loss she knew was coming, but, really, how did one do that? She felt sorry for her brother. He was sick in far-away Ranchi, and so unable to say his goodbyes.

As the bus approached Mahbubnagar, the landscape became more arid, with fewer trees and more rocky outcroppings. Despite this, Mahbubnagar was home to Pillalamarri—the children's banyan—the eight-hundred-year-old tree that spread out over four acres.

Finally, the bus reached the terminus, and she spotted her father, waiting on his Maruti Suzuki scooter, his unshaved jaw dotted with white whiskers an indication that all was not well. She got off and walked towards him. Their eyes met, and he shook his head slowly. She got on the pillion of the scooter, resting a hand on his shoulder. Sitting sideways with both feet on the footrest, she tucked her sari so it wouldn't billow, and they were off.

Ten minutes later, Renuka was by her aunt Mithila's hospital bed. As Renuka gently cradled the hand of the childlike woman who had been her beacon of love throughout her life, the weight of the Bhopal Gas Tragedy seemed to permeate the very air around them. Mithila's laboured breaths and the beeping of the medical equipment served as a constant reminder of the ongoing consequences of that fateful night.

Renuka's mother sat on the other side of the bed, her eyes swollen with grief and exhaustion. She looked up at Renuka, anger in her gaze.

The Ghosts of Bhopal

"It's been thirty-three years since that dreadful night," Lakshmi said, her voice heavy with emotion. "Thirty-three years, and we're still grappling with the aftermath. Union Carbide simply wrapped up its operations and went back to America, leaving us to pick up the pieces."

Renuka nodded, her throat tight. She knew the story all too well—how the toxic gas leak had claimed thousands of lives and left countless others, like her aunt Mithila, with lifelong health problems.

"They never truly faced justice," Lakshmi continued, gently stroking Mithila's hand. "And now, here we are, watching our loved ones suffer, day after day. When will it end, Renuka? When will the ghosts of Bhopal finally be laid to rest?"

Renuka felt a surge of emotion—grief, anger, and a fierce determination to make a difference. Leaning in to tenderly press her cheek against her aunt's, Renuka felt a tremor pass through Mithila's frail form. Then, as if finally finding peace, Mithila exhaled softly, her final breath dissolving into the hushed stillness of the room. Her beloved aunt left the world at thirty-two years of age, free at last from the suffering that had burdened her all her life.

A single tear rolled down Renuka's cheek as she whispered, "I won't let you and grandma be forgotten, Mithila pinni. I won't let your suffering be in vain."

Renuka returned to Hyderabad, her sense of loss deep. She couldn't get over how tragically brief her aunt's life had been. To never get to go to school, to have no friends, life experience, romantic love, nothing. Just pain, and more pain. What kind of life was that?

Weeks turned to months. The projects that Neelima was assigning her seemed like busywork. When she brought it to Neelima's attention, her manager assured her that once they were past the launch, she would be assigned more challenging work. As the launch date neared, the excitement seemed all-time high. Priya ordered dinner for the entire division, showing appreciation of them working overtime. Lots of swag was handed out.

Renuka appreciated both the free food and the fact that she was beginning to make friends. She and two other girls regularly ate lunch together. She was invited to be part of the larger group, and Renuka realized that it had never been the group that was the problem—they were nice enough. She was the one who did not like hanging out in large groups.

Despite all the positive changes, nothing felt meaningful. Sudha, one of her new friends, suggested that she was still depressed over her aunt's death. Regardless of the cause, she felt unsettled.

Restless, Renuka pulled up the technical specifications and test results for the contaminants project one morning. She noticed that the system's claimed removal efficiencies for nitrate and arsenic were extraordinarily high, almost too good to be true. Too unmotivated to do the work assigned to her, she decided to collect water samples from various points in the treatment process and analyse them independently.

Late one evening, a week after she returned from Mahbubnagar, Renuka glanced over her shoulder at Siddharth. Earphones plugged his ears, a clear indication that he was not to be disturbed. She grabbed her purse and headed down to the lab. The door opened and the lab attendant/peon—universally recognizable in colleges and government and private offices across the nation by the tailored loose, dark grey shirt and pants—walked out. "Namaste, Madam."

Renuka smiled noncommittally, mentally beseeching him, It's 9pm. Please go home. Please don't ask if I need help. Luckily for her, he did just that.

Renuka hooked the strap of her purse on a hook next to the door. The lab was large, with uncluttered workstations and surfaces to prevent cross-contamination of samples. Biosafety cabinets enclosed workspaces to provide a sterile environment for handling water samples and conducting microbiological tests, protecting both the samples and the lab personnel. Luckily, it was also empty. Most of her colleagues were hanging out in the large gathering spaces, socializing as they worked.

Renuka put on her lab coat, gloves, and safety glasses before proceeding to a workstation. The lab was spotless, a faint smell of disinfectant in the air. She took a quick look over her shoulder, even though she was the only person in the lab. She eyed the ceiling for cameras. Nothing obvious there.

Renuka took a deep breath. Ignoring the water samples in the biosafety cabinet, she reached into her purse for the water samples she had collected near various factories around the city. She knew she was breaking all kinds of rules here, but she hadn't joined EcoTech to do busywork.

The next evening, Renuka sat in her cubicle, staring at the test results in disbelief. Her tests seemed to indicate that not only was the system failing to remove nitrate and arsenic as claimed, it was actually releasing additional contaminants back into the treated water. The nitrate levels in the output water were even higher than in the untreated water, suggesting that the system was concentrating the pollutant instead of removing it.

She leaned back in her chair, not sure what to make of it. Not only was their much-touted filtration system failing to address the site-specific issues, it was actively contributing to the deterioration of water quality.

That couldn't be right. She had to be misreading the data. This was EcoTech, after all—the company that defined sustainability and ethical practices in India.

She looked over her shoulder. Siddharth was busy. Needing to do something, anything, she grabbed her purse and walked so fast she was almost running.

She slowed as she stepped out of the air-conditioned monolith. A wave of hot March air slammed into her. She almost staggered from the summer heat. June, with its cooling monsoon rains, couldn't come soon enough.

She walked across the tiled quad, where the greenery drooped, trying to ward itself from the wrath of the sun. After it cooled down, the gardeners would be out with their long hoses, reviving the plants long enough to battle another day.

She walked across the cemented driveway, which led to underground parking in the basement. The other end led to the gate and beyond. Nodding at the wilting security guards in their narrow booth, she crossed over from gated luxury to unpaved reality for many of Hyderabad's denizens. That is where she would end up if she didn't stop her imagination from running away.

EcoTech's new filtration system had support from politicians and the general public alike. Noted environmental activists had pushed for other states to adopt this system. A girl fresh out of college, an inexperienced employee, couldn't possibly know more than all of them combined.

She stood in line—a long one despite the heat—for a plate of idli-vada from the pushcart vendor who was steaming fresh idlis, even as his helper fried up fresh vadas. Renuka's, gut tightened as she considered the implications of her findings.

The days passed, the worry gnawing at the edges of her consciousness. She'd triple-checked her calculations, tested many more samples. Despite her lack of experience, her gut told her that she wasn't wrong. She turned off her monitor. Siddharth was staring at her, a troubled look on his face. When his eyes met hers, he jerked back to his screen. Renuka agonized over what to do. She was still a junior employee, and the thought of challenging her superiors made her palms sweat. But the more she learned, the more she knew she couldn't stay silent.

She started by voicing her concerns to Siddharth, hoping that as her mentor he would guide her. But to her surprise, he brushed her off, telling her to focus on her own work. Undeterred, Renuka began discreetly gathering evidence, staying late to access restricted files and collecting samples to run her own tests.

Weeks turned into months, and the weight of what she uncovered began to take its toll. Dark circles formed under her eyes, and she

The Ghosts of Bhopal

jumped at every unexpected sound, paranoid that someone would discover what she was doing.

The haunting photographs of the aftermath of the gas leak that had devastated an entire city were never far from Renuka's mind. If the tainted water was released as safe, they would be headed to an environmental and public health disaster of catastrophic proportions.

As she walked past the double doors of the executive wing on her way to the restrooms, her gut cramped in indecision. She had a sudden recollection of being seven years old and sitting beneath their guava tree on a warm night, snuggling up to her frail grandmother, listening to the story of Trishanku.

Trishanku was a king who desired to ascend directly to swargam, the heavens, without experiencing death. To fulfil his desire, Trishanku sought the help of his guru. Sage Vashishta was unwilling to grant Trishanku's wish because it went against the laws of nature and dharma. So Trishanku sought out another sage, Sage Vishwamitra, who was known for his ascetic power.

Impressed by Trishanku's determination and resolve, Sage Vishwamitra initiated a yajna. The sacrificial ritual would allow Trishanku to continue residing in his mortal body. As the ritual progressed, Trishanku's body started to ascend to the heavens. However, the celestial beings, the Devas, outraged by this audacious act, denied Trishanku entry. Instead, they pushed him back, where he was suspended upside down, trapped between heaven and earth.

Undeterred, Sage Vishwamitra vowed to create a new heaven for Trishanku. He continued his penance with severe austerities until Indra, the king of the Devas, was compelled to grant Trishanku his own separate heaven. Thus, Trishanku Swargam came to be inhabited by beings who were neither mortal nor divine, existing in a state of perpetual suspension.

While it was true that what Trishanku had attempted went against the laws of nature, he was still caught between two worlds. That's how Renuka felt now. She could go back to her workstation to gather evidence and then walk through the swinging doors that led to the senior management.

Or, she could forget about the results and continue working her way to bigger and bigger salaries. Anartham ledu, anaahutham ledu—no loss, no hurt—like her younger brother was fond of saying. Did she really want to risk her future? She had a prestigious job. Her parents, both school teachers, were so proud of what their older daughter had achieved. She could help them out even as they continued to pay off the medical loans.

She thought back to the night before she'd left home to come work here. Her parents sat on either side of her on the sofa, her father's hand on Renuka's shoulders. "Child, when in doubt, let your conscience be your guide."

"If your gut is telling you something," her mother added, "there's a reason for it. Ignore at your peril."

Decision made, Renuka returned to her workstation. As she compiled her findings into a report, her mind raced. She had to tell someone—that much was clear. But who? Priya, the woman who had brought her into EcoTech with such high hopes? Neelima, her manager who had stuck her with projects that made a mockery of her skills? Siddharth, her brilliant colleague who was so uninterested in anything but work that he was completely unaware of goings on in their internal messaging app?

Renuka closed her eyes, her grandmother Lakshmi's face swimming before her. She remembered the day, years ago, when they visited the Bhopal memorial as a family. In 1985, survivors, activists and Dutch sculptor Ruth Waterman had come together to build a memorial right across the Union Carbide factory that proclaimed: No More Bhopal, No More Hiroshima. Renuka was too young to understand the magnitude of what was commonly referred to as the Bhopal Gas Tragedy. But she saw the pain in her grandmother's eyes, and she remembered.

Chapter 4

Now that the launch was less than two weeks away, Renuka knew she couldn't wait any longer. She scheduled a meeting with Priya, rehearsing her speech a dozen times. She reminded herself to speak calmly, lay out her findings piece by piece.

The next morning, Renuka clutched the folder with her findings, her heart thudding painfully against her ribcage as she stepped into Priya's office.

Priya was on the phone, but she waved Renuka in with a smile. Renuka tried to smile back, but her face felt stiff, frozen.

"Renuka!" Priya said, as she ended the call. "Hope you're settling in! You have no complaints, right?" She smiled, inviting Renuka to join in the joke.

Renuka swallowed hard, her mouth suddenly dry. "Actually, that's what I wanted to talk to you about." She laid the folder on Priya's desk, her hands shaking slightly. "I've uncovered some disturbing data about the water treatment process. The filtration system isn't working as it should. The processed water is contaminated. This could be catastrophic."

Priya's smile faded as she reached for the folder. As she flipped through the pages, Renuka tried to decipher her superior's expressions. Did she see what Renuka saw? She had to. The deception was as obvious as the difference between the pure water on her desk and the toxic sludge they would be peddling.

"We've had senior engineers test and retest this, Renuka," Priya said gently. "More times than we can count. You know how much we have riding on this. Do you honestly think we could afford to release a system like this?"

"I guess not," Renuka stammered. She felt like a fool.

"I can't tell you how much I appreciate your diligence," Priya said. "We changed the testing methodology, but we're keeping it closely guarded because, you know, leaks." She smiled at Renuka. "But, if it makes you feel better, I'll have our Principal Engineer take another look. Sounds good?"

Renuka smiled, relieved. "Thank you so much. I should have known I was looking at this wrong." She reached for the folder.

Priya put a hand on it. "I want Raunak to take a look at this. The Principal Engineer?"

"Of course!" Renuka smiled widely. How stupid of her to think she would find something that no one else in the company had.

She closed the door. She walked a few steps, then turned back. She had never told Priya that she had inspired an entire generation of young women to study environmental engineering. She opened the door and poked her head in. Priya had Renuka's file in her hand—she was shredding the papers one by one.

Renuka quietly shut the door behind her. She stumbled out of the management block in shock. What had just happened? Priya, the woman Renuka had admired since the time she spoke at their college, had just brushed off the truth as if it were a pesky fruit fly. Worse, she had lied to Renuka's face.

She collapsed against the rails of the balcony, looking down at the soaring atrium.

"In life, you will face many challenges, Renuka," her grandmother had said, her voice weakened by illness but still full of conviction. "There will be times when you must choose between what is easy and what is right. Always choose what is right. It may be harder. People may try to stop you. But in the end, you will have something far more valuable than wealth or success—you will have your honour. And that, my child, is worth fighting for."

Renuka walked the halls of the building in a daze, not sure what to do next. She thought of the thousands in Bhopal condemned to a lifetime of suffering because corporate greed was put ahead of safety. She thought of the fragile trust society had placed in companies like EcoTech to safeguard public and environmental health. Whether this was incompetence or cover-up, she wasn't sure. The end result would be the same.

Could she betray that trust and live with herself? Her grandmother had named her Renuka—born of water, of dust. Her destiny was woven in with the environment; predetermined at birth.

Mind reeling, she made her way down. She found herself wandering to the underground storage facility, where the treated water from their purification process was destined to be held before distribution. The air grew cooler and damper as she descended the concrete steps, the sound of her footsteps echoing in the cavernous space. Was this how it felt inside a tomb? Hindus were cremated, not buried, so this was an alien thought to her.

A familiar voice cut into her daze. Something prompted Renuka to duck behind a column. It was Siddharth and Neelima. They were standing in front of the tanks, arguing in hushed tones.

"I told you, we need more time," Siddharth was saying, his voice strained. "The filtration system isn't ready. If we move forward now, the consequences could be disastrous."

"Don't be so dramatic, Sid," Neelima said. "We're behind schedule as it is. We can't afford any more delays."

"But the contamination levels—"

"Will be dealt with," Neelima cut him off. "We have contingencies in place. The important thing is to get the plant operational. Once the water is flowing, we'll have the revenue to fix any... issues."

Renuka couldn't believe what she was hearing. They knew. They knew about the contamination, about the danger. And they were willing to risk it all, to put lives on the line, and for what? Profits?

She must have made a noise, because suddenly, Siddharth and Neelima went silent. Renuka held her breath, pressing herself against the column, praying they wouldn't find her.

"We'll talk about this later," she heard Neelima say, her footsteps echoing as she walked away.

Renuka counted to fifty before peering around the column. Siddharth was gone. She was alone with the tanks, and the truth that she could no longer ignore. Her legs felt shaky as she made her way back to her cubicle, her mind reeling. She looked around at her colleagues, at the buzz of activity and purpose that filled the office. Did they know what was really going on? Did they care?

In their shared cubicle, Siddharth caught her eye, his expression unreadable. Renuka looked away, unsure what to make of him.

Chapter 5

Renuka spent the next few days in a state of constant anxiety, jumping at every shadow, every unexpected sound. Was she being watched? She couldn't decide if she was being paranoid or not. Regardless, she'd never had circles under her eyes before. Or lost weight she could ill afford to lose.

She tried to act normal, to focus on her work, but her mind was consumed with the knowledge of what she had uncovered. She pored over the data every night, looking for any shred of evidence that might convince Priya or the higher-ups to take action. She went back to the previous tests she had run. There was nothing there. She sat back, not believing what she saw on the screen.

"Not able to run tests?" she messaged Neelima.

"Focus on real-time monitoring capabilities of filtration system," Neelima messaged back.

Renuka blinked twice to make sure that she wasn't reading it wrong. This was a slap on the face. Shaking, she shoved her chair. It rolled halfway to Siddharth's side of the cubicle, but she was too humiliated to care.

She strode to the restroom, hoping that it would be empty. Thankfully, it was. She scooped her hands beneath the tap, bent forward and splashed water on her warm cheeks. Devuda! Where did she go from here?

She returned to her desk and rested her head on it, trying to simmer down. Noticing a folded note stuck under the base of her monitor, she reached for it listlessly. "Meet me at the Hayathnagar park at 9:30. Trust no one."

She sat up. It looked like Siddharth's scrawl. She looked over at his desk. He was gone. Could she trust him? What choice did she have, though? With her cards laid out in front of Priya, her days here were numbered. If this corruption was to come to light, she needed an ally. Grabbing her purse, she strode out.

They met in a small park near the office, sitting on opposite ends of a bench. Siddharth looked around nervously, making sure they were alone. "I want to help," he said, his voice low and urgent. "What you found… it's not right. We can't let them get away with it."

Renuka was startled. "How do you know?"

"I know it was you behind the tanks."

"Oh."

"Besides, I'm your mentor. I have access to all your work."

The Ghosts of Bhopal

"So you know my data has disappeared."

"I deleted it to protect you."

"And the access."

"I was the one who revoked it. I told Neelima that I was doing it so you could focus your attention on learning real-time monitoring."

At her sceptical look, he said, "You don't trust me, do you?"

"Would you, if you were in my place?"

He sighed. "I guess not. You know, when I joined EcoTech four years ago, I thought I was going to change the world. I believed in their mission, in the idea that we could make a real difference." He leaned back, his eyes clouding over with a mix of emotions. "I didn't want to believe it at first. I thought if I just kept my head down, focused on my work, everything would be okay."

"Is that why you brushed off my concerns?"

He nodded. "But then I overheard a conversation I wasn't meant to. Priya and some of the higher-ups, talking about 'acceptable risks' and 'damage control.' They know, Renuka. They know the system is flawed, but are willing to put lives at risk to meet their deadline." His hands clenched into fists. "I couldn't live with myself if I didn't do something. So I started digging, just like you. And the more I found, the sicker I felt. EcoTech's supposed integrity is a sham."

Renuka nodded, a sense of solidarity settling over her. "What changed your mind about helping me?"

"I have a younger sister, just starting college. You remind me of her. I mean, not you, but your passion. Uh, you know what I mean." He flushed a bright red.

Renuka's cheeks warmed.

"She wants to study environmental science," he said. "Wants to make a difference like I did. And I realized...I couldn't look her in the eye and tell her to follow her dreams if I wasn't willing to fight for what's right myself."

"Is Neelima part of this?"

He shook his head. "I don't think so. I think she sincerely believes that what she's doing is for the greater good. Despite the hype, we'll get the next level of funding only if we can show that we have a working system. Which means—"

"We're caught in a vicious cycle," Renuka interrupted. "The system we're about to unleash upon the unsuspecting public is a ticking time bomb."

Siddharth dropped his head in his hands.

"We're caught in a web of lies and half-truths, Sid. And corporate greed."

He sat up. "Tell me what to do."

He looked so helpless. Renuka was startled. He was the senior engineer. She'd been looking to him for answers. But it was up to her, now.

She looked up at the sky. She could make out a star here and there, mostly because the city lights drowned them out. She could ignore what she'd uncovered for the sake of her brother's fees and her parents' bank balance. Or—she took a deep breath—she could do what was right.

He was saying all the right things. But could she really trust him? "I understand the pressure Neelima is under, Sid. Believe me, I do. But we have a chance to make this right, to expose the truth. It won't be easy, but we have to try."

Siddharth met her eyes. "You're right. Whatever happens, we're in this together."

Renuka studied his face, trying to gauge his sincerity. "Are you sure?"

Siddharth flinched, looking away. "I didn't... I never wanted any of this. I thought we were making a difference, you know? Helping people. But the more I saw, the more I realised... this is not right."

Renuka felt a pang of sympathy. She knew what it was like to have your illusions shattered, to realise that the company you had idealised was rotten at the core.

"You're offering to help," she said, trying to keep the hope out of her voice. "What can you do?"

Siddharth took a deep breath. "We need proof. Undeniable proof of what's really going on. Emails, documents, recordings... anything that will expose the truth to the world."

Renuka nodded, her mind already racing. "I don't have that kind of access."

Siddharth nodded. "If you did, you'd have been fired by now."

"Show me I can trust you. Give me that test data.

Siddharth dug into his pocket and held out a pen drive.

The Ghosts of Bhopal

She stared at him. He must have been as uncertain of her as she was of him, for him to have hung on to the data.

She took it from him and carefully zipped it in her purse. "Something they can't sweep under the rug. But I can't do this alone. I don't have that kind of access."

Siddharth leaned forward, his eyes intense. "I might know a way. But it's risky. If we get caught..."

Renuka met his gaze, her resolve hardening. "We have to try. We can't let them poison more people, create more Bhopals."

"You've changed," Siddharth said.

"How?"

"You're more assertive."

"You taught me that."

He smiled briefly. He dug into his pocket again. "This is Priya's access card," he said abruptly.

Renuka was shocked. "How did you do that?"

"Bribes were involved. That's all you need to know."

"Okay." She reached a hand out for it.

He shook his head. "You'd be putting yourself at risk."

"I've been wondering about that. Why haven't they fired me already?" She explained the episode with Priya.

He groaned. "You had to do that, didn't you?"

"Where does that leave me?"

"They can't afford to fire you right before the launch, and risk a scandal if you go to the press."

"So they'll fire me after." The grand opening was scheduled for the 27th. So, ten days away.

"That's all the more reason for you to give me the badge," she argued. "If what you say is true, I should have the documents to back me up."

"It is dangerous," he said. "They are stepping up security for the Prime Minister's visit."

"Which means we have to act fast."

"I can't let you put yourself at risk."

She clicked her tongue impatiently. "Siddharth, you know more about the company than I do. And they're going to fire me anyway. Let me do this. You can help me more if you're on the inside."

Siddharth sighed in defeat.

It was past 1:30 a.m. when he walked her to EcoTech. As they parted ways, Siddharth leaned down to her, his voice urgent. "Be very careful. If this thing goes as high up as we think," he said. "They'll do anything to stop you."

Renuka swallowed hard before nodding.

Chapter 6

Renuka's heart pounded as she used Priya's badge to get into the building. She walked through the deserted halls of EcoTech, the stolen access card clutched in her sweaty palm.

It was late, long after the last employee had gone home for the night, but Renuka knew the risk of discovery was still high. She walked past the Records room—where one would assume hard copies of files were kept—to the innocuous-looking door with "Maintenance" on it. She scanned the card with shaking hands. The light flashed green, the lock whirring open. Before she could change her mind, she slipped inside.

The room was dark, lit only by the glow of the solidary computer screen. Renuka reached into her bag, pulling out a small flashlight. She played the beam over the shelves, scanning the labels with a growing sense of urgency.

She was looking for the quarterly reports, the ones that would show the discrepancies between the claimed and actual contamination levels. Siddharth had told her the top management distrusted storage servers because nothing was hack-proof. So the hard copies were in this room.

The Ghosts of Bhopal

Renuka's breath caught as her light fell on a familiar label. "Project Amrit," it read, the irony of the name not lost on her. Amrit, or amrut—depending on who was spelling it—the nectar of immortality, the elixir of life.

With trembling fingers, Renuka pulled the folder from the shelf. She opened it, her eyes widening as she scanned the pages. It was all there, laid out in crisp black and white. The falsified data, the hidden toxicity reports.

This wasn't exactly the smoking gun she'd have liked—in an ideal world, she'd have names. Names of politicians and regulators who had been bought off, silenced with bribes and favours. But this would have to be enough.

As she reached for her phone, dust trickled down from the higher shelves. Sneezing, Renuka snapped pictures, hoping it would be enough.

The next day, Renuka arrived at work to find her access badge no longer functioned. Confused, she tried to go up to Neelima's office for answers, only to be met by two stern-faced security guards.

"Renuka Prasad, you are hereby suspended pending further investigation into violations of company data access policies," one of them intoned, handing her a formal notice. "You are to leave the premises immediately and refrain from contacting any EcoTech employees."

Renuka's mind raced—they must have discovered her unauthorized access. She considered arguing, but one look at the guards' implacable expressions told her it would be futile. Gathering what dignity she could, she left the building, a mix of fear and determination swirling inside her.

That evening, Siddharth contacted her through an encrypted messaging app. "I heard what happened," he typed. "I'm so sorry. But I managed to grab copies of some key files before they locked everything down. I think I know why they suspended you—they're rushing to destroy evidence before the launch."

Renuka's heartbeat quickened as Siddharth sent her the files—emails, reports, even surreptitiously recorded conversations proving EcoTech's top brass knew about the filtration system's flaws and covered them up.

"We have to get this to the authorities, the media, anyone who will listen," Renuka replied, her fingers flying over the keys. "Can you set up a secure drop box? I have some trusted contacts from my activist days in college who can help spread the word."

Siddharth agreed. Fuelled by anger and adrenaline, they spent the night organizing the evidence and strategizing their next moves. They knew the risks—EcoTech had proven they would stop at nothing to protect their interests.

The next morning, Renuka couldn't get out of bed. She collapsed.

When Renuka woke up, she was in a hospital bed, her body aching with a pain she had never known before. Her parents sat on either side of the bed, the strain on their faces evident.

Her mother, seeing her opened eyes, bent down with a sob. "We almost lost you."

Renuka opened her mouth, but nothing came out.

Her father put his arm around her, helping her sit up.

Her mother brought a glass of water close to her mouth.

Renuka sipped a few drops, then leaned back, exhausted. "What happened?" she forced out. Her voice came out hoarse.

"The doctor said, stress exhaustion."

Renuka closed her eyes again, too tired to talk.

Her parents took her back to Mahbubnagar in an ambulance—more expense than they could afford.

Two days later, her parents took her home.

"I'm so sorry," she said to her parents. "I wanted to make enough money to help you buy your own flat. I wanted to pay for Sridhar's college. Instead, I am yet another patient you're forced to take care of."

The Ghosts of Bhopal

"We're not used to having so much time to ourselves," her mother joked. "It's good to fill our time with caretaking again."

"Amma!" Renuka protested, and her mother relented.

"Don't be silly," her father said. "You can never be a burden—"

He choked on his words, so her mother picked up. "If someone had been as honourable in Bhopal, the gas tragedy might have never happened."

Renuka was shocked. "What are you talking about?"

"When you didn't respond to messages, your friend Siddharth tracked us down. He told us that you were fired, and why."

Renuka was glad the two of them had exchanged emergency contacts. "I am so sorry. You're stuck spending more money on hospital bills."

Her father clicked his tongue in impatience. "I wouldn't have been able to spend corrupt money."

"That boy," her mother said, "Siddharth. He gave us this." She inclined her head at the files.

Renuka reached for the files. Paper versions of everything in the drop box. He had left a yellow sticky note on the last page, which said, "When you no longer need me to be on the inside, I'll resign and join you in the fight."

Renuka smiled.

Epilogue

The story of the EcoTech scandal broke like a tidal wave, crashing over the nation with unstoppable force. In the weeks and months following Renuka's firing, it dominated headlines worldwide, as Renuka's professors and classmates from college ensured the story spread like wildfire. Public outrage grew as more and more details came to light, leading to raids on EcoTech's offices, the arrest of top executives, and a plummeting stock price.

Government inquiries revealed a deep web of corruption and negligence within the company, with bribed officials and silenced whistleblowers going back years. Renuka emerged as a symbol of courage and integrity, her story inspiring a new generation of activists. Despite ongoing threats, she threw herself into the fight, testifying before parliament and collaborating with NGOs to push for stricter corporate regulations and accountability.

However, Renuka's story did more than just expose corporate corruption; it sparked a broader societal conversation about the often-overlooked contributions of women in various fields. The media coverage surrounding Renuka's activism led to a surge in the representation of women's achievements in popular culture, education, and public discourse.

Siddharth resigned from EcoTech and joined Renuka's movement, standing by her side every step of the way. Together, they founded a watchdog organization dedicated to exposing environmental crimes and advocating for the rights of affected communities.

As Renuka's story spread, it challenged long-held gender stereotypes and biases. People began to recognize the crucial role that women played in the fight for justice and equality. Women scientists, activists, and leaders who had long been overlooked were finally given the credit they deserved.

This newfound recognition of women's contributions extended beyond the realm of activism. In the months following the EcoTech scandal, there was a noticeable shift in the way women were portrayed in the media, in textbooks, and in everyday conversations. The narrative was no longer solely focused on men's achievements; women's stories were finally being told, and being heard.

Change didn't come overnight, as powerful interests pushed back against reforms and greenwashing remained a constant threat. However, as Renuka stood on stage at yet another rally, looking out over the sea of determined faces, she knew they were making a difference. The ghosts of Bhopal, EcoTech, and countless other tragedies would not be forgotten, and this new generation, empowered by the recognition of women's strengths, would make sure of that.

For Renuka, the greatest victories were both personal and societal. She felt immense joy at the rise of a society that finally recognized and celebrated the contributions of women. The weight of the ghosts finally lifted from her shoulders when she visited the Bhopal memorial,

The Ghosts of Bhopal

bringing her a sense of peace in the knowledge that she had honoured the memories of her grandmother and aunt by fighting for the voiceless and helping to create a world where women's achievements would never again be dismissed or ignored.

As she stepped up to the podium to begin her speech, Renuka knew that the fight was far from over. There would always be those who put profit over people, viewing human lives as acceptable collateral damage. But with a society that now valued women's voices and contributions, she was ready to continue the battle, never stopping in her quest to speak truth to power.

A Winter's Day

Lorraine J. Anderson

The Year of Our Lord 1597

Sitting at her desk, Anne Hathaway Shakespeare stabbed at her manuscript with her quill and growled. She straightened up in her chair and glanced across the room. Judith, her younger daughter, was concentrating on her book and paid no attention to her. Her older daughter Susanna looked up from her embroidery. After all, Anne reflected, an accomplished wife just needed to know how to embroider, right? And find a husband and keep him happy and run a household and …

"What's the matter, Mama?" Susanna said, her eyes wide.

"Oh, darling, it's nothing." In spite of herself, Anne started to frown.

She laid down her quill and looked around her apartment. It was relatively small, considering her family, but comfortable. She was so happy she could have the children with her after William passed away. The apartment had six rooms—three bedrooms, a short hallway leading into a large common room with seven chairs (in case she had visitors when her children were home,) a kitchen with a fireplace for what little cooking she did these days and a long thin dining table with more comfortable maple chairs. She had set up her writing desk in the common room, and the girls were next to the fireplace. Her boy was supposed to be doing his reading beside his twin....

Anne looked around again. "Where's Hamnet?" How had she lost track of her son?

Susanna shrugged.

"He's probably with John, mama," Judith said, twirling her dark hair. "You know that John and him like playing around the Thames."

Anne frowned, letting Judith's grammatical error pass. "John is not a good influence on him," she said to herself and then aloud. "He should be starting to learn a trade, and so should John." And, sadly, he seemed to have as much ambition in a regular trade as his late father. Hamnet even looked like Will. But she hadn't yet had the heart to force Hamnet into a trade, not after almost losing him last year.

"What kind of trade?" Judith said. She dropped her book, then picked it up with a guilty look. Anne winced. Some women never learned how to read, but Anne insisted that her daughters be educated, even if she had to do it herself. The family was comfortable, but not so that they could hire a full-time tutor, so she taught the girls and Hamnet herself. She couldn't bear sending her girls off to be Ladies' maids or cleaning women, and she never wanted to force them into marriage.

She focused her wandering mind back to Judith's question. "It depends on what Hamnet's interested in. I write plays. Your father wrote plays. Mr. Worster on the corner tends horses. Mr. Cooper makes shoes."

"I wish I could learn a trade." Judith opened her book again, but looked up hopefully.

"Women don't have trades, Judith." Susanna frowned, poking at her embroidery. Susanna looked more like Anne. Her light hair was in a ponytail, like Anne's was at the moment.

Anne made an exasperated noise. "You didn't hear that from me."

"No, but that's what everybody says," Susanna said, frowning. "I'm supposed to find somebody and get married."

"And if that man passes away, like your father?"

Susanna shrugged.

"Well," Anne said. "I most certainly have a trade. I had to work after your father passed."

A Winter's Day

"You write plays!" Judith exclaimed.

"Yes. I do." Anne smiled at Judith's enthusiasm. But her comment brought her back to why she was so angry.

A knock came from the front door. "Can you get that, Susanna?" Anne said.

Susanna made a face. "Yes, Mama," she said, slowly put down her sewing, and left the room. She came back, leading two ladies into the room.

"Good morning, Mistress Hart, Mistress Jonson." Anne looked curiously at her sister-in-law and her good friend. "What brings you both here today?"

"Men," Mistress Jonson spouted.

Anne had heard that the Jonsons didn't always get along; looking at Mistress Jonson's costly attire, Anne could understand why. Master Jonson likely didn't appreciate the expense. Mistress Jonson was wearing the highest of fashion; her dress and ruffles made Anne's everyday outfit look plain. Anne looked down at her own dark brown gown over a plain off-white chemise. She owned a nicer dress, but couldn't see the point of wearing it around the house. Besides, the dark brown hid any stray ink stains.

Mistress Hart nodded. "I thought the two of us might speak sense to Mistress Jonson."

Joan Hart (née Shakespeare) dressed more simply than Mistress Jonson. She wore a plainer blue dress over a lighter blue chemise. Her husband was a hatter, and it seemed as if business was good, because she had at least three or four different dresses. Like her late brother Will, her hair was dark. She looked like a female version of him.

"Actually, I agree with Mistress Jonson. Men are exasperating." Anne quirked her mouth. She looked at the other woman's red face. "You've broken up with Master Jonson again?"

"Are we ever together?" Mistress Jonson growled. She swept her skirts around angrily and plopped down on one of the benches.

"You sound like mama," Judith said. She closed her book again, looking interested in the conversation.

"Hush, Judith," Mistress Hart said.

Judith glanced at Mistress Hart and nodded.

Mistress Jonson glanced at Anne's still-red face, then her own expression softened. "Who are you mad at?"

"Your husband. Master Jonson."

"Really? Mad at Master Jonson?" Mistress Hart said. She looked a little surprised and glanced at Mistress Jonson, who shrugged.

"Yes. He wrote that I lack art." Anne pursed her lips, rising from her desk and moving to Mistress Jonson. Mistress Jonson's perfume was cloves and lavender, and Anne sneezed.

Mistress Jonson screwed her face up. "That sounds like him."

"It is him, and it reminded me of Robert Greene." Anne moved away slightly from Mistress Jonson so the fragrance faded and the urge to sneeze went away.

"The late playwright?" Mistress Hart nodded. "What did he do?"

"Have you seen the 'Groats-worth of Wit'?" Anne said, sitting back down at her desk.

"No. Maybe Ben did, but since we're not talking, I'm not asking," Mistress Jonson frowned.

"He attacked me. In print. He accused me of reaching above my station." Anne's face grew hot.

Mistress Hart cocked her head to one side. "Anne. That was years ago. But aren't you? How many female playwrights do you know?"

"Not you, too. And what does being female have to do with it?" Anne shook her head.

"What would Mr. Greene have said about Will?" Mistress Hart said gently. She laid her hand on Anne's arm and squeezed, probably trying to calm her down.

But while Anne appreciated the effort, she was still too angry. She had picked her quill up, but slammed it down again, crushing the end. "Probably the same thing. Will was not university-educated. Greene and his friends called themselves the 'university wits.'" She turned to the children. "But what was I supposed to do for my children when Will passed? My father was gone. Turn to prostitution?" She looked to her side, grabbing a fresh quill.

"Anne!" Mistress Hart said. "None of this talk in front of the children." The girls looked at each other and shrugged.

A Winter's Day

Anne grimaced at the girls. "They're around enough actors. They know how they talk." She sighed. "I'm not being taken seriously."

"Did you expect to be?" Mistress Jonson said.

Anne glanced at her manuscript, then glared up at Mistress Jonson. Her face seemed innocent of guile.

"I'm serious," Mistress Jonson continued. She cocked her head to one side. "How many females write anything more than stories or poems?"

"Queen Catherine Parr wrote Bible studies. Our Queen has been known to write poetry. She speaks five languages," Mistress Hart said, turning to Mistress Jonson, with a small worried glance at Anne.

"They say Anne Boleyn wrote songs, and you see what happened to her," Anne said bitterly.

Susanna looked up, interested. "What happened to Anne Boleyn?"

"Hush, Susanna." Anne turned away.

"She lost her head," Mistress Jonson said. "Literally."

"Mistress Jonson!" Mistress Hart exclaimed.

"She's old enough, she might as well know about the ways of men," Mistress Jonson declared.

Anne closed her eyes. "Girls, could you go and try to find your brother? It's about time for supper."

"If he's not at the Thames, he's probably hanging around the theater," Judith said to Susanna.

"He hangs about the theater?" Mistress Hart said. She opened her eyes wide, glancing at Anne.

"Yeah. He looks through the holes in the walls," Susanna added.

Anne raised her eyebrows. "Oh. Dear. I shall have to have a talk with him about that. Now go."

"Yes, mama," Susanna said.

"Don't stay out too long," Anne rose and looked out the window. "It's already late afternoon."

"Yes, mama," Susanna said. The two girls left the room.

"Why is looking through holes in the wall at the theatre a problem?" Mistress Jonson said.

Mistress Hart glanced at Anne. "The holes outside the changing rooms."

Mistress Jonson closed her mouth. "Oh. But the actors are men."

"Yes." Anne sighed. "But occasionally they invite their female friends or their male friends to join them."

"Ah. Oh. Yes." Mistress Jonson sighed and frowned. "I should have known."

"Please. Don't get her started about the male actors," Mistress Hart warned.

"Why?" Mistress Jonson glanced at Anne curiously. She shifted on her seat.

"I'm writing a play right now—a romance between a young man and a young woman from two feuding families."

"Sounds interesting," Mistress Jonson said. She waved her hand across her face, as if she thought it was hot in the room. Curious, Anne thought it was slightly chilly.

"I'm having a hard time imagining the play between the two actors," Anne said, "especially if my Juliet has the beginnings of a mustache."

Mistress Jonson shrugged. "What choice do you have? Women, as the weaker sex, cannot act on stage."

"Please tell me, Mistress Jonson, that you are joking," Anne said. She turned to Mistress Jonson, looking angry.

"Modern sensibilities tell us so," Mistress Jonson said, calmly.

"I believe, Mistress Jonson, you are thinking of twenty years ago." Anne rolled her eyes at Mistress Hart. "Consider this. I had twins. Will was down at the pub because he couldn't handle my screams." She put her pen down and vigorously poured sand over the ink, even though she knew the ink was already dry. It was either that or pound her hand on the desk in frustration. "After Will died, I moved from Stratford-on-Avon to here to support the children. And I took care of Father's household long before I met Will."

"We know," Mistress Hart said gently, laying her hands on Anne's arm again. "He married you for the money. But I believe that he had a great regard for you."

"Do you?" Anne said. "I loved him, but I sometimes wondered if he loved me."

"He did," Mistress Hart said quietly. "When he was dying, he told me so."

Anne grimaced. "He told me that he loved me, but I always had a feeling that his affections strayed."

A Winter's Day

Mistress Hart nodded. "I know you would prefer me to be honest. He told me that, also."

"I knew he had cuckolded me." It was always surprising to Anne that she was not mad at Will; she supposed that she knew whom she had married when she married him.

Mistress Jonson cocked her head to one side. "Can a wife be cuckolded?"

Anne smiled ruefully. "I believe the term is 'cuckqueen'." She sighed. "But Will's infidelity is not the issue here. I reconciled myself to that a long time ago."

"So what is the issue?" Mistress Hart said, curiously.

"Men," said Mistress Jonson and Anne together.

"Yes. Men." Mistress Jonson repeated, looking angry again, slamming her hands beside her on the bench.

"However," Mistress Hart said, "you do have the favor of the Queen, do you not?"

"I do," Anne said, "as had Will before me. It was a kindness of Will that he revealed me to be co-author of his plays."

"Perhaps," Mistress Hart mused, "You should say something…" She shook her head. "What I'm thinking is preposterous."

Anne stared at Mistress Hart. "Are you suggesting that I use my influence to have the Queen censure my opponents?" She shook her head. "I am fortunate that I have as much influence as I have with the Chamberlain's Men."

"All men, of course," Mistress Jonson said.

"Of course…". Anne stopped and her eyebrows went up. She smiled slowly. "I may have an idea."

"I don't like the expression on your face," Mistress Hart said, standing up and looking at her.

Anne picked up a new quill, pointing it at Mistress Hart. "You shouldn't." She smiled.

"Well," said Mistress Jonson, looking from one to the other. "What are you thinking?"

"Joan. You have read my thoughts on a play I call 'As You Like It'?" She pointed the quill at her desk.

"Yes." Realization dawned on Mistress Hart's face. "Oh. Oh!" She shook her head. "Anne. No."

"What?"

"Mistress Jonson," Mistress Hart said. "We shall talk later." She took Mistress Jonson's elbow and stood her up. "The less you know, the less you'll be in trouble."

Mistress Jonson shook her head. "You forget. I am not happy with Mr. Jonson. If this play that you talk about cuckqueens Mr. Jonson, I am all for it."

"Well," Anne said, pointing her quill at the two other ladies, "rather than using the Chamberlain's Men, what if we form a troupe and name it the Queen's Ladies?"

"And perform this play called 'As You Like It'?" Mistress Jonson said.

"Yes." Mistress Hart and Anne watched while Mistress Jonson processed this idea. Her face lit up. "I like it. When do we start?"

"No, Mistress Taylor, try again." Anne shoved away the impulse to drop her head into her hands. The lot of them crowded into her apartment made for close quarters, but she resisted the urge to open the window. No good would come of everyone outside hearing them at work.

Mistress Taylor was a large woman with long dark hair, a broad face, and a deep voice. She was, probably, what Will would call a peasant, but Anne knew her as a steady, reliable woman who rarely spoke up against her husband—in fact, she was surprised Mistress Taylor had agreed to this. She looked uncertainly at Anne, frowning, wiping her hands nervously on her plain brown dress. "Mistress Shakespeare, I'm not certain I can do this."

Mistress Hart, sitting opposite Anne at the kitchen table, looked sympathetically at Anne, then addressed the other woman. "Mistress Taylor, I have seen you embroider without missing a stitch while watching your children climb over your lap. I have seen you dance without missing a beat. This is simply another kind of memorization.

A Winter's Day

And remember," she said, "we have all the time in the world to get it right." She got up, going over to the fire. "Care for some more ale?"

Anne shook her head at Mistress Hart. It wasn't her fault, she didn't know, but Anne had planned to premier this play at the Rose theater in the fall. While she admitted that it was still months away, she wanted to make sure that the Queen was present. Not that Her Majesty didn't attend all of her play premieres, but…

Hamnet wandered into the room. "Mama, can I go to the river? I want to see if John is there."

Anne smiled at her son, who reminded her so much of Will—so animated and so enthusiastic. She was thankful that he had survived his latest sickness. She had thought she was going to lose him. "I think I need you here, Hamnet. You can help me," she said, tousling his hair. "Can you get your sisters?"

Hamnet frowned. "Do we really need them here?"

"Would you like a part in my play?"

He seemed to think about it a second. "Sure!" He ran off.

"I thought you didn't want males in your play?" Mistress Hart smiled after her departing nephew.

"I would rather have him in my play then looking through the cracks of the dressing room," Anne said tartly. She glanced at Mistress Taylor. "I know you can do this. I believe in you."

Mistress Taylor took a breath, looked at the manuscript, then looked up at the far wall. In a deep voice, she started, her voice shaking and then more confident. "All the world's a stage, and all the men and women merely players; They have their exits and their entrances…". She continued, her voice getting more conversational.

Anne watched, entranced.

Mistress Taylor concluded, "Last scene of all, that ends this strange eventful history, is second childishness and mere oblivion; Sans teeth, sans eyes, sans taste, sans everything." She stopped short, her confident look fading, and she wiped her hands on her dress again.

Anne stared at Mistress Taylor.

"Is that all right?" Mistress Taylor said uncertainly.

"That," Anne sighed, "is wonderful!"

"I knew you could do it," Mistress Hart said, getting up and hugging Mistress Taylor.

"You are an actress," Anne said, "and don't let anybody tell you you're not."

Mistress Taylor smiled broadly.

Hamnet came back, dragging his sisters. "I don't want to be in your play as a Lord, Mama," Susanna pouted.

Anne smiled. "How about the lead, then—Rosalind?"

Susanna smiled.

"What about us, Mama?" Hamnet said.

"I think you can be shepherds." She held up her hands to forestall the upcoming objection. "My shepherds have lines. Do you think you can learn lines?"

"Yes, of course, Mama," Judith said.

"I can learn everybody's lines!" Hamnet said.

Anne smiled at her son. So much like Will... but noisier.

They heard a knock on the door, then swiftly buried the manuscripts under the desk in a covered basket with the manuscripts she was currently work on. "Mistress Jonson?"

The door opened. "Yes. My husband has also come." They walked in the room. Mistress Jonson's face was neutral, but Master Jonson looked around, curiously, as if he were looking for something.

Did he know? Anne was thankful that the manuscripts were out of sight. She rose. "Master Jonson. It's a pleasure to see you." And a surprise, she thought. "What brings you to our gathering?"

"My wife has told me what you are doing," he said disapprovingly, then his face softened. He was a large man, with tousled dark curly hair and a beard. He started smiling. "And to her surprise, I wholeheartedly agree with you."

"And what are we doing?" Anne said, still cautious.

"Planning on putting ladies on the stage as actors."

Anne raised her eyebrows. "I am surprised, Master Jonson. I presumed you thought that women could not act on the stage."

"You'll need to prove it to me," Mr. Jonson said, walking up and down the common room, "but I am a proponent of anything that

A Winter's Day

pushes beyond the normal fare. I believe that art that promotes the same thing, time after time, becomes stale."

"So…" Anne cocked her head, curious.

"At the very least, I am going to legitimize your efforts." He glanced at a chair. "May I sit?"

"Mr. Jonson," Anne said, ignoring his request. "I do not need anyone to legitimize my efforts, as you say. I have the favor of the queen."

"I doubt it," he said baldly. "Not in this." He looked pointedly at a chair, then remained standing as Anne still refused to take the hint. "I am not known to be friendly with the authorities. If anything causes the authorities to sweat, I am for it. If you are caught practicing lines from your play, I can say that you're doing it under my direction; that I wished to see whether women could act. You do not wish to be put in prison for indecency, but if I as a male, put you under my direction…?"

"I don't like that we need to do that," Anne said, frowning. "It is not illegal for women to act on stage."

"It is not," Master Jonson agreed, "but it just isn't done." He took a deep breath. "I admire you, Mistress Shakespeare. I didn't think anyone could surpass your Will, but you have equaled him—indeed, you have surpassed him,"

"I am surprised, Master Jonson." Was he sincere? She still wasn't sure.

"I am surprised at myself, Mistress Shakespeare." He looked at a chair again.

Anne sat back and considered. "Please have a seat, Master Jonson."

He sat down heavily, his wife beside him. "Do you have all of your actors?"

"We do." She looked at Mistress Jonson.

"I am playing a Lord, Ben," Mistress Jonson said, with an expression that told him not to argue.

He glanced at her and smiled. "Then I shall be your understudy," he said, "with your permission, of course."

"Under one condition, Ben," Mistress Jonson said.

"What condition, Ann?" Master Jonson put his arm around her tenderly.

She pushed his arm off. "You shall stay away from the pubs until after the play has premiered."

83

He put his hand to his heart. "You betray me, wife."

"I know," she said, and her lips pursed, "how you act when you're in the heat of your alcoholic haze."

"O God," Anne said, "that men should put an enemy in their mouths to steal away their brains!" She moved to her desk. "I need to write that down. And yes, Master Jonson, you may stay."

"Thank you, mistress. I held your husband in high regard, but I hold you in higher regard." He slowly put his arm around Mistress Jonson's shoulders again. "That being said, I don't believe that you should practice in one place all of the time."

"You may be right," Anne said. She got up and started pacing. "But I'm not sure where else to rehearse, apart from each other's homes."

"I understand some other playwrights are wondering what you are doing." His head followed her back and forth. "You usually don't have this many visitors."

"Yes?" She continued pacing.

"I've heard tell of spying."

She stopped to stare at him. His face was bland. "How can they spy in my house?"

"They're watching all of the ladies come to your house day after day." He held up his hand. "So far, they are not suspecting what you are doing. Their speculations are far cruder."

"Oh," Anne said, startled. "I see. Mistress Jonson, perhaps shall we meet in your place, next?"

"Tomorrow?" She said, glancing at Master Jonson. He nodded. "Tomorrow. I will practice my part. We will expect you." She glanced at her husband again with something like—did she see respect? And love?

She smiled as the couple left, then turned to Mistress Taylor. "Now, Mistress, shall we go over some more of your part?"

Mistress Taylor smiled. "Thank you, Mistress Shakespeare. For everything. You have all made me feel like I'm a part of something bigger." Her arms spread as if to encompass the world.

"You're welcome." Anne took out the manuscripts from the basket. "Now, let us go to Scene V, where Amiens and Jaques are in the forest. Master Amiens?" She turned to Mistress Hart.

A Winter's Day

"Under the greenwood tree, who loves to lie with me…" Mistress Hart sang.

After a month of going to each others' homes, the ladies had begun meeting at the Rose a week ago. Anne walked quietly down the street towards the theater, glancing from side to side. She didn't want to be arrested, especially with her children with her. The street smelled as if all of the horses in London had used it and they had to walk carefully to not step in the piles. At a couple of spots, she even got a whiff of the middens. She reached a dark alley, looking right, then left. She motioned her children in front of her. "It's the doorway at the end of the block." She pointed at a tall building that looked like three walls. Anne knew the building to be a three story octagonal shape, but it didn't look that way from this side.

"Why are we whispering, Mama?" Hamnet said, matching her tone.

"Because we're not supposed to be in the theater at night," she whispered back. Judith cuffed him lightly on the side of his head, and Hamnet glared at her. Susanna, as normal, ignored the two, watching carefully at each doorway and window, but all were bolted shut. They approached the Rose and slipped in through a door Master Jonson had already opened. They made their way to the stage, where much of their troupe, fifteen younger ladies and a couple of older ladies, had already assembled. They were a motley group, upper class and lower class, ruffles and silk, and plain dresses. She wondered how they would look in doublets. A couple of ladies were sewing costumes for those ladies who couldn't fit into what was at the theater.

The wood stage creaked slightly, and Anne cautiously looked up at the seats. Like most theatres, the audience was in a half-round facing the stage. The wood seats looked rather foggy in the shadows created by the half-lit chandeliers.

"Anne," Mistress Hart whispered. "I thought you may have forgotten." She smiled to take the sting out of her words.

Anne smiled. "The stage that is the world—is hard to manage with children. Particularly the one who wants to play in the tepid puddles in the middle of the street to annoy his sisters."

Hamnet grinned and Susanna tossed her head.

"It's a few short weeks, Susanna, and then you can do what you wish." Anne loved her older daughter, but she could be obstinate and opinionated. Much like Anne herself.

Susanna looked sideways at her, as if she didn't believe it. "Really, mama?"

"Well, no, but at least you won't have to act."

"I don't mind that so much, Mama," Susanna pouted. "I like acting. I learned my part a long time ago. But it seems like we've been doing this forever."

"Susanna," Anne said. "It's only been five weeks."

"I love acting," Hamnet said loudly. His twin shushed him.

Anne looked around. "Is our Orlando here?"

Mistress Hart looked around. "I don't believe Mistress Gracy has come yet."

"I see." It wasn't surprising; Mistress Gracy had five children, had had problems with the oldest, and her husband was in the tavern all of the time. "Well, I shall do Mistress Gracy's part, and if she does come, we'll fit her in."

"The Queen's Ladies" glanced at each other. Along with Mistress Taylor, who played Jaques to perfection, there was Mistress Hart, Mistress Jonson, Mistress Cole, young Miss Smith, the elderly Widow Mistress Hale and her two maiden granddaughters, the three Shakespeare children, skinny Mistress Smith, overweight Mistress Jones, and the overworked Mistress Gracy. A couple of the actresses played two parts. There were various shades of abilities, but what they lacked in acting ability they gained in enthusiasm.

They had gotten through to act three when Mistress Gracy came in, panting. She led in her two youngest while carrying the baby in her arms. "I am so sorry, Mistress Shakespeare. I could not get Thomas to settle, then he fell asleep on the way over."

"I understand," Anne said kindly, "but this is the third time you've been late. Are you sure that you want to do Orlando?"

A Winter's Day

She chewed her lip. "Perhaps I should play another Lord. I don't seem to be able to memorize the lines."

"Anne," Mistress Hart said quietly, "you should play Orlando. You haven't looked at the script once."

"But that would mean I would play Rosalind's lover, opposite of Susanna, my daughter."

"And you both are quite believable," Mistress Hart said. "Susanna is playing Rosalind to perfection."

"But I'm the playwright!"

"That doesn't mean you can't act." She stepped up, placing her hands on Anne's shoulders.

Anne shook her head. "Will was the actor. I am merely a woman trying to fill his shoes."

The ladies surrounded her. "I didn't think I could act," Mistress Taylor said, glancing around at all of the troupe, "but you told me I could."

"We know you can, too," Mistress Hale said. She hugged her granddaughters. "Who knew I could act at my age?"

Susanna, who was downstage, stormed up to her mother. Anne was taken aback at her ferocity. "Mama. You are not merely a woman. You are our father and our mother and a very good actor. You write plays and are in the favor of Her Majesty." She shook her head. "Mama, you are my inspiration."

Anne had raised her eyebrows. "Thank you."

"Even if you are my Mama," Susanna added.

"Thank you, I guess."

Ben Jonson came from the entrance. "I can only watch out for you so long," he said. "Are you through yet?"

Anne straightened. "Let's continue."

The actresses were at Mistress Carter's house when someone knocked at the door. Swiftly, they buried the manuscripts under the table as Mistress Carter slowly ambled to the door. "Yes?" She said slowly.

Master Jonson slipped in. "Someone has told one of our friends that something is going on at the Rose late at night." He smiled slightly at Mistress Jonson, who smiled back, then turned his attention to Anne.

"So," Anne said, "if we want to keep the production secret, the Rose is out." She thought a second. "Or maybe not." She walked around the room, considering. "What is the next play due there?"

Master Jonson harrumphed, then smiled. "I believe Her Majesty wanted a repeat of Will's 'Taming of the Shrew.'"

Anne smiled ruefully. "You know, he had me in mind when he wrote it."

"Indeed?" Master Jonson's face looked innocent, but his voiced dripped irony.

"He was never fond of the portrayals of women and tried to tweak the authorities every chance he got."

"Ah," Master Jonson smiled. "More like me than I realized." He glanced at his wife, who nodded.

"He was always trying to have his actors play 'the shrew' more sympathetic, but—if you will excuse me—they were men who had no idea how to play women." She shrugged. "Anyway, I have an idea. Is Burbage free?"

Mistress Hart was listening to the interchange. "What are you thinking?"

"We start a double production, one openly, the other secretly. Lord Chamberlain's Men start at the normal hour and rehearse. I believe the ladies are as ready, so we will hold one rehearsal at my house, one at Mistress Hart's house, and one at Mistress Jonson's house. On the last day before the show, I will arrange that our ladies watch the men rehearse "the Shrew." They will stay as the actors leave, then the ladies will rehearse."

"But," Mistress Hart said, "will the actors have enough time to stage a production of 'the Shrew'?"

Anne nodded. "Lord Chamberlain's Men are actors used to fast production times. And Burbage is always a good draw."

"But..."

"We can explain the unexpected audience to the actors as an experiment. That my new friends wanted to see how a play production

A Winter's Day

worked." She looked back and forth from Master Jonson to Mistress Hart. Despite her confident words, the plan still seemed a bit shaky to her.

Master Jonson shook his head. "Some actors will not be happy."

"What about Master Burbage?" Anne said. In spite of her success in the theater, the famous actor, Richard Burbage, still intimidated her by his presence.

"We can tell him that he will never act in either of our productions if he causes trouble with the actors," Master Jonson mused. "He has often told me how he enjoys your plays."

"Then 'Taming of the Shrew' should start rehearsing." She started pacing back and forth, firming the plan in her mind. "We ladies keep going to each other's houses and practiceing—we already know our moves. We rehearse the play the last night before the production, after the men leave, then switch plays for opening night when Her Majesty attends. 'Taming of the Shrew' will go on the next night after that, as originally planned."

"Who is going to tell Lord Chamberlain's Men about the change of dates?" Master Jonson said, then stopped short. "Perhaps I should. I can threaten them with never acting in your plays or in mine ever again, if they don't cooperate." He looked at Mistress Jonson, who smiled at him. "Would that make you happy, luv?"

Mistress Jonson smiled at him, then her smile faded. "I'm not entirely sure what you're doing."

"Actually, neither am I," Mistress Hart said gently. "Could you two geniuses explain?"

Anne blushed slightly and glanced at Master Jonson. "Sorry. So that the activity at the theater will be less suspicious, Lord Chamberlain's Men will start rehearsing at normal rehearsal hours. The ladies will continue to rehearse, but at our houses. At the last rehearsal of "Shrew", the ladies will be my 'guests' to watch the play and have a 'tour' of the theater. After the men leave, we will rehearse 'As You Like It' one more time. The next evening, rather than 'Taming of the Shrew,' played by Lord Chamberlain's Men, 'As You Like It' will be performed in front of the Queen by 'The Queen's Ladies.'"

"Oh." Mistress Jonson glanced at her husband.

Anne stopped pacing and sat down. "I will take all of the responsibility."

Mistress Hart grimaced. "It sounds like a quick trip to the Tower for you," Mistress Hart said. "I am certain that Her Majesty would not be pleased, and I would rather not have my sister-in-law in prison."

"It will be worth it for that one night."

Mistress Hart grinned. "My sister-in-law, the revolutionary."

"Someone has to do it." Anne stopped pacing and smiled at her sister-in-law. "If not me, who?"

Ben Jonson shook his head and grinned ruefully.

The actors were all in the back of the theater, gathered behind a wall behind the stage. Anne had made certain that all of the peepholes in the dressing rooms were blocked. She hoped that the secret was safe. She looked encouragingly at the actors. Some looked nervous, others looked excited, Elderly Mistress Hale looked calm, and, after glancing at Anne, moved from actress to actress, calming them.

"Mama," Judith said, coming to her side. "I'm scared."

Anne leaned down. Her doublet felt odd against her body, and her false mustache scratched her. "Can I tell you a secret?"

"Yes, Mama."

"I'm scared, too."

Judith stared at her. "You don't look scared."

"That is called acting, my dear Judith." Anne leaned over to hug her, started slightly that she didn't have to lean over so far anymore.

"I'm not scared," Hamnet said. She hugged him too, and he pulled away.

Anne smiled, but not too broadly. She had already discovered that her mustache would fall off if she smiled too much. "I know you're not, Hamnet. You take after your father."

Ben Jonson came backstage. "Are you ready?"

"Has Her Majesty come yet?" Anne whispered.

"She has."

"Are we ready to make an impression, ladies?" Anne said.

They all nodded. She suddenly realized how dear all of them had become to her, and she would miss them after this night. She went down the line and hugged all of them, then stepped back. "You all realize that there is a possibility that we will be shunned from society. Are we prepared for that?"

More nods.

"Then let us start." She strode onto the stage with Mistress Cole, "As I remember, Adam, it was upon his fashion bequeathed to me…"

While onstage, Anne could hear the murmurs of the audience, but kept going. She noted some audience members were leaving as they caught on that it was an all-female cast, but she kept her eye on Her Majesty. It was hard to tell her reaction, especially with her face covered with the "venetian ceruse," a white makeup made of vinegar and lead. Anne herself preferred a natural look, even though her actors could overcome any sort of makeup.

Her Majesty did not smile throughout the play. But, as Anne considered, neither did she shut it down.

The play finished with Susanna's speech as Rosalind. Anne sighed as she reached the last sentence: "… will, for my kind offer, when I make curtsy, bid me farewell." Susanna left the stage and went into her mother's arms. She was shaking.

The audience was silent for a second, watching the queen's reaction. She looked sober, then started clapping. The audience then seemed to breathe, and as she watched, stood and clapped their hands. They looked happy, the Queen less so.

"Everybody go out and take your bows." While they were receiving their applause, Anne was watching the Queen. Her Majesty smiled, but it was not a happy smile. She seemed to be judging the audience. After an interval, she motioned to her Ladies-in-waiting and left the theater.

Anne kept smiling, but this was not a good sign.

The watchmen came for her the next morning. Anne was prepared for this; she had sent her children home with Mistress Hart after explaining why she felt that she would be taken that night. Susanna had objected.

"Mother! I was acting, too. Why should you take all of the punishment?" She stood before Anne, her arms crossed.

Mistress Hart smiled ruefully. "Are you sure you don't want me to stay, Anne?"

The twins copied her. They glanced at each other. "We want to stay, too."

"No, Joan. Please take the children with you." She wanted to say "if I get arrested," but refrained. She turned to her children. "Because," Anne said gently, hugging her children, "I wrote the play. And it was my idea to put on the play." She released them, drinking in the sight of them, wondering when she would see them again. She banished the tears from her eyes.

"Do you really think the Queen is angry at you, Mama?" Hamnet said.

"I don't believe she was happy," Anne said lowly, frowning. "But whether she is displeased enough to punish anyone but me, I don't know."

"We love you, Mama," Judith hugged her swiftly.

"I know."

"Come along, dears," Mistress Hart said. She put her arms around Susanna and Judith. Hamnet also seemed upset, but being a boy, he wasn't going to show it.

"I will be fine. I love you, dears." She resisted the impulse to tousle Hamnet's hair but didn't want to upset his dignity.

And they were gone.

Anne spent an anxious night. Just as she thought that the watchmen may not come, she heard a knock on her door. The young man took his floppy hat off and bowed. He had a club, but didn't seem to know what to do with it, finally storing it under his arm. "Mistress Shakespeare. If you will come with me."

"Yes." She picked up her satchel, filled with her quills and some papers. "May I be allowed to bring my materials?"

"Of course." He seemed nervous.

"Shall we be going to the tower?" She ushered him out of the door, closing it behind her.

"Yes, Mum." He lowered his head as he took the lead, walking swiftly down the street. He was tall and gangly, and she had a hard time keeping up with him..

A Winter's Day

"Do you know if I can have visitors?" She grabbed his arm, slowing him down. He looked at her startled, then nodded his head.

"I don't know, mum." He kept his head lowered but extended his arm so that she could take it.

She glanced at him as they started walking again. "You seem very young." He barely had any peach fuzz on his chin.

"Yes, Mum. I'm seventeen." He dropped the stick he was carrying, stopping to pick it up.

They were silent for a second. She could feel the trembling in his arm. "Why are you so nervous? I will not protest. I'm coming with you peacefully."

"Mum, I watch your plays." He hung his head. "I'm sorry." He slowed down even further.

"You were sorry you watched it?" Anne smiled to show that she was not mad at him. "Did you enjoy it?"

He looked up at her shyly. "I did, Mum. And I enjoyed the one last night. I'm sorry I have to arrest you." He stopped to look at her. Did he think she was mad at him?

"You saw it?" She smiled. "I'm surprised."

"I did, Mum. I was in the back of the theater with my betrothed."

Anne stared at him. She couldn't help but ask. "Did you and your fiancé enjoy it?"

"Lizzie and I did, Mum." He looked away and blushed.

She smiled at him to show she wasn't mad. "How about others around you?"

"Most seemed to like it, Mum. Some left and…". He seemed more nervous.

"And…?" She pulled at his arm slightly to start him walking again.

"They seemed disgusted. Mostly men." He blushed, then started walking a little quicker. "I'm sorry."

"Do not be sorry. I expected that people may be disgusted." She nodded slightly. "Your name?"

"John, mum." He looked down at her. "You aren't mad at me?"

She snorted. "Why would I be mad, John? Good solid name." She nodded and started leading the way to the Tower. "Do your duty."

"Mum?" He seemed even more nervous, if possible. "Do you think I could be an actor?"

"I don't know." She thought a moment. "My sister-in-law's husband is William Hart, the hatter. Do you know him?"

He nodded.

"After you take me to the Tower, please talk to my sister-in-law, Joan Hart, and tell her I told her to keep in touch with you," she nodded and squeezed his arm. "She will let you know when I'm looking for actors." If I ever look for actors again, she thought. She noticed that they were gaining an audience. Some of them looked friendly, some did not. She pretended to ignore all of them but looked at them covertly.

They finally approached the Tower and he led her to the West gate, passing by the Beefeaters. Anne looked at them curiously. She had thought that the Beefeaters were only to protect the Queen. She shrugged.

"This way, Mum."

He led her across the courtyard to one of the towers. Anne didn't know which one—she had never been to the Tower, and she looked around curiously.

He opened the door. Another man was behind the door. "Thank you, John," Anne said.

"I'm praying for you, Mum."

"I appreciate that."

The new man led her though a room to a hall and opened the door in front of her. A whiff of perfume wafted out at her. Rose and civet musk and ambergris—

She entered the room and gasped. She curtseyed. "Your Majesty."

Queen Elizabeth bowed her head, then continued to look at her. She was sitting in the only chair in the room, at a table set by a window. On the other side of the room was a canopied bed. The room was not bare, but not luxurious, either. At least it wasn't the dungeon.

Anne kept her curtesy until her legs were starting to ache. She concentrated on the Queen's dress. The dress today had highlights of gold and embroidered flowers. She tried very hard not to collapse and kept concentrating on the dress.

A Winter's Day

"Oh, Anne, you have given me a dilemma." The queen made a gesture. "Stand up."

Anne nodded her thanks.

The queen continued to stare. "Anne, you are a talented playwright, as was your husband before you. I suspect you wrote some of his plays."

Anne nodded her head. "Some of the acts, Ma'am." There seemed to be no point in denying it.

"I suspected so." She motioned Anne to proceed.

"Will was a playwright, but I did help him." Anne bowed her head. "I believe that he would have been a great playwright if it weren't for his untimely sickness and death."

"Would he have? I wonder. I believe what you have accomplished is greater than Master Shakespeare's efforts." She looked out the window, then turned back to Anne. "As you know, I have gone through many trials. Even though I was highly educated, many doubted my ability. In fact, I had to agree to rule 'by good advice and counsel.' And though I was almost forced to marry, I still remain the bride of England."

Anne nodded. She wasn't sure where the queen was going with this, and she was, in fact surprised that Her Majesty entrusted her with this speech.

"It has only been a few years since John Knox insisted that we are the weaker of the two sexes. Do you believe that?"

"Ma'am, respectfully, I do not believe that."

The Queen smiled. "I understand that. Neither do I. Is that why you staged the play with all females and replaced the play I had expected?"

"Yes, Ma'am, partly." She hesitated. "'Taming of the Shrew' will be presented tomorrow."

"I did enjoy this play and your ladies. I understand you call them 'The Queen's Ladies?'" She held up her hand before Anne could answer. "However, I am getting pressure from my advisors to sanction you."

"I am sorry." She stood up straight. "I will accept any punishment."

"Of course you will." The Queen smiled ironically, and Anne blushed. "You may speak freely."

Anne took a breath. "Ma'am, I consider it a travesty that female characters in plays need to be played by males. Most of the 'females' in my plays have the beginnings of a beard. I believe that I have showed that females can play any role and can play them well."

"And I agree, Anne."

"You do?" Anne burst out.

Elizabeth ignored the breech of protocol. "However, I believe that we should tread delicately. In spite of my reign, we, as women, are still considered as incomplete men, and some still believe that we should not rule or have any other position of authority, such as you as a playwright."

It seemed to Anne that the Queen was thinking out loud. She wasn't sure what to say, except, "Yes, Ma'am."

"From what I observed from your audience," the Queen went on, once again focusing on Anne, "most seemed to embrace the concept of lady actors enthusiastically. After, of course, I applauded."

"Yes, Ma'am."

"Do you have some actresses who are ready for the stage?" She looked at Anne intensely. "That large woman is a wonderful actress. And the young lady who played Rosalind."

"Yes, Ma'am. Mistress Taylor and my daughter, Susanna. I believe that my daughters will consent to act. And my son, Hamnet. I am not so certain of any of the other ladies."

"I thought I spotted a young man in your play." She smiled ruefully.

"Yes, Ma'am. He enjoys it and it keeps him out of trouble."

The Queen stood up, and Anne curtseyed again, nervously. "We will keep you at the Tower for two weeks." She looked around. "These are the chambers that I was kept in." She shook her head. "You will have as much paper as you wish. Do you need anything from your apartment? Are your children safe?"

Anne shook her head. "I brought my latest manuscript with me, ma'am. And my children are with my sister-in-law's family, Master William Hart and Mistress Joan Hart."

"Good. I will see you in a couple of weeks."

The Queen swept out, leaving Anne to shake her head in astonishment.

A Winter's Day

"A glooming peace this morning with it brings. The sun for sorrow will not show his head. Go hence to have more talk of these sad things. Some shall be pardoned, and some punished. For never was a story of more woe then this of Juliet… and her Romeo."

The theater was silent. Only a few sobs could be heard. Then the Queen enthusiastically started applauding and the crowd stood up.

The actors bowed—including the watchman, John, who had taken her to the tower—and then Anne stood on the stage. She hugged her daughter and bowed to the Queen, who nodded back.

The Queen stood up and the crowd silenced. "Mistress Shakespeare, with this play, has shown to Us that ladies may act on the stage effectively. From this day forward, We officially rename the Lord Chamberlain's Men as the Queen's Players. Also, from this day forward, both male and female are accepted as actors. Should any persons object, they will need to object to Us." She once again nodded to Anne and left the theatre.

Anne smiled broadly as she hugged all of her children. Her future was bright. In fact, she had an idea for a new play which she thought Elizabeth would appreciate—Love's Labor's Lost, about four men trying to be celibate and not succeeding.

In fact, she could anticipate ladies on the stage for decades to come. Oh, she supposed, women would have eventually taken the stage, but she felt happy that she was the one to make acting a respectable occupation for females.

She glanced at Mistress Hart. Did she realize what was happening? This was the start of a new revolution. If ladies could act, society would accept them in other roles. After all, Anne ran a household, was teaching three children, and could run a production efficiently. She knew of other ladies who did much the same. If they could run households and teach children, why not women-run businesses and other trades?

"You've created a revolution," Mistress Hart said underneath the crowd noise. "Will would be astounded and proud." She smiled. "As am I."

Yes, the future looked bright!

The Phoenix Dynasty

Mariah Southworth

My first meeting with Empress Wu Zhao was seared into my memory.

I had seen her before. I had been one of the tens of thousands to travel with the court for the Fengshang ceremony at Mount Tai, when Emperor Gaozong and Empress Wu gave offerings to Heaven and Earth. I knew Empress Wu Zhao when she was draped in silken robes, her black hair piled atop her head in a cloud and hung with golden phoenixes. I knew the flawless, white powdered face, lips, and cheeks red with rouge, the red lotus painted on her forehead.

I did not know her as she was when I was summoned to her quarters that early spring morning. She stood before the round window overlooking her garden, a cool breeze laced with jasmine and plum blossom flooding the room. The dawn light framed her in a golden haze that shifted seamlessly into the yellow silk robe she wore. Her hair, black as midnight, fell down over her shoulders to the small of her back.

Even without the trappings and make-up of court, she was beautiful, her face ageless, her figure full and curving. But of course she was beautiful—she had been a court concubine, like my own mother. Concubines were chosen for their perfection and their beauty.

What burned that image of her in my mind for all time was the fire in her dark eyes. They filled my mind even as I kowtowed to her, my forehead on the cool, polished wooden floor. I knew at that moment what my husband meant when he said that the courtiers would walk over coals for Empress Wu. And if they didn't go willingly, she made them.

The Empress had been regent for two years, but the rumors of her ruthlessness had circled in the court since my infancy.

They said she had killed her own daughter in the crib, though the crime was attributed to her rival, Empress Wang.

They said when she had displaced Wang, she'd had her hands cut off before whipping her to death with iron chains.

Her oldest son, Prince Li Hong, died after speaking out against his mother's treatment of his half-sisters. They said Empress Wu arranged his death for his rudeness.

Her second son, Li Xian, was killed for treason, and they said Wu had a hand in that as well.

They said she'd forced the emperor's uncle, Zhansun Wuji, to kill himself.

They said so many things, and I, daughter of one of the Emperor's lesser concubines, was terrified.

"You may rise, Lady Mei," the empress said, voice as cool and calm as the dawn breeze that drifted through the room.

I did so, and Empress Wu inclined her head towards the table in front of her, where a teapot and cups waited.

"A shame if it were to get cold," she said.

It took all of my will not to shake as I poured the tea. The pot was a beautiful delicate thing of fine porcelain, glazed in swirling gold and blue. The spout was shaped like an open phoenix mouth, whose wings swept back over the belly of the pot. The empress waited silently as the steam from the cups curled in the air. She gestured for me to sit, and then folded herself down opposite me.

I looked at my cup and hesitated.

There was one long, silent moment. Empress Wu broke it with a laugh. I jumped at the brazen, braying sound and stared at her before remembering my place and glancing away.

"Smart girl," The Empress said, the memory of her laugh coloring her voice. "Will you not drink?"

"My Empress," I demurred, back straight. "I would not presume to drink before you."

"And if I told you that you must?"

Steeling myself, I met her fiery black eyes and picked up the cup. The thin porcelain warmed my fingers. I forced myself not to look at the silent guards waiting in the shadows. They would not bat an eye if I fell choking on poison, as so many children of other concubines supposedly had.

A smile twitched at Empress Wu's lips, and she shook her head. "Enough, enough," she said, half-laughing. She raised her own cup and drank heartily, downing half of it. She put the cup down without a sound. "I did not bring you here to poison you, child. Though I won't give the rumors you no doubt have heard the dignity of protest." She sat back, and the flame in her eyes banked itself to an amused sparkle. I found myself relaxing, despite the fear. "Li Mei Niang," she said, tasting my name with a small, secret smile on her face, as if she knew something I didn't. "I have invested too much in you to have you killed."

I blinked, startled. I didn't quite know how to handle the directness of Wu Zhao.

She saw my confusion, and laughed again. "Let me explain. Your mother was my dear friend, did you know that?"

Another surprise! My mother had been a forgotten wallflower in the garden of Emperor Gaozong, disregarded and abandoned after she had borne only a single girl. "Forgive me, Empress, I did not," I managed to say. How could my mother have been friends with an Empress? Although Wu had not been Empress then. Only a concubine, albeit a high ranking one.

She nodded. "Of course you did not know. Your mother was wise, and when things became difficult in the court, she kept her tongue and faded into the background. It saved her life and yours as well. But for a long time she was my friend and companion. When she died, I ensured there was a place for you here."

My cheeks heated, and I bowed my head to hide the fact. "Forgive me for my ignorance, Empress." If what she said was true—and I had no reason to doubt it—then she was my patroness. And here I had been accusing her of murder in my mind!

Empress Wu waved her hand in the air, brushing away my apology. "Had I wished you to know, you would have known." She smiled and tilted her head. "But yes, I am the one who saw to your education, and you have repaid my patronage with your excellence."

"I– "

"When it came time for you to marry," she continued, not acknowledging my surprised interruption. "I whispered in my husband's ear that his doctor should be rewarded."

"Oh!" I forgot myself entirely, and stared at her, mouth parting slightly. No one was so fortunate as a wife who loved her husband, and who was cherished and loved in return. Many a day I had thanked my ancestors for giving me the chance at an education and for bringing me to Ming Chongyan, but all along it had been Empress Wu Zhao.

"Empress, I find that you are the source of all that is good in my life," I managed to say, "I am robbed for words by your generosity."

"Good," she said, smiling again. "You are happy with Ming Chongyan, then? And your son?"

"Oh yes," I said, brightening as I thought of my family. "Chongyan is all I could ask for, and little Tai is so like his father. He is walking early, and already speaking."

"Good." She nodded decisively. "I am pleased with your Chongyan as well. He has served my husband well during his sickness. A better doctor could not be found in all of Asia."

"You honor us, your Majesty," I said. I was starting to warm to Wu Zhao's bluntness. She had a causal charm about her, and it felt as if I were sitting with an old friend. "Of course we hope that Emperor Gaozong will not need my husband's skills for much longer."

She tilted her head. "That hope is granted. Emperor Gaozong is dead."

I froze.

As I sat in shock, the empress turned her head to look out onto the garden. Blossoms fell from the twisted, black-barked plum tree. The white petals drifted slowly down through the air. I can still see them, even after all these years. I only need to close my eyes to watch the petals falling, and the sun-soaked empress gazing out at the garden.

"So deep in thought while watching reds turn to greens..." Empress Wu said, her voice softer than the fall of the petals. For a moment I saw the grief in her face. Then she put it aside as one might put a scroll back on the shelf. "You're afraid," she said frankly. "Afraid that I will blame your husband."

Since this was exactly what was on my mind, I nodded meekly.

"Don't be. He gave my beloved relief and comfort through long years of pain." She leaned forward, catching me in the intensity of her gaze. "I did not summon you here to speak of our husbands, Mei Niang," she said. "I want to speak of you."

"I am at your disposal, my Empress," I said.

She nodded and sat back. "Tomorrow they will announce the emperor's death, and Prince Li Zhe will enter a month-long period of mourning. I will continue to be regent for that time."

I managed to shake myself from my shock. Although technically speaking, Emperor Gaozong was my father as well, I had never met him. He was a stranger. But Li Zhe I knew, if only by reputation, and the realization that he would be emperor broke me out of my stupor. The crown prince's impulsivity and impatience were no secret in the palace. Behind closed doors, where such musings were safe, my dear Chongyan had often lamented that Li Zhe was more interested in cockfighting than being the crown prince. "The heavens frown upon him. Li Dan would surely be a better heir," he'd said.

To this I would laugh and say, "Li Dan does not want it. He is a poet and scholar at heart, not a ruler. His time would be better spent compiling histories."

"Ah, but they say that the best ruler is the one who does not want it," Chongyan would counter. "He will put the people before his ambitions."

"Or let them fall to ruin as he indulges his own pleasures."

I am fortunate in my husband; he enjoys and encourages our debates, something that would scandalize his Confucian rivals. I had no intention of telling this to the Empress, of course, but by the way she scrutinized me, I could not help but feel she read it on my face. "Gaozong's consorts will be sent away to the nunnery," Wu continued. "As is customary. New concubines will be found."

"For Prince Li Zhe," I said.

She smiled her small, knowing smile. "Tell me, Mei Niang. Why does the emperor fill his harem with so many girls? A hundred women for one man, and why?"

I knew this, everyone in the empire did. "To ensure his lineage continues, my Empress. To bear him sons."

She shook her head, still with that small, knowing smile. "To preserve the dynasty, Mei Niang. There will be a new process for choosing concubines, and I want you to head it."

"Me?"

"Yes. You will speak with them, interview them, and ensure that their intelligence is a match for yours and mine. Some of them will not be as educated as we would like, that is the way of the world. Find a way to ferret out their potential." She lifted her cup of tea and finished it, looking at me with the fire of the phoenix in her eyes. "At the end of the week I shall be announcing a new addition to my North Gate Scholars. It will be you, Mei Niang."

I didn't know what to say. It was true that I had taken and passed the Imperial exam when the constraints had been eased to allow women. I was nobly born, technically. I had every qualification to be admitted to the North Gate Scholars, who wielded almost as much power as the Chancellors themselves. Except, of course, I was a woman.

But then, so was Wu Zhao.

What else could I say? I bowed my head.

"As my Empress wishes."

Then I finally drank my now-cold tea.

The month passed, and Wu Zhao appeared to hand the reins of the empire over to her son without complaint. But I had been with her during that time. I knew that she had spent it consolidating her power in the court, assuring the loyalty of her armies, and, most importantly, maintaining the love of the palace servants and staff. They, I learned, were her true secret weapon. They were her spies, and they served her with the undying loyalty that only a servant treated like a human being for the first time in their life could wield.

Li Zhe did not have his mother's wisdom or patience. He had only been on the throne for a week before the servants were scowling and muttering among themselves. He was brash, cruel, entitled; all things that emperors had been before, surely, but it had been a long time since the palace had been faced with a leader with such traits.

Luckily, Li Zhe had his own wife, and his advisors encouraged him to focus on getting her with child, so he did not bother my girls.

Funny how they were my girls; mine and Wu Zhao's, and not Li Zhe's harem. Wu Zhao certainly never referred to them as concubines. No, they were pupils. My pupils, and though they still practiced grace, etiquette, and handwork, I also schooled them in politics, history, and critical thinking. The girls I had chosen ate it up with a fierceness and joy that even the fire-eyed dowager empress was proud of. It was certainly good that no officials bothered with the women's area of the palace. Surely if they knew the army that Wu Zhao was building, they would quake with fear in their Confucian slippers!

And then...

Then...

How can it still pain me, after all that has happened since? After almost four decades, how can the thought of all I had lost, of all that could have been, break my heart so?

Ming Chongyan, my love. My son's father, who laughed with me, and debated with me. Who asked after the well being of my new charges. Who praised my mind as well as my beauty. My Chongyan, dead. Murdered on the outskirts of the palace, dropped into a bush like so much trash, his blood feeding the roots.

No one who has not experienced the loss of someone they have loved can know what was in my heart during those dark weeks. I woke up each morning surprised that the sun could still rise.

I didn't know then, just how much Wu Zhao cared for me. We had only known each other for half a year. But as I grieved, she set to work, and she appeared herself in my quarters at the end of the month, dressed and painted for court, with such rage in her that I recoiled from the heat of her gaze.

"Lady Li Mei Niang, you will come to court today," she said with all the command of heaven behind her steel words. "Choose two of your pupils to accompany you to observe the proceedings."

For a moment, anger to match her own kindled in me. My love was dead! No one, not even the gods themselves, could bid me to show my tears to the world.

But this was not the gods. This was Empress Wu. I touched my forehead to the ground. "As you wish," I said, my voice as flat and dead as I felt.

To my surprise, I felt her touch my shoulders. Shocked, I looked up, allowing Wu Zhao to draw me to my feet. The fire of her rage had banked, and as she looked at me with those dark eyes, I saw a hurt so deep and cold that I could drown in it.

"Niang, my polar star," she said, voice soft and sweet. "I would not ask this of you in your time of grieving if I did not have a reason." Her voice hardened. "But I know who killed your husband, and he will be avenged this day."

I chose Shangguan Wan'er and Zhangsun Feiyan to accompany me. Both highly intelligent young ladies, who had shown their skill and eagerness to learn early on. To my surprise, Empress Wu did not take us into the court itself, but rather one of the adjourning rooms, separate from the court by an intricately carved panel. The panel and lighting were such that we could see into the courtroom, but those inside could not see us. Empress Wu bid us sit on silken cushions, then gestured for our silence as the court entered.

The air smelled of incense and sandalwood. I watched as the officials entered. They murmured among themselves, and adjusted their silken robes. The Emperor strode in, the beads from his imperial headdress swinging in front of his eyes. Li Zhe, or rather, Emperor Zhongzong, sat on his throne and looked over his courtiers with a frown.

"My generals are not here," snapped Li Zhe. "Nor my chief chancellor. What is the meaning of this meeting?"

One of the lesser chancellors, the jade tablet that marked his rank cradled in his arm, spoke. "My Emperor, we received word from you that this was to be an emergency meeting. How can we tell you the meaning if we do not know it ourselves?"

The emperor paused, frown deepening. "What folly is this? I sent no such word."

Then, as if waiting for just such a cue, the doors to the meeting room swung wide. The missing Chancellor, Pei Yan, strode in, chin tilted up with determination. The generals of the imperial army flanked him, kitted out in full armor. With an audible gasp the court drew back, and Pei Yan held up a gold-gilt edict scroll. He unrolled the scroll, and began to read. "The emperor is without capability. By order of the empress dowager, the emperor shall be demoted to Prince of Liuling."

Behind the carved panel, I turned to stare at Empress Wu. A small smile tugged at her lips, and her eyes blazed with victorious wrath. It sank into me suddenly that I was not only witnessing a coup, but that here was the murderer of my husband, being pulled from his throne by the very generals he thought he had commanded.

I knew that Li Zhe hadn't wielded the knife himself. But if Wu Zhao said that he was the cause, then I knew it to be true. I watched as he was bodily removed from the throne, headdress falling from his head, and my heart filled with black joy.

"What did I do to warrant this? Unhand me!" Li Zhe cried, pulling at the general's iron grip. His eyes widened as no one in the court moved to help him, though they shuffled uneasily.

Wu Zhao straightened. "You want to give the empire to your father-in-law. Is that not severe enough of a crime?" Her voice echoed through the room. The courtiers froze into statues. The empress stepped out, yellow and red robes trailing behind her like wings of fire. She walked past the screen, and her son glared at her. I had no idea what the empress dowager was speaking of, but Li Zhe apparently did.

"Lies!" he spat angrily.

"Did you not tell me in your own words that you would give him the throne?" Pei Yan said calmly, pitching his voice so that all could hear.

Li Zhe glanced at the chancellor with a snarl, tugging again at the armored hands that held him back. "I did not mean that and you know it! I am the Emperor!" He stamped his foot like a petulant child. "I should be able to appoint my own chancellors, and yet you said my father-in-law was unsuitable! So what, if being emperor gives me the power to promote who I want and when! It's the truth!" Rage dyed his face red, and his struggles had only allowed strands of hair to escape his top knot. Compared to him, the calm and collected Wu Zhao was a mountain; a steady, calm monument, and he the useless, howling wind that thrashed itself against the stones.

"No," Empress Wu said, tilting her chin up. "For you are not emperor any longer." She waved to her generals. "Take him away."

And they did, and there was nothing the shocked courtiers could do or say about it.

When all was over, and only Wu Zhao, myself, and my two pupils remained in the empty council chamber, Wu Zhou called us around her. "Ladies, listen to me now," she said, face grim and serious. "As long as you are alive you have a second chance. But that goes for your enemies as well. Do not give them that second chance."

It was no surprise then, when we received word six months later, that Li Zhe had killed himself during his exile.

Several days after the dramatic expulsion of Li Zhe from the council room, I was sitting in the palace garden on a stone bench. The red and gold flush of autumnal leaves surrounded me, and my son, Tai, played at my feet. I sat, and I grieved. How would Chongyan feel if he knew that his predictions had come to pass, and that Li Dan would take the throne? Ah, but that prediction is no doubt what got him killed. How would he feel knowing that his murderer had lost everything?

A deep, shuddering breath rattled in my throat, and my son looked up at me and smiled. He had a leaf in his hand. I picked him up and held him to my chest.

What a world ambition created. I could not imagine my dear son turning into the monster that Li Zhe was. I could equally not imagine tearing his world to shreds, as Wu Zhao had done with her own son. How lucky I had been, truly, to be born of a mother whose only ambition was to live and who had shared only that one ambition with me.

But perhaps that was all Wu Zhao's machinations were for, in the end. To live, not as a flower in the emperor's garden, but as herself: fiery and defiant. And without that fire, Chongyan's killer would have faced no consequences.

It was not fair! Chongyan had been too important under Emperor Gaozong's rule for anyone to even dream of hurting him. And everyone knew that it was really Wu Zhao who had been the power behind Gaozong's throne. If only the Imperial crown had passed to her instead of her murderous son...

I laughed. A female emperor, who had ever even heard of such a thing?

These confusing thoughts and the toddler in my lap kept me distracted, and I did not realize I wasn't alone until I felt someone sit beside me.

I looked up and jumped, clutching Tai to me for fear of dropping him. He squirmed, wriggled out of my arms, and climbed back down to the grass, only to clutch and hide behind my skirts, gazing solemnly at the stranger beside me.

"Prince Li Dan!" I cried. I moved to bow, but he waved me back. Like his mother, he seemed to have little patience for decorum when in a private setting.

"Lady Mei," he said, cutting right to the point. "You have my mother's ear."

I put a reassuring hand on Tai's shoulder. "I have the honor of being the dowager empress's chief scholar," I said politely.

"Yes, yes, as I said." He nodded eagerly. He was still very young, barely twenty, and looked at me with boyish earnestness. "You speak with her, you advise her. You must tell her that I do not want to be emperor. I am not like her, or Father or my brothers. I do not want the weight of the empire on my shoulders."

I looked at him, and for the first time saw a little of myself in one of Empress Wu's sons. It was true, Li Dan and I shared the same father, but what a difference between the daughter of a concubine and the son of an empress! I had never thought of the imperial family as part of my family. And yet Li Dan and I had the same narrow nose, the same arch to our eyebrows, the same love of history and knowledge.

He was, technically speaking, uncle to little Tai, who had gone back to collecting leaves on the grass before us. Only an accident of birth separated Li Dan's situation from my own. And for the first time, I felt that small, bitter rage that Wu Zhao must feel every day. Would I, had I been him, tried to run from my responsibilities as he was doing now? Begging a lowly female to come save him? I struggled to keep the disdain from my face.

On the other hand, maybe I couldn't blame him for not wanting to be emperor. All his brothers had died because of that desire.

"Li Dan." The chilling voice rang out over the garden, and the prince jumped, scrambling to his feet as if caught with his hand down my dress. He stepped away from me, bowing his head to his mother, who stood watching us from the edge of the garden.

"The mandate of heaven will pass to whom it passes to," Empress Wu said sternly. She tilted her head, and a smile that did not meet her eyes pulled at her lips. "Pressuring my scholar will not change that."

Li Dan was at least more humble than his brother. He inclined his head politely to me. "Your forgiveness, Lady Mei."

"You already have it, my lord," I said, glancing between the prince and empress dowager. Wu Zhao held out her hand to Li Dan. "Walk with me, my son. We have many things to discuss."

Without a backwards glance, Li Dan did just that, leaving me and Tai to our chosen corner of the garden.

I do not know what they discussed, but I know that it was announced that Li Dan was too distraught over his father's death to shoulder the burden of administration. He was emperor, certainly, but council meetings took place with the imperial throne empty. Chancellors and strategists spoke and planned with Wu Zhao, who sat behind a beaded curtain behind the throne.

"The Divine Mother has graced the mortal realm. May she reign forever."

The phrase was being whispered all over the capital and beyond. It was a phrase that several Buddhist monks had found carved upon a stone in the Luo river. The stone had, of course, been presented to Wu Zhao, and now many of the commoners were calling her The Divine Mother Holy Emperor. Of course, the fact that Li Dan was the actual emperor annoyed many of the noble officials, but what could they do? The people loved Wu Zhao—she gave low ranking officers and officials raises, her edicts saw the rise of the silk industry and economy. It didn't matter what the few, dogmatic nobles thought—the people and the army were with Wu Zhao.

And yet the anger that had sparked that day in the garden, when Li Dan bemoaned his good fortune, still haunted me. It irked me that all this glory and power would be attributed to Li Dan—Emperor Ruizong, that is. I had been working for Empress Wu for three years by that time. Three years was all it had taken for her to open my eyes, and see the constraints that bound women for the chains they were. We were as smart and capable as men! Who had ever heard of such peace and prosperity when the empire went through three emperors in as many years? No one, and that was because Wu Zhao was the real stability and power behind the throne.

And I was tired of no one acknowledging it.

I said as much to her when she brought me a text to translate. She laughed at me. Time was finally starting to show its mark on her if you knew where to look for it. Her hair had dulled, showing iron gray among the black. The skin beneath her makeup was soft, and showed the lines of governing around her mouth and between her brows. Not for the first time, I wondered if this slip of time was intentional on her part, to make her look wiser. I had no doubt that had she wished to, she could have held onto her youth for a decade longer.

"There's the fire I knew you had," she said. "You are too quiet about it, Niang. Do me a favor, and the next time you want someone dead, you tell them that to their face."

I was not in the mood for her humor. "Only when I am as fearsome as you, my empress," I sighed.

She handed me a scroll. "You'll get there," she said. "I need this translated into a more modern language."

I took the scroll and unrolled it. "This is part of the Great Cloud Classic," I said, skimming the Buddhist text. I read the passage, and my eyebrows rose. It described how the Buddha had promised a heavenly spirit that she would be reincarnated as a woman, and rule over a mortal kingdom before ascending to Nirvana.

I looked up at the empress, and she smiled down at me.

"Be sure you understand which heavenly spirit the Buddha is talking about," she said. "I do not need to tell one as learned as you that it is of course, Maitreya Buddha."

I immediately knew why she wanted the change. The Maitreya Buddha was well known and recognizable. A more auspicious figure to claim to be then a random spirit.

My slow smile matched hers. I should have known that Wu Zhao would not be content with the feminine constraints the world put on her, even now.

"It will be done, my Empress," I said.

And it was. Over the next few months, all the Buddhist temples received copies of the Great Cloud Classic, and the whispering that the mandate of heaven belonged to Wu Zhao, and not her son, grew stronger and stronger.

And finally, when Wu Zhao was forty-six, a court official gathered a crowd in front of the palace and petitioned her to take the throne and become Emperor in her own right.

And she said no.

The Phoenix Dynasty

"You're angry, Niang. It would serve you well to hide it better."

I looked up from the blotch of ink my pen had left on the scroll I was writing. Wu Zhao, stacking her own reading material into the hands of a servant, reminded cool.

"Why should I hide my anger around you, my Empress?" I asked her, the audacity enough to cause the servant to raise her eyebrow.

I didn't care, in that moment, if I scandalized the staff. I set my quill down and stood, calligraphy be damned. "Why did you say no?" I demanded. "I don't understand. Do you not realize how much better things would be for the empire with you truly at the reins? For the rest of us women?"

Wu Zhao snorted, folding her hands into her sleeves. "Don't be naive. You are too old for fairy stories. If I were emperor, it would still be a long, slow fight for the women of the empire. Thousands of years of culture do not disappear in a day. And all of history wants nothing more than to fit us in our proper place."

"It would be better," I insisted.

"And when I die? What then?" She shook her head. "It would be worse, for no one would ever again allow a woman to fly as high."

I stared at her, heart breaking. "So you won't even try?"

The small, knowing smile that I had come to know so well bloomed across her face. "I did not say that." Suddenly, she seemed to change the subject. "Why did Li Zhe lose his position?"

In my current mood, I did not want to hear that name. "He was a murderer and spoke rashly," I said sulkily.

Wu Zhao shook her head. "No. He was emperor. He could have gotten away with snapping at Pei Yuan. He could have gotten away, I am sorry to say, with the murder of your husband. No, he lost his position because he was impatient. He worked too quickly, tried too hard, to put his people in power. He was impatient and made enemies instead of friends." She stepped forward, suddenly, and placed her cool fingers on my chin, tilting my face up. "Wait, Mei Niang. Wait and see. And trust me."

The next week, ten thousand people stormed the palace and demanded that Empress Wu become the emperor. She demurred, protesting that she could not possibly overstep herself. I saw the nods of approval from the old Confucian officials at her humility, and then I looked out over the mob in front of the palace gates. I began to get an inkling of what she was up to.

Wu Zhao asked me, casually, if any of my pupils were good with animals. I sent for three such girls, whose fathers had kept menageries, and who had an interest in husbandry. She sent all but one of them back; all but Wei Xindu, a small girl of sixteen, whose interest and skill lay with birds.

Sixty thousand came for the next round of petitions, a sea of people from all over the empire, demanding that Wu Zhao take the mantle of emperor. She appeared atop the wall, with her guards and several of her ladies, myself included. I had caught on by now that most of this was staged. And indeed, some of the rallying cries felt a trifle over the top.

"The time for humility is at an end!" one official screamed at the palace gates. "A virtue when used to defy the will of heaven is no virtue!"

"You must take up the mantle of emperor!" another cried.

It took all my self-control not to laugh. They were angry with her! Angry, for not doing what she wanted to do!

Wu Zhao looked out over the crowd and shook her head, hiding her face behind her sleeve like an embarrassed maiden. Some of the crowd started to demand to know who exactly was holding her back, which officials they should draw and quarter.

Then Li Dan appeared, the beads from his headdress catching the sun, and a hush fell over the crowd. No one had seen the Emperor since he had taken the throne.

Really that was because he had been in the library with the rest of us scholars, quite happily compiling his histories, relieved to have nothing to do with modern politics.

As the crowd watched, Li Dan removed his beaded headdress and dropped to his knees. He held up the headdress and spoke, his voice ringing out over the silent crowd. "Take it, Mother. It is meant to be yours. Be mother to the people! Be our emperor!"

The Phoenix Dynasty

The crowd howled with glee, and whatever Wu Zhao said in response was drowned out by the cheering. Then, just as she was shaking her head once more, someone cried out, "A phoenix!"

To be heard over the crowd, they must have been standing in the precise perfect spot with something to amplify their voice, but no one thought of that. They were all staring at the huge, golden bird suddenly flying overhead.

It was, as I later learned from a bright-eyed Wei Xindu, a pheasant covered in turmeric, but no one in the crowd knew that, and even the ones who Wu Zhao had planted were struck with wonder. They screamed and howled, and fireworks were set off, and finally, finally, Wu Zhao gave in, with great reluctance, to the will of the people. It was a fantastic performance by all involved, and now even her loudest critics would not dare say that Wu Zhao had stolen the throne, or that it was no place for a woman. They would be ripped to shreds if they dared.

And so she was given the imperial name Wu Zetain, and the Wu Zhao dynasty began.

"Funny how they were all fine taking her orders when she sat behind the throne, but now that she is sitting on it, they argue," I thought as I stood among the squabbling councilors. I was a councilor myself now, and though I still got sidelong glances from the others for being the only female in their ranks, no one said anything. Unlike Li Zhe's infamous father-in-law, I actually was qualified for this position.

The current subject of debate was Wu Zetain's new edict, that, regardless of rank, anyone could come to the palace and report corruption in the government, and that said reports would be taken with all seriousness.

It was Pei Yan whose voice finally cut through the rabble. "Emperor Wu," he said, standing proud with his jade tablet in hand. "The fact of the matter is that the common folk cannot be trusted not to abuse such a privilege. Even the common-born who have come into new money think only of their own ambitions, and not the good of the empire. Leave such things where they belong, with the families who have long safeguarded the interests of the people."

Shangguan Wan'er and I exchanged a glance from across the room. Now that I was a chancellor, she had taken my place as chief scholar and secretary for the Emperor. I knew from her face that she was wondering the same thing I was; if that had been an intentional insult to the Emperor, or if Pei Yan had merely forgotten that Wu Zetain's own father was a new money merchant, whose rise to power had begun with his success in the lumber industry.

Wu Zetain smiled at him, and I knew that his intention didn't matter one way or the other. "Forgive me, Chancellor, for I am suddenly struck with nostalgia. Shall I tell you the anecdote that comes to mind?"

Pei Yan blinked and found suddenly that no other officials would catch his eye. "If it pleases my Empress," he said carefully. I had to stifle a laugh, for I was close enough to see the beads of sweat break out across his forehead.

"It does. I am reminded of my youth when I was a part of former Emperor Taizong's court."

Several of the courtiers had the intelligence to look alarmed. Wu Zetain rarely brought up the reminder that, before Gaozong, she had technically been a concubine to his father as well. Pei Yan, evidently, was either ignorant of this or too secure in his assumption of her good favor. He nodded and waited.

"The emperor had brought a horse to court," she said smoothly. "A wild, willful thing, with hide as black as midnight and eyes of obsidian. The Emperor, of course, wanted such a powerful beast for his own, but it would not submit itself to be ridden. So he looked to his courtiers and bade them to come and tame it. Unfortunately, the wild, kicking thing intimidated them, and none stepped forward."

Now the fire blazed in her eyes, and though her smile remained sweet, I could see Pei Yan's face twitch with uncertainty.

"So I stepped forward, and I told the emperor that I could tame the creature if he would only give me three items. An iron whip, an iron club, and a knife." She held up three fingers as she spoke, and her dark eyes traveled the silent room before settling on the chancellor once more. "A whip to command the beast, and if it would not listen to that sting, a club to bash its head. The knife, of course, was for when all else failed, and I slit its throat."

She looked into Pei Yan's face, and she laughed that wild, brazen laugh of hers. "Ah, age settles on even the noblest of shoulders! Thank you for your indulgence in remembering my younger years. Now, Pei Yan, what was it you were saying about fulfilling my commands?"

Pei Yan was not a stupid man. He would not still be in court if he was. He bowed low to the emperor. "That your new edict will be announced throughout the provinces, my Emperor. It shall be done."

"Excellent," she said, waving him away. "Now, to the next order of business…"

Not that Emperor Wu did not listen to her advisors. She knew talent and expertise when she saw it and listened well to wisdom. But she also knew when it was only petty pride or dogma talking, and she did not hesitate to bully and threaten when that happened. And if the accounts of corruption and treachery that came to her from her new edict proved to be true, she came down on the culprits with such wrath and violence that no one dared duplicate the crimes.

And it showed. The empire prospered under her care. I have my bias of course, for by then I had become what my husband had long ago told me of, one of those who would walk over coals for Wu Zetain. But even her worst critics couldn't deny that she was a superb leader.

And she had those critics, to be sure.

Li Jingye was one of them. Li Jingye, who posed as a provincial governor, opened all the prisons, ordered the criminals armed and marched them on the capital. The rebellion claimed to be fighting to restore the Li Clan to their rightful place as rulers.

The council chamber was full of uneasy shuffling and sidelong glances. No one was sure that the Emperor, despite her vicious reputation, could stand against this threat. Many of them, cowards that they were, were considering joining it themselves.

Wu Zetain looked out over the assembly with a smile. She tapped the scroll waiting in front of her. "I have something I think you all should hear," she said with calm amusement. "The manifesto of this little rebellion." She unrolled the scroll and began to read.

Two lines in and I could already feel the rage building in my chest. A paragraph down, and I was ready to spit fire. The things that were written out on that scroll in simple ink! Accusing, no, stating as fact, that Wu Zetain was a vicious tyrant, who had tortured and murdered her way to the throne! That she had forced Taizong and Goazong to perform incest by playing consort to both. That she had tortured Empress Wang to death. That she had poisoned her own sons!

Never mind that, long ago, I had half-believed rumors not dissimilar to these. Never mind that there was a half-truth to many of them. Wu Zetain was ambitious and powerful, but what good emperor wasn't?

I peered through my rage, and I saw with a cold shock that Wu Zetain was not angry. She was half laughing as she read it, and her eyes sparkled.

I looked around, and I realized that the more she read, the more the tension bled away from the officials surrounding us. They saw what I saw—that Wu Zetain was not threatened by the rebellion. Her confidence was their confidence, and by the time the long list of slander came to an end, the court was practically laughing alongside their Emperor.

And as I listened, I smiled too, and my anger died. Not one word, not one word against her capability as a leader! All of it was attacking her moral fiber. Even the rebellion could not deny that the empire prospered under her rule.

"Such skill," Wu Zetain said, lowering the scroll. "The grammar, the penmanship. Truly we must archive this as one of the great literary triumphs of our times." With a smile she handed the scroll off to Shangguan Wan'er. "Make it so." She folded her hands in front of her and shook her head sadly. "A pity that we had not realized the author's talent before. We could have used him well. Now then..." she raised an eyebrow at all assembled. "Tell me, my advisors, what shall I do about this revolt?"

"Surely it is clear, this rebellion was sparked because you took the throne from Li Dan," Pei Yan said, confidence making his voice ring through the hall. "Step down, give up your power, and the rebellion will dissolve."

Silence descended.

I turned and stared, aghast, at the chief councilor. He had been so eager to pull Li Zhe from the throne for our Emperor!

"Ah," I thought, my heart hardening. "But that was when he thought Li Dan would be emperor."

"Pei Yan must be in cahoots with the rebellion!" an official yelled, breaking the silence. "Why else would he say such a thing?"

I did not know the official, but he was a smart man. Wu Zetain graced him with a nod. "Yes. Arrest him."

Pei Yan barely had time to realize his error before he was dragged from the council chamber, babbling in protest.

Wu Zetain waited for his cries to fade, then turned her smile to the advisors. "Now then, who else has an idea?"

To their credit, the removal of Pei Yan did not entirely rob them of their voices, and one strategist stepped forward. "My Empress, this rebellion is not a trained army. Its bulk is made up of random criminals, armed with stolen armor and weapons. Its morale is low. Cut off their branches rather than the trunk, and they will scatter to the winds."

Wu Zetain listened, nodding thoughtfully. "That makes good sense, Strategist Han. You will accompany one of the nobles of the Li Clan. Let the rebellion see that the Clan's true loyalties lie with me." She gestured to the rest of her chancellors. "I will now hear suggestions for who will accompany Strategist Han."

As the chancellors and strategists clamored to have their own suggestion taken, I noticed several officials slip from the chamber. I smiled grimly. They were the ones known to be allies with Pei Yan. They were trying to run, the cowards. Foolish, to think they could outrun the Emperor.

The rebellion lasted forty days. When it was over, the Emperor gathered her court together. "If any of you think yourselves to surpass those I have defeated in intelligence, nobility, and leadership, take me down now, or else serve me with all the loyalty your frail bodies can manage." Her fiery gaze swept the chamber. "Do not make yourself a laughingstock of the world."

All the officials, scholars, strategists, and chancellors knelt before her. We touched our foreheads to the ground. "We are yours to command," we cried.

The years that followed were bright for the empire. Wu Zetain opened the Imperial exam system to all of her people, be they noble or commoner. Ambassadors from far-flung nations were welcome in her court, and new ideas from Japan and Greece inspired our artists and philosophers. The lack of corruption and chaos in her government meant that the people were happy and prosperous.

Buddhism flourished under her rule. No surprise there; it had led to her taking power, and the propaganda she had installed said that the Buddha himself had sent her to rule. No wonder that she wanted to build as many monuments and statues as possible to honor the philosophy. Only once did I need to step in and remind her that the imperial purse was not endless, and though statues were all well and good, the money would better go to serve the people. She listened, and it filled me with pride that my advice was valued and welcomed.

Then I made a mistake.

It should have been a small mistake, but I had forgotten that the court, even under Wu Zetain's rule, was a maze of machinations and complex ambitions.

My beloved son Tai had grown into a man with a brilliant, tactical mind. He was more his mother's son then his father's, and rather than enter medicine he was on his way to becoming one of Wu Zetain's most brilliant tacticians and war strategists. I was proud when our household could play host to him and his friends. One such friend was Zhang.

The Phoenix Dynasty

Think what you will of me, but when my son went off to the border to advise on a skirmish there, Zhang stayed. Such romantic affairs were more common under Wu Zetain's rule. She herself had enjoyed a string of lovers. What I shared with Zhang was not love—not like I had held for my long-gone beloved Chongyan. It was only fun.

So I was without jealousy or resentment when Zhang left me to warm the Emperor's bed. I could only admire her passion, and hope that I could match it when I was in my early seventies.

But I did not like how Zhang, and soon his brother, started to swagger around the palace giving orders where they had no right. I did not like how they spoke to the pupils under my teaching, and I did not like how the officials listened to their opinions. Suddenly they had the ear of the Emperor, not me, and everyone knew it.

The trouble was, it was becoming increasingly difficult to speak with the Emperor without one or both of the Zhangs in earshot. They hovered over her, fawning and complimenting.

In the end, I needed to use Wu Zetain's own tricks against her. It was one of the palace servants whom I had befriended who managed to help me lure the Zhangs away, and I slipped into the Emperor's private garden.

She would not listen to me, though, despite all the suspicions I laid at her feet.

"I do not trust them," I finally said with exasperation.

She waved the concern away. "They are well in hand."

"But my Emperor..."

The fire in her eyes flashed toward me. "You do not trust my ability to see to my own people, Lady Mei?" she asked, voice hard as steel.

"Of course I do. It's just that you are giving them more power then they deserve, or indeed, have been proven trustworthy of."

She snorted at that. "They are playthings, Niang, nothing more." Her eyes hardened, and her lips twisted bitterly. "Men have long used women as toys. Have I not earned the right as emperor to turn the tables on them for once?"

I bowed my head, defeated. How could I argue that when I had thought much the same thing? "My Emperor, it is your affair. I would only say that you were once a toy. Look what you have done."

A heavy silence settled over the garden.

"Get out," she said.

My bow deepened. "As my Emperor commands."

I could not see the Emperor after that. I was not strictly forbidden to, of course. But she did not call for me, or seek me out, and I found that she did not appear as she used to in the places where we would meet and talk. Her displeasure was a dangerous thing, but I missed her more than feared her, and that loss weighed on my shoulders.

I threw myself into my responsibilities. No one referred to the collection of young women as the Emperor's harem anymore. No, it was The Ladies Academy, and those who completed the many years of study went on to become governors, scholars, and government officials. Many stayed, though, and became instructors for the next crop of girls.

One thing I did personally was prepare those who were to take the Imperial exam. I was in just such a lesson with my two senior pupils when Wan'er came bursting into the library with a storm in her expression. She saw I was teaching and stopped, but the lesson had already been disturbed, so I waved her over with concern.

"Wan'er, whatever is the matter?"

She didn't need any further invitation to vent. "It's those Zhang brothers," she said with a grimace. "They won't let me see the Emperor."

I stared, aghast. "What?"

Wan'er huffed and waved a scroll through the air. "I was bringing the Emperor the itinerary for the next council meeting, and they would not let me in her quarters. They said she's ill and asked to have it instead."

"Did you give it to them?"

"Of course not!" she said with a snort.

Xiran, one of my pupils, spoke up with a frown. "Lady Mei, if I can be so bold, the Emperor has not come to our debate practice as she usually does."

Her companion, Yichen, nodded. "I heard one of the North Gate Scholars say that one of the Zhangs had accepted the new translations the Emperor had asked for in her stead. None of the scholars have seen her in weeks."

Fear spiked through me. I had assumed that I had not seen the Emperor because of her displeasure, but if what I heard now was true, no one had seen her. My heart began to race, and I forced it to be calm. Wu Zetain had all the rage of a fire within her, but she was always calm, always in control. I stood.

"Wan'er, come with me," I ordered. "Xiran and Yichen, fetch the guards and meet us at the Emperor's quarters."

It was the elder Zhang who opened the door for me, not the one whom I had taken into my own bed. I was glad of that. He looked down at me with disdain. "The Emperor does not wish to see you, Mei Niang," he said.

"I will hear that from her own lips," I told him.

A frown creased his pretty face, and he all but sneered. "Go, or you will face the consequences."

I held his gaze with steely determination. "No."

Before anything else could be exchanged, my girls rounded the corner with a pair of guards. I glanced at their faces. I knew them, and I fought to keep a smirk from my face. Jinzong and Goajun, good. My girls were smart. They had chosen guards who knew and trusted me and did not like the Zhangs.

Zhang nodded to the men. "Guards, good, take these women away," he demanded, flicking his hand towards me and Wan'er. "They are disturbing the Emperor."

"We will see the Emperor," I said loudly, loudly enough that surely, surely, Wu Zetain would hear.

She didn't, but the other Zhang brother did. He appeared in the doorway with a scowl. "The Emperor will have your head if you do not leave now!" he said.

"I will have your head if you do not step aside this moment!" I snapped back, barging forward. Zhang, shocked, almost let me pass but then grabbed my arm at the last moment.

"You take your hands off of Lady Mei!" Jinzong called.

Shifting, Swirling HERitage

I jerked forward, and the sound of silk ripping rent the air, but I was through, and the sudden crush of my ladies chasing after me stopped the Zhangs from holding me back any longer. I rushed through the Emperor's quarters, no sign of her anywhere, as behind me the guards and the Zhangs shouted.

I found her in her bedchamber.

The guards, ladies, and Zhang brothers clamored in after me.

"You see? She is sleeping," Zhang said.

Her breath was too fast, her face too pale. "She has been poisoned!" I countered.

I didn't actually think it was true until the Zhang brothers reacted. The one I had loved for so brief a period lunged for me, a knife appearing from his sleeve. The other whirled around and shoved Wan'er into the guards.

I lurched back, throwing myself across the body of the Emperor, and even that did not wake her.

I thought of the Emperor, but my girls thought of me. With a shout Xirin jumped onto Zhang's back, throwing off his gait, and Yichen drove her shoulder into his side.

Twenty years ago, no female would have even thought of acting as such. But these two had grown up under Wu Zetain's rule, and they defended their Emperor with all the ferocity that she had instilled in them.

The Zhang brothers had also grown up under Wu Zetain. They should have realized that they were not fighting two guards, but six loyal and devoted courtiers.

It was over in seconds—the Zhang brothers on their knees with the guards restraining them, swords at their throats. Yichen had a small cut on her face that she held her sleeve to, but that was the only injury among us.

I towered over the Zhangs, my wrath clear on my face. "As much as I want your heads," I told them with all the fire I had learned from Wu Zetain, "I am leaving them to you. I know the Emperor will want the privilege of removing them herself."

The Phoenix Dynasty

I sat by the Emperor while the doctor tended to her. It was not lethal poison, he told me—but drugs. Enough to make an old woman sleepy and lethargic. A feigned illness, and one the Zhang brothers could take advantage of. I saw the treachery, and I was respected and liked enough that everyone else saw it too. But would the Emperor? After everything, I was still not sure whose head would roll when she awoke. Still, I sat with her, and waited until she awoke.

She listened calmly to what I, the doctor, and Wan'er said. Her only reaction was to close her eyes now and again. For the first time she looked her age, with her iron gray hair, sagging face, and frail hands folded on her lap. I was not so much shocked and disappointed at the sight of this old woman before me but enraged that the treacherous Zhangs had rendered my goddess human.

Of course, when the subject of how to deal with them came up, that old fire lit her eyes, and her spine straightened with imperial authority.

"Mei Niang already told you what to do," she told her guards. "She wants their heads, and so she may have them. But I will first have their hands, lips, and manhood."

That was the Wu Zetain we all knew and feared, and what a relief it was to have her back.

Then she turned her eyes to me. "I would speak with you, Lady Mei." she nodded to the rest. "Leave us."

They bowed and left, and I was alone with the Emperor. I opened my mouth, but she raised a hand, forestalling my questions. "I need to tell you a story." She closed her eyes and took a deep, shuddering breath. "Many, many years ago," she said without opening her eyes. "I had a daughter. My first, and only daughter." Her lips turned into a smile, and the ferocious face of the Emperor softened. "My beautiful little girl. I cherished her from the moment I laid eyes on her." Now she opened her eyes, and they were so full of grave sorrow that I almost wept. "And that was my mistake. Remember I told you that your mother was my dear friend? Well, the night her own daughter died, I was there for her."

I blinked, startled. "But—"

"Shh," the Emperor said. "She cried on my shoulder and held the poor little thing in her arms. I was just persuading her that she must set the baby down, when one of the eunuchs came rushing in. The eunuchs and the servants of the harem loved me like they loved no other, for I treated them like people rather than convenient objects. The eunuch warned me that Empress Wang had gone into my quarters, where my little girl was sleeping. I rushed to my rooms, and your mother came with me, still clutching her dead baby."

A scowl crawled over her face, emphasized by the deep lines time and her sickness had set there. "We turned the corner and caught only a glimpse of Empress Wang leaving, but dread filled my heart. We rushed inside. My daughter was alive, but barely. Wang had tried to strangle her, for she knew I loved my daughter. She wanted to hurt me."

Emperor Wu Zetain looked at me, and there was no fire in her eyes, no iron in the set of her jaw. She looked at me with something I had never seen on her face before. Love, pure, unfiltered, and tinged with deep pain. She reached out and touched my hand in hers.

"No, no surely not..." I thought, eyes wide with wonder.

"I made a decision then," she said. "I gave my daughter—I gave you—to my best friend, and I took the dead child from her. It was the dead child that I showed Goazong. Remember, the two girls were half siblings, and looked almost identical. Empress Wang underestimated Goazong's love for me; she thought she would only hurt me. She did not realize that Gaozong would be enraged at the death of a mere girl. And your mother took you, and she faded into the background, so that no one would discover the truth."

She moved her hand and cupped my cheek. I felt tears burn hot in my eyes. "You are my daughter, Niang, and I could not be more proud of you."

Then the mother was gone, and the Emperor was back. She folded her hands in her lap and sat up with regal pride. "Tomorrow I will tell the other chancellors that I am officially adopting you, and that you are my heir. I will be stepping down as Emperor by year's end. It is up to you, my polar star, to carry the dynasty."

Her stern mask cracked, and she smiled at me. "But I will still be around to advise you, of course, and scare off the usurpers. If you will take lessons from an old fool, that is."

The Phoenix Dynasty

Today is the two-month anniversary of Emperor Wu Zetain's death. Tomorrow I will go out, and, as tradition dictates as her successor, write the epitaph on her funeral stele. I only pray that they have made it large enough to encompass her life story, and the legacy she has left for us.

~Empress Wu Mei Niang, second Emperor of the Wu Zhoa dynasty.

So deep in thought while watching reds change to greens,
so frail I've become in memory of you.
If you do not believe the tears I have wept,
open this chest and see the marks on my pomegranate dress.

~Wu Zhao to Emperor Gaozong, Tang Dynasty

The Empire Builder's Wife

Shabana Kayum

Guiana is a country that hath yet her maidenhead…
— Sir Walter Raleigh, 1596

Mourn not for us who died but for our brothers everywhere who live in bondage and in mourning turn away to act.
— African Liberation Monument
Georgetown, Guyana 1974

1.

"MY LADY," HER LADY'S MAID SARAH CALLED FROM THE DOOR, then hesitated. "He is talking now of doing something about you."

Bess did not answer the warning about her son Carew. When she heard the door close, she faced the ceiling and counted all the cracks. Durham House was falling apart and no one else saw it. Or believed her.

With Sarah's words ringing in her ears, Bess grabbed the nearby candlestick and ventured out into the dark and empty halls. When Walter lived and she woke up alone, she would find him in his library poring over a conquistador's map, making plans for long ship journeys without her.

Memories of those days were so vivid and tangible they usurped the air around her—they held her up and kept her standing tall. They kept the walls up, too.

When she arrived at the library door, it was slightly open and candlelight flickered within. A man sat in Walter's favorite wingback.

She took in her late husband's features with surprise. His length, his cross-legged position indicating deep thought, the opened book balanced in one hand. But it was not her husband. It was Carew.

Someone else was in the room with him, speaking to him. Bess could not see his face, and she dared not move any closer.

"We could have beaten the Low Countries there had your father lived. We'll have to settle for the second outpost there. Regardless, this is a victory for England's future empire."

It was the sniveling Robert, Earl of Somerset and the king's favorite, who stole away Sherborne Castle from her during Walter's final imprisonment in London Tower. Bess did not know they were even hosting, and here Somerset was in her husband's library. What could Carew be thinking?

"I daresay the Raleigh family will have cause to hold their heads high once again," Somerset continued, "when the Guianas and the riches your father wrote about finally belong to the Crown."

"Do you believe in the city of gold, then?" asked Carew. "Do you think we'll find it this time?"

"The privateers setting sail in the morning will be searching for El Dorado. Later, we shall send more ships to make headway with the savage nations. We will need a good, strong breed of them to plant our coffee and sugar." He came into view now behind Carew's chair, stretching an odious hand for the open book. "Your father wrote extensively about his travels there. And he knew the hostiles from the docile of the inhabitants. His writings will be most invaluable to us."

"I hope His Majesty will be pleased to learn how pivotal my help has been." Carew remained seated, allowing Somerset to hover over his chair.

Bess cringed at the sight. Her Walter would have never tolerated this man!

"Our most benevolent king shall know all," said Somerset. "Your father's legacy will once again serve the Crown. Your mother will be pleased, will she not?"

"Yes, perhaps it will finally pull her out of her grief. I've been told she managed well while I was in Oxford. But now that I've taken over the estate, she refuses to be strong anymore. Let's hope this news brings her back to her senses. Else something will need to be done about Mamma."

Bess did not stay to hear what Somerset might have to say on the matter. She retreated as quietly as she could to her rooms, taking care that her candle was steady and did not cast wild shadows the men might see. That Carew should speak of her this way, with such a man! She had always known Somerset to be detestable. No doubt he now advised her son to lock her up in the attic.

Walking back, her body felt heavy with the knowledge that this was no longer her home.

Else something will need to be done about Mamma.

When she reached her rooms, she opened up her cabinet and took out her red reticule.

"Come, my dearest love," she said. "It is time for us to find a new home."

The Seafarer's Tavern became a second home for Captain Dorset when his ship was in port. The keeper allowed him access to the dining hall to conduct his last-minute affairs before heading over to his ship. *Destiny* would set sail at dawn, in just an hour's time.

When Lady Bess Raleigh appeared at the hall's entrance, cloaked in a heavy hooded cape, he thought of all the lost youths he had acquired as privateers over the years. She had the same look in her eyes.

"Dear Lady," he said, catching her attention, for she seemed not to notice him. "What can you be doing at the waterfront at so early an hour?"

"I came to see my Walter off," she said, once again looking far off. Perhaps to a place only she could see.

"Your…" Dorset had heard the lady was not well. Now that her son was grown, the poor lady had given up all pretense of mental strength.

"Yes, of course," he told her. He motioned her to sit in his chair. "I shall call him. But first let me get you a glass of water."

There was no telling what she might do if he corrected her confusion. He retreated into the kitchen to pour dear, befuddled Bess a glass of water and tonic to calm her nerves. He did not hear the lady herself follow.

A sudden sharp pain washed over his head, and from a distance he heard the glass crash and then a great thud. He knew nothing else until he awoke three days later. His ship to the new world was long gone.

2.

A fortnight into the ship's journey, the boatswain Samuel Berrycloth stood upon the bow watching a peaceful sunset. The sea had calmed for the first time since they set sail, and there was just enough light to see two distant vessels move across the horizon. Berrycloth recognized the billowing sales as part of a Spanish fleet.

"Them is pirate ships," said Fletcher, one of the gunners on board. "Not 'spectable ships like this here."

Berrycloth hadn't noticed the gunner before and stifled a spooked yelp. Prickled, he replied, "And where do you suppose this here 'spectable ship be going if not to steal some gold and riches?"

"It's not piracy if it's on behalf of the Crown."

"A pirate's life is a pirate's life. 'Spectable or nay," said Berrycloth.

Fletcher remained by his side, silent until the horizon disappeared and darkness took over.

"I bet a pirate ship is not brimming with these here white-livered crewmen afeard of the dark. Of the ocean even," said Fletcher, through gritted teeth.

So, this is why Fletcher approached him, Berrycloth thought. The situation aboard *Destiny* did not just affect him, then.

Sailors were superstitious gossipmongers even when journeying through fair weather and smooth sails. Life aboard *Destiny* was neither.

The Empire Builder's Wife

Life, in fact, had been misery from the moment the ship set sail. The more experienced crewmen, like Berrycloth and Fletcher, expected hardships. Wobbly sea legs, stormy ocean waves, nights so dark and enveloping it felt like a sentient void staring back at them. But Captain Dorset had yet to make his way above board, and his mates began to whisper bad omens. The ship's pilot, Dudley, had given them some vague excuse about mild malaise and suddenly every illness, every tussle of the ship, every spoiled ration of salted pork got them going again. They decided their bad luck was the doing of a woman.

Berrycloth would have dismissed rumors about sporadic sightings of a woman on board as fishhusband superstitions. Except he had seen her for himself. Or bits of her. A train dragging around the passageway, a ruffle caught in the breeze on deck. He almost suspected Dorset of smuggling one of his favored companions to be his mistress for the season. Yet this journey was longer and riskier. Why would he have done such a thing?

A few men fell ill, and some had perished this week. It was the way. It was life at sea. But Fletcher's apprentice ran around below deck yelling to all who would listen that the captain was dead, murdered by a mad woman who haunted his quarters. Berrycloth had helped to restrain the boy and the pilot assured the crew the lad suffered from a little "sea madness." But Berrycloth could not help believing the boy. Ghostly or nay, he was convinced a female presence on this boat was somehow at fault for all these woes.

Fletcher remained by his side and the two watched the horizon recede into darkness.

"Do you reckon it's true," asked Fletcher. "You reckon our captain lies dead in his bed while we sail on into treacherous waters?"

Having both sailed with the late Sir Raleigh to the Caribbean and beyond, both men knew how much worse was in store in their journey. To have had such a hard go of it already did not bode well.

Berrycloth turned away from the long-gone sun and made his way below deck.

"What I reckon," he said, "is a ship needs a captain. We owe it to *Destiny* to find out what happened to hers."

"And if Dorset be dead?" asked Fletcher, following him. Their boots upon the planks were the only sounds on the quarterdeck.

"A ship needs a captain."

"Reckon it's our turn to take the helm?"

Though Berrycloth could not see his face in the dark, he heard the smile. Fletcher did like to climb the ranks.

"If there ain't no Captain Dorset," said Berrycloth carefully, "perhaps it's Captain Berrycloth's time ... and his First Mate Fletcher."

Fletcher's footfalls paused behind him.

"Come now, Fletch. Do you want to be captain, or do you want to keep my men in line?"

It was decided. Either they find the captain, or they ascend the throne themselves.

Later in the night, while others snored in the lower decks, Fletcher and Berrycloth gathered outside the captain's quarters. Perhaps they, too, were overcome with sea madness to have hatched such a feeble plan. Still Berrycloth felt something had to be done.

The two drew strength from their brotherhood and screwed up their courage for whatever they found on the other side of the captain's door. Berrycloth kicked the door once, twice without it budging. Fletcher wrapped the head of his musket with cloth to reduce the sound and used it as a battering ram. The door gave way, and both men spilled into the room, lifting their swords high, ready to do battle.

There on the bed lay a woman, propped up against the stuffers. She was a striking elder woman dressed in finery. She was also not alone.

Upon her breast was a man's head, and despite the lady's many ruffles and the layers of bedding, Berrycloth could not locate the rest of the gentleman's body. As they looked on, the lady continued to stroke the hair of the bodyless man with a dainty gloved hand.

Berrycloth felt frozen in time, unable to move until the lady acknowledged his presence. He did not dare turn to Fletcher, but he imagined Fletch was just as speechless at the sight.

"The devil take me!" Fletcher's voice came from beside him.

Well, perhaps not.

Bess did not startle at their presence. She slowly lifted the head at its base, and the men were treated to the sight of the two faces gazing upon each other. She then turned her face in the intruders' direction.

Berrycloth and Fletcher put down their swords and backed away slowly.

"Beg pardon, Ma'am," mumbled Fletcher before closing the door. It now flopped to one side, having come off its hinges. Giving in to their instincts, the two bolted down the passageway and headed for crew quarters.

Once in Berrycloth's cabin, they did not speak for a long while.

"Sam," Fletcher started. Berrycloth did not realize Fletcher knew his given name. "Was that a ghost?"

"No," said Berrycloth, unsure if his answer consoled either of them. "I reckon that was a real lady."

"And that…phantom head?"

"I reckon that was a real head of a real man who was alive once." Berrycloth could not unsee the image of the lady raising the gaunt and expressionless face by where its neck should have been. How she pondered it, as if communing with it.

"The devil take me!" Fletcher seemed to be having a harder time with it.

"I knew him, Fletcher, ole boy," said Berrycloth. "As did you. He is– he was the head of our last expedition. Sir Walter Raleigh. Do you remember?"

"What, you mean to say he'll be heading up this one, too?"

"He'll not be good for much else, will he?"

Fletcher stared at Berrycloth, his mouth agape.

Around the time Berrycloth and Fletcher whispered to the men about just how lost this vessel had become, Bess made her way up to the weather deck.

It was high time she made her presence known.

The pilot Dudley, an old friend of Walter's, had been hiding her, and the two seamen who barged into her cabin last night set an angry mob on the poor man. The way the crew feared the very idea of her aboard their ship made her feel invincible. This must be how men of status feel every day, she thought.

Amid the chaos of high winds roaring and angry men shouting at poor Dudley, Bess felt a great calm in her arms and legs. Her fluttering dress was outlet enough for the chaos in her mind, and she walked in peace and grace before the men.

She made her way to the stern, and men quieted as she drifted past. When she came to a stop and turned to them, they were rapt with attention. Some marveled at the strangeness of her layered skirts and petticoat in such a setting, upon a quarterdeck between the ship's banners and ropes that held the mizzenmast taut. For others the billowing parts of her gown gave her the appearance of a winged creature, and she resembled the figurehead upon the bow. The one modeled after a Grecian statue.

All eyes upon her now, Bess withdrew from her many folds the head of Sir Walter and held it above her own.

If the men gasped, it could not be heard above the wind.

"We have common goals, do we not?" she asked them, her voice strong. "To find a new empire and to bathe in the majestic waters of Lake Parime. To find the golden city of Manoa, what the Spaniards call El Dorado. You know the place. You see it in your dreams at night. Gold in their temples, gold hammered into shields, gold in the grains of the earth. You will take me there." Here she brought down her hand to hold her Walter to her chest. "We shall reside there for the rest of our days, my husband and I. And then you can go your way with whatever gold you can carry back to that dreary land you call home."

The men, Berrycloth and Fletcher among them, did not know whether to be more afraid of the woman before them or the head of her husband, whose countenance in this light was as fearsome as any sea monster. Its eyes followed each and every one of them, stern in its reminder of the evil fate that could befall them should they not heed its wife.

To Lake Parime they would go, and may God help them!

The Empire Builder's Wife

3.

Bess seldom brought out Walter. Despite what her crew thought, she was not a mad woman. She did not expose him to the elements. Sometimes her red velvet reticule was enough to keep her men in check. Often her gown alone did the trick. Her cumbersome, wild in the breeze, oppressive garments hid so much. The clothing had given her the appearance of innocence all those years ago when it hid her growing belly and the evidence of her secret marriage under the queen's nose. Now it gave her the appearance of grace when her legs wobbled, and her men eyed her suspiciously, wondering if her husband's decapitated head hid beneath it.

When they reached Trinidad, she brought Walter out to share the moment. Berrycloth ferried a small party to land, and her eyes feasted on lush foliage and cascading waterfalls and birds of indigo and scarlet, so vibrant she mistook them for flowers. One of her men told her the native tribes called the island the Land of the Hummingbirds. Walter had once used those exact words when he returned from his first journey here. She laughed at herself a little at having thought he invented such a pretty moniker.

The shore they reached seemed empty of any natives. Berrycloth explained that Spain once built an outpost nearby and the natives kept their distance. He and Fletcher escorted her to a fortress in ruins. Burned bricks and mortar, whittled down to heaps of uneven, jagged slabs on the ground.

"Who could have done such a thing?" she asked him.

"The English did," said Berrycloth. "We needed a base for our last expedition. We seized it, and after we returned, it was no longer needed."

"But why burn it to the ground?"

"I am but a boatswain, Ma'am, not a war strategist for the king."

"War? What war?"

Berrycloth seemed disinclined to answer her. She looked over to Fletcher, who had yet to speak to her directly. His eyes did not meet hers.

She walked along the outpost's broken walls. It was as large as a hamlet on the outskirts of London. Behind a cornerstone lay an open field scattered with piles of ash. Like the ash that fell from the sky in her visions.

"What is the meaning of this?" she demanded. These ruins lay outside the walled fortress.

"It might have been a small fishing village, Ma'am," said Berrycloth. "Of natives."

A settlement of ash led to a riverbank where men once fished, and women wove, and children played. All for a war between distant nations. She held her Walter to her breast. This would not do for news to share to her beloved.

What do you make of this, my Walter? Did you know about this?

In the corner of her eye, she caught Fletcher staring at her in her private moment.

"Are our noblemen so badly behaved when away from home, Mr. Fletcher?" she asked him.

"Seems to me they do as they please at home or nay," he answered, startled out of his embarrassment. "But here they seek the gold they promised their king."

"The Crown has permitted this bad behavior?"

Growing bolder, he replied, "Like your husband who came before ye–"

"Fletch!" Berrycloth warned.

"The king's men are authorized to cut down what stands between England and her goals," Fletcher finished, with less bite to his words.

"And the men and women and children of this small fishing village? How did they stand in England's way?"

"They helped the Spaniards," said Berrycloth. "They traded with them."

Bess looked about her at so much destruction.

"It is the way, Ma'am," said Fletcher. "God save the King, eh?"

Bess did not answer.

Berrycloth offered her his arm without another word, and she let him guide her back to the boat.

They would now journey further south, through eighty miles more of the Caribbean Sea's choppy waters and then to the empire of Guiana. For the very first time since she left home in search of this paradise, Bess was afraid of what she would find once there.

The Empire Builder's Wife

Soon the vast green hit her eyes as it slowly replaced the infinite blues of the sky and ocean. They approached an endless wilderness, and Bess's excitement grew once again. When it came time to send out a scouting party to explore the rivers, some of her crew insisted that the lady stay with the ship. It was an anemic show of chivalry from what remained of her crew. Bess would have none of it.

With Walter safely tucked within the folds of her petticoat, she climbed into the ship's barge and sailed with Fletcher, Berrycloth and a few of the quieter voices aboard *Destiny*. She had little patience for the sharper-voiced sailors. She left the rest with Dudley. He would see to it they did not mutiny.

They sailed two days down a river called Orenoque before they found land with sparser trees. She was eager to explore the banks where her Walter once walked. The forest foliage was so abundant, it overflowed into the water. Lotuses and lily pads floated down the river with them. Bess's tranquility was often disturbed by the most haunting of sounds—real sounds the men heard as well. Fletcher clutched his musket tighter at every howl or roar. But the call of beasts deep behind the wildwoods soothed her in a way the daytime sounds of London never could. There was no pretense in this place.

On the second morning, they disembarked where two rivers met, mooring the boat to an overgrowth of tall-rooted shrubs that created a leaky dam across the narrower channel. The gunner in the lead, the group followed a path mapped out on an earlier expedition. It would lead, Berrycloth said, to helpful Arawaks.

Exploring the terrain was no easy morning walk in St. James Park. Bess's gown snagged and the uneven ground wore out her ankles. Though her men, with their muskets and cutlasses, surrounded her, the howls coming from the canopy no longer soothed her.

The sun was just a few hours from setting when the group came across another river and walked along its bank. They spotted two men in the water, rowing little boats Fletcher said were canoes.

Berrycloth pulled her and the others behind a line of trees to provide them with cover. Their weapons lowered, he and Fletcher walked to the marshy edge and waved their arms in the air.

"Oy there," they called before shouting again in another language. "*Pawana, Pawana!*"

The natives rowed toward her men, and Bess could not help marveling at them as they drew near. They were young and handsome. Their bare chests did not scandalize her—it had been more than thirty years since her blushing days. But she was slightly embarrassed to be wearing so many layers herself. While the men of her crew found it impressive, would these native men? And what of their women? She envied their nakedness a little, so at ease in the heat of this rainforest. The hues of their bodies so in line with all the colors around.

Berrycloth pointed out their hiding place to the men and gestured for Bess to come forward. She approached, relying again on her wide skirt to give her the appearance of grace. One of the natives held a small cross that Berrycloth often wore around his neck. The other had Fletcher's pocketknife. They had agreed to trade with her men.

But they backed away as she approached, their eyes widened with shock at her presence. It was less than flattering.

Berrycloth turned to her and said, "You make a striking figure, my lady."

He did not fool her. But she was used to striking fear in the hearts of her men by now. She didn't even have to bring Walter out.

"*Woryi poto*," Berrycloth told the strangers.

The older one repeated Berrycloth's obviously stilted sentences with words of their own, but Bess could only make out the two she heard Berrycloth enunciate slowly. He spread his arms wide when he repeated "*Poto.*" The natives nodded to each other in what seemed like acceptance, and Berrycloth bid the rest of the party to come out into the open. With more gestures and words Bess could not possibly catch, the men started walking away. Their party followed.

"They will be taking us back to their village and to their leader—a chieftainess," Berrycloth said, smiling at her.

She eyed him with suspicion.

"What did you tell them about me?"

"I told them you are an important woman."

"What does *poto* mean?"

"Important," he said, not looking at her. "…and also big."

Far from being offended, Bess was pleasantly surprised to know she would be taken to a chieftainess. She was curious to be among a people where a big woman and an important one were one and the same.

Their small fishing village was built around a natural pool the river created with the help of large river rocks and a depression in the land. Berrycloth continued his translations as their new friends pointed out curious trees and other features of the landscape. They called the river the Cuyuni, and their people were Warao. As they walked further up the riverbank, Bess made out more canoes and wooden rafts. She saw shelters peeking through trees. They were covered with thick layers of dried tropical leaves, which were large and man-sized when green and on the trees.

As the party drew closer, she saw children at play and women tending a fire near a large rotund structure she later learned was a ceremonial meetinghouse, an *umana yana*.

The fisherman, Yi-Me, explained as they guided the party over to the chieftainess that the village was under "*ewapo*," which Berrycloth interpreted as a great sadness. The more he explained, the more worried Berrycloth appeared. He waited for Bess and offered his arm as they followed.

"Perhaps it's best if you walked ahead, my lady. It appears we are not the first Europeans this village has encountered. The chieftainess lost her son last month in a run-in with another party. Perhaps from the Low Countries or the Spaniards. It is hard to say."

Bess remembered that *Destiny* was not the only English ship bound for this part of the world.

"How do we know it was not an English party?" she asked.

"There is no way of knowing, Ma'am," he said. "But it is important that the village elders see you as a prominent member of our party. The men who caused an earlier destruction would not have had a noblewoman, or any woman among them. We must make it known that we are not the same people."

"You mean they could see us as their enemy?"

"I am counting on a different outcome, Ma'am."

In the eyes of this fishing village, did her presence alone separate her party from those who bore ill will against their families? Back home, it was easy to tell apart a Dutchman or a Spaniard from an Englishmen. But for the Warao, they may well be all the same. It didn't help that the tribe's attackers might have been other Englishmen. It discomforted her on a level she had never felt before—a feeling she could not explain—to be lumped in with men so frivolous with human life.

Yi-Me did not stop to speak to anyone as he led them into the heart of the village. The children stopped their play, and all eyes were on their group as they moved carefully to the village center. The chieftainess, her breasts bare, wore more beads than the other women surrounding her. They were prominent in her hair, around her neck, her wrists, and even her forearms.

Her name was Naubai, and she spoke in a stern tone with Yi-Me and the other fisherman who brought them here. Berrycloth did not translate what she said and replied to her words with careful calmness. He often gestured to Bess, who kept her eyes low and bowed to the woman, though she did not know whether such a gesture would be understood.

Naubai began speaking directly to Bess and Berrycloth rushed to translate.

"Are you a mother?" she asked. "Men who look like your men killed my son with the same weapons I see your men carry. They said they looked for a golden land, a place even our elders do not know."

Berrycloth must have registered Bess's confusion and he added, "My lady, they must have been searching for El Dorado."

With a deep breath, Bess gathered her courage and tried to mimic the chieftainess's poise as she spoke of her own heartbreak.

"Tell her, Mr. Berrycloth," she said. "Tell her we are not those men. We do not seek any such place. Tell her we only seek peace ... a place to rest. Tell her they killed my son, too. Tell her they killed my husband."

Berrycloth did as she said. Naubai's eyes softened as they fell upon her.

Indeed, this was the land where her second-born had died. Wat was twenty-two. He had wanted to follow in his father's footsteps. They told her the Spanish had killed him.

Bess patted the place beside her right hip, where Walter was.

"Tell her I would like to show her something in private," she said.

The Empire Builder's Wife

The chieftainess agreed and gestured for the fishermen to stay behind.

Bess also asked her men to stay, and she and Berrycloth set out with Naubai and a female companion. They followed a narrow, manmade path through the forest to a large clearing. Naubai led them to a tree, explaining that her son was newly laid to rest there. Bess marveled at the burial mound at the base of a great tree. She listened to Berrycloth's translation with her eyes focused on its large, protruding roots. They bent in such a way that she thought it cradled the late prince.

"My son was to guide my people when my time came to go with our ancestors. I pray every day that this tree should accept my son and take him into itself. The tree gives life and will grant a second life to my son, that he should also give life, give shelter, give food."

"I am sorry for your loss," Bess told her.

"It is a second loss to me to know the men who took my son's life—and with him the future of my village—have also taken your son and your husband. But if you have come to this land to avenge them, I ask that you do not provide more dead men for these trees. If you should carry out a blood feud with these men, go away from this place. Three days east, where the forest ends and the great river stumbles over sandbanks, a new people have settled. They are like you, they have weapons like yours, and they have driven away Carib nations deeper down the river. We have heard talk of entire villages, neighbors to these new people, simply fall ill and die. Others traded with them and then learned what they traded for had no value. They were also killed. We do not know how to reason with the new people, and we do not want war with them."

"Who are these men, Mr. Berrycloth? Are they Englishmen or Spanish?" Bess asked.

"They are from the Low Countries. The Dutch Republic, they are now called. They have set up a trading post."

"Are they after El Dorado, too?"

"Nay, they are looking to expand territories and build up their empire."

Bess looked upon the burial mound and upon the faces of the chieftainess and her female confidant. What strong women they were.

"Mr. Berrycloth," she said, "Please tell her I desire nothing to do with such a people as those she has described. I do not seek treasure. I do not seek to collect on any blood feud. What I seek is a place to rest. For myself and for him."

Here Bess reached into her overskirt, pleated at the front of her gown, and withdrew from her petticoat her red reticule.

"Lady Raleigh, I do not think..." Berrycloth began to protest.

Bess pulled Walter out and held him to her breast.

"I have come here to lay my husband to rest in a land he loved."

The two women backed away slightly from Bess, and their faces registered shock.

"Please do not fear. The men who killed my husband bestowed his head to me. I do not know if they meant to be cruel or kind. I could have carried him with me in my heart alone. But now I have the chance to restore head and heart. I do not wish to take your land or your resources. But if you will share your part of the great river with myself and my men, I will see to it that they train their loud weapons on any group that comes along wishing to harm you."

"My Lady," said Berrycloth, a little taken aback.

"We are not here for England," she told him.

She waited for Berrycloth to translate all she said and watched the chieftainess's expression. Naubai's eyes never left Walter. But when Berrycloth finished, she looked up and met Bess's eyes.

"Your garments serve as a unique burial mound," she said. "There are nations south and west of us, the Makusi People and the Wapishana People. They also have strange funeral processions. Though yours might be even more strange."

"We all have our traditions," Bess replied, smiling.

4.

Holding Naubai's baby girl was Bess's favorite morning ritual. In the months since Bess first arrived at the Waitopo Village, Naubai had given birth to a new future for her people. And though the chieftainess would have simply carried her babe with her as she performed her daily duties, she allowed Bess the pleasure of playing nursemaid.

This morning Bess left her little hut, its roof thatched with palm leaves in almost as watertight a pattern as the village *benabs*, and made her way to the meetinghouse to collect the baby. The village was always up before her, ready to start the day's rituals—praying and fishing, eating and communing. And she walked in leisure amid their bustle to her favorite place, the palm-covered pier by the water's edge. Pampered as she had been all her life, she came to enjoy the simple luxury of sitting by a river with a babe in arm while children played around her.

Berrycloth and her men were on the opposite bank today. They canoed there in the small boats they'd made with their own hands, and they planned to explore the narrower tributaries that led deeper into the forest. Her men were easy to spot from this distance. Divested of the cumbersome costumes of the old world, they were pale against the darker hued trees and river and Waitopo fishermen. She often hid a well-bred English titter at their bare chests when she saw them.

The welcome the Waitopo families gave Bess and her men had been enough to convince a handful of them to stay in the village with her. They hunted with the women and fished with the men. They even drank cassava beer with the elders, which was Fletcher's favorite pastime. When everyone came together in the evenings, Bess remembered her own sons' unbreeched years. They spoke to each other in their own languages and communicated with smiles and gestures. After almost a year in Waitopo, Bess had still not surpassed the stage when small children learned how to put words together. Her crew were more successful, being decades younger. But Bess was content to point to the trees and the sky and the river and call out the Warao words for them.

As she spent most days with the village children, she did not need more than this. She had found her place in the world, here under the palm-covered pier by the edge of the water. Her French farthingale around her head in place of a hat and a granddaughter in her arms, she watched the children play. The boys mastered their fishing and rowing skills in tiny canoes. The girls, fearless in their cotton skirts and beaded hair, ran into shadowy thickets and skipped across river rocks.

Not long after her men disappeared into the woods, a wooden barge appeared from the south. It ambled along at a slow pace, reminding her of lizard-like monsters gliding through the water before they pounced on unsuspecting prey. The barge headed their way, and as it got closer, Bess could make out men with muskets at the ready. Then all the random words Bess knew failed her.

"*Aky*," she called. It was the word for both dirt and danger.

She pointed to the barge and raced to find the warrior women.

"*Ruruma*," she called again. It was the word for ambush and also a dirty look. She hoped they knew which she meant.

One of Naubai's advisors called the children back to the *umana yana*, along with the elders. The warrior women took position side by side in front of the smaller *benabs* that hid the meetinghouse and waited. Naubai took her baby from Bess's arms and ordered her into the meetinghouse. But Bess ran as fast as she could, barefoot like the children, to her own little hut. With her bare hands she dug into the sandy ground to extract Walter from his hiding place. As fast as she could, faster even than young Sarah back in London, she tied the farthingale around her waist and wrapped the silk rolls she'd been using for a pillow along her hips so she could keep Walter inside her petticoat. There was no time to look upon him.

She hurried to take her place among the warriors. At the very least, she could help them tell an English tongue from a Dutch one. But a young woman, Naubai's sister Aruku, spoke gently to her and gestured to the *umana yana*. She only understood the "*nopoko*"—the word for grandmother—and walked back to the village center to sit with the children and hold Naubai's baby again in the darkened meetinghouse.

For a long moment all they heard was their own shallow breathing. A good sign the visitors were not here to harm them.

Then the musket fire started, and the women's screams traveled to the ears of their children. It did not matter, Bess realized, if their attackers were English or Dutch or Spanish.

Huddled together, the children began to whimper at the sounds, at the frightful men who had found them so deep in the wilderness. The gentle strokes of their grandparents' hands upon their backs did not console them. The elders were just as frightened and just as confused about what was happening to their people.

Bess remembered the ruins of another fishing village in Trinidad.

Had she brought this on? She had allowed others from her group to leave, the ones who did not wish to stay in Waitopo. They set out to hunt for treasure with the understanding that none of the Warao was obliged to guide them.

Was it wrong of her to let them go? Were they the men who ran rampant outside? Perhaps they had reunited with Somerset's fleet and led them, with their vast weapons and delusions of El Dorado, to this village and its people.

Had she brought the crumbling pieces of Durham House to her new friends? To come tumbling down on these children who now leaned into her body for warmth and comfort?

A thunderous blast jolted through the meetinghouse. The children trembled and began to cry. Voices from the elders, some stern, some soft, reminded the children to remain quiet. But it was too much to bear for Bess. How could she possibly comfort anyone else?

Bess closed her eyes to their faces. The visions that made her so wretched in her last days in London returned, and not even the feel of Walter under her gown could stop it now. Ash and debris fell from the sky like rain. She could not even close her eyes to it, and tears flowed down her cheeks and soaked the babe she clutched to her chest.

When the visions subsided, her head was against another elder woman's chest. In her distress, the grandmother must have turned her away from the children, so as not to frighten them. She cradled Bess and chanted soft prayers for protection.

Her face was wet with tears, but Bess smiled through them to let the woman know she was better now.

The musket blasts told her the fighting still raged on. Mothers and fathers of little children could already be dead outside. And she could not even be trusted to offer comfort. Disgusted with herself, Bess passed Naubai's baby to the elder woman and extracted herself from the group, caressing little faces and tousling heads. She exited the meetinghouse and, keeping her body low, crept along its curved structure until she came closer to the fighting.

The battle before her now, she covered her mouth so as not to cry out in panic. Men and women fought together and against each other in an angry, hateful dance.

The fisherman had returned from this morning's exploration, and they wielded their spears and hurled their bone fishhooks, as if the intruders were the man-sized catfish they hunted. Bess's own men had retrieved their muskets and provided cover for the fishermen. The warrior women held the enemy off at the riverbank, but the nearby *benabs* had caught fire. Bodies lay on the ground beside them. And this time it was not a vision. It would not disappear.

The warrior women worked together to push the attackers back with their hunting bows and their blowpipes. Berrycloth entered the fray from the other side of the river, aiming his weapon at the barge. The Waitopo outnumbered the invaders, who struggled with the sheer variety of weapons aimed at them. Perhaps the sight of such strange allies distracted them, as well.

But where was Naubai? Bess could not make her out.

Her sister, Aruku, hid behind a tiny *benab*, its conical roof ablaze. She refilled the long bamboo blowpipe with a sharpened palm stem. It was a process that involved first dipping the stem in the pulp of poisonous vines. Bess willed her to hurry.

Fletcher, always ready for a fight, swung at his opponent by the remains of the covered pier. Broken palm fronds and wooden planks floated in the water. Fletcher used his cutlass to strike down his opponents with all-too-easy, almost graceful swings. Just a month ago he had stumbled clumsily with it while cutting down thorny bushes to clear a trail for her.

Sighing with relief, Bess spotted Naubai alive and fighting in the water not far from Fletcher. She hurled herself at one of the men. He was heavy in his many layers of wet clothing, and she grabbed hold of his short jacket to pull him under. She seized another's musket and tossed it to Yi-Me. Without stopping, she hoisted herself onto the pier to help Fletcher, who was surrounded on the unstable pier. Both bare-chested, they moved together upon the well-dressed attackers, using their shoulders and elbows and legs to bring the men face down.

The Empire Builder's Wife

Fletcher began to tie them up, but Naubai grabbed him by the back of the breeches and tossed him onto the bank. She then leaped onto the marshlands at the same moment a blast from the barge destroyed what remained of the pier. Broken planks fell into the water.

Fletcher, a little dazed, paused to survey the fray before leaping to his feet. Aruku, equipped with her blowpipe, circled the *benab* to take aim. Fletcher ran toward her. His arms out, he knocked her to the ground, taking the bullet meant for her. From her place on the ground, Aruku aimed her blowpipe at the still approaching musketeer and her dart pierced his neck.

She reached for Fletcher. He did not move. He would never move again.

The wind whipped and the fire from the surrounding *benabs* fanned out wildly. Bess wished to cry out to Aruku to be careful of the flames, but she dared not give her position away.

Only a handful of invaders remained standing. The women had disarmed many of them and tied them with ropes made of the yucca tree. These men bucked and threw their bodies against the women, seeking to brawl with them. But the women held them by their naked arms and strong legs and were unconquerable.

Bess's men cheered as they seized the barge and its weapons.

One sailor seemed to realize too late that his side had lost the fight. Waist-deep in the water, he watched women tie up his crewmates. Berrycloth and another closed in on him, but he was armed. Before Berrycloth could grab him, he fired his last bullet at the nearby huts, already on fire.

Flames engulfed the *benabs*, which crackled with little explosions. Smoke and flames bubbled up and out, enveloping the area where Aruku still sat with Fletcher's body, consuming them along with the structures.

Bess ran toward the place where they disappeared. But soon more huts caught fire. She could no longer see the riverbank or the village center. And she could not find her way out of the flames, which billowed around her. Ash fell from the sky again. The thatched palms of a nearby *benab* collapsed from the structure and fell on top of her. The screams Bess heard came from her own lips.

Shifting, Swirling HERitage

When Bess came to, Yi-Me was above her, his sturdy arms wrapped around her. He pulled her away from the flames and the place where Naubai's sister disappeared within it. In tears himself, he carried her closer to the water while mothers ran past them to protect their homes and the *umana yana* where their children hid.

Satisfied that she was fully conscious, he joined the procession of villagers putting out the fires, passing back and forth clay pots and hollowed-out gourds of river water. Bess splashed water onto her face and breathed deeply, coughing out the smoke from her lungs. She was too weak to join the fire fighters. Yet another thing she could not do for these people.

Further up the river her crew trained their weapons on the foreign invaders, now captives. Brought to their knees on the sandy earth, they looked on at the destruction. Berrycloth dragged the last of them, the one who killed Aruku, to take his place among them. He was a young man, no older than Bess's own living son.

Somewhere behind her, Naubai cried for her sister. Aruku was gone. Fletcher was gone. How many more?

Bess struggled to her feet. Pain rippled through her body as she approached the prisoners. But she ran at them, screamed at them. She pulled out Walter from her petticoat and held him out to them. Their eyes widened with fear at the sight of her.

Bess looked into their faces. They were all English youths. Glory seekers for a richer man, safe across a whole ocean. She paced back and forth before them and mumbled to herself. She cradled Walter in her arms and spoke to him as if she expected him to answer, every bit aware of how she looked to them.

"Would you have led these boys into the wilderness to do what they did?" she asked the weathered head. "Is this the legacy you left me with?"

Berrycloth walked silently to her side. Worry was in his eyes as he attempted to block her from view, but she turned from him to face the captives. Some sneered at her. Others fixed their eyes on Walter's blank stare.

"So, you seek to fill your ships with stolen goods, then sail back to your little king. Tell him here in this land be gold and riches." She could not hide the disgust in her voice.

Berrycloth, who seemed to understand her intentions, repeated her words in the Warao language, as he had done for her every day for the past nine months. But there were no villagers around to hear. The prisoners looked at each other, unbalanced and bewildered.

Good.

"Will you boast about the men and women you killed today?" she continued. "The children you orphaned? Will they sing songs about you and call you heroes? You are not heroes. You are fools. Little fools who believe in a city made of gold. Do you believe in leprechauns as well? Should I tell you nursery tales about fairy queens and little elves?"

The fires still raged behind them, and the villagers raced to save what they could. Bess wanted these men to feel some of their distress. To regret what they did.

"Look at him!" she shouted, waving Walter at them. "This is where your wars will get you!"

Above all else, she wanted them to regret coming to such a strange land, one to which they did not belong.

"But they will keep on coming, won't they, Walter?" she said, turning him to her. Though his eyes had shrunk, it still thrilled her to look upon him. The preserved head had changed much in this humid climate, but so had she.

She turned her back to the invaders and fixed her eyes on the villagers, on their women, their fierce protectors. When Bess fell apart, they remained strong and defiant against ruthless invaders. But would their fierceness alone be enough against an entire fleet of such men, who were assuredly coming?

"We are the ones who must stop it, Walter," she said. "We must cut this off at the head."

5.

When men died on *Destiny*, they were given sea burials. They were wrapped in cloth and any heavy weaponry the ship could spare, and away they went into the ocean. When a sailor died on a distant shore, his captain would order a quick grave to dispose of the body, leaving him forever alone and thousands of miles from home. It was the way. But this was not how Fletcher's story would end.

The villagers saw Fletcher as one of their own, deserving of a burial mound at the root of a great tree in the surrounding forest, to be granted a second life. He had protected them while he lived and would continue to do so after his death. Bess could not think of a better send-off for the eager gunner.

After the burials, Bess strolled through the little huts of her camp, admiring her men's handiwork. She had already gathered up her belongings and placed them on the barge, which would take her back to the sea, where *Destiny* waited. And her men had found and seized the intruders' ship, *The Lion's Whelp*, at the mouth of another river, and unloaded its guns and cannons. With two ships now at her command, the only thing left to do was say goodbye to a place and people she had come to know as home.

One of the prisoners, young with childlike blond hair, walked toward her on the way to his new lodging. Berrycloth must have released him from his restraints for good behavior. He stopped dead in his tracks when he saw her. She smiled at the lad, who walked around her with ginger steps, his eyes everywhere but on her. She was tempted to pull Walter out, but let it be.

The camp would now house the prisoners. Berrycloth would remain in Waitopo to help them reform. The villagers they killed were game huntresses and fisherman. They were friends. They were people. If these men returned to England, they would not face justice for what they did. When Bess and Berrycloth explained this to Naubai, she agreed to keep them. To show them her mercy, she buried their dead, though in a more distant grove of trees. They, too, would be granted a second life, one in which they gave more than they took.

Since the attack, the English camp on the outskirt of the village had grown into a soldier's barracks. Bess could hear the musket fire in the distance as she made her way to the riverbank. Her men were training Naubai's warriors how to aim and shoot guns and fight with English

The Empire Builder's Wife

swords. They learned it in Aruku's name. Like Bess, they were determined that the loss they suffered at the hands of the Englishmen would never happen again.

When she reached the bank, Bess took in the village. The shape of it moved with the land and flowed with the river. Larger *benabs* built where the land permitted it, smaller ones where it did not. All of it showed movement, an acceptance of change from dense foliage to marshland to the river. The Waitopo understood what it meant to change. But were they prepared for the greater changes to come?

A makeshift, raft-like little pier replaced the one the Englishmen destroyed. Its rough planks swayed, caught between the tides of the river and a sudden gust of wind. A handful of the Waitopo would accompany her back to England, and they gathered in front of the pier, in their ceremonial skirts and spears, to say goodbye to their loved ones.

Once in England, Bess would present them to the king. She loathed James I, but she had faith the Waitopo could make him a better ruler as they had made her a better woman. Perhaps the beauty of her warrior women, with their grace and strong legs, and the broad shoulders of the handsome Yi-Me, might soften his heart long enough to listen to their wise words. And with their own voices, for they knew more English than she knew Warao, they would appeal to him.

"There is no El Dorado," they would tell him. "There is only a worthy people and their land. Our people are your equals. Respect our land, respect our sovereignty. Let us live like neighbors."

You there, I know what you're thinking. This would never work. But Bess has suspected this, as well.

If King James did not have a better self to appeal to, Bess had another ship at her command. *The Lion's Whelp* would follow *Destiny* back to England with English sailors to tell him again there was no gold. "The Waitopo are armed with Old World weapons," they would say. "They have their own army, cannons from our own ships, and privateers who were once in our command. Should we risk more of our English boys for fool's gold?"

And should James fail his people once again, the Waitopo army would be waiting for them, ready to resist British settlers, ready to protect their land.

Berrycloth, Bess's steadfast companion, escorted her onto the barge. More than half her men wished to stay in Waitopo. Berrycloth agreed to lead them.

"I am sorry to again commandeer *Destiny* from you, Mr. Berrycloth," she said, shaking his hand.

"No matter," he said, smiling. "In the village, they call me *kapiteni*."

Naubai brought her baby to Bess. She took the child in her arms gratefully, holding her to her breast one last time. The child wiggled in her arms, and Bess laughed through her tears. How she had hoped this would be the place she spent the rest of her days.

"It still can be," Naubai told her, Berrycloth translating. "When you have spoken to your English chief, you will come back. We can put your husband to rest in these woods."

Bess thanked her and grasped her hand, holding on for as long as she could. When her new crew was ready to set sail, she handed over the little babe and allowed Naubai and Berrycloth to disembark.

Naubai had offered her the chance to bury Walter this morning. But it would be a lie to have him in the same grove as Aruku, or even Fletcher. Unless she could undo the king's desire to claim this land and wipe out its people, a seed her own Walter had planted, then her beloved belonged in the more distant grove where Naubai had buried the invaders.

The villagers, both Warao and English, stood side by side on the bank, waving to the barge as it set sail. Bess waved back until a bend in the river hid them from view and the vast green took over. But visions of her people stayed with her. She kept them in the folds of her dress. They spurred her on. Whether she would meet them again, she did not know, but as she journeyed toward *Destiny*, she did so with hope.

6.

Meira Chandra adjusted her white sari. With all this wind aboard the steamship, and the thin fabric fluttering so wildly, she should have remained below deck. Twice already the garment had exposed her blouse and bare legs to the deckhands. But she had no reason to fear them. She was headed to Warao territory. She was headed to a haven.

She had made friends with the bosun, who promised to call her the moment Guyana's wild coast overtook the horizon.

"Land, ho!" he yelled. It was the only English she knew, and she ran toward the bow, her young daughter trailing her.

The vast green hit her eyes and it took several moments, sailing only thirty-seven kilometers an hour, to make out the *umana yanas* scattered across the highlands. Great cities peaked through the rainforest and its tangle of rivers, all of it run by true Amazon warriors.

She'd held fast to the girl's hand. The child had wanted to play with the bosun's mooring lines. Being eight, she'd lost interest in staring so long at a distant and fuzzy green blob. But now there were landmarks she could make out. And Meira lifted her up so she could see the estuary island and its harbor.

"Look, Rani, our new home. See that gap in the forest? That is the great Essequibo River. We will live on an island at the mouth of the river. And you'll go to school and learn all the Cariban languages, and you'll teach your *Amaa*, yes?"

Little Rani promised she would.

The bosun, an older Englishman who did not know Bhojpuri, asked her a question in his own language. He gestured to her, pointed to the coast and then made a show of shrugging his shoulders.

Meira smiled in understanding. He was asking her why she traveled to Guyana.

"*Mosiro*," she answered him—a Cariban word for collective work. She wanted to find work among the warrior women. She would seek their protection and make a new life with her daughter.

The bosun nodded, taking in her white garments and the young girl in her arms, who quickly wiggled away to play. Perhaps he knew she was a widow, which explained his kindness. British Colonialism had not spared Hindustan the way it had spared Guyana. She could not build a new life on her own there, not under the British Raj.

But she'd heard stories of Guyana since she was a child. Legends said its diverse nations were forewarned by an oracle. They formed a mighty army that resisted every attempt to conquer them. The Spanish. The French. When the Dutch dared to bring stolen people to their shores, the Warao and the Kalina joined together to defeat them and take in the abducted men and women. Over the years their armies grew strong enough to move south and free the Tupinamba and West Africans from the Portuguese.

The history books said Guyana owed its sovereignty to the kindness of a British king and his fondness for its warriors. But Meira suspected his colonists aboard *The Lion's Whelp* had no longer found desirable a land and people they could not suppress. The thousands of women from South Asia, Africa and even Europe who journeyed there every year would agree with her.

The warrior women of Guyana grew in numbers each year, and each year they moved out into the wider world to right some of its wrongs. Some wrongs would take hundreds of years to right. And some might never be made right. But the women turned to action and did their part. Even the old bosun did his part by ferrying new warriors to the land. Meira would do her part by joining the famed band of sisters.

History is Written by the Losers

Diana Dru Botsford

> Briton Encampment
> Droche-Brig, Britain
> A.D. 61 (814 A.U.C.)

TAUNTING SHOUTS FROM THE ENEMY CAMP FAR ACROSS THE VALLEY pierced the night, hounding Queen Boudica's inspection of her warriors' fortifications. Behind her, the druid Borvo, cloaked in green wool, clutched his oaken staff and prayed softly.

She loathed the priest's words of hope. "Come, Elder. The Romans' promises of peace, if we surrender, are lies enough for one night. Let us walk in silence without strain to my disbeliefs. I yearn for an hour's rest."

Borvo offered her a rag. "So you may present yourself as queen."

"To what end?" She wiped her hands on her torn leather trousers. "Our people know I fought beside them. Do you wish that truth erased?"

"By no means."

"Then let us visit with those still among us."

Boudica continued through what remained of the Breton encampment, her limbs heavy with fatigue. The air reeked of loss. Blood mingled with tears. Smoke hung with the stench of sweat. She despaired, searching for signs of optimism amidst the shards of hope.

Until that day, the Bretons had been victorious. But then the Roman Governor-General returned from the north, bringing with him two legions, ten thousand new troops with three hundred cavalry.

Fresh, disciplined, and with war engines aplenty, they destroyed the Bretons. A quick head count by the Breton's tribe leaders confirmed: Nearly 150,000 Bretons fell that day.

Boudica's rebellion had failed.

As the sun set, only a meager fifty, maybe sixty thousand remained to face tomorrow. The Roman rules of battle allowed a respite until sunrise. Some sought rest, others clung to hope, huddled by their fires, saying goodbye to loved ones lost.

Boudica struggled to keep her eyes open. Mortified, she walked away from the encampment, lest her people see her weakness. Borvo followed. Together, they stopped by the river, the irony of flowering blooms along the banks not lost on her.

She stifled a yawn.

"My queen..." Borvo said grimly, "the best bridge between despair and hope is a good night's sleep." He raised a hand. "Impossible, I know. We may never sleep again, but a moment's rest might allow..." He trailed off, unable to finish.

"Victory, Druid?" She did not bother to hide her scowl. "Victory is the very least the Gods can spare for all the sacrifice required."

Borvo smiled with a confidence she could not share. "With sacrifice comes great power, my queen."

"This sacrifice is too much." Boudica referred not just to the horrors of battle, but to what had led them there. Her husband, King Prasutagus dead. Roman soldiers demanding she renounce her rule. Her young daughters raped when she refused.

Thank the Gods she had sent her daughters north away from Roman hands.

She shivered; her body determined to conspire against her.

History is Written by the Losers

"A sudden chill will not aid our people." Borvo took off his cloak and placed it on her shoulders.

Boudica pulled the hood over her mud-caked red hair, unable to believe anything would help. "Go now, so I may be alone with the Gods as company."

Borvo bowed and left.

The truth was, Boudica needed to decide if she should surrender to the Roman general in hopes of saving her people.

Or trust the Gods to save them all from the Roman dogs.

Boudica walked on through the night, her feet and mind sore from the day's combat. A breeze blew through, clearing the heavy air. She strode toward the river banks where young trees populated each side, swaddled in tall grasses. Along the shore, large rocks dug into the sandy beach.

Hit by another wave of weariness, she sat down beside one such rock.. She needed rest, if only for a moment.

She laid her head against the rock, its cool surface soothing her brow.

Grateful for Borvo's cloak, she wrapped it tight around her shoulders. Her eyes then closed with a will of their own.

She slept…

…only to awaken to golden daylight's caress upon her eyelids. The sensation of a hard stone floor beneath urged her eyes open.

She bolted to her feet. Impossibly far above, a golden roof glowed in splendor. If there were walls, they were too far away to see. Instead Boudica saw only shelves. Miles upon miles of shelves. Endless rows laden with an astonishing array of boxes and clothing, metallic statues, oddly colored wooden objects, vessels of liquid, ice, and smoke, and other obscure items.

Somehow, she had been transported to a great Hall of Everything.

Refusing to allow to panic to steer her actions, Boudica inhaled deeply. She must be in the realm of the Gods, but even that felt wrong and unlikely.

DING.

Boudica spun around, unsure from where the chime had come. Her leather boots glided across the shiny stone floor. She grabbed the nearest shelf to steady herself and listened.

She inhaled. The pungent sting of battle no longer clung to her nostrils. The air was clean, warm. She removed Borvo's cloak, allowing the cloth to drop to the floor.

DING.

A distant laugh. A cough. An odd whirring noise.

Her hand went to her hip. Her belt and sword were gone.

Her pulse quickened. Had she passed into the Overworld?

"Not now," she mumbled. Not when her people were in their time of need. Not when justice was yet unserved.

DING.

Perhaps the source of that sound held the answer.

And the means to return home. Emerging between two towering shelves laden with blankets, she found herself in a vast, open space that seemed to be the hall's center. There were no immediate shelves. Instead, she faced a large, low wooden table covered with more unrecognizable objects.

Rectangular objects were stacked one upon another, each made of thin, smooth sheets bound together. They varied in size and color, some bound in leather, others in stiff, colorful materials. The objects reminded her of Roman scrolls, but these were different - more compact and substantial.

Surrounding the wooden platform was an enormous white couch, its plush surface divided into sections that curved and angled. Boudica had never seen anything of its size before.

Curiosity drew her to the table, her fingers brushing against one of the rectangular objects. It felt cool and slightly rough, unlike anything she had encountered before with thin sheets bound on one end, with writing on each side.

She looked closer at the writing, the letters at first obscure. The letters became clear. The words understandable.

There were messages in these bound pages. She could read them. The word *book* came to mind. These were all books. From different eras. From different lands. With different tales.

History is Written by the Losers

What magic or knowledge could they hold? In this strange, timeless place, anything seemed possible. She picked one that looked promising, bound in a deep crimson, the title *The Annals* embossed in gold. A weathered bust of a Roman emperor, his expression stern and brooding, gazed out from the cover, silently passing judgment on the ages.

Could the answer to defeating Rome lie within these pages?

She opened the book, determined to find her answer.

"Found them!" Ona slipped the red plastic sunglasses into a pocket of her gray wool vest and began her descent. Since becoming the infinite Hall of Everything's Curator, she'd spent her days finding bits and pieces to bring a moment's solace to visitors in their darkest hour while their bodies slumbered somewhere in the universe.

Ona yawned. Another ridiculously busy day, but visitors mattered. True, the Hall's bits and pieces weren't end-all solutions, but Ona hoped a moment's respite helped somehow.

Her left velvet-clad slipper hit something bulky. She nudged it deeper into the shelf.

All this climbing around… Was she really helping?

Mind your footing, whispered the Liaison in her mind.

The Hall's AI, known as the Liaison, was a white metal orb currently hovering beside her. Self-sufficient, no larger than a beach ball, the orb was a sometimes self-serving, sometimes arrogant, always a know-it-all, mind-reading, pain in her ass who frustrated the hell out of Ona, but whom she admittedly thoroughly adored. The two were closer than close, and, despite their differences, the orb's curiosity never ceased to inspire Ona.

That and the visitors from all walks of life and eras in time. Everyone had a darkest moment. The Hall provided answers.

The Liaison's ability was sending each visitor's life story to Ona, giving her the information to help. Ona referred to those nuggets of information as info-dumps. They helped determine what object from a visitor's past would help them resolve their life's challenge.

She jumped down from the last shelf. No question, without the Liaison, Ona couldn't do her job. She would be screwed.

The feeling is mutual.

She patted the orb's hard shell, appreciating the sentiment.

DING.

Ona froze. That chime meant a new visitor had arrived from some*when* in time.

"Hello?" called a distant voice.

The Hall is in popular demand.

"Maybe a little too popular," Ona muttered.

Or perhaps the Hall is attempting to overcome a backlog of visitors in need.

"Maybe... Here you go!" Ona handed the red sunglasses to a twenty-fifth century waste disposal specialist named Nancy whose father had just passed away. The glasses had been a childhood gift.

"Oh, my!" Nancy lit up, her grief-stricken face softening as she donned the glasses. She glanced at a reflection of herself in a metal trophy. A sliver of a smile and—

Nancy dissolved in a glittering glow. The sunglasses fell to the floor.

Ona sighed. Giving a visitor a happy moment should've made her happy, too.

Instead, she felt oddly empty.

DING.

The Liaison swooped up the glasses and flew them to their spot on the top shelf. *You usually find our work gratifying.*

"I know. I...." Ona searched for the words. "I just wish... I wish we could do more. I wish we could make a difference in these people's lives."

You want to change the visitors' outcomes?

She gasped. "Can we?"

DING.

The Liaison drifted down to eye level. *I have never considered that possibility.*

"Hello... Is anyone here?!?" called a voice at least ten or more rows over.

"Oh yeah, our next visitor. Hold that thought!" Ona darted into the main aisle and headed toward the voice with the Liaison close behind.

History is Written by the Losers

While the Liaison's admission raised all sorts of questions, she had to prioritize. Ona knew visitors came first.

But maybe... Just maybe, they could become more effective.

Maybe they could make a real change.

Unfortunately, the day became impossible. The chimes rang closer together. Overlaps happened, visitors left to wander unattended.

At one point, Ona tripped over a green wool cloak. Ona rolled the thing up and shoved it next to a pink contraption labeled Barbie Easy-Bake. Then another set of chimes announced a new visitor. She rushed to greet them, priming herself for yet another info-dump.

As Ona rounded a corner into an aisle, she said, "Sorry about that! It's been a busy day."

"Too busy to attend me?" An older man in a bleached white toga and sandals strode down an aisle, pausing every few steps to straighten an object or fix a haphazard pile. He picked up a small mermaid statue. "Ornamental nonsense."

Putting the statue back, he turned away from Ona and headed down the next aisle toward the main waiting area.

Ona snorted. "Huh."

That is Publius Cornelius Tacitus. The Liaison glowed blue, accessing new information provided by the Hall. *A retired Roman senator, best known for his historical annals. His father-in-law was a Roman general. Tacitus's work significantly underscores the idea that history was written by the victors.*

"Because it's bull——?"

"Precisely."

"Sounds like trouble." Ona gritted her teeth, readying herself for an info-dump.

Until a woman's voice cried:

"Roman dog!"

Shifting, Swirling HERitage

A visitor slipped past our notice.

Ona raced to the central waiting area, the Liaison at her side, to find a tall, imposing woman with waist-length red hair and wearing leather pants, a sleeveless shirt, and a leather breastplate. She stalked the much shorter Tacitus around the book-laden coffee table, the only thing that seemed to be keeping the two from coming to blows.

This is Boudica. Your newest visitor. The Liaison's central band glowed, promising an incoming info-dump.

A buzzing pressed against Ona's ears, forcing her eyes shut. She grabbed a couch as the images bombarded her, nearly overwhelming.

Smoke, blood, and fear filled Ona's senses. Then the images sharpened.

—Boudica as a child, watching her home consumed by flames.

—Boudica as a teen, in a grove of oaks, her eyes locked with the man who would become her husband and king.

—Boudica bearing her daughter, Andra. A year later, Draste.

—Boudica laying a torch on her husband's pyre, her daughters singing farewell.

—Under the Roman lash, the agony a gift as she watches Romans rape her daughters.

—Bretons charging into battle, swords raised, chanting "Boudica! Boudica! Boudica!"

—One bloody battle after another, the Bretons triumphant.

Until…

—A sunset by the river. Mothers. Fathers. Sons and daughters. A battlefield filled with the dead.

Ona shook off the fog as the British warrior-queen and the Roman historian glared at each other, each refusing to break the stalemate, until–

Boudica whirled on Ona. "I demand an explanation. He is no ally of mine."

Tacitus crossed his arms. "Says the barbarian whose kind impaled our children on stakes and hung our most distinguished, hacking—"

"Lies! Those few responsible were dealt with severely. Who told you these lies? I do not recognize you from the battlefield."

"If I may," the Liaison said aloud, moving to Boudica's side. "*Senator, you were not part of the Imperial envoy who met with the queen or her husband, King of the Iceni.*"

History is Written by the Losers

"Certainly not," Tacitus scoffed. "I was a child at the time."

"A child?" Boudica whirled on Ona. "What magic is this?"

"I understand your anger." Ona held up her hands.

Boudica snorted. "More like perplexed. Confused." She gazed up at the ceiling. "I know this is not reality." She grabbed a bulky picture book entitled, *The Roman Empire Lives Today*. "Would my mind devise such nonsense? Worse yet," Boudica scoffed. "How can we speak the same tongue?"

"You understand each other," said the Liaison. *"A benefit of visiting the Hall of Everything."*

"An exceptional benefit." Tacitus scurried to the other side of the table. "There is purpose."

"Not just yours, Senator, but—," Ona began.

"This so-called Hall of Everything is here to serve me as a visitor." He placed a hand on his chest. "To offer solace in my dark times."

"Your dark times?" Boudica scoffed. "What possibly could compare to–"

Ona grabbed her elbow and hurriedly explained the Hall's purpose. "The sooner we handle his needs, the sooner he leaves so we can help you out."

"No." Boudica yanked free. "What possible darkness has brought you here, in such dire need of comfort?"

"Darkness, indeed." Tacitus raised his chin. "I received word that my dear friend Gaius Valerius Marcellus was assassinated."

"That is not the entire truth," warned the Liaison. *"Speak in earnest here."*

Tacitus dropped his gaze. "I may have been responsible for Marcellus's demise."

"You sacrificed your friend to save yourself." The Liaison floated closer. *"Did you not?"*

Ona stared at the orb, surprised by its directness. Normally, the Liaison stayed silent, speaking only when prompted. "Explain, Tacitus," she said.

The queen has been reading, the Liaison shared privately with Ona. *She recognizes the name and yet holds back.*

Since when do you care?

I care when one visitor disrespects another.

Me, too. Ona turned to Tacitus. "What happened?"

"The emperor—"

"Nero," Boudica spat.

"Incorrect, savage. Our emperor is now Hadrian. Any citizen suspected of disloyalty faces his executioner's dagger. When the Praetorian Guard questioned my loyalty, I urged them to look to question my known associates.

"They questioned Marcellus. I never meant him harm. I am an honorable man. My father-in-law, Gnaeus Julius Agricola, and his mentor, Gaius Seutonius Paulinus—"

"General Paulinus?" Boudica asked sharply.

"A man of great honor."

"Honor?" Boudica grabbed a book from the coffee table. "As our hosts have explained, visitors are brought here during our darkest hours, searching for solace in an object. Some item from our past that might bring us joy or respite."

"Impossible." Tacitus smoothed down his toga. "Forgive me, Curator. I have little faith that any object could assuage my uniquely profound and significant feelings."

"Poor Roman citizen." Boudica's voice dripped with sarcasm. "The great injustice you have—"

"That's enough." Ona placed herself between the two.

"Oh, but I've just begun." Boudica held out the book to Tacitus. "Senator, I believe I have just the thing to assuage of your sadness."

Ona glimpsed the title: *The Annals* by Publius Cornelius Tacitus.

"My work..." Tacitus reached for the book with trembling hands. "The culmination of my life's efforts to record the truth of our times."

"You wouldn't know the truth if it was right in front of you."

"More lies!" Tacitus snatched the book and hugged it against his chest. "General Paulinus was a man of honor. That is the way of the Roman citizen! We conquer all. We make all great!"

Boudica surged forward, but the Liaison cut her off. *"Wait."*

Tacitus flipped through the pages, and something near the beginning must have caught his attention. "'*Ancient* Rome?' To know my work is still read two millennia later—"

History is Written by the Losers

"Your work is a lie."

"Lie or truth, my barbarian queen, the Roman Empire will persevere while you die on a battlefield somewhere, left to rot in an unmarked grave." With a final, grateful smile toward Ona, Tacitus became enveloped in a golden glow, soon after fading from view, returned to his own time and place.

His book fell to the ground.

Boudica stared down at it, sneering. "He lied. His people lied. All to maintain power and erase our truth."

Ona placed a comforting hand on Boudica's shoulder. "Your story, your fight... They really do matter. We just need to find the very thing to help you believe that."

Boudica kicked Tacitus's book aside. "Show me."

The parasol was pink, frilly, and covered in flowered appliqués.

Ona glanced at Boudica's narrowed eyes and hurriedly collapsed the Victorian era umbrella. "Not your style, of course."

The Liaison hovered beside Boudica. *What you intend will not satisfy the queen's needs.*

Give it a chance, Ona replied silently. She returned the parasol to its shelf in the British mementos aisle beside a few jars of Marmite and Cooper's Oxford Marmalade.

There were boxed wine gums and packages of Digestive Biscuits, Shortbread, and Jaffa Cakes. Boudica picked up a box labelled *Tunnock's 6 Tea Cakes, Milk Chocolate*. "These are Britain's future?"

"Your country loves its sweets." Ona carefully opened the box, handing a red and silver foiled cake to the warrior-queen.

Boudica raised the wrapped tea cake as if to bite into it.

"Hold on!" Ona grabbed the treat and carefully unwrapped the foil, revealing the chocolate-covered sweet. She nodded encouragingly.

Sweets are not memories, the Liaison warned. *Not for her.*

Just wait. Her object is one aisle over, but let's first get her in a better mood. Ona gave the treat back. "Maybe a taste of your country's future will inspire you."

The warrior-queen bit into the treat, past the chocolate shell and cake base. She hit the gooey center and froze.

"It's called marshmallow. Delicious, isn't it?"

Boudica swallowed. "It is exceptionally sweet."

The Liaison floated toward Boudica. *"Italian confectioners in the late 1500s were critical to the marshmallow's development."*

"Italian…You speak of the people of Rome?" Boudica dropped the uneaten portion of her tea cake on the nearest shelf.

"Okay, let's forget the desserts!" Ona chimed in. She pushed aside more boxes, finding what she was looking for in the far back of the shelf. Knowing its weight, she climbed onto the shelf, using both hands to pull it out.

"Hold out your hands." She set the foot-tall bronze statuette in Boudica's hands.

The warrior-queen stared at the statue. "Who is this?"

"You!" Ona gestured at the powerful image of Boudica atop her two-horse chariot, her young daughters behind her, one on each side. More muscular than in real life, the statue's version wore flowing robes, conveying strength, determination, and undeniable defiance. The robes billowed, adding a sense of movement and dynamism. Her right arm was raised high, holding a spear, while her left hand grasped the horses' reins.

Boudica handed the statute back. "I do not see the relevance."

"It's proof your legacy mattered centuries later."

Boudica crossed her arms. "In this small statute?"

"Well, no…" Ona put it on the nearest shelf and squeezed her eyes shut, allowing herself a moment to access information about the original. "The full-sized one's in London. It's an homage to you, celebrating your bravery. "

"Did the statute foist the Romans from our shores? Did my image prevent the subjugation of women? Were conquered lands permitted to keep their cultures?" Boudica turned her back on the statute. "I am not a Roman emperor. I do not need tribute."

Ona took Boudica's hand. "It must all feel so impossible."

"Feelings are not the problem." Boudica peered down the aisle. "Shall we move on? No object will revive my spirits, but it's your duty so let us proceed, Curator."

History is Written by the Losers

Ona winced at the accusation, but one glance at the orb as it moved down the aisle was enough to remind her that Boudica was right. She was the Curator. Even if what happened next might seem futile, she needed to try. She needed to get Boudica home.

Ona led Boudica down the Hall's next aisle, which was set up with racks that went almost all the way up to the ceiling. High ladders fixed on lateral pipes ran down the full length.

Weapons from throughout time were crammed onto each rack, odd objects that to someone, somewhere, held significant meaning. From rocket launchers to slingshots, from lasers to needle guns, any weapon devised in the history of humanity had a place on those racks.

Boudica took it all in, perplexed. "You truly believe some object here will be enough to turn my spirits round?"

The Liaison floated to the nearest rack. *"The laws of this hall have held for billions, if not trillions of visitors. Many suffered circumstances as dire as yours."*

"Forgive me, sprite. You are right." Boudica bowed her head and placed a hand to her chest. "It is only that I cannot see how this hall, or its objects will help my people."

With a grateful nod to the Liaison, Ona strode a dozen paces further down the aisle and stopped beside a marble bench. The rack beside it carried an object from Boudica's info-dump.

"Look familiar?" She pointed at a ceremonial Roman spatha sword and scabbard. The hilt glinted with intricate swirls of gold and silver. The whole thing spoke of pomp, ceremony, and the hallowed whispers of power and glory. Along its double-edged blade was inscribed the words, *Prasutagus Rex Icenorum.*

Prasutagus, King of the Iceni.

Boudica's lips curled in a rather sardonic smile as she approached the sword. "To see this again…" She shook her head. "So many years have passed."

She ran her fingertips along the broad blade. "I can see the day the Romans gifted us this sword as if it was yesterday. It was meant as a gesture, a symbol of our alliance, believe it or not. The Brigantes to the north had rebelled, causing much trouble for Gallus, Rome's previous governor-general of Britain before Paulinus."

She lifted the blade from the rack's brackets. "Gallus was desperate for an ally and so reached out to the King of the great Iceni tribe, my husband, Prasutagus." Swinging it down to her side, she raised an eyebrow. "In turn, Prasutagus believed a pact with our occupiers would give the Iceni status, providing a level of political influence and prestige among Britain's other tribes. The pact with Gallus would serve as a guarantee of protection for our people."

"And the sword?" Ona asked, almost afraid of what the answer would be.

"Well, that brings us to now, does it not? This sword was a gift at the signing of that pact. A token of Roman friendship. A symbol of support."

Boudica raised the tip, closing one eye to study the sword. "Prasutagus believed the symbolism would keep us safe. Protect our family, our future. Because I loved my husband, I believed it, too."

She turned the blade, watching the light gleam off the metal. A stray glint flared against the polished white marble bench. "That belief was his first mistake."

"First?"

"Indeed. His second? Trusting Gallus. He believed the alliance would endure." She swung the blade under, testing its weight.

"But the greatest mistake? The big one?" She stared through the blade, gazing into the past, hungry for the impossible. "Believing this trinket, these fantasies would become real. That this object, this thing," she spat, "would be better than being free.

Boudica slammed the sword down on the marble bench. Shattered shards of brittle lead and rusted iron scattered across the marble floor.

Ona jumped back, barely stifling a yelp.

The hilt fell from Boudica's hand, the clatter echoing in the hall. She raised tearful eyes upward. When her breathing quieted, she turned to

History is Written by the Losers

Ona. "I am sorry, Curator, but no thing will change what's to come. You cannot help me."

Ona stared at the brittle shards scattered across the floor. "I want to… I just don't know how. I don't know how to change history."

A soft whir, a short series of beeps. The Liaison floated over to Ona and said aloud, *"But I do."*

The Liaison led them through unfamiliar aisles at a fast clip. Ona and Boudica had to run to keep up. As far as Ona knew, no visitor had ever been through this section of the hall. The nearly empty shelves showed why. No objects meant no memories. It was as if humanity's history had been swept clean without a new direction forward—yet.

Their footsteps echoed against the cream-colored marble, an underlying unease building with each step. Ona wondered if something here could've made more of a difference for other visitors and not just Boudica.

If there had been, the orb told her privately, *we would have come sooner.*

Ona felt better. Not much, but enough to reach out and give Boudica's hand a reassuring squeeze.

Boudica managed a smile.

Ona silently asked the Liaison, *Can I ask where we're going?*

You can ask. I will answer with a question of my own. What is the hall's mission?

Ona glanced at the grim and determined Boudica.

To give visitors the strength to return to one of the most difficult moments in their lives, restored by some positive memory of their past.

The Liaison flew further down an all-but-empty aisle. *Having heard the Iceni queen's tale in addition to the info-dump—as you like to call them— do you genuinely believe some object exists that will give her the strength for when she returns to her life?*

Ona shook her head. *Not in her past, no.*

Then our mission cannot be complete unless her future changes instead.

But it's not just her *future you're changing,* Ona warned.

True. The orb veered left. *But perhaps the future should be changed. Aren't you tired of the grief?*

"Of course I am!" Ona stumbled, forcing everyone to slow down. "Will a future where Boudica wins against the Romans make the world better for everyone?"

"Is that possible?" Boudica stopped.

Ona covered her mouth, realizing she'd spoken aloud instead of in her mind to the Liaison.

"Indeed." The Liaison took a hard right into another empty aisle.

With a nod to Boudica, Ona picked up the pace again. "You can do that?" Ona asked the orb as they ran past oddly barren shelves. "You mentioned something earlier, but… Can you really create an alternate timeline?"

"Where we're going is not an alternate."

Boudica grabbed Ona's elbow. "Is this possible?"

Ona pressed, but the orb wouldn't answer. Instead, it continued down the aisles, pausing only long enough for Ona and Boudica to catch up. Then, it was off again. They had little choice but to follow. The deeper in they went, the more the hall changed. The golden ceiling faded to a dull gray, draining the warmth from the air. The smooth marble turned to rough, dark slate, each step a harsh reminder of the shifting surroundings. Venturing deeper, the aisles closed in, the shelves changed from warm woods to black stone, each shelf absorbing the light and casting eerie shadows.

And then finally, objects began to populate the shelves again. Humanity's memories had found a new history, a new reason and new means to thrive.

In an aisle carrying musical instruments were combinations of different cultures. On one shelf was a bamboo flute similar to a Japanese shakuhachi, but with holes and leather fringe like a Native American flute. On another shelf was a sitar-like instrument combining African and Indian elements. A third shelf held a Belgian-style trombone with a painted wooden body and brass bell, but a mouthpiece shaped like an Australian Aboriginal didgeridoo.

Halfway down the aisle, Ona discovered a soot-covered, wooden lyre with a Latin inscription. She handed it to Boudica. "Care to translate?"

Boudica swiped away some of the black dust. "Nero Claudius Caesar Augustus Germanicus." She raised her eyes to Ona, stunned. "This belonged to Emperor Nero?"

History is Written by the Losers

Ona recognized the significance, her head packed with the knowledge of both timelines. In the original timeline, a devastating fire had ravaged Rome for six days, leaving much of the city in ruins and thousands homeless. They rebuilt the city, but blamed Nero for playing while Rome burned.

In the new timeline, that rebuild had never happened. Feeling like a failure, Nero abandoned his people. The Empire fell apart. Dispirited Romans fled the city, spreading out across Europe, to mingle with other cultures.

She explained as much to Boudica.

"Good." The warrior-queen tossed the lyre on the shelf. The instrument protested, sounding off with a dull, hollow thud and a discordant twang.

DING.

Ona whirled around. "A visitor... Now?"

The Liaison rose up above the shelves. *"Consider him an introduction to the shape of things to come. The differences may be subtle, more apparent on the shelves than in the visitor himself."*

DING.

Ona braced herself for the inevitable info-dump. Images flooded her mind of an eighteen-year-old's life in the early twenty-first century. Gadgets and gizmos. Weddings and funerals. Laughter, tears, a mother's call to come in for the night, a father's words of encouragement.

DING.

"Hello?" The young man's voice called out from nearby.

Ona exhaled. The onslaught subsided far faster than normal. No head pain. No overload.

Footsteps echoed against the slate floor. "Anyone around?"

Boudica grabbed Ona. "Explain."

Ona waved an arm, indicating all the wonderful objects having appeared on the shelves. "These objects changed because history changed. All thanks to you winning against the Romans. Because of your success, meritocracy, equality, and ambition became global virtues."

"Global virtues?" Boudica turned toward the Liaison. "Is this your doing, sprite?"

"No. It is your efforts that bring us here, Queen Boudica."

"But what did I do?" Her eyes widened. "Please… I need to know."

"Anybody there?" the young man called out again.

Ona put up a hand. "Let's take care of him and then figure out how to send you back."

"When I laid my head to rest," Boudica said hurriedly, "I did not believe we could win. I could not find the means." She shook her head. "With so many of my people gone, I do not know how we can possibly succeed."

"You can and you will." Ona side-eyed the Liaison. *What should we do? Let the queen have time to adjust to her new reality?*

Is it her reality… Or everyone's?

That depends on her actions.

Ona jerked a thumb toward the new visitor's voice. "Let's go meet this guy from the new timeline. We can see how the world changed, then figure out how to send you back."

"To see a new world changed for the better…" Boudica's face softened, and she smiled slightly. "I would be honored."

Will Matthews was eighteen with hands tucked into black jean pockets, dark eyes heavy with the weight of recent trauma, a rumpled, long-sleeved gray Ghostbusters t-shirt, and scuffed Converse sneakers.

Ona knew from Will's info-dump that life had shattered his innocence. The best way for him to heal was to open up. Slowly. Gently.

"Hello, Will." Ona gestured to the gadget-filled shelves. "Amazing, aren't they? Objects from across the world and time."

She explained how the Hall worked and made introductions, noting the recognition on his face at Boudica's name.

"Is my mom here?" Will looked around the hall.

"No. Typically it's one visitor at a time."

He pointed at Boudica. "So she lives here?"

"No. She's a visitor like you. I see you've found some of humanity's more collaborative technological advances. Do you like technology?"

History is Written by the Losers

Will shrugged. "I guess."

Ona couldn't get a bead on the young man. Nothing in his info-dump connected any profound memory with an object.

Boudica picked up a slim translucent box surrounded by multi-colored stacks of thin sheets marked with a blend of Hebrew and Japanese Kanji. "How extraordinary."

Will frowned. "It's a dictation box, so?"

"Anything look familiar?" Ona asked.

She pointed across the aisle at bizarre objects she'd never seen. One shelf carried a half-dozen smooth, polished hand-held objects, each bearing a brass label marked *Neuro-Nexus*. Another shelf held a thin pole covered in black and gold beads labeled *Zulu Sonic Spear*. On yet another shelf sat a set of translucent teacups covered in silver and turquoise Arabic lettering with Navajo animal designs, all shifting and changing under the hall's lighting.

Ona asked , "Why are you here?"

"My mom..." Will wrung his hands. "I asked her not to go out with her friends, but she didn't listen. Then the next day, she didn't come back. She struggles with depression so…"

Ona nodded, encouraging Will to continue.

"Dad got a call from one of mom's weirdo friends. They'd found her passed out in her car, deep in the woods. When we got there, she was barely coherent, near death." Will's eyes welled up with tears. "Seeing my mom like that... I thought I'd lost her."

As Boudica patted Will's shoulder, Ona hoped his story might resonate with the mother of two.

"Dad managed to get an ambulance to take her to the hospital. They said she'd been drugged." His voice cracked. "I feel like it's all my fault."

Boudica stepped back, aghast. "Are you a terrible son?"

He shook his head.

"Did you steal or lie? Or beat your mother or drive her into the arms of this 'weirdo' friend you mentioned?"

"Of course not!" Will scowled.

Ona held back, recognizing how being a mother made Boudica perfect for this.

"It's not like that." Will slid to the floor, elbows on knees, head in hands. "Seeing mom hurting... I should've done something."

Boudica knelt beside him. "All you can do is love your mother as her son."

"I guess..."

"Allow her *her* life. Live your own. You are young. Be brave. Be a good son but be true to yourself. That is the greatest gift for a mother."

"Mom says that." He sighed. "It just sucks to see her hurting. I feel like I'm ten years old all over again."

Boudica winced. "I know."

Will looked up at Boudica, his anguish subsided. "Man, my mom would dig you."

Boudica glanced up at Ona. "Dig?"

Ona grinned. "It means you did good."

"I can't wait to tell my mom we met." A light smile tugged at Will's mouth. "Every kid learns about how you stopped Rome before it was too late."

"Do you remember any of the tactics used?"

He shook his head. "Nah. They don't teach that in second grade."

Boudica frowned. "I wish to win tomorrow's battle so that all children may live in a land of equals. One where all may flourish, not by a show of weapons or troops, but on merit."

"It's a work in progress, but I think we're heading in that direction" Will flung his arms wide, taking in the shelves around them. "As awful as Mom's situation was, she's gonna be okay. The world's gonna have her back..." A grin broke out on his face. "And so will I."

Boudica crossed her arms. "Yet none of this answers how I may gain victory."

Ona ransacked the warrior-queen's dual info-dumps for any clue that could help.

And came up empty.

History is Written by the Losers

DING.

"No, no, no…" Ona shot a glance at the Liaison. "Another visitor?"

"Soon, yes." Then the orb replied privately, *Transmission of our new visitors will be withheld until Will's departure. Focus on him.*

Visitors… As in two of them? Together?

Together. The Liaison gave her no new information. Instead, it flew over the shelves, heading deeper into the new timeline.

Ona glanced from Will to Boudica. The Liaison was right. Will should be her focus. He was certainly the easier of the two problems to solve. It wasn't like the young man was trying to change the future course of history (although one never did know). Ona sifted through her memories of his past, present, and future until an image rose from the mayhem in her brain. A woman's hands. A feeling of purpose, of connection, and belonging.

Somehow all tied to Will's object.

I know where we need to go, she told the Liaison.

You always do.

They found Will's object nestled between a set of Norse rune stones and a golden torc covered with Celtic knotwork, tangled up with a set of amber mala beads. Ona unraveled the rosary beads; his info-dump supplied the rest. The beads had belonged to Will's mother who in turn had gifted them to Will.

Ona lifted the string of beads from the shelf, their deep azure color pulsing with life, each bead a tiny universe of love and devotion. The warmth emanating from the beads seeped into her fingers, as if the essence of a mother's eternal love had been woven into them, providing a tangible reminder of the unbreakable bond between a son and his mother.

Ona offered them to Will. As he reached for the beads, a ripple ran over his face. His shoulders broadened. She wasn't sure, but he also seemed to have grown another few centimeters.

And a small beard appeared on his chin.

"What dark magic is this?" Boudica stepped between Ona and Will, blocking him from the beads.

"It's okay." Ona sidestepped, handing the beads to Will. "Same person, different age?"

Will stroked his new-grown beard. "Twenty-seven with the memories to prove it." A wistful smile played across his face as he draped the beads over his fingers. "I don't remember leaving here at eighteen, but I do remember Mom giving these to me just yesterday… Like yesterday-yesterday. I'm twenty-seven now. Mom's in a good place and I've finished school."

"What does the cross signify?" Boudica pointed to the silver cross at one end.

"It's a religion thing." Will shrugged. "Not really my jam. I'm more an atheist, except visiting here makes me wonder." He tilted his head back, taking in the Hall's impossibly far-off ceiling. "The beads meant a lot to my mom, so she gave them to me."

"May I?" Boudica rubbed a finger across the metal cross. "This is not a Druidic symbol, and yet I recognize the Celtic knots."

Will shrugged. "Just another symbol. There's plenty of them. Kinda like life, huh?"

Boudica raised an eyebrow. "Meaning?"

"It's kind like if you're trying something and it's not working, try something else. Don't get stuck."

Boudica's face flashed with recognition, making Ona wonder if Will had somehow inspired the warrior-queen.

It was time for Will to go home. To that end, she deliberately asked, "Why the rosary? Why this object?"

"I know Mom's gonna be okay." He slid the beads along the string, creating a soft, melodic clicking. "She's pulled her life together, inspiring me along the way. I want… No, I *need* her to have a good life because I know she wants the same for me. Her beads feel like a way of keeping that connection going." He sheepishly shrugged. "I can't really explain it."

Ona beamed. "I think you've explained it well."

"Extraordinarily well," Boudica added.

"Yeah?" Will glanced down at the pooled beads in his palm. "I guess I'm ready."

Ona cocked her head. "As an eighteen-year-old or–"

He raised his eyes to Ona, a golden glow rippling across his face, changing him back to his younger self. Sparkling stardust bubbled up around him. He began to dissolve.

"My Gods." Boudica reached out to Will, her hand going right through him.

A great sigh of contentment escaped him. "Yep. I'm ready."

And with that, Will disappeared. Ona swooped up the rosary and returned it to the shelf.

One down, one to go.

"What you did for William was extraordinary," Boudica said.

"He would've got there on his own."

"Perhaps. Perhaps not." Boudica joined her at the shelf, gazing on all it held.

The shelf housed diverse spiritual artifacts, including Jewish Stars of David, Christian crucifixes, Islamic crescent moons, Hindu Om symbols, Wiccan pentacles, Buddhist wheels, Sikh khandas, Native American medicine wheels, and more unrecognizable by Ona. The array reinforced the idea of no single faith dominating the others; intricate Celtic knots adorned many pieces. Each unique piece contributed to a rich tapestry of faiths woven harmoniously through this new timeline.

The implications of such an existence equally humbled and frustrated Ona. Humbled, because it was a promise of a better place for all humanity throughout time and space.

Boudica picked up a translucent spring-green teardrop pendant, shimmering with a soft, apple-like hue. A tree was etched onto one side. A hole was drilled through one end with a black cord passed through for tying around one's neck. "I do not recognize most of these icons, and yet…" She slipped the cord around her neck, the pendant falling to lie against her chest. "I would readily fight for their existence."

Ona remained silent about the pendant. The green corded stone would never leave the hall. If it gave Boudica the smallest glimmer of joy, that was a step in the right direction. Instead, she wracked her brain, focusing on what mattered.

Sending Boudica home to win.

Even from a distance, the Liaison seemed to know what to do next. *Perhaps our latest visitors will inspire both you and our warrior-queen.*

Ona grabbed Boudica's hand. "Come on. Let's go meet our new guests."

Under the Liaison's silent direction, Ona led Boudica toward the wing's new waiting area. A few lefts, a few rights…

Take the aisle a few hundred paces, the Liaison told Ona, *and you will find me waiting with the new visitors.*

Boudica kept up, her hand often touching the green pendant on her chest.

"We're close to figuring it all out. Just two more visitors and then—"

"What did Will mean about getting stuck?" Boudica stopped beside a display of miniatures of historical spaceships. Some were recognizable, others changed. More streamlined, sleeker. More flightworthy.

Humanity's reach for the stars had found more success in this new timeline.

"You'll figure it out." Ona leaned in, reading the ship names.

"The solution eludes me."

"How's this for proof?" Ona pointed at a sleek spaceship named *I.S.S. Boudica*.

"That means nothing to me." Boudica turned away. "Nor have you answered my question."

"Yeah." Ona sighed, realizing that spaceships weren't exactly a thing in Boudica's era. "I was afraid you were gonna say that."

The answers sought do not exist within, but inspiration sparks their inception.

That's obtuse even for you, Ona told the Liaison. *While we're at it, you haven't given me visitor information. How can I help if I don't know who I'm dealing with?*

Turn left, was all the reply she got.

With Boudica beside her, Ona followed the Liaison's silent directions. They emerged from an aisle packed with old paperbacks onto an upper platform overlooking a sunken amphitheater made of mahogany-colored marble. Across the way, shelves and aisles bore objects from the original timeline.

On a leather couch at the amphitheater's bottom level, two red-haired women sat, sobbing. The Liaison hovered behind them, waiting patiently.

Ona descended with Boudica. The Liaison had yet to supply any info-dumps. Ona had no idea who they were or how to get them to their respective homes. Although… While each was dressed radically differently—one wearing unbleached linens with a leather breastplate like Boudica's, the other a dark red tartan toga—she sensed they were family.

Boudica gasped. "Daughters?"

They lifted their heads.

Their mother raced down the remaining stairs and into their arms.

Ona knew the reunion would be short-lived but would do all three family members good. Their collective trauma thanks to the Roman Empire deserved that, at the very least. She hung back with the Liaison as Boudica sat between Andra and Draste. Platters of roasted meats, breads, and apples sat on the central table with jugs of rich, frothy ale. They ate and drank ravenously, as if it were the first and last meal they'd ever know.

Somehow, the sisters were in their late thirties, and from a far later chapter in the Boudica's life. Each took a turn admiring Boudica's newfound pendant. She did introduce them, but as Curator, Ona thought it best to keep back. She gave them a friendly wave, which was readily returned.

Boudica handed a cup of ale to Andra. "You wear the cloth of our people, my daughter, but with the style of a Roman citizen."

"I wear the toga of the Consul of Britain." Andra accepted the cup and drank deeply.

Boudica's eyes widened. "You rule our people?"

Andra and Draste exchanged glances.

183

"In a manner of speaking," Andra said. "The Empire fell. Shifting sentiments allowed us to ally with many nations."

"Including Rome." Draste took the other cup. "And beyond."

Boudica leaned back on the couch. "Hence your breastplate."

"I am a general in the Jewish forces of Galilee," Draste said. "At your encouragement, I traveled to Galilee once Rome had truly surrendered. There I joined forces with Yosef ben Matityahu, commander of the Jewish forces. We managed to push back against the Romans before they could destroy Judea's second temple. Once Andra convinced what remained of the Empire to become allies, hostilities ceased. Relations have been strained, but we take each day as it comes."

Andra put down her cup and counted on her hand, "Rome, Britain, Gaul, Judea, Morocco, Persia... It is our ambition to ally with as many as will have us. Each nation lends its strength to bolster the others."

Draste grabbed Boudica's other hand. "What happened before... When the Romans attacked..." She inhaled deeply. "The memory is always there, but at a distance, fueling each day we awaken, but insuring that we separately–"

"And jointly," Andra added, "make the most of our lives."

"You have turned bad into good, my daughters." Boudica embraced them both. "I could not be prouder. Your father would be pleased if he knew."

Draste scoffed. "Father was proud when one of us tied a knot."

Boudica stared into her cup. "Prasutagus was a good father."

"But not a great husband," Andra said. Boudica's head shot up, to which the eldest daughter added, "You and father rarely agreed on anything."

"Except on how to be battle-ready," Draste offered. "Father knew who wielded the blade in the family."

All three chuckled.

Ona mentally whispered to the Liaison, *this isn't exactly the stuff of a darkest hour.*

Wait.

Andra nodded to the Liaison. "Thanks to the sprite, we know what brings us here, but–"

"Daughters..." Boudica shook her head. "Only a fool would not see why you are here together."

History is Written by the Losers

Draste's eyes welled up as Ona realized the why. In their world, their mother had died.

Draste dashed her tears away. "Borvo claimed the Gods kept you alive to inspire the world."

Andra sniffled. "He was not wrong."

"Borvo is still alive?" Boudica chuckled. "That druid was born old."

"He refused to visit the Overworld until securing your company."

"May he now rest." Boudica touched her newfound pendant. "Tell me of my final battle against Paulinus and his troops. It has not yet occurred, and any guidance would assist."

Their sobs stopped short.

Boudica sat up taller. "You do not know?"

"How could we?" Andra said.

"You sent us north," Draste added. "We only know what you and others told us."

"Which was?"

Draste shrugged. "Even Borvo would only say that your brilliant maneuvers took the Romans by surprise. Nothing more."

"Ah, well… whatever happened," Boudica put her arms around her daughters, "I am thankful for this day."

Andra pulled back. "This day upon our mourning of your passing?"

Boudica smiled, her eyes glistening. "Death comes, whether on the battlefield or years later." She pulled her eldest back into the embrace.

For one extraordinary moment, Ona found herself yearning to be loved so simply, truly, deeply.

It was an extraordinary gift.

Unsurprisingly, a golden glow arose, swirling from sister to sister, sparkling lights wrapping around each daughter's arms as they jointly held their mother close, and then…

Boudica gasped, her arms empty, her daughters gone. A mother's tears had brought them solace.

DING.

DING.

DING.

In Andra's place sat a woman. She smiled broadly, her rich brown skin aglow as if kissed by the sun itself. She wore an intricately embossed, red-painted leather breastplate, marking her as a warrior as well. Beneath her armor, she wore a black cotton tunic and matching pants adorned with geometric patterns of red, gold, and blue.

The woman gazed at Boudica, smiling wide. "You found my pendant!"

As Boudica returned the pendant, Ona explained the Hall's rules and how they might help Chengetai. As introductions were made between the two woman-warriors, Chengetai took in every detail around her with curiosity, hinting at an insatiable appetite for new experiences and knowledge. Coupled with her confident posture, her persona easily spoke of a brilliant mind ready for a challenge, whether it be leading troops into battle or unraveling the hall's mysteries.

Her keen eyes darted around the hall, her smile never disappearing. At worst, she seemed a bit wistful, but certainly not deep into living her darkest hour. She appeared calm, clear-eyed, amused, and maybe just a bit mirthful. Without an info-dump, Ona was uncertain why the woman was there.

"I never believed I'd see this pendant again." Chengetai patted her pendant. "The last time was… I believe it was during our year of freedom."

"Was your land occupied?" Boudica asked.

The new visitor waved her hand. "Nothing like that. When you become sixteen, you are encouraged to explore the world before assuming responsibilities at home. I sailed for the Americas with Zuva, my childhood love. I lost this very pendant during our adventures."

"His passing is why you're here?" Ona asked.

For a brief moment, Chengetai's face stilled. "Zuva was more than a spouse. He was my other half. My best friend and companion. We knew each other from birth to matching armor."

"You were both warriors." Boudica indicated her own breastplate.

"And much more than that, I hope."

History is Written by the Losers

"Tell us more."

"Zuva was my shoulder. I was his arm. He taught me the value of winning a battle without loss for both sides!"

Boudica shook her head. "An exceptional warrior."

"I'm forever grateful to have known him." Chengetai mumbled a soft prayer. "He gave his life so that others might keep theirs. Our enemy has surrendered. Peace will be restored."

"And the pendant?" Ona asked, puzzled by the woman's serenity.

Chengetai wagged a finger at Ona. "You know all my answers, don't you?"

Ona gave her a half-smile. "Not all of them. Besides, it's good for you to talk through what's happened. What you've lost."

Chengetai stroked her chin, "My darkest moment is of my own loss. I am now alone with no other to challenge me, with no other to share strategies, no other to provide tactictal inspiration, no other to inspire my mind. Perhaps between you both, I will find a new path. A new reminder of who I am and how I may walk in the world."

Ona glanced at Boudica, hoping she felt the same. "What's your pendant made of?"

"Chrysoprase." Chengetai held out the green pendant. "A remarkable stone composed of crystals so fine they cannot be seen separately without a looking glass. Much like our marriage. We were one to all who looked our way."

Then, she laughed. A joyous laugh from deep within.

Boudica furrowed her brow in disbelief. "This is your darkest moment?"

"That moment has passed!" Chengetai slapped her hands on her thighs. "It is over. I am now in the next moment. With you. With the Curator and her magic ball who speaks and knows things. The past cannot hold me back. If it does, it wins.

Chengetai shook her head vehemently. "I refuse to lose."

"I do not have that choice." Boudica outlined the strategic nightmare awaiting her on the battlefield.

The Shona warrior shrugged. "Then to win, you must change the rules."

"Impossible." Boudica jumped up from the couch.

"All things are possible," Chengetai insisted. "Simply change the rules."

"General Paulinus has shown up with ten thousand more troops and three hundred more cavalry." Boudica began to pace. "I can't change that. At dawn, they will strike."

"At dawn." Chengetai crossed her arms. "Let me guess. The rules of engagement dictate you fight only in the daylight?"

"Of course." Boudica slowed down.

Ona could see what Chengetai was trying to point out, but–

The warrior-queen must arrive at the answer herself.

But none of this matters, Ona railed privately to the Liaison. *When she goes back to the real world, she won't remember a thing.*

If timelines can change, then perhaps as Chengetai suggests, our rules can change as well. Then, without reason, the orb headed upwards, toward the shelves that led back into the Hall's original section. *I will return shortly.*

"Ten thousand new troops…" Chengetai mused. "That is a great many more bodies."

"A *great* many more bodies. The battlefield will not hold them all…" Boudica froze, her expression transforming from confusion to clarity.

"Is it possible?" Boudica hurried over to Chengetai, clearly transformed—her steps lighter, her posture more confident, her entire being radiating a newfound sense of clarity and purpose.

"You know what you need to do." The Shona warrior-woman stood up and took Boudica by the forearms.

"I do." Boudica mirrored Chengetai, the two warrior-women of different eras and different lives, thriving in their mutual strengths. "Zuva was a lucky man to have you as his arm."

"Oh, he knew." She grinned, touching her pendant. The hall's signature golden glow circled around her, sparkles dancing within its light. "And now his shoulder will carry me forward."

Boudica bowed her head. "Farewell, Chengetai of the Shona. You have my thanks."

"And you have mine, Boudica of Britain. Go win your war!" Chengetai began to dissolve in a shimmer, becoming translucent, transparent, and then–

Ona felt compelled to shout out, "The pendant stays in the hall!"

History is Written by the Losers

Chengetai disappeared, leaving only a whisper in the air. "Remember what I said about rules?"

The Shona warrior-queen disappeared.

As did the pendant.

Stunned, Ona reached out to the Liaison, hoping for a sanity check at the very least. Objects never left the hall. What had happened, shouldn't.

Unusual, but not unexpected. The Liaison crested the top of the amphitheater stairs, floating down toward them. A clamp extending from its base held a green wool cloak. Ona recognized it as the warrior-queen's.

The cloak was dropped into Boudica's arms. *When you are ready."*

"My thanks, sprite." She threw the cloak around her shoulders, her eyes glinting with newfound resolve. "I have what I need."

"Which is what?" Ona asked, confused. "I'm glad you feel sure of what to do, but you're not going to remember any of this. You're going to go back to that final battle and—"

"Have a little faith, Curator." Boudica's face lit up as the golden glow of departure prepared to send her home. "I told you, not everyone requires the memories of an object to regain their strength. Some need a friend to show us the way. You were that friend. I am thankful."

She dissolved into a shimmer of sparkles, leaving Ona to truly hope that somehow, someway, the warrior-queen of Britain would, indeed, remember.

Briton Encampment
Droche-Brig, Britain
A.D. 61 (814 A.U.C.)

Lapping water, rustling leaves, a mournful bird's call echoed in the darkness.

Boudica shivered awake, wrapped tightly in Borvo's cloak. She sat up, pulling it closer for warmth.

And remembered.

She jumped to her feet. "Borvo!" she called into the night.

A glance toward her people's encampment told her why he failed to answer. She had been asleep a short while, but long enough for the fires to burn low. Huddled masses spoke of sleep. As much from exhaustion as from the night's rhythms. This was when people usually slept. This was a rule of life. A rule of war.

The war that she would end by morning.

She strained her ears and heard nothing from the Romans.

Boudica raced to her people, shaking three men awake.

"Cut down those trees by the river's bank," she ordered, pointing toward her sleeping spot. Grabbing a dozen other men, she added, "Those large stones jutting from the bank... Stack them on the other side. Dredge the area for more if needed."

She grabbed a trio of young boys and told them, "Go throughout the camp. Repeat my orders to each lieutenant. Tell them the rules have changed, but softly. Let our Roman adversaries sleep. We have work to do!"

No one moved. Not at first.

Borvo stumbled to her side. "My queen. It is night. The rules of engagement—"

"Can be changed, my dear Druid." She gently returned the cloak to his shoulders, motivated by the knowledge that he would hold onto life for her in the years to come.

It was up to her to ensure those years existed.

Ona strode to the middle of the amphitheater. She looked toward the old timeline's shelves and then turned around, taking in all of the new timeline's aisles stacked with shelves that seemingly went on ad infinitum. What objects existed there? What gadgets and gizmos and artifacts existed in a world where the rules had been changed?

"Do you think we made a difference?" she asked the Liaison.

History is Written by the Losers

"There is one simple way to find out."

Together, they climbed the stairs toward the new shelves, toward the new timeline.

They saw humanity's new past, present, and future.

Briton Encampment
Droche-Brig, Britain
A.D. 61 (814 A.U.C.)

The sun had risen high, yet the battlefield remained still.

The river was crowded, its sides blocked by fallen trees and rocks trapping several hundred legionnaires. The rank and file could not pull their swords from their hilts. Centurions stomped in the water, cursing. Horses splashed, kicking at the barriers, neighing in protest.

All of them protected one man, and yet any means of escape was long gone for this particular segment of the Roman army.

Boudica strode to the center of the trapped riverbank, her army guarding her rear flank.

She clicked her tongue, urging a horse from the river forward. The tall, regal horse splashed the water with each step, its brown hair wet from the river.

She offered the horse an apple, which it swallowed in two bites. With gratitude, the horse nuzzled her outstretched hand.

Boudica looked up in the morning light at the horse's rider. She offered a conciliatory smile. After all, she had just trapped his most essential armed forces. There was nothing else he could do except…

"Good morning, General Paulinus. Shall we discuss the terms of your surrender?"

The Mercury 13

Rigel Ailur

TWIST-A-WHIRL, THAT'S HOW GERALDYN "JERRIE" COBB THOUGHT of the centrifugal equipment that simulated high Gs.

She enjoyed it, but not everyone did. It gradually slowed and then came to a full stop. As quickly as she could, she peeled off all the electrodes monitoring her vitals. Not a single tremor in her hands as she unstrapped from the seat and climbed down, a broad grin on her face.

"Great job, Miss Cobb. That's the last one," Dr. William Lovelace said. One of the sponsors of the National Aeronautics and Space Agency's Lady Astronaut Program, he offered a hand down.

She winked, but ignored it and jumped the two steps. Unless a male astronaut looked unsteady, she didn't imagine Lovelace would make the same gesture to any of them.

The attending nurse clutched a sheaf of medical papers more tightly as she turned away and hustled out of the room, but not before Cobb spotted the woman's disapproving frown turn to a contemptuous scowl. Oh well. Many if not most women supported her enthusiastically, but some could be just as sexist as any man. Maybe they preferred the familiarity of tradition. Maybe they simply lacked imagination or ambition—or tolerance. Cobb didn't understand them in the least, but she knew all too well that they existed.

"Well, Doctor, what's next?" Cobb asked, even though she suspected the answer.

She was acing all the tests, the same tests that the male astronaut candidates were taking. After some discreet digging, she'd learned that twelve other women were passing them all as well. They'd dubbed themselves the Mercury 13. NASA, and then the national press, had caught wind of the term and adopted it as well.

"Now I compile my findings and make my report and recommendation."

She waited and fixed him with a look, her silence tacit prodding. When he glanced around as if to ensure no one else were around to hear, she almost laughed—until she gleaned he was totally serious.

Lovelace lowered his voice. "There are rumblings the Soviets want to put a woman in space," he told her. "They beat us with Sputnik, and with Gagarin. The US needs to beat them at this."

Wow. Cobb hadn't realized. But if that twist added incentive, so much the better. It should be enough that doubling the candidate pool made a ton of sense, but she'd accept any assist she could get. Even from the Russians.

"Will that help you get us the jets?" Their final—and so far biggest—hurdle. The women needed the military's planes so they could qualify flying jets. Of course NASA could waive that requirement. They'd waived the college degree requirement for one or two of the men.

Cobb didn't expect reciprocity on that count.

Lovelace's dour tone didn't bolster her hopes. "We'll see."

Mouth twisted in derision, Cobb stood in the doorway and regarded her office at the NASA complex. She supposed she should be grateful that the closet—er, room—at least contained a desk and a chair. No telephone or window, but the overhead light worked.

And revealed the wall decorations.

The Mercury 13

Once again, posters and pinups from *Queen of Outer Space* adorned her office walls. Because naturally every astronaut needed pastel mini-dresses, perfectly coiffed tresses, and exquisite make-up.

Someone had oh-so-considerately supplied a wastebasket as well. At last.

They'd even filled it for her.

As diligently as Cobb had distributed her memo to everyone and anyone in any position of authority or influence at the Space Center, someone else had collected them.

No matter. Cobb would continue to beat that particular drum, as well as fight for women astronauts.

Her complaint was at once tiny and huge, and exemplified the battle she faced.

After the current Mercury program, NASA planned to name the next phase Gemini. Then—although they didn't dare even whisper 'moon mission' in public yet—they privately already called those missions Apollo.

Apollo.

Sun God.

For the moon missions.

What the hell?

Despite her derision and ire, Cobb had pointed out quite calmly and rationally that naming the moon program after the Moon Goddess made far more sense.

Artemis.

One change, both tiny and huge. "Just" a name, right? Some chuckled; others sneered, snickered, or scoffed. But Cobb knew that names mattered. Awareness and acceptance mattered. She'd keep pushing on that front as well.

First things first, however. She had more time to deal with future mission names.

Right now, the Soviets planned to put a woman in space. The first woman in space.

Not if Cobb had anything to say about it.

Good—and no doubt deliberate—that Dr. Lovelace had told her.

She could leverage that competitiveness, hope that national pride and patriotism would supersede sexism. The USSR had already won stages one and two of the space race by launching Sputnik and then Yuri Gagarin into orbit.

Now the US really needed to step up. In order to come from behind, America needed to ramp up its space program and put the first woman in space and the first people on the moon.

For the US to win stage three and permanently take the lead, NASA needed women astronauts.

Yes, Cobb wanted it for herself. Desperately. She didn't deny that. But the country also needed it in order to fulfill its potential by claiming and staying at the leading edge of this new frontier.

Cobb promised herself that she and the rest of the Mercury 13 would triumph over the huge obstacle before them. Who knew that passing Dr. Lovelace's and Gen. Flickinger's tests—the same tests the male astronaut candidates needed to pass to qualify—would be the easiest hurdle to clear?

Hot dry air smacked Cobb in the face as she descended from the plane to the tarmac of Lackland Airbase. Time was of the essence and she'd arrived last, so she'd changed into her flight suit during the short hop from Ellington Airfield. Evidently planes and pilots at Lackland had incredibly tight schedules.

She spotted Dr. Lovelace and Gen. Flickinger amidst a group of twelve women.

Cobb grinned so broadly she figured her face might crack. They'd heard of each other, some had even corresponded, but the Mercury 13 had never assembled in one place until now. She loved seeing them all together.

Joy quickly fading, anxiety replaced it at the officer striding toward them.

A lieutenant approached Gen. Flickinger from the hanger and somehow managed to both ignore all the women, and still make a point of whispering to the general so no one else could hear. Neat trick.

"I'm going to assume a USAF airbase does have planes available and ready, especially considering we were expected." The general did not

The Mercury 13

raise his voice, yet the lieutenant took a quick step back. "Otherwise I'll be having words with your base commander and then working my way up the chain of command from there."

Funny how quickly things happened after that.

The women had all flown jets before—mostly thanks to fortuitous connections and/or happenstance. They needed official acknowledgement of the skill.

Cobb climbed into the cockpit of the F-86 Sabre, settling into the seat as she pulled on the helmet.

Last to arrive, last to take off, not that she minded. Fair was fair. The metal body encasing her rumbled with barely contained energy she could feel in every cell of her body. She adjusted the throttle, pushed the stick forward, then with the faintest bump, the roughness of the runway gave way to the lift of the air.

Air traffic control gave each woman very specific instructions as to direction and altitude to eliminate even the most miniscule chance of colliding with regular flights or with each other.

She was flying.

Cobb soared through the cloudless azure sky.

Exhilaration still filled her when her feet touched the ground hours later. Last to take off, last to land. She didn't mind in the least.

Days later, they got the news. Yes, they'd qualified to fly jets, but people still had 'concerns'. So much so that Congress needed to hold hearings on the matter. And evidently Jacqueline Cochran—who should have been their staunchest supporter, considering her own history—was doing her utmost behind the scenes to sabotage them.

After Cochran's triumph leading the women pilots in WWII, she had effectively prevented them from becoming a permanent part of the army. Now she wanted to sabotage the women astronauts before they even had a chance.

Not if Cobb had anything to say about it.

Off to Washington, DC.

The longer Cobb sat still in the previously charming restaurant, the more the gentle hum of conversation, the muted clink of cutlery and china and glassware, and the formerly tantalizing aroma of garlic, tomato sauce, and freshly-baked bread got on her nerves. Nothing—not even her twelve fellow pilots at the long table with her nor the scrumptious food—assuaged her aggravation at seeing her nemesis seated nearby enjoying her own delicious meal.

Cobb had thought long and hard about what to do, how to possibly persuade Jacqueline Cochran to change her mind. Just maybe, Cobb had come up with a solution—and it all depended on Cochran's ego being as huge as Cobb thought it was.

Now or never. Cobb shoved to her feet and strode over to Cochran at a corner table.

Clearly pushing sixty, the legendary aviator "Jackie" Cochran nevertheless wore the decades as effortlessly as she did her stylish powder blue suit. After just a beat, Cochran realized the person who'd stopped at their table wasn't a server.

"You were a goddess to me growing up. I wanted to be you. You are why I fly." Cobb's flat statement interrupted Cochran with a forkful of pasta halfway to her mouth. "You are why hundreds of women fly. Little girls idolize you."

Startled, Cochran lowered the utensil as Cobb leaned closer and continued her tirade barely above a whisper. "But now look at you. You've turned into those men you used to fight, men telling women to stay in their place. I don't get it."

Cobb shook her head, voice staying low yet betraying deep anger. "Your legacy won't be forgotten. Ever. You could have been the giant whose shoulders we stood on. Instead you're tarnishing your own legacy. Now you'll also be the person who stomped others down, and who set the space program back decades."

Cochran's perfectly lipsticked mouth fell open and her skillfully made-up eyes flared then narrowed as her jaw clamped into a scowl. Even as Cochran drew breath to reply, Cobb turned and marched off.

Cobb sailed past her still-seated friends—stunned and nearly as aghast as Cochran—and out of the restaurant.

The Mercury 13

She skidded to a halt just outside the restaurant and waited on the sidewalk under a tree. Its shade gave welcome respite from the blazing sun overhead and temperatures still in the eighties. Typical Washington DC in July. Her hand clenched around the keys in her pocket as she took deep, measured breaths, allowing her pounding heart rate to slow.

Only time would tell if her gambit had succeeded. Time they didn't have.

No one else in the restaurant seemed to have paid any attention. Just as well. The last thing she and her fellow pilots needed was news reports about some hysterical woman trying to start a catfight in a restaurant. Not that Cobb regretted even the tiniest bit speaking her mind. She felt better having had her say, and dared to hope her tirade would have the desired effect.

Her grip on the car keys relaxed.

She briefly contemplated returning to the hotel immediately. The others had enough cars among them that she wouldn't strand anyone. But she didn't want them worrying or wondering where she'd gone. She'd wait. They'd all finished dessert before she'd gotten up to confront the legendary pilot working so hard against them. They'd likely all emerge in another five or ten minutes.

After lunch but before rush hour, as confirmed by the steady yet not heavy traffic on the four-lane road. Pedestrians sauntered, strolled or sped by, occasionally giving off a waft of too-strong cologne or perfume. For the most part, though, Cobb smelled the car exhaust and the aroma emanating from the restaurant.

She heard the restaurant doors open, and the fragrance of food overwhelmed all others before fading. Cobb turned, expecting to see her friends with various expressions of rebuke on their faces.

Instead, Jacqueline Cochran stood there, hands on hips, an indecipherable hard set to her countenance, breeze tugging at her blond curls.

Cobb almost walked away. She thought better of it, not wanting Cochran to misconstrue that as avoiding a fight. Instead, Cobb folded her arms across her chest and raised a brow in silent inquiry.

"You're awfully young," Cochran said. "But you're right."

Not what she'd expected. Both Cobb's brows now arched high. She'd been prepared to ignore Cochran's initial declaration—youth wasn't a failing, after all—when her second statement registered fully.

Definitely not what Cobb had expected. She waited.

"You are right." A tremor of exhaustion touched Cochran's voice. "I can remain at the vanguard of this, of progress, or not. But I've done a lot of damage. Probably more than you know."

Cobb frowned. "I know pretty much." Cochran had sent a lot of letters to a lot of powerful people in government and in the military. Impactful letters.

Cochran gave a facial shrug. "Maybe you do." Then Cochran smirked. "So I'm a goddess and a giant, am I?" She turned dead serious. "I don't know about that, but I do have resources. Ones I've grossly misused until now. So now we'll see if you're right and I can turn it around for you."

Still Cobb frowned, dubious as the sudden turnabout. She wanted exactly that, but dare she trust it? "Meaning what?"

"Meaning, those hearings will still rest on your shoulders. I'll revise my testimony, but they won't want to hear that. I'm afraid that particular damage is done, and I'm sorry. I can get you backup, though. I can get you a lot of backup. It's high time my power served good, instead of my own short-sightedness."

"What do you have in mind?"

"Like you said, I've fought this battle before. I won, and hundreds of women pilots proved exactly what they could do. Time to remind everyone of that. Be sure to show up early for the hearings. You'll enjoy the view."

Cochran turned on her heel, took her husband's arm, and the pair wandered off, leaning close and chuckling softly as if they didn't have a care in the world. Cobb stared after them.

What the hell had just happened? Cobb had hoped for just that but still couldn't quite let herself believe. Had Cochran really turned around that easily? Cobb would find out soon enough. Which had swayed Cochran, the reminder of her past or the description of two potential—opposite—futures?

Maybe both, or a little of each? Cobb didn't care. However shocking, she'd definitely take the win.

The other women pilots followed almost on the heels of Cochran, exiting the eatery barely a minute after Cochran had vanished around the corner.

"What? No bloodshed?" Janey Briggs made a show of studying the nearby surroundings. "I don't see any signs of bloodshed."

"No bloodshed." Cobb pulled a face, annoyed at her own doubt but unable to get past them. "She claimed she's changed her mind and is now going to support us."

"And you believed her?" Wally Funk scoffed.

"I didn't say that, but I'm willing to reserve judgement. Doesn't mean we ease up. I'd say we still need to redouble our efforts. I'm sure she expects that regardless, though, so why lie? She can't seriously believe we'd back off due to anything she said. Anything anyone said, for that matter."

Funk remained unconvinced. "We'll see."

Exactly. Cobb's initial reaction remained: What the hell had just happened?

By the time Cobb got back to the hotel, she knew. Or, rather, she already had thirteen messages waiting to tell her, and more kept flooding in.

Rich, charismatic, and influential, Cochran inspired people and knew how to get what she wanted—a true force of nature when she chose not to hold back. Plus a ton of her friends or acquaintances owned planes, or had easy access to them.

Cochran had called on the women WWII pilots she'd led.

And they'd answered.

All of them.

As if that weren't already beyond impressive, Cochran had also rallied the Ninety-Nines, the international association of women pilots founded by Amelia Earhart, among others.

Paul Simpson's gruff voice rang out across the television studio newsroom, easily cutting through all the background noise of conversations, typewriters, and people wheeling cameras into place.

"Macht, get to the Capitol now. Take Kraft with you. Some huge ruckus with the Mercury 13." The editor Paul Simpson always called her 'Macht', never 'Veronica' or 'Ronnie,' or 'Miss Macht.' Just 'Macht', same as he addressed all the guys by their last names.

Macht waved in acknowledgement from her desk and he retreated into his office. Simpson didn't waste words. Besides, her camera operator Sharon Kraft and Macht knew that he knew all about the women trying to get into NASA's astronaut training program.

But... huge ruckus? Evidently something had happened.

"Oooo, deploying the Rockettes." The newest hire—still a snot-nosed kid despite an alleged quarter-century behind him—smirked at his own cleverness as Macht went by.

He tried too hard. The other men all rolled their eyes despite agreeing with him. They'd already coined the label. The rest of the newsroom called Kraft and Macht the Red Space Rockettes. They sneered—to their faces, not behind their backs—that they were partners because no one else would deign to work with a woman.

Macht wagged her middle finger at them as she went by.

They could snicker and scoff all they wanted. Macht and Kraft didn't care; they always said they'd laugh all the way to their Emmy. Simpson had three Pulitzers from before he'd switched over from print, and they intended to earn the tv journalism equivalent. In his own way, he backed the pair and they took full advantage.

Macht found Kraft in the tech room checking supplies and cleaning up her camera. Meticulous, she perpetually battled weather as well as wear and tear on the equipment.

"We're up. Mercury 13 hearing this morning. Simpson wants us to get there now. Something's going on."

"Good." Kraft flashed a pirate's smile. "I hope the flygirls trounce 'em. And we'll be there to see." Her tone grew solemn, matching the sudden seriousness in her eyes. "They aren't going to win this in Congress. They'll need something more."

Macht agreed, but Kraft already knew that. She and her camerawoman may not be aspiring astronauts, but no one wanted women reporting the news either. Even though Simpson often tried to hide it, he was exceptional in that respect: He backed them, and they appreciated it.

Their working together likely saved Simpson from a ton of complaints. It also saved them a ton of aggravation. Drop-dead gorgeous Kraft couldn't hide her amazing looks and voluptuous—yet somehow still athletic—curves no matter what. She lived in oversized sweats (lighter fabric ones in summer), kept her dark red hair in a messy ponytail (i.e., gorgeous cascading fiery tresses) hanging out the back of a Pittsburgh Pirates baseball cap, wore no make-up (not that her immaculate alabaster skin needed it), and concealed glorious sky-blue eyes behind dark sunglasses she often wore even inside. Men still hit on her nonstop. So did the occasional woman.

At 6'0" even, Macht stood a smidge shorter than her partner, and kept her lighter red hair chopped short. She was a field reporter, not some news anchor worried about a chic, stylish coif. No supermodel by any stretch, she didn't hurt anyone's eyes either. And copper hair with her height stood out regardless. Much to her guilty chagrin, she liked working with Kraft as much because the camerawoman drew all attention away from her as because Kraft was a great person and incredibly talented behind the lens.

A quick drive to the Capitol later, the pair exchanged astounded glances at the scene that awaited them.

Kraft immediately raised the camera to her shoulder and began panning the crowd. "WASPs," she murmured. "A friend of my uncle was a WASP." At Macht's questioning look, Kraft added, "The Women Airforce Service Pilots. They ferried military planes during WWII."

Other news reporters were just beginning to arrive. Kraft quickly claimed a prime spot that would give her a good view of the building and the park across from it and continued to film.

What a crowd! Hundreds of women in flight suits—not dresses or skirts and pumps and sharp jackets—filled the area at the base of the Capitol steps.

Mostly in their forties and fifties, the women wore their flight suits and work shoes or boots. Hundreds of women, maybe even more than a thousand—almost all of them? Just under 1,100 had served—who had flown military aircraft in WWII. The crowd across the street behind them included women and men, girls and boys of all ages. Clearly the women had brought family and friends, as had a whole bunch of members of the Ninety-Nines.

Kraft signaled Macht with a nod when she'd gotten enough background footage. She followed Macht as they threaded their way closer to the Capitol stairs. Macht got statements from several congressmen as they entered, basically all variations on, "We admire the little ladies; no further comment."

A silver-blue sedan pulled up, with Jerrie Cobb, Jane Hart, and Wally Funk getting out. Roaring with cheers and applause, the crowd parted to allow them to climb the steps and make their way inside. Not that Macht needed confirmation, but she glanced at Kraft to make sure she was getting all this.

Of course she was.

Macht had already interviewed the Mercury 13 in depth; She could wait this time and catch them coming out. Instead, she talked with a few of the WASPs and several people on the street to gauge their mindset.

Then a midnight-blue limo pulled up. The passenger didn't wait for the driver to come around. The door opened and Jacqueline Cochran stepped out of the vehicle. Lt. Colonel Jacqueline Cochran, in uniform—dress blues, of course—and wearing all her medals.

All on film thanks to Kraft's prime location and height.

After catching Kraft's eye—no cameras allowed in the chamber; she and Macht would meet up afterward—Macht slid into Cochran's wake and followed her inside to take notes on what transpired. That way she could reference it in their ongoing coverage.

Macht recognized the rest of the Mercury 13 in the gallery, sitting not far from her and the other members of the press. They exchanged friendly encouraging waves.

That the hearing went precisely as she'd expected didn't lessen her disgust. She slipped out as they were wrapping up so she could catch up with Kraft before the session adjourned and the participants came back outside. They wouldn't announce any results for at least a day or two.

Panning over the crowd, Kraft continued to film, getting tons of great footage. Behind the WASPs, tens of thousands more people filled the plaza and the park across the street. Finally getting wind of the demonstration, even more press had shown up while Macht was inside. She and Kraft struggled amidst the shifting sea of bodies to keep their prime location.

Macht tapped Kraft's shoulder, and she swung around to face the Capitol.

As the pair watched the top of the Capitol twin staircases, Cochran, Cobb and Hart emerged, with the rest of the Mercury 13 right behind them. In tandem, they started down the broad left staircase. Whatever their former relationship, no matter her previous stance, Cochran made it clear that she now stood with the Mercury 13 as she now, literally, stood with them at the base of the Capitol steps.

Cobb touched Cochran's arm. "See the two redheads over there? They're good. They'll air what we actually say; no sketchy editing. No stupid questions like whether or not we cry a lot, or are we positive women can actually fly."

The women pilots maneuvered toward the reporter and camerawoman, who saw them coming and helped close the gap.

Cochran clearly had her quote ready. "Our esteemed congressmen expressed some concerns," Cochran said, "But we are confident that when they have time to reflect, they will conclude that women and men must soar into the future together."

'Soar Into the Future Together' headlined almost every major newspaper and led nearly every television news broadcast that evening.

The next morning, pounding on her hotel room door woke Cobb. She rolled over in bed, her hand flailing for her wristwatch on the nightstand and not locating it until she'd found the light switch on the lamp.

She squinted at her wristwatch.

5:13 a. m..

Three more sharp, loud raps on the door. Who the hell could possibly be out there before the crack of dawn? Something had to be seriously wrong.

Shifting, Swirling HERitage

Heart lurching in her chest, Cobb scrambled out of bed. She slept in pajama bottoms and a big tee shirt, so she didn't bother grabbing a robe as she stumbled to the door.

Cobb yanked the door open and stared in utter confusion. The reporter? With her partner? With the camera? Macht and Kraft?

Huh?

Clutching the door with one hand, Cobb blinked and rubbed her eyes with the other. Irritation began to mingle with the bewilderment. "Are you crazy? What are you doing here?"

Absolutely beaming with barely-contained ecstasy, the reporter simply held up the morning edition of the *Washington Post*.

WOMEN ASTRONAUTS

Two huge words emblazoned across the paper right below the masthead on page one.

The subhead below that in letters half the size:

CONGRESS APPROVES NASA PROGRAM.

Tears welled in her eyes and a scream rose in her throat. Cobb clamped her hands over her mouth to stifle it, then snatched the newspaper as if it would suddenly vanish into thin air. Forgetting to breathe, she skimmed the article. 'Congress announced the approval... Lady Astronauts Program... The Mercury 13 will be officially added... Thanks to an assist from Lt. Col. Jacqueline Cochran and her legendary WASPs...'

A horrible thought struck Cobb. "If this is some kind of sick joke..."

"What? No!" The reporter burst out laughing. She waved a thumb at her camerawoman. "Her cousin works for the paper. Got us this copy literally hot off the press. Woke her half an hour ago; she came and got me, and here we are. Any comments for on camera? You have twenty minutes for us to make the morning news broadcast."

Cobb's brain kicked into gear. "It'll take me one to get dressed. Those rooms, the very next ones, six on either side," she pointed down the hotel corridor, which her room was at the end of, "get the others."

The Mercury 13

Cobb pulled on her most presentable blouse and trousers and ran a brush through her hair. Then she joined Macht knocking on doors, replacing Kraft who went and shifted around the hotel room so that two chairs sat in front of the window. She left the drapes pulled shut to prevent any reflection from the glass.

Eighteen minutes later, Macht and Kraft had film and quotes from all of them. Lastly, Kraft used a 35 mm to get a group shot of the thirteen together. She promised them copies.

With 100 seconds to spare, the two intrepid newswomen raced off, leaving the Mercury 13 standing looking at each other in Cobb's hotel room.

Hart stated the obvious, "This was the first battle. Still going to be a long war." Still, her beaming smile glowed as brightly as everyone else's.

"Exactly." Cobb hugged her. "But victory is victory, and we'll take each one we can get. Gotta start somewhere."

Riding a wave of triumph, Macht and Kraft roared into the mostly-empty WWDC newsroom. While Kraft went to do a quick edit of the footage, Macht found Simpson already in his office.

"We've got a scoop! Sharon's setting the footage now."

He looked caught off guard at her explosive entrance. "I didn't send you on any story," he said pointedly, the lines in his face deepening. He ran his hands through his curly dark hair, then leaned back in his chair and folded his arms. "We go live in five."

She tossed a second copy of the newspaper on his desk. "Congress approved the women astronauts. We have interviews with the Mercury 13."

One brow climbed high on his forehead, way high. "You interviewed them? At five in the morning?"

"All thirteen." She sounded smug, she knew, but didn't regret it. Usually she tried to avoid it—but not in this particular instance.

"Let's see it." He pushed to his feet. "It's not the lead story, but maybe the second or third."

Macht watched Simpson watching their story and saw the tiniest trace of a smile playing about his lips. Then his mouth tightened and he gave her a solemn look.

Her jubilation plummeted as Simpson removed his glasses and rubbed his eyes, a stalling tactic she'd observed from him before.

His next words made her stomach roil. "I've been told to back off anything with the Mercury 13."

"What? Why?" her jaw dropped. "By whom?"

"Some people want them to fade away."

"I don't understand. Why?" she repeated. "Who?"

"There are still a lot of people who don't like women doing men's jobs."

She glared at him, barely believing her own ears. When he just stood there, eyes unfocused and clearly deep in thought, she finally couldn't stand the silence any longer.

"What are you going to do?" Macht demanded.

He held her gaze but still didn't reply for a long moment. Then he heaved a huge fatalistic sigh. "If we cover the story, hopefully others will as well. And if not, well, the *Washington Post* is good company to go down in flames with."

"Is there really that much opposition?"

Simpson just gave her a look, and she realized how naïve the question sounded. She knew how everyone else in the newsroom—everyone but Simpson—treated her and Kraft. Suddenly she could only imagine what the women astronauts dealt with every day.

"But you'll air the story?"

"Oh, yeah. My daughter loves to watch you Red Space Rockettes in action. And she's totally over the moon for the Mercury 13. But even if that weren't the case," he said, "Everyone needs to see you all in action."

Back in her NASA office two days later, Cobb gleefully regarded the collection of newspapers someone had stacked on her desk. She could guess which intern had gathered them for her and resolved not to forget to thank them.

The Mercury 13

A week later, training began. Not surprisingly in the least, most of the men wanted nothing to do with them. But Dr. Lovelace (former military himself) and Gen. Flickinger (also an MD) ran interference, reminding their fellow astronauts that the woman had qualified by passing the exact same tests.

Cobb overheard one grumbled exchange that the Mercury 13 weren't military pilots, and the tart reply that not all the men had degrees. If NASA could waive requirements for the men, the women deserved no less consideration.

The second official astronaut group, announced August 1962, ended up including seven of the women and nine men, not all military test pilots this time. Public interest continued to grow, and with it government support and—most importantly—funding. Notably, NASA was drifting ever-so-slowly but unmistakably away from the Pentagon and building closer ties with scientific institutions.

Alan Shepard had already flown; so had Gus Grissom. Next up: John Glenn, then Scott Carpenter. All the while, the USSR and a woman named Valentina Tereshkova loomed over them. Thus far, despite training toe-to-toe with the men, none of the Mercury women were scheduled yet for a flight. Cobb's frustration and trepidation grew.

At a knock on her office door, Cobb looked up from the engineering specs she was reviewing.

Janey Hart stood in the doorway, an inscrutable expression on her face. "I just came from the Director's office. Dr. Roman gave me a preliminary copy of the latest flight schedule," Hart said. "I wanted to be the one to show it to you." She stepped inside and offered Cobb a thin sheaf of papers.

Cobb accepted them warily and glanced at them. Mission parameters, training specs, pilots' names.

It instantly jumped out at her. More names added to the list. Women's names! One scheduled for January 13, 1963.

Jane Hart.

Cobb leapt out of her seat, papers flying, and crushed Hart in a bear hug. "We did it! Do you realize what that means? We did it! We'll do it. And we'll send a woman into space before the Russians do!"

"I was just the tiniest bit worried you'd be mad at not going first."

"Are you nuts?" Cobb said, wounded and offended. "I mean, sure, we all wanted to go first. So I'm third. I can live with that. This, this," Cobb hugged her again, "this is fantastic! This is historic!"

"Yes, well, we're all qualified, that's for sure." Hart hesitated, mouth tight. "Dr. Roman told me how they picked me to go first," chagrin filled her voice. "All-American happily married mother of eight. Then Wally, the brash daring young flygirl. Exciting and sexy."

Cobb scoffed and rolled her eyes. "Oh, for– Like you said, we're all qualified. I don't really care what order we get to fly in." She added with a glint in her eye, "Well, yes, I do. It would have been great to go first, but 1964 will be here in no time."

On January 13, 1963, Jane Hart launched into outer space, the very first woman ever to do so. Celebrations erupted across the country. Congratulations poured in from all over the world—even from Russia, whose own woman astronaut followed months later.

In October 1963, NASA announced the Group 3 astronauts: the remaining seven of the Mercury 13 plus two additional women, and sixteen men (eight civilian and eight military).

The countdown lasted forever and sped by at an unimaginable speed. The Titan rocket thundered and roared to life beneath Cobb and her fellow astronaut Jim Lovell. Gravity pressed her back into the seat until she felt like her heart would explode—from pure joy.

Three minutes.

Three minutes, and she would officially—finally!—be in space.

It exceeded her wildest dreams. As the gravity of Earth and then the added gravity of launch fell away, Cobb floated and gazed out the small portal at the tiny blue and white globe. She and Lovell exchanged triumphant looks.

Surreal.

Profound.

Transcendent.

The Mercury 13

Life-altering.

Communications continued with Mission Control. Their space capsule worked flawlessly. Three days later, re-entry and splashdown went off without a hitch as well.

Over a month after returning to Earth, Cobb still found herself processing the experience. The breathtaking view of their delicate blue planet from space. Floating against the vastness of deepest black, an orb without borders or any lines of demarcation.

She may have landed, but her feet still hadn't touched the ground. Cobb still found herself walking on air.

In the inaugural speech for his second term, President John F. Kennedy on January 20, 1965 reinforced his praise of and support for the space program. Standing behind him on the stage with a bunch of other dignitaries—the term only loosely applicable in her case, she'd joked; she knew Hart and Funk hadn't been able to attend—Cobb's spirits soared as President Kennedy repeated his determination to put men and women on the moon. The feeling didn't quite equal when she'd flown in space, but it came awfully close as he boldly declared they'd reach their goal before the end of his presidency, maybe even, he added with that twinkle in his eye, before the end of 1967.

Cobb's office telephone rang. It had taken NASA a year, but they'd finally gotten her one in '63, a year after the hearings. Even though it was now well into '65, this was maybe the fourth time the telephone had rung. Or not. She wasn't often in her office, normally either training or traveling instead. She might well have missed some calls.

She picked it up and balanced the handset on her shoulder as she continued perusing paperwork on the Artemis project. The revised name still elicited a satisfied grin every time she saw it, adding to her euphoria. "Hello."

"Hi, Miss Cobb. This is Veronica Macht from WWDC-tv. If you have a minute, I'd love to hear your comments on the NASA/Pentagon teaming, and potentially barring women from future astronaut service."

"What?" That couldn't be right. Cobb put down the papers and gripped the phone as if it had attacked her.

What was Macht talking about? After a—yes, epic—battle, NASA had included women astronauts since 1962. It had sent three women into orbit, with Cobb the last one in December 1964. Now in 1965, Gemini was flourishing, and still-preliminary plans nevertheless were proceeding at full speed to put people on the moon. Why would anyone think women were about to be barred again from participating?

"You didn't know," Macht stated flatly. "I'm sorry to spring it on you. Then again, maybe not. I'm glad you know now. What are you going to do? That I can quote you on."

"That can't be right. I haven't heard a thing." Head spinning, Cobb struggled to gather her thoughts. "Why would you ask that?"

The silence on the other end of the line stretched. Apparently finally reaching a verdict, Macht spoke quickly. "Listen, we're sure. Sharon has a cousin in the Pentagon. The information is not classified, but they aren't doing press releases or interviews on it either. So please do not tell anyone how you know."

"Let me call you back in an hour. Or, Macht, do you want me to call someone else first? So this doesn't trace back to you."

Another contemplative pause, then Macht said, "No, you can call me. In fact that's better." Cobb could hear the rakish grin in the other woman's voice as Macht continued, "Then I can honestly say that you called me. People will remember we have a professional relationship. They won't think anything of it."

"An hour then." Cobb put down the phone and stared at the far wall, mind whirling.

Now what? What could she do? Had decisions been made, or were they still pending?

What would be more effective? Talking up the program's successes so they'd look foolish canceling it, or pointing out the flaws and total lack of logic in their 'reasoning' and shaming them out of canceling it? Did they even have any shame?

Did she need an all-out publicity assault, or to work behind the scenes? Did she even still have any pull behind the scenes? Had they not told her because she did, or because she didn't?

Cobb's thoughts kept circling back to her conviction that absolutely no rational justification existed for barring women from the space program.

NASA had, almost by itself, revolutionized science not just in the US but across the world. It had severed the previously unavoidable link between science and the military-industrial complex. Technological advances no longer applied automatically—or solely—to weaponry. Communications and transportation, medicine and entertainment, manufacturing and infrastructure—practically every aspect of life, they all benefitted from progress made thanks to the space program.

Especially education. Little girls flocked to the sciences in record numbers. People—some well-meaning, others not so much—no longer discouraged them. They couldn't insist that 'girls can't do that; it's too tough.' Little girls knew better. They recognized the names not just of Jane Hart and Wally Funk (and yes, Jerrie Cobb), but also of Dr. Nancy Roman, Katherine Johnson, Margaret Hamilton, Dr. Dana Ulery, and Pearl Young, who'd retired amidst great fanfare in '61.

With the potential talent pool doubled, science flourished in the US. Other countries saw this and emulated it. Scientific advances accelerated exponentially. The ripple effect touched the entire globe, and not just the US and Europe. Attitudes in lesser-developed countries gradually shifted as well, improving conditions for all, but especially for women demanding to be seen as more than property.

Cobbs rage and frustration grew in tandem with her brainstorming.

Should she have seen this coming? Perhaps not exactly, but it didn't surprise her either. Just look at what had happened to the women who'd comprised the massive workforce during WWII that had enabled the US to help win the war. Sent home with nary a thanks once the country no longer needed them. The women drivers, and welders, and riveters—even the WASPs.

WASPs. Cochran.

Cobb reached for the phone. She and Cochran hadn't become friends by any stretch, but they respected each other. If anyone could navigate behind the scenes, Cochran could. With her fame and money, she maintained powerful friends among the most elite of the elite, the very highest of the upper crust.

Cochran, it turned out, had heard a few faint rumblings but not enough to have given her any real cause for concern. Cobb filled her in on what she'd just learned without saying how.

"I'm at a loss as to how to best fight this," Cobb admitted. "Public or private or both? Emphasize positive or negative?"

"Definitely both," Cochran's voice crackled in her ear, yet Cobb still heard Cochran's certainty and boundless confidence clear as a bell. "Always praise in public; always criticize in private," Cochran declared. "There are people I can get in touch with, people in government, and industry, and the military—and academia. I'll contact them and have friends contact them and others as well. Quietly. Phone calls and letters."

"Much appreciated." Cobb put the phone back in its cradle.

She pondered Cochran's words as she debated how best to proceed. What could she leverage to best highlight the worth of the entire program?

A plan slowly took form.

It took nearly the whole hour, but she called the rest of the original 13 and gave them a quick rundown of her conversations with Macht and Cochran. They agreed to do everything possible to head off the catastrophe, not just talking to reporters but visiting as many schools as they could.

Not happy by any means, but more than a little relieved that they least were taking action, Cobb called the reporter back.

To Macht's credit, she quickly grasped the gist of the message Cobb wanted to convey. Cobb noted that the announcement about the Artemis 13 crew—for the third crewed moon landing—hadn't gotten much press after its release. Of course that wasn't planned until 1969, over three years away. Reporters were concentrating quite understandably on Artemis 11, now scheduled to land men on the moon in July 1967.

Cobb still bristled at the all-male crew, but at least the Artemis 12 crew included a woman. Artemis 13 also included a woman: Geraldyn Cobb.

Assuming she hadn't lost her job by then.

Macht listened dutifully, and Cobb heard the scratch of a pencil on paper, indicating that the other woman wasn't just listening but taking notes as well.

Of course Macht wasn't about to forget the original purpose of her call. Cobb didn't expect her to—or want her to.

Macht again broached the subject of women possibly losing their place in the astronaut corps, and of NASA's closer ties to the DoD.

This time Cobb knew how to respond.

Cobb lauded the military for their vital, invaluable work and for their sacrifice and dedication. After expressing her immense—and sincere—admiration for them, she segued.

"Of course NASA's mission is very different. It benefits the military without being military itself. I can only imagine that your information is either mistaken, or perhaps simply exaggerated. Perhaps someone overcome by false nostalgia and wishing for their idea of the 'good old days'—and forgetting that those days included the likes of Rosie the Riveter, not to mention Col. Cochran and the WASPs she led. Plus astronauts train for so many years ahead of the actual mission, NASA would cripple its operational readiness if it lost a full third of its astronauts."

"Can you meet me and say that on camera?"

Cobb felt her gut twist. Either this risk would pay off big-time, or she'd get herself grounded completely, if not outright fired. Then again, it she were already on her way out, she wasn't about to go quietly.

"You do mean today, right?" Cobb asked.

"In two hours?" Macht replied.

"Gee, I'm already going to be having lunch at La Osteria in two hours."

Macht instantly took the hint. "The one on the river?"

"Right. So we'll have to schedule our meeting for, say, two or three weeks from now after I run it through official channels."

"Sounds like a plan."

The phone clicked in Cobb's ear as Macht hung up.

Too bad Cochran was in California. If only she could have come as well. Now Cobb needed to think of someone she could drag to lunch with her at the fairly expensive Italian restaurant. Joan Walsh, one of the secretaries, was a friend whom Cobb owed lunch. Problem solved.

Cobb didn't spot the reporter anywhere in the vicinity, so she and her friend Joan went inside. They still needed to eat, after all. Seated near a window, Cobb tried not to make it too obvious that she kept looking outside.

Her anxiety increased until, halfway through the main course, she spotted the pair of newswomen across the street. Making it plain she'd wait, Macht waved and sat down on a bench in the shade. Kraft strolled around, camera on her shoulder. Cobb wondered if the woman were really filming or not.

Worries assuaged, Cobb enjoyed the delicious tiramisu. Standing, she made a show of counting out bills to leave on the table for the check, then made her leisurely way to the door. Macht and Kraft waited outside.

"Miss Cobb, how are you?" Macht called. "Do you happen to have a few minutes to spare?"

"Come on, you know the routine," Cobb said sternly.

"I know, I know, but when I saw you, well, I just can't pass up the opportunity. Just a minute or two. Please?"

Cobb admired her deft questions—and her acting skill. Macht covered all the easy stuff first, and the more Cobb thought about it, the happier she was that her secretary friend was along. The young woman could confirm the happenstance nature of the meeting and the casual questions.

When Macht broached the question about the Pentagon, Cobb feigned surprise and exchanged a shocked look with her friend. Always insightful, Joan played along without overdoing it. If Joan suspected—and Cobb didn't doubt for a moment that the tiny (short and slim) young brunette knew perfectly well what had happened—she gave no indication she thought the meeting was anything more than coincidence.

"Oh, that can't be–" Cobb repeated her response from over the phone, not verbatim but imparting the same information.

Joan snorted for emphasis and gave a knowing nod at the part about planning years in advance, muttering under her breath about doing all the paperwork for it.

"Thanks for your time." Macht and Kraft shook hands with both of them. "Really appreciate it. Not sure when this'll air, but I can let you know."

"Great."

Joan chuckled at their retreating backs. "What a coincidence."

"I know, right?" Cobb agreed innocently.

Neither ever mentioned it again.

For a second time, the renewed swell of publicity—not to mention Cochran's efforts, no doubt—ensured the women astronauts kept the rightful place they'd worked so hard to earn.

From that point on, Cobb kept a much more attentive ear to the ground. She still heard occasional rumblings but for the time being, the issue seemed to have subsided—again. Still she could never fully trust that it wouldn't ever resurface.

Cobb loved the control room with its rows and rows of instrument panels. The only thing she loved more was sitting in the actual cockpit atop a rocket. The entire room positively vibrated with activity.

After all, in just twenty-four hours, three astronauts would be on their way to the moon. Not just to the moon. To land on the moon.

Janet Dietrich and two fellow astronauts had orbited the moon months ago, the final check—a dress rehearsal, as it were—of all the equipment. Not this time. This time, Neil Armstrong, Buzz Aldrin, and Mike Collins were going all the way to the moon.

Armstrong and Aldrin would walk on the lunar surface.

Alarm bells sounded, and a number of people grabbed for their phones. People rushed about, with security personnel racing in and making a beeline for the director at the front of the control center.

Word spread like wildfire even as someone silenced the alarms.

There'd been a bizarre accident in the parking lot. A driver had lost control of his vehicle and slammed the automobile into a pedestrian.

That pedestrian was Neil Armstrong, now with a compound fracture of his left leg and on his way to the emergency room.

Cobb could barely fathom the turn of events.

How was something like that even possible? Especially right before Armstrong was about to go into pre-launch quarantine. She felt flabbergasted and furious on his behalf. To be so close and be the victim of a fluke accident! Cobb couldn't even imagine the depth of his bitterness.

News spread and the entire space center knew what had happened even as the ambulance left the compound which was still filled with equal parts relief and excruciating anxiety. After a few moments, Cobb realized all eyes in the control room were locked on her. An instant later, it dawned on her why.

She was Armstrong's backup on Artemis 13.

Then Cobb saw the director and two senior scientists huddling in one corner of the room. Alarms blared in Cobb's head and she rushed over to them, catching the words 'cancel' and 'reschedule' as she approached. Her blood froze but she didn't hesitate. Especially now so close to their goal, they couldn't fail.

"No." Cobb interrupted them without compunction.

She didn't raise her voice, yet it rang with conviction.

"No."

They looked at her with great sadness but she forged ahead. "No, no, no. *Cancelling is not an option.* And I'm not saying that just because I want to fly. I promise you I would say the exact same thing regardless.

"All of us, everyone in this room," Cobb waved an arm to include the dozens of scientists at their posts, "plus all the other astronauts, all the staff not in this room, the managers, the clerks, everyone. We have worked way too hard to trash this opportunity. You have worked way too hard. We cannot throw it away. This is exactly why every system is redundant and why we train backups.

"Artemis 13 has to launch. It has to, or we risk all of NASA's accomplishments."

The Mercury 13

Cobb's pulse thundered in her ears. A deafening silence filled the whole room. No one moved. People barely breathed.

She had stated the obvious, things they already knew as well as she, yet which clearly required driving home at the moment.

Not to mention one aspect—equally obvious—that hung unspoken yet dominant in the air between them. She believed without the slightest doubt—no, she knew—that their hesitation would have been fleeting if not for one fact glaring them in the face.

Horror of horrors. Absolute travesty. Complete nightmare scenario.

The backup was a woman.

They desperately wanted to avoid sending a woman. They could, even after seven successful years, still barely conceive of women astronauts. Put one on the moon? Impossible.

Yet not doing so made not just every women astronaut look bad, it made NASA look utterly foolish. All the money and hours of training invested, how could NASA now turn around and say a woman was unqualified? Not to mention, Russia would love the whole fiasco and redouble their own efforts.

A brand new intern, barely into his twenties and looking as if he'd rather be anywhere else on the entire planet, approached and addressed the director. "Sir, President Kennedy is on the line for you."

Cobb crawled into the cockpit and strapped herself into the launch couch aboard Artemis 13. NASA Mission Control sounded in her ear, and she responded on cue, matching her words to checking all the instrumentation.

Aldrin and Collins followed her lead, taking their positions in the spacecraft and doing their portions of the preflight checks.

Green across the board. All systems go without a single glitch—aside from the fact that Neil Armstrong, one leg cast from hip to toes, watched from his hospital bed.

Jerrie Cobb sat in the cockpit.

Time ticked away. Acknowledgement after acknowledgement came from the astronauts and their coworkers in mission control. The crew capsule tremored with the power of the Saturn rocket it perched on.

The countdown hit zero.

The rocket roared to life.

The moorings fell away, and Artemis 13 rose majestically into the air, gathering speed and altitude with each passing second. Arching gracefully through the crystalline azure sky, the rocket climbed higher and higher.

The rocket passed the atmospheric threshold, and Cobb peered out the tiny window into a sea of endless black. Every bit as majestic and awe-inspiring as her first flight into space.

Four days later, on July 13, 1967, Cobb stepped out of the lunar lander and onto the silver surface of Earth's closest companion in space. Her boot stirred a tiny cloud of gray dust. She glanced back at the lander, then up at the crescent Earth above the horizon.

Magnificent.

"Wow," Cobb uttered the first words to cross her mind. "What a tiny step, but what a huge leap for humanity."

Five days later, the trio of astronauts splashed down to a hero's welcome on Earth. Twenty-five days after landing—the quarantine precautions and medical exams all concluded—the astronauts were finally able to participate in all the festivities.

"Macht, is Kraft here yet?" Simpson's voice rang out over the newsroom, one that now echoed with keyboard clicks instead of the metallic clanks of typewriter keys.

The Mercury 13

Macht glanced up from her computer at her boss. His hair now completely iron gray, and with even deeper lines in his face, Simpson looked fifty. Considering he'd just hit his sixty-seventh birthday, Macht hoped she looked as good at his age. Ageless Kraft definitely would.

"No, but any minute." She got up and strode to his office so he wouldn't shout across the newsroom. "What's up?"

"We just got confirmation from NASA. Dr. Ride will meet with you today, but they asked if you can make it at 10 instead of at 1. I told them 'no problem'."

"Great, thanks."

A thrill of anticipation coursed through her. She and Kraft had covered NASA since the sixties, for more than twenty years now. They'd long since outlasted their 'Red Space Rockettes' moniker, transitioning to the unofficial and then official science reporters. They covered every branch of science, but NASA remained her favorite.

She still followed the careers of the original Mercury thirteen, most of whom had moved on to management positions at NASA or retired to take jobs in private industry—or simply retired. A whole new batch of astronauts now followed in their footsteps.

Macht couldn't wait to sit down with Dr. Sally Ride, the astronaut who would be the first person to command the international moon base about to go fully operational with a staff of thirteen from five different countries. According to plan, from December 13, 1985 onward, the lunar installation would always have a full crew in place in staggered six-month rotations. The number of personnel would increase over the years as preparations for the Mars Mission grew more intense.

Macht still thought of it as Simpson's office. She knew she always would. He'd retired seven years ago at the age of seventy, and now sent her postcards from his travels all over the world. She had a desk drawer full of them. Now she ran the whole newsroom, and Kraft produced all the segments.

Still as drop-dead gorgeous as over thirty years ago, Sharon Kraft came and leaned on the doorjamb. "You going to come meet her?"

"Of course," Macht shot her a look. "What kind of question is that?"

Kraft laughed. "A rhetorical one, basically." They both still loved NASA. Thanks to their longstanding contacts, they'd been able to secure this particular interview before anyone else. No way would Macht miss it, although she was more than happy to let the much younger on-air talent conduct the actual interview.

They expected General (retired, USAF) Eileen Collins at the station any time now. Only forty but a long-time veteran of both the US Air Force and the astronaut corps, Gen. Collins would lead the first crewed mission to Mars. Launching on January 13, 1996, their journey would last five months. They'd remain on Mars' surface for two, in the habitats that had been sent ahead for them, then embark on the five-month return voyage landing them back on Earth in January 1997.

From orbit to the moon to Mars.

The Mercury 13 would be proud. And Macht had it on good authority that they all would attend the launch.

The Mercury 13

Author's Notes:

As of March 2024, ninety-three women from eighteen countries have flown in space, including—at long last, in 2021—Mary Wallace "Wally" Funk of the Mercury 13. Five hundred fifty-five men from forty-seven countries have flown.

On June 6, 2007, Representative Steve Kagen [D-WI-8] introduced **H. RES. 421**—Honoring the trailblazing accomplishments of the "Mercury 13" women, whose efforts in the early 1960s demonstrated the capabilities of American women to undertake the human exploration of space. Three representatives co-sponsored the Resolution. One additional sponsor later signed on.

The nonbinding resolution only required committee approval and passed.

On July 17, 2023, Representative Chrissy Houlahan (D-PA-6) introduced **H.R. 4682** - Mercury 13 Congressional Gold Medal Act. Eleven representatives co-sponsored the Act. Eleven additional sponsors later signed on. The summary of the Bill reads: To award a Congressional Gold Medal to the Mercury 13, in recognition of their historic accomplishments and their work for gender equity, and in recognition of their important example of women in STEM fields.

The bill requires committee approval and then a congressional vote. If passed, it becomes law.

Ostraka

Dana Fredsti

Hypatia

"LADY, YOUR LIFE IS IN DANGER."

I'm sitting on a bench in the agora, snacking on olives, almonds, and cubes of creamy goat cheese purchased from one of the vendors in the open-air market. I wash my feast down with Cretan wine from another seller. The afternoon is balmy, a cool breeze blowing in from the sea. I can see the top of the lighthouse from my vantage point and think I might walk over there. My charioteer, currently flirting with the merchant at the wine stall, can meet me there.

And then a hand tugs timidly on my arm accompanied by the ominous warning.

I look down to see a young girl of about fifteen staring up at me with sky-blue eyes framed with a thick fringe of lashes. Hair the shade of dark honey is pulled back from her face by a simple band, curls falling midway down her back. A simple style that accents an undeniable beauty. She wears a pale blue silk chiton, cloak of a darker blue silk covering her arms.

Her name is Zoe and her brother Jason is one of my students. She often accompanies him to my lectures on philosophy and astronomy at the *Mouseion*, sitting quietly off to one side by herself. She wants to learn and she listens, her attention always focused on me. Had I not worried that it might cause her problems—the fact she was there in the first place was unusual—I would have provided her with a wooden slate, wax, and a stylus. Of course, I didn't know if she knew how to read or write. These skills are not common or encouraged amongst women in Alexandria.

Neither is journeying out of their homes without accompaniment from a male family member. And with her father no longer living…

I glance around the plaza and see Jason near the wine vendor's stall, cup of wine in hand, deep in conversation with several other young gentlemen. They're congregated at the base of one of the many marble statues in our city, this one the depiction of an athletic young man, the ideal of Grecian manhood. Jason is standing in an unconscious imitation of the statue's pose—while a good student, he does have a high opinion of himself. Zoe must have slipped away from the group. Well, he could not be angry with her for speaking with me.

"Why do you worry about this, child?" I ask.

"The *parabalani*. I've heard…" She paused briefly as if choosing her words carefully. "There are rumors."

Parabalani. A funny word. It means 'those who risk their lives as nurses.' Perhaps that had been the truth at one time, but now the *parabalani* are used as attack dogs by the patriarchs of Alexandria, most notably Bishop Cyril. The good bishop does not approve of my status as a scholar and scientist, and deeply resents the friendship and respect I've garnered from academics and nobles alike. My astrolabes, for instance, are much sought after and this does not please him. He fears educated women and—dispensing with false modesty—I imagine I'm his worst nightmare in this regard. I was not only educated by my father Theon, a famous scientist and astronomer, but the only woman to attend and then teach at the *Mouseion*. I am also a renowned astronomer and mathematician in my own right.

On his own, Cyril is a weak man. With the backing of the *parabalani*, he has more power than he deserves. And without the Bishop, I imagine the *parabalani* would be undirected and impotent. Ignorant and misguided, they need a leader to help them focus their malice.

The combination is undeniably dangerous.

But I cannot believe they would act against me—not when I have the ear of Orestes, Augustal Prefect of Alexandria, and the love of the people. Still...

"I thank you for your words of caution," I say, placing a reassuring hand on Zoe's shoulder.

"Mistress Hypatia..." Zoe's tone is not reassured, nor is her expression. "I *heard* them. My...my uncle Calix and his friends." This last emerges in a rush of words.

Calix, a former student of mine, had been trouble even before he became a fanatical sheep following a shepherd filled with ignorance, envy, and spite. He had left the school and joined the *parabalani* after I'd refused his suit. He had not been dissuaded easily and I had, by necessity, resorted to a public rejection which turned his supposed love into hate. He would not forgive me in this lifetime.

"They say you're a witch and a...a slut." She looks mortified. "I'm sorry, my lady."

"I've heard worse," I assure her. "And no doubt will continue to hear these things as long as the Bishop and his hounds roam Alexandria. So I must have a thick skin."

I smile, hoping Zoe will smile back.

She does not.

"You don't understand," she says with a flash of anger. "They mean to flay the skin from your body, my lady. While you are still alive. No matter how thick your skin might be."

As her words sink in, I feel cold despite the warm breeze. Even though I do not believe the Bishop or his dogs would dare do anything so horrific, the thought is enough to chill me.

"I will be vigilant," I promise Zoe, scraping up what I hope is a serene smile.

"Is my sister bothering you, my lady?"

Jason, Zoe's brother, has joined us. He's pleasant enough—just entitled and arrogant as is often the case with young, handsome, and wealthy men.

"Zoe, you know better than to go off on your own." His tone is jovial if somewhat forced, and it's obvious that he is not pleased with Zoe. Her cheeks redden and she casts her gaze down.

"Not at all," I hasten to reply, adding, "I have been enjoying our conversation."

I draw Jason into a conversation about a recent lecture of mine on Euclid's *Elements* to distract him from his annoyance with Zoe, who fades quietly into the background as we talk. I give her one last smile and turn my attention to her brother.

Zoe

I can tell Lady Hypatia doesn't take my warning seriously. The *parabalani* are always going on about something, after all, and it is no secret that Bishop Cyril would be happy if she were to up and vanish. But what she doesn't understand is that the rumblings and rumors going around Alexandria are more than the idle boasting of drunks in a taverna. No, I had overheard our Uncle Calix talk to his fellow *parabalani* about their plans for Hypatia less than a quarter of an hour ago.

Bored while waiting for Jason to finish yet another self-important conversation with his friends—I love my brother, but he truly adores the sound of his own voice almost as much as he loves Cretan wine—I had slipped away to look at wares in some of the nearby booths. As long as I stayed within shouting distance, he wouldn't tell Mother that I didn't strictly obey the rules.

I was perusing jeweled hair ornaments when I heard a familiar voice coming from the other side of the fabric wall that backed the stall. The hairs rose on the back of my neck when I recognized my uncle's voice.

Both Mother and Jason have bade me not to be alone with Calix, and I am happy to obey this particular stricture. The way Calix looks at me when he thinks he is unobserved makes my skin crawl. And while I don't know what had happened between brother and sister when they were younger, I see how he looks at Mother as well, especially since Father died last year. Luckily, he is an infrequent visitor to our house—Jason does not tolerate the poison that falls from his tongue regarding Lady Hypatia, and Calix is either unable or unwilling to talk about much else.

And had my brother heard the words that passed Calix's lips this afternoon, I think he would have killed him on the spot.

I don't know if our uncle has passed beyond sanity or is truly evil, but what they plan to do to her is beyond cruel, and it is clear from the conversation I overheard that Calix is the author of this plot. And when I saw Lady Hypatia enter the agora, I knew I had to warn her.

I watch now as she talks to Jason. Dressed in a plain chiton and philosopher's cloak of undyed linen, she is beautiful in ways that transcend the physical, although Lady Hypatia is thought to be one of the most beautiful women in Alexandria. She has no husband, although many men—my brother included—would be her suitor if she would have them. Some of those men she rejected were disappointed yet respected her decision.

Others are not so understanding—Calix, before joining the Bishop's wolf pack, was one of these. He pestered my lady with his unwanted attentions until she presented him with cloth stained with her monthly blood, claiming that it was *that* which he desired, not her. He never forgave her the humiliation, and Jason opined that this was what had driven him to join the monkish *parabalani*.

Bidding Jason farewell, Lady Hypatia makes her way through the agora. I see how faces light up when she passes by. She is truly loved by the people of Alexandria. Maybe with such support and adoration behind her, she will indeed be safe from Bishop Cyril and his thugs.

As she leaves the marketplace and heads toward the Great Harbor, however, I see Calix and several of his brothers peel away from the crowds and follow her, like stealthy hunters tracking prey. My breath catches in my throat as Calix glances back over his shoulder and looks me straight in the eyes. He smiles and it promises nothing good for Lady Hypatia.

Or for me.

I need to talk to Jason. I can only hope he'll listen.

Shifting, Swirling HERitage

Hypatia

Standing at the edge of the sun-dappled water at the Great Harbor, the Lighthouse of Pharos rising like a Titan on the island it is named for, I feel at peace. Not a feeling that always finds me, but today... even with the warning from Zoe, and the trouble brewing between the Christians and the Jews... yes, I feel at peace. Even more than that... I feel joy. A moment of pure happiness and a sense of oneness with the world. Would that I could distill this sensation and spray it like a perfume to share with those around me. Alas, I cannot. But I can try and take it into myself, remember it in my body and mind, and share it as best I can.

Perhaps that would be enough to still the hatred, at least for a while.

In the meantime, I have lecture to teach and preparation to do beforehand.

"Darius," I call. "Please take me back to the *Mouseion*."

"Yes, my lady." He bows and extends a hand. I smile in thanks and accept it. I am capable of getting in and out of a chariot on my own, but it makes Darius happy to help and my ego is not so important as to deny him that.

Zoe

Jason and his friends stare at me in a mix of horror and skepticism. After a brief pause, he asks, "You are certain you heard correctly?"

I nod vehemently. "Yes. And I saw Calix and the rest follow after Lady Hypatia when she left the agora."

"And you're sure you heard Calix mention the Serapeum."

"Yes!" There is definitely an edge to my voice and Jason frowns.

Then he replies, "I believe you."

I have never loved my brother more than I do in that moment. He almost ruins it, however, with his next words.

Turning to his friend Leon—shorter than my brother by a head but just as athletic and arrogant—Jason says, "I must fetch the Prefect and

Ostraka

his soldiers as quickly as possible. Will you lend me your steed and see Zoe safely home?"

"It would be my honor," Leon assures him, flashing me a dazzling smile. He has made no secret of his desire to court me and no doubt sees this as an opportunity to press his suit.

Jason puts his hand on my shoulders. "I will save her," he promises me. Then he dashes out of the marketplace.

I wonder how long it will take Jason to convince the Prefect that this is a genuine emergency. Yes, my brother is well acquainted with Orestes—he knew him before his rise in power and status—and hopefully his word will be good enough to instigate immediate action, but will it be quick enough to stop what Calix and the rest of the Bishop's hounds have in mind for Lady Hypatia?

"Allow me the pleasure of escorting you to your house, my lady." Leon offers me his arm with a flourish.

"Leon," I say, putting a hand on his muscular forearm. "You must help me find Lady Hypatia. We can't take a chance that Jason might reach Orestes too late to help her."

Leon eyes me worriedly. "Your brother told me to see you home. What sort of comrade would I be if I ignored his instructions?"

"And I'm asking you to help me," I reply urgently, for once meeting his gaze instead of dropping mine down demurely. If he wishes to court me, he should know who I am, not who he wants me to be or thinks I *should* be. "To help Lady Hypatia. Our uncle is filled with hatred and spite toward her," I continue. "He and the other *parabalani* will kill her. We have to let everyone," I gesture at the crowds gathered in the agora, "all the people here, know what they plan as well. The more we have on our side, the better the chance of stopping this abomination."

Whether it's the urgency in my voice or because he finds he's not a match for my own stubbornness, after a brief hesitation Leon nods. "Very well. But you must stay by my side."

I promise that I will and together we gather as many people as we can, the words "Lady Hypatia is in mortal danger" enough to gather a crowd large enough to give us a chance to stand against the *parabalani*.

Shifting, Swirling HERitage

Hypatia

When we reach the Canopic Way, Darius has to slow the horses. The street is full of pedestrians, chariots, and wagons filled with goods. The breeze has died down, and it's uncomfortably warm without the formerly swift pace of the horses. Still, I enjoy the sights and sounds of the thoroughfare. We should still arrive at the *Mouseion* in ample time for my next lecture.

No sooner has that thought crossed my mind when there is a disruption in the street and a crowd of black-robed men surround my chariot. A startled scream escapes me as one of the men seizes the horses' reins and another strikes Darius with a wooden cudgel as the horses whinny, one of them rearing up in fright. I recognize Calix immediately.

Darius falls to the ground, blood streaming from his head. I am dragged from the chariot by rough, cruel hands with no care for my clothing or my skin—nails tear gashes in my arms as strong fingers wrap around my wrists like manacles before throwing me to the pavement, knees and hands taking the brunt of the impact. The wind is driven from my lungs. I have no prior experience with this sort of violence to my person and am stunned, both physically and emotionally.

Blood running into his eyes from a gash on his forehead, Darius pushes himself up onto his elbows. "My Lady," he gasps. He is reaching for me when Calix kicks him in the ribs and swings his cudgel down onto my poor Darius's head. The sound as the wood cracks my charioteer's skull nearly causes me to vomit, but they don't give me time. I am hauled to my feet by my hair and dragged down the street by a howling, black-robed mob.

I read my fate in their expressions.

Zoe was telling the truth.

They plan to kill me.

Ostraka

Zoe

As my escort and I hurry down the Boulevard Aspendia—the quickest way to the Serapeum—more people fall in behind us, following the ever-growing crowd even if they don't all know why they're doing so. Enough of them *have* heard our words and are passing them along, outrage and indignation stamped on many faces.

A sudden uproar, the sound of men's voices raised in hateful triumph, rises above the noise of the crowd following us. It comes from the direction of the Canopic Way, the main thoroughfare of Alexandria.

And the most likely route Lady Hypatia's charioteer would take back to the *Mouseion*.

Leon and I exchange a brief look. As with Jason, I see the moment when his doubt turns into belief. We turn towards the sound, down a narrow side street that connects to the Canopic Way, now running, Leon's hand holding mine to make sure we don't get separated in the chaos. I'm grateful for his help as there are *ostraka*—"oyster shells," the nickname for the ubiquitous roofing tiles found throughout the city—scattered along the base of the buildings that line the street, but some have slipped onto the paving stones, making it difficult to navigate quickly.

In what seems like seconds, I see Calix and a mob of *parabalani* heading towards us, Calix at its head. He also is one of two who are dragging Lady Hypatia, not stopping as she stumbles on the *ostraka*, instead dragging her on her knees until she manages to regain her footing. Blood pours from her legs and arms, an expression I've never seen on her face before—terror.

No! I think.

Except I say it aloud.

Rage fills me. Yanking my hand out of Leon's and ignoring his attempt to snatch it back, I stoop and gather *ostraka*, using my cloak to hold them. Not caring that their jagged edges tear the expensive silk.

"Stop!" I cry.

Calix looks up, hand still wrapped in Hypatia's hair. "Step away, niece," he growls, an ugly smile on his face. "This is none of your affair. You would be wise to step aside. You and your schoolboy."

I can feel Leon tense up beside me. "Let Lady Hypatia go," he shouts.

"Out of my way, boy!" Spit flies from Calix's mouth.

He begins to move forward again. I can see the pain in Lady Hypatia's face as he brutally pulls her along by her hair.

"Stop!" I step forward, vibrating with fear and rage. "You will not harm her."

"Zoe," my uncle says, "this witch's fate is already determined. Yours need not be."

"You lie," I hiss. His expression tells me exactly what I can expect if this day goes as he has planned.

"It is the will of the Lord!" another of the *parabalani* shouts.

"It is the will of Cyril!" I retort, glaring at my uncle. "And the will of Calix. Who only wishes it because Lady Hypatia rejected his suit. The will of a scorned suitor and a power-mad bishop."

"Lies!" If Calix could strike me down with his eyes, I would fall senseless.

"Is it? Ask them, then!"

As if summoned, the people of Alexandria stream into the side street, following the commotion. When they see Lady Hypatia in the grasp of Calix, the rest of his mob behind him, they utter a collective roar of outrage and surge forward, a tidal wave of fury.

Calix's certainty wavers. He has misjudged the mood of the streets and the citizens of Alexandria. The realization shows clearly on his face but it does not chase away his poisonous resolve.

Suddenly, he plucks a knife from under his black robe. Jerking back Lady Hypatia's head, he lays the edge against her neck. She is quiet, so still that she might be a statue. I catch her gaze and I can tell she is afraid for me as much as she is for herself.

And that hardens my resolve.

"Calix!" I shout. He looks at me, his expression ugly with triumph as he prepares to slit her throat. And I hurl an *ostraka* at him with all of my strength. It hits him squarely in his left eye with the jagged edge of the tile. He screams as blood and white jelly ooze down his cheek, dropping his knife and releasing Lady Hypatia at the same time.

Ostraka

She scrambles away from him, towards me and Leon. At the same time, the crowd behind us charges the *parabalani*, who disappear under their mass. I hear screams as blood splatters from punching fists, fingers that tear flesh, and feet that break limbs.

I feel no pity as Calix is reduced to a pulp of blood and flesh.

I feel no regret when I see the horrified expression on Leon's face and understand that he will not be pressing his suit.

I feel no guilt as Jason and Orestes, followed by several dozen soldiers on horseback, gallop into the side street, swords unsheathed, only to find that their job has already been done.

The only thing I feel is joy as Lady Hypatia stands before me—her grateful smile radiant despite her injuries—and enfolds me in her arms.

Hypatia

Several years have passed since Cyril unleashed his hounds on me in the failed attempt to wipe me and my accomplishments from the earth. Several years since he saw his power wither and die, the people having lost their faith in his leadership when word spread that his was the hand both holding the *parabalani's* leash and releasing it to see an end to me. He may not have planned as ugly a death as Calix had devised, but the stain of the attempt stuck to Cyril. He left Alexandria under a cloud of shame. Some say he was lucky to leave with his life.

In that time, I started classes at the *Mouseion* for women. Classes in mathematics, philosophy, astronomy, reading and writing. At first the classes were sparsely attended—women were hesitant to go against centuries of tradition and their menfolk even more so. But slowly the idea gained acceptance amongst the pagans, Christians, and Jews of Alexandria, spreading beyond our city and Egypt to other countries. In the next decade or so, I expect there will be as many female scholars as there are male.

And while there are still men who hate the idea of educated women, they are outnumbered by those who support it. Because despite the protests of those who feel this will upset the natural order of things, there seem to be more happy unions than ever, with plenty of children being born.

"My lady?"

I turn and smile at Zoe, who now teaches at the *Mouseion* and is radiant in her seventh month of pregnancy. To her surprise—and mine, I admit—Leon was even more eager to woo her after he had seen her stand up to the *parabalani* than he had been before he'd gotten a glimpse of the strength inside her.

Both of them give me hope for the future.

The Woman Who Would Be Queen

Laura Ware

London, England
September 1987

DIANA WAS GRATEFUL FOR THE LIGHT TAN COAT SHE WORE AS SHE stepped out of the black sedan that had spirited her and Charles out of the palace to this quiet brick home on the outskirts of London. Ivy grew along the walls and tea roses nodded from bushes that flanked the black back door.

A mist gave the early morning a surreal feel, which matched Diana's mood perfectly. She had stood her ground with the Queen when she and her husband Prince Phillip urged Diana and Charles to salvage their marriage before it became impossible.

Over a lunch of ham and pickle sandwiches and sliced melon, the Queen appealed to their love for their children and their country. It would be for the best if they found a way to make their relationship work instead of remaining at odds with each other.

Diana had been willing to give it a go. Despite everything going on, she was fond of Charles—she'd only turned to a lover because she wanted to feel cared for. She felt it was possible for Charles and her to rekindle their relationship.

And she was unwilling to sacrifice her place as Princess of Wales. There were things Diana wanted to accomplish, and her position would make it easier to do so.

But going forward would be on her terms. She had a condition for doing as the Queen asked: the couple needed counseling. The Queen had frowned at that, stating that their business was their own. Diana countered that any attempts that didn't involve some outside help would be doomed to failure.

Charles hadn't wanted to agree to anything, but finally gave in and said they could give it a go. The Queen relented, only asking that whoever they picked be vetted by the palace. The press was quite fond of Diana, and the last thing the royals wanted was their finding out about a counselor.

Charles came to stand beside Diana as she shook her head, pushing her memories away for now. "Are you all right?" he asked, his voice somewhat stiff.

"Yes, of course," she replied. They were not visible from the street where they stood: Doctor Glenda Jacobs has assured them that she would offer them as much privacy as possible. In fact, they stood at the rear of the doctor's private home, rather than her office in London proper.

Diana watched as the driver approached the door. He'd barely knocked before it opened and revealed Dr. Jacobs, dressed in white trousers and a peach blouse. She looked past the driver at Diana and Charles. "Good morning. I have just put on tea. Do come in."

To Diana's surprise, Charles reached over to take her hand. She could see he was nervous, and couldn't blame him—butterflies appeared to have taken up residence in her stomach. She squeezed his hand. "Thank you for doing this."

He swallowed. "It's for the boys and the country. I will do my best."

"I know you will," she said, not missing that she'd been excluded in his list. She stifled the sigh that rose in her.

The Woman Who Would Be Queen

Charles noticed, anyway. He bowed his head briefly, then met her gaze. "I do not wish ill on you, Diana. I hope something good can come from all this."

I do too, she thought as they walked towards Dr. Jacobs. I hope much good comes.

South London
July 1989

Diana alighted from the sedan that had brought her from the palace to Middlesex Hospital. Inside was the new Landmark AIDS Center that she would help open that day. Cordoned off from her and her entourage were the ever-present press, along with some citizens straining for a look at their Princess.

The hospital, established in the mid-1700s, was a huge U-shaped brick building that rose seven stories above her. Diana knew the hospital had a long history; now, thanks to her, another chapter would be added to it.

Her stomach rumbled a bit—she'd picked at her eggs that morning. Diana knew that what she was doing would not be universally popular or understood. There was such unfair terror regarding HIV and AIDS patients, and Diana hoped to alleviate some of that concern.

She felt a wave of contentment wash over her. True, the Queen didn't understand Diana's interest in AIDS patients. The stigma surrounding the disease ran deep in the country. But Diana felt deep sympathy for the sufferers of AIDS or HIV. She wanted to help them become more accepted in their communities.

To her pleasant surprise, Charles had taken her side, telling his mother that Diana's work in this area would be good for the Crown. These suffering people were also her subjects and needed to know they mattered.

The nearly two years of counseling they'd undergone had helped to a certain extent. Sadly, while Charles chose to give up his "Lady," Diana knew that Camilla would always hold part of his heart. Her growing acceptance of that had helped ease the tensions between them. Charles had even come to her bedroom in the last month, a breakthrough for the two of them as they tried to navigate their relationship while dealing with an all-too-curious press that so far remained unaware of their counseling.

As Jonathan Grimshaw, the director of the new center, approached her, she smiled and held out her hand. One of her bodyguards stepped forward. "Your Highness, this man is HIV-positive."

She turned towards the man, her smile reassuring now. "I know," she said. "It's quite all right."

The director hesitated briefly before allowing Diana to give him a firm handshake. "I am delighted to be here and see this grand new center."

Grimshaw returned her smile. "We are honored to have you open it, Your Highness."

As she followed the director into the hospital, she could hear the crowd of press and onlookers murmuring behind her. Yes, a simple handshake had definitely stirred things up.

Good, she thought. Maybe when I don't keel over and die they will realize how silly their fear is.

Buckingham Palace
May 1990

Diana knew when she and Charles entered the White Drawing Room that something was amiss. The Queen sat at a polished cherry desk in the elegant room, her expression solemn. A wall-to-wall multicolored carpet covered the floor. A white fireplace held a bouquet of white flowers, the warmer weather meaning there was no need to light a fire.

The room, often used to receive visitors, was empty of all but the three of them. A fat white and gold teapot sat on the desk with three matching cups nearby. Two cherry chairs with white and gold striped padding on the seats waited for Diana and her husband.

The Queen waited for them to be seated and asked her son to serve the tea. Once that task was completed, she placed her cup down on the desk. "We have been apprised of a situation."

Diana glanced at Charles, who looked as puzzled as she felt. "What situation?"

The Queen frowned. "The Daily Mail has contacted us. Apparently, they have discovered that the two of you are in marriage counseling. They've asked for a statement before they release the story to the public."

Diana knew that the Queen had insisted on privacy in this matter. "Do they know? Or are they guessing?"

"They mentioned Doctor Jacobs." The Queen's frown deepened. "You are certain the doctor can be trusted? Could she have released this information?"

Diana felt shock run through her. "The palace vetted her. I'm certain she has not broken our confidence."

The Queen looked towards her son. "Charles?"

He shifted in his chair. "I must agree with Diana. To release this to the press would be a shocking breach of professionalism. I can't imagine Dr. Jacobs doing such a thing."

"Yet the information is out there," the Queen said. "Someone has broken our trust. Who would do such a thing? Surely neither of you have told anyone else about this."

Diana flinched. The Queen had included both of them in the statement, but she knew it had been aimed at her. "I have said nothing. Our bodyguards know, but no one else."

Charles appeared extremely interested in his cup of tea. "Camilla knows."

The Queen grew still.

Diana felt as if air had fled the room. "What? How?" she asked.

"I…told her." Charles wouldn't look at Diana. "She needed to know why we were no longer seeing each other. But she has no reason to reveal this—she'd know how it could hurt me."

"Perhaps she thought it could hurt us," Diana said, hating how sharp her tone became. "If she could drive us apart, then she might have a chance again with you."

The Queen raised a hand to silence Charles's response. "Whoever the source might be, the Daily Mail is planning to go ahead with this story. We need to get ahead of it. You should end your relationship with Doctor Jacobs immediately."

"But...why?" Diana asked. "She has been of great help to us."

The Queen set her cup down. "Diana, it displays weakness if it becomes known that an outsider had to intervene in your marriage. The Crown must not appear weak."

"What if it were not weakness?" Diana said. "What if it were displayed as strength?"

The Queen raised an eyebrow. "How could this possibly be shown as strength?"

Diana gave Charles a pleading look. "It takes courage to admit you require help to overcome a difficulty. That it is beyond your ability to manage. We sought assistance because we wanted to strengthen our marriage, to benefit the Crown. What good would our not dealing with our problems accomplish?"

Charles sighed. "Mother, Diana has a point. Stopping with Dr. Jacobs now doesn't stop the story from coming out. In fact, it will give it a patina of shame if our response to the news is to end the relationship."

"We do not air our dirty laundry to the masses," the Queen said, her voice cold.

"But we're not," Diana argued. "We're demonstrating that seeking help isn't weakness, it's strength. How many marriages could be saved if a couple knew seeking help was nothing to be ashamed of? How many children would not have to suffer a broken home because their parents got help?"

The Queen said nothing for a long moment. Then she turned to her son. "Charles, are you in agreement with your wife in this?"

Charles finally met his mother's gaze. "I believe I am. Were it not for Dr. Jacobs, our marriage would be in tatters. Surely that is something far worse than getting needed help."

The Queen looked from Charles to Diana. "I want you both to prepare a joint statement that will go out prior to this story's publication. I will need to see it before it is made public."

Diana knew her mother-in-law wasn't happy about the decision. Still... "Do you think we should do a joint interview concerning this? With a sympathetic newsperson, of course."

"An...interview? Is that really necessary?" the Queen asked.

The Woman Who Would Be Queen

Charles appeared dubious. "What if something goes wrong? It could make matters worse."

"That's why we approach someone trustworthy, someone who is predisposed to be on our side," Diana said. She thought a moment. "I may know of such a person. Emma Nichols has done stories about me in the past. They have been favorable."

"Who does she work for?" the Queen asked. "Not the Daily Mail, I hope."

"She is a freelancer," Diana said. "I'm positive she would leap at the chance to do this interview."

"This does not negate the need for a joint statement," the Queen insisted. "I need you both to work on it and give it to our Communications office as soon as possible."

"Of course, Mother," Charles said. "We'll get right on it."

"See that you do." The Queen picked up her cup. "You have my permission to go. You have work to do."

Diana got to her feet as her husband did the same. Once they left the drawing room, Charles turned to Diana. "Are you certain an interview will help?"

"I am," Diana said. "If we act as if we're afraid of this, it will be far worse." She stopped talking, holding back hot words that she knew wouldn't help.

But Charles knew. He touched her shoulder. "Diana, I had to tell her. I never dreamed she might share it with someone. And it might not have been her."

Diana felt her stomach clench as she swallowed her initial reply. "It doesn't matter."

"It matters to you."

She wouldn't meet his gaze. "Shall we go to my office to prepare this statement? We should also instruct the Director of Communications to contact Ms. Nichols."

Charles moved in front of her, stopping her forward movement. "Diana…please, I am trying. Even when things were not ideal between us, I never wished you to be hurt."

"I know," she said. "But she'll always be in the shadows, won't she?"

He dropped his head. "I am trying," he repeated. "Please, don't let this undo all the work we've done these past two years."

Diana sighed. Charles did have a point. She already knew Camilla would forever stand out there as one Charles loved, even if he couldn't be with her.

It wasn't the fairytale marriage she'd hoped for when she was nineteen and naïve, but for now, it would have to do.

Diana's office, Kensington Palace
June 1990

Diana tried not to fidget as she sat on the light yellow couch in her office. She smoothed the skirt of her simple dark blue dress with tiny white dots and a white collar. The young man who was one of the two makeup artists that had shown up for the interview gently dusted her face with powder. "Please don't move, Your Highness. I don't want to get any of this on your clothing."

There was little chance of that, she thought, gazing down at the huge white cloth bib they'd fastened around her neck. She could already see streaks of beige and rose colors on it. As she did her best to become a statue, she felt someone brushing her short hair.

Charles sat next to her, and appeared to be able to shut out the buzz of activity that surrounded them both. He wore a navy-colored suit with a white shirt and a gray tie. His eyes were closed as the other makeup artist hovered over him.

Hot round lights were turned on, making the room unnaturally bright. Two large black cameras were set up on tripods and pointing at Diana and Charles, looking quite intimidating. A buzz of conversation filled the room with sound as men and women moved about the room.

A padded blue chair sat in front of the couch, waiting for Emma Nichols to have a seat. Dr. Jacobs herself, a short woman with thick brown hair pulled back in a ponytail, appeared to be reviewing some papers with a gray-haired man whose name Diana had forgotten already. He was from the BBC and was interested in broadcasting the interview.

Diana usually had no trouble remembering people's names; it was evidence of how nervous she felt. What if this went badly? The Queen would certainly blame Diana for anything less than a successful outcome. That could well bring into question Diana's projects, especially the ones the Crown was uncomfortable with.

Nichols gave a brisk nod to the BBC gent and quickly took her seat. Diana's makeup artist whisked away the white bib and turned his attention to the reporter. "Just a few more minutes," Nichols assured the royal couple. "This will be fabulous. I promise."

Diana clasped her hands on her lap and took two deep breaths. Her gaze went to the wall where she'd hung pictures of William and Harry. Gazing at her beloved sons calmed her nerves.

She glanced at Charles, who opened his eyes as his makeup artist finished. He looked over at her and patted her hands. "Relax, dear. We mustn't appear anything less than calm."

"I know," she said quickly. She struggled to ease the tension in her shoulders and find a place of peace inside herself.

Charles frowned slightly and gently squeezed her hands before flicking off some imaginary lint from his lapel. He faced Nichols and together they watched as the reporter got the finishing touches done on her face.

Once her makeup was done, Nichols smiled at Diana and Charles. "Remember. Look at me, not the cameras. If you can, pretend they aren't there. It's just the three of us having a chat."

Diana wished it were just the three of them. But Nichols had sold her and Charles on a televised interview. Not a live one—the Queen made it clear that the interview needed to be taped beforehand so the couple could review it prior to its being released. Nichols had agreed to a taped interview and promised Diana and Charles could see the finished product before it was aired.

Nichols glanced at a man who held a clapboard like those used in films to indicate the beginning of a scene. "We're just about ready to go. Remember, I'm Emma. Are you both ready?"

Diana took another deep breath before nodding.

"Yes, let's get on with it," Charles said.

Jacobs pointed to the man with the clapboard. He called out, "Roll tape. Interview with Prince Charles and Princess Diana, take one." He quickly snapped the clapboard shut.

Diana turned her attention to Nichols…no, Emma…as she began to speak. *Here we go.*

Diana was relieved that Emma didn't start with their marital troubles. Instead, the reporter asked about William and Harry, especially about William's upcoming eighth birthday. Diana loved talking about her children and felt tension bleed out of her as they chatted. Charles also seemed to loosen up a bit as they talked about their plans for William's party.

After a bit filming was halted so everyone had a breather. The makeup artists returned to touch things up. A young woman dressed casually in jeans and a purple blouse brought a wooden tray with three glasses filled with water on it. Diana took one, grateful for the cold drink.

Emma took two large swallows of her water before putting the glass back on the tray. "Okay, that wasn't too bad, right? You both ready for round two?"

Diana glanced at her husband. Charles toyed with the glass he held. "I doubt the rest of the interview will be so…trouble-free."

"Please, You Highness, try to relax. I've gone over the notes both you and the palace sent over. I know what I'm doing."

Diana remembered how she and Charles had hammered out precisely what they wanted from this interview. Charles had insisted that they insist on no "gotcha" questions. He'd gone as far as to ask if they could see the questions before the interview and had been disappointed when Emma had refused.

Diana had expected that answer and did her best to reassure Charles and his mother that this was still a good idea. Was it a risk? Undoubtedly. But Diana felt they'd done all they could to get the odds in their favor.

All too soon it was time for the next part of the interview. Diana handed her empty glass to the young woman with the tray and tried to slow down her racing pulse. Charles glanced at her. "All right?"

She nodded. "This will go well. I'm certain of it."

"Of course it will," Emma said. She looked towards the man holding the clapboard. "If you're ready, let's get started."

As soon as the clapboard snapped shut, Emma leaned forward slightly. "According to The Daily Mail, the two of you have been attending marital counselling sessions. Would you like to talk about it?"

Charles and Diana had agreed to let her take the lead on this line of questioning. "There is little to talk about. We were going through a difficult time in our marriage, and rather than let it fester and become a worse problem we chose to fix it."

"Some would say that you shouldn't have to get help. That you should be able to deal with such things on your own."

To Diana's surprise, Charles spoke up. "If one of our vehicles develops a problem, I do not decide to ignore it or attempt to fix it on my own. I allow professionals with skill to address the issues and resolve them. That is what Diana and I decided to do when it came to our relationship."

"So you're seeing a professional?"

"We are," Diana said. "That should not be something to be ashamed of. Instead of tossing our marriage into a bin, we've decided to strengthen it."

They talked about Dr. Jacobs for a few minutes. While Diana and Charles had agreed to speak about the doctor, they had both made clear that certain subjects were off the table—Camilla being one of them. Emma had appeared unhappy with the news but had not backed out of the interview.

Still, Diana felt a flutter in her stomach as Emma scanned her notes. "You say your marriage had issues. Some of them must have been difficult to resolve. Would you like to elaborate on that?"

"No," Charles said, before Diana could answer. "There are some things that ought to be between Dr. Jacobs and ourselves."

"But if others are going through similar issues, surely you could help them…"

"People have issues," Diana said. "They are unique to each couple. What works for Charles and me might not work for them. It is important to seek professional help to resolve such things, not simply take what one hears on the telly."

Emma raised an eyebrow. "But you would encourage struggling couples to seek help?"

"Yes," Diana said. "It sounds easy to just toss a marriage into the bin and start over. But it isn't, especially when children are involved. Strong families will make England strong. Charles and I know that we are better for our children and country together than apart."

"Sometimes a marriage can't be saved," Emma said.

"True," Diana said. "But what is the harm in trying? There are certainly exceptions to the rule—an abusive relationship, for example—but so many people divorce over fixable problems. Charles and I demonstrate that it needn't come to that."

To Diana's relief, Emma called for a break. When the camera was turned off, Charles spoke with a touch of anger. "I thought we made clear that some matters were not to be brought up."

"I did not bring any up," Emma said. "I simply invited you to share what you were comfortable with."

Diana shook her head. "You attempted to manipulate us. That was hardly necessary."

"People are curious. Certain issues you have experienced are already known to the public. Why not address them?"

Charles's eyes narrowed. "I am not so certain we should continue with this interview. If you cannot adhere to our agreement, then there is no point of this."

Diana saw Emma stiffen. Before the reporter could speak, she said, "Emma, please. Think of whom we might help. We aren't doing this to satisfy those who gossip about us. We are trying to set an example for our subjects, one they might do well to emulate."

Emma said nothing for a few seconds. Then she seemed to relax. "I understand. While I think the interview would be better served by dealing with those questions people have, I did agree to your guidelines. I shall endeavor to align myself with them, Your Highnesses."

"That is all we ask," Diana said quickly as she accepted some water from the same young woman who'd served them before.

Charles stared at Emma, then sighed. "Very well. We will continue."

Diana suppressed a sigh of relief. She knew that Charles was doing this to put a good face on the Crown. That was what the Queen wanted.

Diana hoped it would be so much more.

Hackney, a neighborhood in London, England
September 1992

Diana gazed through the tinted windows of the unmarked black sedan that had brought her to this buzzing neighborhood. Even though it was September, it was uncomfortably warm outside and she was grateful for the cool air that came through the vents.

There was a time she would not have visited Hackney—the village had once held a poor reputation. But these days it attracted families and young professionals to it. The vibe was upbeat in the neighborhood and Diana had seen several art galleries, bars, and eateries that displayed tasty looking selections in their windows.

Her driver parked the car in front of a bakery. Diana was tempted to roll down the window to catch a scent of the loaves of bread that sat in the sparkling-clean window of the shop. In addition to the bread, someone had placed some tea cakes on display, their soft white frosting promising a delight for the tongue.

Today she was accompanied by a single bodyguard who also served as her driver. Harriet Lawson was a cheerful redhead whom Diana had picked for this particular occasion. The situation called for a female guard only. While Diana trusted her male bodyguards, her contact for this visit had asked that they not be present.

In fact, the car Diana rode in had been stripped of any identification that would tie it to the palace. That was in large part to keep the hungry media away from her. For the safety of those Diana would visit today, this trip had to be kept a secret.

A small green car came to the corner where Diana's car sat. A tall woman with long brown hair and tired eyes got out and cautiously approached the sedan.

Diana noticed that Lawson had come alert when the woman got out of her car. As she drew nearer, Lawson said, "Stay here, Your Highness," and slipped out of the sedan, shutting the door behind her.

Diana watched as the two women spoke even though she couldn't hear what was said. She assumed the brown-haired woman was Karen Martin, the one she'd spoken to over the phone when she had arranged for this visit. The location of the woman's shelter here in Hackney was a closely guarded secret, and Martin had insisted on precautions before she agreed to let Diana come.

Lawson shook her head, crossing her arms in front of her. The other woman glanced at the car Diana sat in and gestured towards it. Lawson turned and stomped her way back to the vehicle and Diana rolled down her window. "What is it?"

"She wants us to get in her car and let her drive us to the place." Lawson's tone made it clear that she thought this was a bad idea. "We can't just leave our car here. If something were to happen—"

"These women aren't dangerous," Diana said, her voice soft. "I appreciate your concern, but I believe we should follow their lead on the matter."

Lawson appeared alarmed. "Your Highness, I'm supposed to look after you."

"I know. And I trust you to do so under these circumstances," Diana said. She glanced over at the two black bags of clothing and toys they had brought that sat in the seat next to her. "Shall we transfer the gifts to her car?"

She watched as Lawson's gaze went from her to the bags and back again. "Your Highness…"

"Please, just trust me," Diana said. She rolled up the window and placed a broad-brimmed straw hat on her head. A pair of large sunglasses went on next. Then Diana stepped out of the car. She'd dressed simply in dark navy slacks and a pale blue blouse with less jewelry than usual—the goal was not to draw attention to herself.

She took a deep breath, the aroma of the bakery tempting her. She hadn't eaten much that morning—a bit of buttered toast and some tea completed her breakfast—and she wished she had time to get a snack.

Lawson went with her to the woman who waited for them. "Karen Martin, Your Highness," Martin said. Dropping a brief curtsey (which was a neat trick given she was dressed in jeans), she continued, "Thank you for your interest."

Diana extended her hand and shook Martin's. "I am glad. We brought clothing for your clients. May we place it in your car?"

"That was thoughtful of you. Yes, of course. But we shouldn't dawdle here."

Lawson went to retrieve the bags. Diana glanced around but while people walked about the clean streets, going in and out of the shops, no one paid attention to them.

It was a bit of a relief, to tell the truth. It was getting harder and harder for her to avoid the press, who loved to keep tabs on her and report every move, every word, every twitch.

While she was glad they'd lost her for the moment, she intended to take advantage of the opportunity they offered her. And not just her, but those she could speak for.

A few minutes later they were in Martin's green car. Martin appeared to take a circuitous route to their destination—at least that was how it appeared to Diana. She also noticed that Martin constantly checked her mirrors, at one point asking Lawson to look and make sure they weren't being followed.

Eventually, they pulled up in front of a pale blue two-story house with white trim that resembled the other houses in the neighborhood. The front door was flanked by two pink rose bushes that appeared to be well kept.

Diana got out of the car. She reached inside to grab one of the bags, but Lawson waved her off. "I have it, ma'am."

Diana pulled back, grateful that Lawson had remembered not to address her as "Your Highness" here. No telling how nosy the neighbors were, and it wouldn't help for her presence to be advertised here.

She hoped the clothes would do. Martin had mentioned that clothing was in short supply at the shelter, as many women arrived only with what they were wearing at the moment. Diana had gotten her staff to assist her in purchasing some clothes in various sizes. Working through her staff had helped keep her name out of it for the moment.

Martin led them to the door. "We do the best we can for the women here," she said. "But it can be difficult. Funding is an issue."

"I'm certain we can help with that," Diana said.

Martin's look was skeptical. "Does the Crown really want anything to do with this? It's not pretty."

Diana felt herself straighten up. "These women are the Crown's subjects. Of course we should want them well cared for."

Martin stared at her for a long moment. "We'll see," she said finally, unlocking the door. "Please don't wander off. I will be happy to show you around."

"Of course," Diana said. She took a deep breath, hoping she could put pounds behind her words. Ever since she'd learned of this shelter, she'd wanted to offer some aid. Not because Charles had ever harmed her physically—he hadn't—but because she knew what it felt like to be lost, overwhelmed, and unsure.

These women had taken a brave first step towards becoming stronger. Diana wanted to help them go further. She hoped this initial visit was just the beginning.

New York City, New York, USA
April 1995

Diana flipped through her speech as the limo she rode in carried her to the Waldorf Astoria where the first International Women's Symposium was being held. Diana felt a thrill of pride mixed with concern. She, along with some other female leaders in the world, had spearheaded this symposium that would take place beginning that evening. She hoped it would become an annual thing, but that would depend on the next three days.

She would have loved for it to have taken place in London, but Hillary Clinton had made a New York City venue attractive. She and the President were fully on board with Diana's take on women's issues, unlike the Queen, who still questioned some of Diana's ideas. Some distance helped Diana navigate that tricky road.

She tried to ignore the tall buildings and crowds of people they drove by, but even though it wasn't her first trip to the city, her attention kept wandering.

The city had a hum to it so different from London. She could almost feel the energy under her skin, the energy of so many people in one place. She wondered why London, which had a similar number of residents, didn't affect her in this way.

At a stoplight she looked out of her tinted window and saw a bearded man sitting in a doorway. His clothes appeared worn and he held a cardboard sign that Diana couldn't quite read from where she sat, though she could imagine what it said.

With a sigh, she went back to her speech. The Queen had given her approval of it after a lot of back and forth between Diana's people and hers. Diana had been tempted to not let the Queen see the speech until she gave it, letting…what was that American phrase? Oh yes…letting the chips fall where they may.

Charles had persuaded her not to go that route. The counseling that had ended the year before had enhanced their mutual respect for each other and left them with a strong bond of, if not burning passion, solid friendship that included genuine caring.

"You aren't just representing yourself in New York," he said to her as they ate a simple breakfast of scrambled eggs and bacon in their apartment in Kensington Palace. "You're representing the Crown. Of course Mother wants to vet your speech."

Diana sipped her hot tea. "But she might gut it. The things I speak of are things she isn't comfortable with."

Charles gave her a small smile. "Mother may not be comfortable with some of your words, but she knows they come from your heart. And from what you've shown me, the things you speak of would benefit a number of our subjects."

"Subjects that no one wants to talk about."

"You do. One thing Mother knows is that you are a voice for those who cannot speak. She sees that. Work with her so that you can be that voice for the Crown as well."

So Diana had worked with her mother-in-law, trying to preserve as many of her ideas as possible. She was forced to admit Charles had a point—here, she was not simply Diana. She was Diana, Princess of Wales, a member of the royal family. Like it or not, she represented them as well as herself.

But today she would also represent the women who could not speak for themselves. The woman in the homeless shelter she met several years ago, her face still carrying bruises from a beating her husband had given her. The homeless woman who, according to a recent news report, had nearly died from exposure to the cold before some kind soul rushed her to a hospital. The woman struggling to raise two children alone, her husband dead from a terrible cancer.

Diana wanted these women to be heard. To be seen. That would be the first step to their getting the help they desperately needed and deserved. She knew from talking to other leaders that this was not simply a problem for England—it was a problem for the world. And it was time for the world to do something about it.

As they pulled up to the front of the hotel, Diana noticed the crowd. Many were obviously from the press, given their cameras and microphones, but there were some regular people sprinkled among them, craning their necks to see who was arriving now. Police and barricades allowed a passageway for one to gain access to the hotel proper, but it wasn't an easy task.

Her security people had attempted to persuade her to enter the hotel from a back way. While she understood their concerns for her safety, she'd insisted on a public arrival. The press still loved her, applauding her and Charles's recovery of their marriage as "the right thing to do." They were always looking for her, wanting pictures, quotes, anything to feed a hungry public.

Today, Diana intended to use them to conduct her message beyond the symposium. To send out her call for action to those who might influence their leaders to act. She prayed that this would be just a beginning step to bring real change for women in the world.

Lawson, who had accompanied her as part of her security detail, got out of the limo and held open her door. After securing her speech in a dark leather binder, Diana put a smile on her face and stepped out of the car, listening to the clicking of the cameras and trying to ignore the flashes. A smattering of applause could be heard above the voices of newspeople reporting her arrival.

Diana nodded and waved in greeting, keeping the smile on her face. She permitted her detail to form a circle of protection around her as they made their way to the hotel's glass entrance. Some called her name; others shouted out questions that she felt she could ignore. A press conference had been scheduled for the following morning, prior to the day's events. Diana would have spoken by then, and she was sure what she said would lead to questions.

Let it, she thought. The more attention brought to these issues, the better. She and the others intended this to be the beginning of change for women around the world. Change for the better.

It had to start somewhere. Diana chose for it to start there.

London, England
September 2001

Diana rubbed her tired eyes as she forced herself to look away from the horrors on the television screen. She and Charles had visited New York City just two months ago, visiting their friends Bill and Hillary Clinton. They'd driven by the Twin Towers during their visit. To see it now...she could hardly breathe.

She'd just returned to the palace after a long and delightful lunch with some friends when one of her staffers came to her, her face pale, followed by members of palace security.

The security staff had insisted that she remain in her apartments and promised to bring William and Harry there as soon as possible. Charles was out of town in Wales but safe. Diana spoke to him briefly on the phone while she watched the chaos unfolding in the United States.

She sat in a private sitting room on a rose-colored sofa, gazing at the large-screen television across from her. The cherry coffee table in front of her held her cold cup of tea that someone had brought her hot a while back. William and Harry sat with her, shock rendering them quiet for the most part.

William frowned. "Mum, didn't they say they'd grounded all the planes in the United States?"

"Yes," Diana said. "They've cancelled all the flights."

"Well, what about people here who were going to fly to the United States from here? Can they?"

Diana shook her head. "I don't think so. They want no planes in the air there right now. I can't say I blame them."

Harry scratched his chin. "Mum, what will the people at the airport do?"

Diana blinked. It was a good question. She could picture it in her mind's eye: tired travelers, being told their flight was cancelled. Stuck at the airport, perhaps without a place to go, or any idea what to do…

"Come with me," she told her sons, turning off the television. She brought them to her office in the apartments, a security team following after her. Before going in, she asked her staff to please get hold of Tony Blair if possible.

Twenty minutes later, the Prime Minister was on the phone with her. "I don't have much time, I'm afraid," he said, his tone apologetic. "What can I do for you, Your Highness?"

"My sons and I are wondering about those Americans here whose flights have been cancelled. Is anything being done for them?"

"To be honest, I'm not entirely certain. The airlines might be providing vouchers for rooms and food."

"With so many flights cancelled, the airlines might be overwhelmed. Is there something the government could do? Or even the Crown?"

"I have instructed Parliament to convene—this is certainly a matter we can consider. As far as the Crown, you would know better than I what could be done."

"True," Diana allowed. "Please, keep me posted on what kind of aid might be required."

"Of course," Blair said. "I will be sure Parliament considers options as well."

"Thank you." Diana considered her next move. She needed to speak with the Queen. But her security had been adamant that she not leave

Kensington Palace. It was one thing tracking down the Prime Minister. Her mother-in-law was another matter.

The problem was solved for her a few minutes later when a member of her staff informed her that the Queen wanted to speak with her on the phone. Diana quickly picked up the receiver.

She let the Queen ask about her grandsons and express sorrow over the tragedy "across the pond." After that, Diana raised the issue of the stranded passengers. "Is there something we might do for these poor people?"

"What did you have in mind?"

Diana thought for a moment. "We could assist with helping them find places to stay. An appeal to our people, perhaps. Surely there are people willing to help."

"We have prepared a statement, expressing our condolences to our American friends. What has happened is truly heinous. Do you think we need to do more?"

"If our positions were reversed, would they not help us?"

The Queen sighed. "You raise a valid point, Diana. Very well. We will add a call to action to our statement. Is there anything else?"

"I would like to go to Heathrow myself, meet with some of these travelers. This must be so difficult for them."

"Diana, we cannot approve of that. We are on high alert. You do not need to be at an airport right now."

Diana sighed. She'd known it would be a long shot. But she had had to try. "Would you mind terribly if I also put out a statement? Since I can't go to them."

"That would be acceptable." The Queen's tone softened. "Diana, we know you want to do something…over the years, we've seen that passion to make things better for others in you. But for now, you must think of yourself and your sons. You need to stay safe. Charles would never forgive us if we allowed you to take such a risk."

"I understand. I will have a statement ready shortly."

"Very well. Do give my love to the boys."

Diana hung up the phone and looked at her sons who sat on the golden couch in front of her desk. "Your grandmother sends her love. Do you mind remaining here with me for a time? I need to prepare a statement."

The teens nodded their agreement. Diana was grateful for her sons. They had their moments—what child didn't?—but in general were good boys.

She contacted her staff and asked that tea be brought in. She had work to do.

Kensington Palace
September 2022

Diana felt a thrill of nervousness as she looked at herself in her dressing room mirror. She sipped some hot tea with lemon as she considered her reflection that morning.

So much had changed over the years. Threads of silver graced her short hair now, and she had lost the glow of youth she'd managed to hang onto well into her thirties. Now sixty-two, the press, who still loved her, claimed she had "aged gracefully."

The room she sat in had changed some over the years. The wallpaper had been freshened up to a patterned pale blue that Diana found soothing. Her dressing table still sat by a window that she'd drawn a white curtain over to have a little privacy.

The wall next to the dressing table still held pictures of William and Harry—but now included wedding pictures and family photos. While most had known her as the Princess of Wales until yesterday, she found that she valued the title of "Nana" just as much.

Yesterday...Diana felt her eyes fill with tears. Queen Elizabeth, who had reigned longer than Diana had been alive, had passed away. She and Charles had been with her until the end, and Diana's heart had cracked as her normally stoic husband wept.

He had not cried alone. Over the years, Diana and her mother-in-law had grown closer, especially as the queen had seen the benefits of Diana's efforts for the women of not only England, but the world. She grew to support Diana more and more, but always reminded her that the Crown was to be preserved at all costs.

The Woman Who Would Be Queen

Even with that caveat, Diana had accomplished a lot. Thanks in no small part to the work of the annual International Women's Symposium, violence against women had gone down worldwide, with victims gaining important assistance that helped them to leave and stay out of abusive relationships. In addition, abusers faced stiffer penalties and authorities that were less sympathetic to their view. While not all countries subscribed to these changes, the naysayers became fewer and fewer each year.

Diana and Charles' telling of their own marital difficulties and counseling had caused other leaders to speak out on their marital issues and in some cases seek help themselves. Charles and Diana's journey helped them deal with issues close to home, especially helping Harry and Meghan walk the royal path.

The symposium had, among other things, sought to find and encourage talented women to rise to leadership in their respective countries. Women took the reins and proved well able to manage the responsibilities. Even in the United States, a young woman governor named Nikki Haley surprised everyone by defeating Donald Trump in the primaries and eventually becoming President of the United States.

Another issue Diana had championed was that of the homeless in the world. Women in communities spearheaded a movement to provide those without a home a safe place to land while they gained skills that led them to eventual independence. Changes in local laws made it easier for groups such as churches and other religious groups to offer such services, and homelessness had dropped significantly in first-world countries over the years.

Diana smiled at the image in the mirror. So much had been accomplished—but there was still more to do. However, momentum was on their side, and with her new status as Queen, her influence would only grow.

She looked around the comfortable room and sighed. She would miss the apartments here—but tradition could not be ignored. She and Charles would move into Buckingham Palace that very day. Soon people would come to pack up those things Diana wished to take with her from this room.

She drained her teacup and then stood, her gaze drawn to the gold and white gown that lay on the four-poster bed. Two young ladies in waiting stood quietly nearby, ready to aid her in getting ready for the coming day.

Shifting, Swirling HERitage

She smiled at them. "I'm ready," she said.

And she was. Not just for that day, but all the days to come. For all the challenges and opportunities that lay before her. And the people she spoke for.

There would be people who would say it couldn't be done, despite evidence to the contrary. People who would call her ideas too lofty to succeed.

Let them. She'd proven them wrong before; she would continue to silence the naysayers with her successes.

There was work to be done.

And she could hardly wait.

Westminster Abbey, England
May 2023

Diana smoothed the skirt of the brocaded cream-colored gown she wore. The cool, damp day made her grateful for the thick material as she entered Westminster Abbey. The butterflies in her stomach made her glad she'd stuck to toast, cut-up fruit, and tea that morning.

So many people! The press was there, of course; the BBC along with foreign reporters were everywhere, snapping pictures and speaking into microphones to let the millions tuning in know every detail of the first coronation in seventy years.

Diana was glad they had rehearsed things the day before when the crowds were much smaller. There was tradition, pomp, and ceremony to be observed and no one wanted to get it wrong.

Flanked by the two bishops who would assist in her coronation, Diana walked towards the massive building. It was a long walk across the tiled floor to where she and Charles would be crowned. On either side of the path outside were throngs of people, dressed in every color imaginable, all craning their necks for a glimpse of the new royal couple.

As she passed, some people bowed their heads in acknowledgement. A few women curtsied. One or two of the older women blew kisses to her. After all these years, she was still "the people's Princess," beloved by the common folk who couldn't get enough of her.

That was about to change. In a few minutes, she would officially be crowned Queen Consort. Would the people still feel the same way about her? She fervently hoped so.

At the same time, she knew that, in a way, she needed to take a back seat when it came to attention. Yes, she would be Queen Consort, but it was Charles who would rule. The day really belonged to him. The last thing she wanted to do was take that away from him.

Music swelled as she walked young voices raised in song. She resisted the temptation to look behind her, where six lads serving as pages carried a red train behind her. The heavy gold-edged material was fastened to her shoulders, and she was grateful for the help of the lads carrying it.

She finally arrived at the wooden chair she would sit in. She sat and found herself able to watch her husband coming down the aisle. Bareheaded, dressed in black and white royal vestments, a train like the one behind her carried by six lads. Remembering the weight of her own train she was grateful he didn't have to drag his about either.

Once Charles was seated, the ceremony began in earnest. As she listened to the archbishop speak, Diana wondered if any changes had been made since the last coronation so many years ago. She doubted much had been altered. This was steeped in pageantry and tradition.

Diana watched as the archbishop took the heavy crown (framed in solid gold and lined with a purple velvet cap and an ermine band) and placed it on Charles' head. Diana knew that at the end of the ceremony he would change to the lighter jewel-encrusted Imperial State Crown, since the first was only for crowning him king.

Becoming king suited him. He had waited years for this moment, even though he'd not been in a particular hurry for it. But this was what he'd been born for, just as their son William had and would one day rule in his father's stead.

Then the archbishop stood in front of her, speaking from a script he'd referred to when crowning Charles. First the consort's ring was presented to her, a gold ring set with rubies. Then the crown that had been made for Queen Mary so long ago was presented. The large crown looked quite similar to the one Charles was crowned with.

As it was set upon her head, Diana felt the weight of it settle on her. The ceremony continued with a traditional prayer and the presentation of the royal scepter and the Rod of Equity and Mercy.

The rod spoke to her. Equity and mercy—that was what she wanted for her people. All of them, not just a few who were fortunate or privileged. She'd been able to do so much as Princess—how much more could she do as Queen?

As the boys' choir sang the Andrew Lloyd Webber hymn "Make a Joyful Noise," Diana rose and approached Charles. After she offered a brief curtsey, the priests with her guided her to the seat a few feet away from him on his left. She sat, aware of the weight of responsibility that was now theirs.

Today would be a day of celebration and ceremony. Diana was grateful that she was able to be a part of it. There was still much to be done.

But today, she would rejoice with her countrymen.

Buckingham Palace, England
May 2040

Diana smiled as she looked down at her sleeping great-granddaughter, Diana Frances, second in line to the throne after her father George. The fact that George and his wife Amanda had chosen to name their firstborn after Diana touched her deeply.

The newborn was swaddled in a soft pink blanket. Tufts of blond hair peeked out from under the white cap on her tiny head. Her eyes closed, the baby was the picture of peace. And so light, Diana felt as if she could hold her all day without getting tired.

She sat in a sitting room in her apartments in the palace. The wallpaper here was cream-colored with gold stripes. The pale blue couch she sat on had been in her office when she was Princess and had been carefully restored. A flat-screen TV, currently off, sat across the room. A cherry wood end-table at one end of the couch held a small Tiffany lamp and Diana's e-reader.

Diana sighed. Charles would have loved to see this child. But cancer took him away from them in 2026. Their son William sat on the throne now, and Diana was Queen Mother, still living in the palace, still, at seventy-nine, speaking out for those things she believed in.

She carefully picked up her porcelain cup of lemon tea and took a sip. Baby Diana was three days old and unaware of the attention her birth had brought. Cards and gifts had poured in from people in England and all over the world, some people quite emotional at the little girl's name. Diana still retained the love of her people, and she prayed the babe would receive the same affection her great-grandmother enjoyed.

Diana let her thoughts drift to all the changes that had taken place since she'd been a shy naïve girl of nineteen. There had been many challenges over the years, but she'd succeeded in overcoming almost all of them.

Domestic violence worldwide had dropped greatly as countries took an active role in dealing with the problem. Women were empowered to seek help and given tools to live without their abuser. Those who chose to harm their partner found themselves arrested, prosecuted, and looked down on by society. Those willing to seek help and change were given the opportunity to do so.

Through the work of the International Women's Symposium, which had just held its annual meeting in Taiwan the previous month, communities were now geared towards helping those homeless and/or in poverty instead of demonizing them. Parcels of land were devoted to building and providing inexpensive shelter for those without a roof over their heads, thanks to a cooperative effort between the private sector and local governments.

True, poverty still existed in the world. Diana recalled the Bible passage where Jesus stated that the poor would always be with them. Still, tremendous progress had been made and far fewer children went to bed hungry than there had been back in the 1990's.

Through it all, she had been the voice of these downtrodden folk: men and women who couldn't speak for themselves and be heard. Diana spoke. And the world listened.

Many changes had come about. More women had taken on leadership roles and added their voices to hers. Ten years ago, after much research, a cure for AIDS had been developed. The death toll from the disease had dropped significantly. And those who contracted it were no longer looked at with fear and loathing.

Diana softly pressed a kiss to her namesake's forehead. The baby stirred but didn't awaken. Amanda came into the room, smiling, dressed in comfortable leggings and a loose-fitting t-shirt. "She's still sleeping?"

"She is. Did you get sufficient rest?"

Amanda shrugged. "I got some. It's close to feeding time for her, so I thought I'd take her off your hands."

"I don't mind holding her."

Amanda laughed. "I know you don't. But you can't exactly breastfeed her. I promise you'll hold her again."

Diana chuckled as she handed the baby to her mother. "Thank you. I won't ever get tired of holding her."

Amanda cuddled the baby. "I know. She's quite special, isn't she?"

Diana thought again of how bright a future lay in store for baby Diana, thanks to her great-grandmother's work and the work of other women. A future that didn't seem possible sixty years ago.

"She is special," Diana told Amanda. "And I look forward to showing her the world we've helped make for her."

J'ai Deux Amours

K. Ceres Wright

August 12, 1939
Paris, France
Casino de Paris

THE INTENSITY OF THE MAN'S STARE UNNERVED JOSEPHINE, EVEN as she traversed the stage away from him. His gaze burned into her back, and she tamped down the urge to flee backstage and run down Rue de Clichy. He sat away from the glare of the stage lights, half shrouded in shadows, but his scrutiny of her was obvious…at least to her. The other patrons continued to chat and nod in huddled twosomes, or silently sing along as their lips moved in time with the lyrics. His glare made her sweat even more than the hot lights did.

As the last notes of her last song faded, she waited for the upswell of applause and cheering, took her bows, and hurried backstage to her dressing table. The bouncer at the door would keep strangers from entering, and her driver was waiting outside the back entrance. She quickly changed into a pair of wide-leg trousers and a chiffon short-sleeved shirt, said goodbyes to the other girls, and dashed out the back. She waved to the driver, who slowly pulled the car up to the door. He opened his door to alight, but Josephine had snatched open the rear door and climbed inside before he could step out.

"Home, please, Yves."

He sat back in the driver's seat, his bulky weight stretching the leather. Curly brown hair peeked out from under his cap. "No late partying tonight?" Yves eased the car into the street and slowly accelerated.

She smiled, despite her uneasiness. "No, I just want to soak in a hot bath. I'm not as young as I used to be."

"Don't say that. You look younger every day."

"Liar!" She laughed. Somehow knowing she was on her way home helped calm her nerves, but when she looked back through the rear window, the shadowy figure stood outside the back entrance, and she fell silent.

Le Beau Chêne
Paris Suburbs

They arrived home close to midnight at Le Beau Chêne on the western outskirts of Paris in Le Vésinet, a garden suburb that had been built for the wealthy bourgeoisie of Paris. This time, she let Yves open the door for her. Josephine checked for the shadowy figure along the driveway, but he was nowhere to be found, and all she heard was the occasional cluck from her chicken hutches. Still, she hurried inside.

"See you tomorrow, Miss Baker."

"Good night, Yves."

The housekeeper usually left a late supper in the refrigerator, but Josephine wasn't hungry, and headed straight upstairs. She opened the door to her bedroom, looking forward to a hot bath. Her room was decorated with layers of white, blue, and pink muslin and ribbons atop multicolored cushions. Bouquets of pom-pom roses dotted her tables and bureaus in art deco vases.

J'ai Deux Amours

A body pressed against her from behind and a hand closed over her mouth, trapping her scream. She struggled to free herself, but her captor held fast. A husky voice whispered in her ear.

"I'm not here to hurt you. I'm an American, and I need your help. Please." He paused, and she stood still. "Now, when I take my hand away, do you promise not to scream?" She nodded. He slowly withdrew his hand and took a step back. She craned her neck to see the shadowy man who had been at the show. Josephine backed away.

"What do you want?"

"My name is William McKee. I'm with military intelligence."

He peeled off the fedora he was wearing, revealing a head of wavy sandy-brown hair, brown eyes, and a kind smile. He looked far less sinister than when she had first seen him, Josephine thought.

"You were at my show. I thought you might be a mobster or something. But what's military intelligence? Smart people with guns?"

William chuckled. "No, it's…spies, basically."

"Spies? What do you want from me? I'm just an entertainer." She heaved a sigh of relief. "I don't know about you, but I could use a drink. You want something?" She headed to the bar cart on the opposite side of the room and pulled out a decanter of brandy.

William sat in a flowered chair next to a lamp. "No, thank you. I'd really rather get right to it. I don't want to be here longer than I have to."

"Well, that sounds rather intriguing, Mr. McKee. Please, continue." After having poured herself a drink, Josephine sat on her bed, cattycorner to William.

"I don't usually take strangers into my confidences, but you're not really a stranger, it seems. Your posters are everywhere. Everyone knows who you are. And I've seen and heard enough about you to know you'd be more than capable. So…what I'm about to tell you is in the strictest confidence. Can you give me your word you won't breathe a word of this?" William leaned forward.

Josephine nodded stoically. "Yes, of course."

William gave her a pointed look, his eyes at once laced with both sadness and wisdom. "I'm also Black, Josephine."

Her eyes widened as she realized what he was telling her. "You're passing," she whispered.

William nodded. "I was there, during the Houston riot in 1917, like you were at the race riot in St. Louis a month earlier. Only in Houston, soldiers had fought back. But it didn't make a difference. They were still hanged like dogs. When I turned 18 later that year, I enlisted in a white part of town, said my parents were dead. Truth was, I had told my parents my plans and they agreed it was a way out for me. And at that point in the war, the government was taking pretty much everyone who showed up who didn't have an amputated limb. And even then, they might put you on desk duty.

"I was assigned to the Corps of Intelligence Police and sent overseas to the American sector north of Toul, facing the St. Mihiel salient. We reduced the flow of civilian traffic by setting up a system of travel controls that detained people who did not have proper identification, which helped to clear the area of potential enemy agents. Sounds simple, right? But…the things you see in war. I saw the effects of chemical weapons that the Germans used on us…that German scientists invented. And I knew then what they were capable of. And that if we ever got into another war, they would be the ones to watch for new types of weapons. So after the war, I got out and went to night school at the City College of New York to get a degree. Worked during the day as a clerk at an insurance firm. But I would hang out when I could at bars around Columbia University, try to pick up information on what the upper crust was up to. They're the ones who wage the wars, you know. Over the years, I kept a few bartenders on my payroll to let me know if anything interesting happened. I had moved up in the insurance business, but truth was, I found it boring. It paid well, and I was sending money back to my parents, but I couldn't wait to sign up for the army again, this time as an officer. My chance came when I got a call from a bartender in late January, who told me there was buzz on campus about something called nuclear fission. And guess who had discovered it?"

"The Germans, yes." She sighed, knowingly. Her answer seemed to bring him up short.

"You knew?"

J'ai Deux Amours

"Frédéric, Hans, and Lew were talking about it one night at a party, huddled in a corner. Naturally, I gravitated toward the hushed whispers. They explained it was about the release of energy from splitting an atom. I didn't think much of it until last month, when Frédéric said he thought it could lead to a bomb that's much stronger than anything we have now. I always pretend as if I don't understand, so they'll speak more freely, and I keep things in the back of my mind…" She paused as realization hit. "Well, look at that. I guess I am a spy after all." Josephine took another sip of her brandy, beginning to feel the tendrils of relaxation extend through her body.

"So you are," said William, grinning. "So you know Frédéric Joliot, Marie Curie's son-in-law?" William now sat on the edge of his seat, as if he would spring up any moment. Josephine found it amusing.

"Yes, well, everyone likes a night out every now and then, even physicists. But what do you want from me? As I said, I'm just an entertainer. And people don't want another war. We're still clawing our way back from the last one." Josephine got up from the bed and went into the bathroom. She turned on the water for her bath and sprinkled in oil for bubbles, hoping the hint would drive the man away, but he came to the bathroom and stood in the doorway.

"You're much more than that. Men everywhere fall at your feet. From ministers to garbage men, and everyone in between. You're in a position to gather secrets from high-ranking admirers. Surely you've heard things already. You know what's going on in Germany, Hitler and his thugs, beating up Jews in the streets. He's already annexed parts of Austria, Czechoslovakia, and Lithuania. He won't stop there, no matter what our friends across the pond in England think. War is coming, Miss Baker, whether you believe it or not. And I need people in place who know things."

Josephine laughed. "You need people in place? What are you, a one-man war department?"

William squirmed and shrugged, as if offended. "No, I'm someone with half a vision. After the news in January, I was able to convince my old boss in the military intelligence division at the war department to start up a small counterintelligence branch to monitor the Germans and

Japanese. And international communism. The FBI is obsessed with it. But it took them 3 months. America could be a powerhouse if it could just get rolling. The Europeans will still be fighting their Great War, with a trench warfare mentality and decades-old military equipment. The Germans are already years ahead. We can't let them get a leg up on this nuclear fission. We have to at least delay them as much as possible, until other countries can get their scientists up to speed. Think back. Did Joliot say anything about what materials they were using?"

Tiredness crept over Josephine, but she tried to maintain a focus on what William was saying. What he said made sense. There had been rumors of war, and she more than anyone knew about Herr Hitler and his dark deeds. "Of course, I know what the Germans are doing. I was harassed and run out of town in Austria, Berlin, Dresden, and Munich in 1927. I was called the Black Devil and Jezebel. Denigrated in the papers. And that was a decade ago. No one's stepped up to stop Hitler and his persecution of Jews since. I'm married to a Jew, for heaven's sake. I am a Jew!" She thanked the stars her husband, Jean, was away on business. He would have likely strapped on a gun and gone stalking after Hitler himself.

"Then help me, please. Find out what Joliot needs to continue their experiments. And try to determine how far along Germany is with theirs."

Josephine's anger rose as she recalled her tour in Germany, and as she had read of the British Prime Minister's appeasement agreement with Hitler a year ago, and not two months later of Kristallnacht. Appeasing Hitler hadn't helped.

She searched William's eyes, looking for a hint of insincerity, a trace of a lie. But there was none. He was the real deal. And if the powers that be wouldn't do anything, then she would do the best she could. In facing Goliath, David was just a shepherd boy with a slingshot and five smooth stones. And he only needed one.

"All right. I'll do it," she said. She turned off the water to the bath. The piled-up bubbles shone under the bright overhead light. "Getting information won't be too big of a problem. For now, anyway. German soldiers still take their leave here. And they may say one thing in the open, but behind closed doors and liquored up good, let's just say, they like their chocolate. But how do I get the information to you?"

J'ai Deux Amours

The corners of William's mouth stretched into a broad smile. "Thank you, Miss Baker. Thank you. Now, for getting me information, do you know the Japanese bridge in the park?"

"Yes, of course."

"Take a piece of chalk and make a mark on the end of the north-side hand rail. Not an X, maybe a slash. That way I'll know you have something for me. And put whatever you have under the chicken nest on the bottom right of the coop. We can't afford to be seen together but I want to make it as easy for you as I can. I'll retrieve the information at night."

Josephine nodded. "Chalk mark on the bridge hand rail, information under the chicken nest on the bottom right. Got it. Oh, and Frédéric had mentioned something about…water? A type of water…weighty water?"

William wracked his brain, but came up with nothing. "I don't know. Could you ask him?"

"Not ask, per se. I'll have to wrangle it out of him." Tiredness came crashing down on her and she just felt like crawling into bed and staying there for a week. William must have sensed it, for he turned and headed back into the bedroom. Josephine followed him as far as the bathroom door.

William reached into his pocket and pulled out a small book, then threw it on her bed. He turned. "This is a code book. Use this to code your messages. Keep it safe, someplace where only you know. I'll let myself out."

Josephine nodded, then took the quickest bath she had ever taken. After drying herself off and putting on a nightgown, she flopped on the bed and hid the code book under the mattress. Sleep overtook her.

August 15, 1936
Portuguese Embassy in Paris

In 1936 European diplomatic relations, the Portuguese were one of the few powers who could host an Embassy party, as they mostly kept to their own affairs and confidences...at least on the surface. They had had a treaty with Britain since 1386, but maintained cordial relations with the Germans. When asked to perform at an embassy party, Josephine had gladly accepted, and had asked for the guest list to help tailor her song list, or so she had said. In truth, she hoped as many foreign ministers as possible would attend, even the German one, von Ribbentrop. Rumor had it that he slept with the former British King's mistress, Wallis Simpson. Other rumors circulated that the Italian Foreign Minister Galeazzo Ciano had had an affair with her and left her pregnant, leading to a botched abortion that left her infertile. Still others said she had learned sensual tricks from prostitutes in brothels in China. Truth was, Josephine enjoyed being close to power and money, despite the scandals. It invigorated her, and she chased it. She supposed it was a product of her childhood...always afraid that grinding poverty would rear its head again in her life.

After arriving at the embassy and surveying the scene, she knew she would have to make do with the Italian minister, Count Ciano. He looked upset, blustery even. Josephine would have to lay her claim. She picked up two champagne flutes from a waiter holding a tray and traipsed past a row of busts of Roman Caesars that fronted ionic columns draped with red velvet. She landed in front of the minister, whose eyes first roved over her, then to his companion—who was tall and thin with a monocle—with a look that screamed, "Leave." The thin man scurried away forthwith.

"Galeazzo, ciao," Josephine purred. She delivered the requisite two-cheek kiss greeting before handing him the flute. She had met him several times before, at clubs and parties. "You are looking quite well, but...come, come. Whatever is the matter? You seem upset."

"La Baker, you are looking exquisite, as always." He took a draught of the champagne, and Josephine beckoned to the waiter to grab another one. He finished the one he had and began on the second one. "It is monstrous, I say. But..." He looked shyly at her. "I should not say, no."

Josephine could tell he was dying to say, but needed a bit of prodding, and with something stiffer than champagne. "Wait right here.

J'ai Deux Amours

I'll be back with something you will appreciate." She meandered her way across the room, after several quick hellos to fellow guests, to the bar. "Two whiskeys, double."

The bartender smiled and poured them with a flourish. Josephine winked at him and hurried back to Galeazzo. By the time she returned, he was practically sweating. "Here, drink this," she said, handing him a tumbler. He nodded thanks and downed it in two gulps. She offered him hers, insisting she preferred champagne. He obligingly accepted.

"Let's go sit somewhere quiet. Out on the veranda." Josephine headed for the French doors in the back of the room and opened one side. She slipped out onto the tiled patio and sat in one of the wrought-iron chairs. The minister soon followed, and she patted the seat next to hers. He sat down, then retrieved a handkerchief from his jacket pocket and wiped his large forehead. Josephine placed her hand on his and squeezed it.

"Galeazzo, you look as if you might soon have a fit. Please tell me what is going on. Relieve yourself of your burden. My lips are sealed, and there's no one around to hear."

"My dear Josephine…" He craned his neck around to verify that, indeed, no one else was around. Then he leaned in and spoke in a whisper. "Germany is set to attack Poland quite soon, which leaves us no time to prepare for war. We signed the Pact of Steel, which obligates us to follow Germany's lead, or declare neutrality. The former would make us look unprepared. The latter would make us look cowardly."

The news stopped her breathing and set her mind to racing. If Germany attacked Poland, Britain and France would declare war…if they had the guts. She closed her eyes in disbelief, but then remembered to gather herself. "When will they attack?"

Galeazzo shook his head. "I'm not sure, but I think it's a matter of weeks. And there's more."

She squeezed his hand again, as if to give him the strength to speak further. "Yes?"

"There's a rumor that von Ribbentrop is traveling to the Soviet Union, but he was very tight-lipped about it."

"You saw him?"

"This past Friday, in Salzburg." Galeazzo's body relaxed and he sighed heavily. "Oh, it is a relief to talk to someone."

"What do you think Mussolini will do?" A breeze blew, bringing with it the scent of lavender, one of her favorites. She paused to breathe in the fragrance, now knowing that such carefree moments would soon become scarce.

"I do not know. Maybe stall for time."

Josephine's heart sank. Another world war would devastate everything…the land, the people, the economy. She didn't know if she would have the stomach for it. God give me strength. Galeazzo put his hand on top of hers, covering it with his meaty palm.

"My dear, why don't we go to my hotel? I can order us dinner and…"

Josephine popped up like a jack-in-the-box, retrieving her hand from his grip. "I'm afraid I have to sing. I am obligated to deliver a show tonight. Perhaps I'll see you after?" She moved quickly to head to the doors. After pausing for a second to blow him a kiss, she slipped through the door and headed toward the band that was playing light jazz on a small dais. She clenched her fists to give herself strength to sing prettily, knowing that dark days would soon come to her beloved Paris…and all the world. But she bit her lip and thought back to previous shows, where gaiety and the relief of an ended war had permeated the atmosphere, and people danced and sang freely. She wanted that Paris back, and she vowed one day to have it.

As she sang to her small audience, she noted two Germans, both blond, with steel-grey eyes. They looked like brothers. One of the men looked at her greedily, the other with barely concealed contempt. But she ignored them and sang on. She sang seven songs, ending with J'ai Deux Amours, where she sang of her love for both the United States and Paris. After the applause, she descended the dais and mingled with the guests. After 20 minutes or so, she made a dash for the door while Galeazzo was preoccupied with the buffet table, barely able to contain her yearning to code her message for William.

As she stepped outside, a figure to her right moved, startling her, and she turned to see who it was. It was the contemptuous German. He was smoking a cigarette and when he saw her, he flicked it into a potted

J'ai Deux Amours

plant near the entrance. She backed away from him, but he lunged toward her and grabbed her wrist.

"Ah, the Black Jezebel. Strutting about like a pretty ape. Believe me, when the Reich takes over, subhumans like you will be eliminated," he growled.

Josephine tried to wrench her wrist away, but he held tight. She brought her right foot back and kicked forward with all her might. The German doubled over in pain, sputtering in anger, and stumbled onto the ground. Josephine resisted the urge to kick him in the head. The sound of a car horn punctuated the air and a car screeched to a stop in the driveway. Yves jumped from the driver's side and hustled Josephine into the back of the car. The other German walked out the front door as Yves shut the car door and exclaimed when he saw his fellow officer on the ground. Yves roared away, leaving the German yelling after them.

"Thank God I saw you," Yves said. "But you got him good, Miss Baker."

Josephine's heart was pounding in her chest and she gulped air into her lungs.

"It's okay. You're safe now. Just breathe," Yves said, reassuringly.

When her heart slowed, she smiled at Yves in the rear-view mirror. "He did go down like a pile of bricks." They both erupted in laughter...but with an undercurrent of wariness.

Le Beau Chêne
Paris Suburbs

Josephine was too on edge to take the time and code the information she had. If William wanted to find out what she knew, he would have to hear it straight from her. She snuck out to the park in the dead of night and made the mark on the bridge hand rail, then stuck a message in the chicken hutch for William to come to her living room to talk, and that she would leave the back door unlocked. She knew it would be dangerous, but speaking face-to-face would be more efficient. Josephine made a pot of coffee, grabbed a kitchen knife, and sat down on the couch to wait. It did not take long, however, before the rattle of the back door handle alerted her that someone had arrived. Josephine had kept the lights off, and she leaned back into the shadows and gripped the knife, in case it wasn't William.

The floor creaked lightly as a figure stepped into the room. A voice whispered, "Josephine. It's me. I saw the mark."

She sighed in relief and put the knife on the table next to her. "I'm here on the couch. Come, sit. I daren't turn on the light."

"Quite right." William edged over to the couch and followed the sound of her patting the cushion next to her. He sat down but did not look in her direction. Instead, he scanned the room, as if expecting someone else.

"Why didn't you code your message? This is risky."

"Just be quiet and listen to me. I got this from Ciano. Germany is about to invade Poland in a matter of weeks. Italy is upset because they are not prepared for war and since they signed the Steel Pact...or whatever it was called...they have to back Germany or declare neutrality, neither of which they like." Josephine sensed William's agitation as he clenched his fists in the dark, evidenced by the moonlight streaming through the window, catching the edge of his knees.

"Shit."

"There's more. Von Ribbentrop is set to go to the Soviet Union, but Ciano didn't know why."

"Fuck."

"What?"

William huffed. "In the war, Russia lost a lot of territory...Ukraine, Poland, Belarus, and the Baltic and Caucasus provinces. My bet is they're looking to get it back. If Germany invades Poland from the west, and while the world's preoccupied with that, the Russians could march through Belarus on the east and mop up the Poland leftovers." He put his head in his hands. "This is another world war for sure."

The two fell silent for a moment. Josephine was the first to speak. "There were no scientists there. I couldn't find out what the Germans..."

"It's all right. I did some digging of my own. The element you were talking about was heavy water."

J'ai Deux Amours

"Yes, that was it. What is it?"

"The details don't matter. The only place that produces it in large quantities is the Norsk Hydro plant in Norway. We're going to commandeer their stockpile for France."

"But they'll still be able to make more."

"Yes, for now, but at least it will delay the Germans. That's all I can ask for at the moment. We're not officially in a war yet. And I doubt the U.S. would follow Britain and France into a war…at least not right away. The American people are in their isolationist bubble."

Josephine arose from the couch and began pacing. "Someone has to warn the Polish. We can't let them just sit there while Hitler marches in on them."

"I'm sure the embassy and their communications are being watched. And who knows if the Germans have spies in the embassy."

"But…" Josephine stopped and whirled on William. "The ambassador's wife. I know her. Halina. I'll invite her to lunch."

He snapped a finger. "That's an idea. No one will be watching the women. Make it someplace secluded, not a lot of eyes."

"What could be better than here? I can send my car for her." Excitement crept into Josephine's voice. Perhaps their plan would work after all.

"No, not your car. Look, I can lift a driver's uniform somewhere and a car. I'll pick her up and bring her here. That way, I can make sure we're not being followed, and no one would recognize me as your usual driver."

"It's perfect."

William guffawed. "Don't count your chickens yet. I just hope she's not busy tomorrow."

"I'll ring her first thing in the morning. Who can refuse La Baker?" She did a flourish as if she were wearing a feather boa as she twirled in a circle.

"Good luck. Tell her I'll be by at noon. No excuses. Now, I'll start arranging things. Have a good night."

Josephine let him out the back door and made sure to lock it. The fate of the start of a war would be settled tomorrow…one way or another.

Shifting, Swirling HERitage

Le Beau Chêne
Paris Suburbs

Halina Łukasiewicz paled as Josephine told her the news over a lunch of chicken salad sandwiches and lemonade in the Louis XV salon, with its décor of gilded wood walls and chintz curtains. The vacant face of a suit of armor looked on from the corner. Halina stood up with a stricken look on her face, her napkin falling to the floor. Josephine had to caution her.

"Halina, you cannot act as if anything is wrong. We don't know who is watching the embassy. You must remain calm. Tell your husband, Juliusz, yes, but away from prying eyes and ears."

Halina fixed an inquiring gaze on Josephine. "You are sure?" she said in perfect French.

Josephine nodded, gravely. "Unfortunately, yes. I cannot tell you my source, but it is of the highest caliber."

"I believe you. We've all been afraid these past months." Her voice lowered to a whisper. "I had a sick feeling." She looked up at Josephine. "I must—"

Josephine stood. "Yes, of course. I will accompany you back to the embassy. In disguise, of course. I want to make sure you're all right…well, as much as can be."

"Not another war." Halina looked as if she would burst into tears. Josephine walked over to her and hugged her.

"All we can do is be strong, and pray this will be the last one. Come on, we have work to do." Josephine walked over to the sideboard and opened the top. She pulled out a hat, long brown wig, and sunglasses, then put them on. They headed outside.

William had put signs on the car for the Le Bon Marché department store to fool observers into thinking Halina was going on a shopping spree. He reported that they had not been followed on the way in.

"What are you doing? You need to stay here," he said, pointing to Josephine.

Josephine waved him away before climbing in the car after Halina. "I'm making sure Halina arrives back safely. I wouldn't be able to rest until I knew she was okay."

J'ai Deux Amours

Halina started to protest, but Josephine wouldn't hear of it. "The matter is settled." She figured William knew she meant business, because he did not say another word. He merely got into the driver's seat and they pulled slowly out of the driveway and onto the street. They rode in silence. Josephine surmised they were each lost in their thoughts and fears about the future. Her husband, Jean, would soon return from his trip, and she wondered what she would tell him.

Josephine felt the car take a hard curve as her face pressed into the window. She reached out to grab the back of the front seat to keep from mashing against the door. Halina had slid over to her side, her face locked in surprise. Josephine looked up at William. His eyes were focused on the rear-view mirror as he swerved tightly around the corner. "We've got company," he said. Halina and Josephine both turned to look out of the back window. A black Peugeot followed behind them.

Halina's face grew even more stricken than before, and Josephine figured their present situation was the limit of her espionage capabilities.

"Desperate times," William said. He sped up and rounded another curve, then screeched to a halt on the side of the road and hurriedly got out as he pulled a gun from his jacket pocket. As the Peugeot roared around the corner, William steadied his aim on the roof of the car and shot the driver. The Peugeot veered right, then skidded off the road and crashed into a tree. William ran across the road to make sure the driver was dead, and delivered two more bullets. The shots echoed off the nearby trees.

"Wait here." Josephine got out of the car and followed William. The driver lay slumped across the front seat, with a sizeable chunk missing from his skull. Josephine's stomach turned and she had to avert her gaze to keep from regurgitating her lunch. William began to pull the body from the car.

"What are you doing?"

"We have to take the body with us. No one can know what happened to him or prove we had anything to do with it."

Josephine nodded. "Okay, I'll open the trunk." She ran back across the street and pulled the keys from the ignition. Halina's eyes rounded as William carried the body to the rear of the car, but she said nothing. Perhaps she had seen some things as the wife of a diplomat, Josephine thought. After William loaded the body, he and Josephine piled in and William took off, a bit faster than before. Josephine knew he couldn't speed, but she wanted to get rid of the car as soon as possible. They rode in silence again, as the impact of things to come hit home more than any of them could have guessed.

"You can drop me off two streets over from the embassy," Halina said. "I can walk since it is such a nice day, and no one will be watching you, except perhaps a nosy neighbor."

William nodded silently. As they pulled up to let Halina out, she turned toward Josephine. "Thank you. I appreciate all you've done." Then she got out and headed up the street.

William then eased left onto a side street and meandered between neighborhoods before heading for the main road. Josephine had slumped into her seat and pulled her hat down to fully cover her face, afraid the police would pull them over. But they did not. William drove a circuitous route before heading for Josephine's house. She felt more relieved the closer they got to home.

After William pulled into the driveway, he turned around to face her. "You have no doubt changed the course of Hitler's plans, Miss Baker. I suspect the intelligence branches will see the wisdom of using more women as spies. I think it will turn the tide in our favor. You should be proud."

"Then why do I feel so anxious?"

"Good spies are always nervous on missions. Keeps them sharp. But let's lie low for a moment. No chalk marks for at least two weeks, and I'll think up another way of communicating. Perhaps a radio."

"All right." Josephine opened the door to get out.

"One more thing."

She turned toward William. "If the French and British are smart, they'll try to recruit you. I only ask that you share their information with me. The Deuxième Bureau is French military intelligence. I would prefer you chose them over the British."

"Always. But why?"

"The Brits still use the old boy network to vet their spies, boarding school chums and all. The FBI's obsession with communism isn't totally misplaced."

J'ai Deux Amours

Josephine nodded, a bit puzzled. "Thank you, William. I'll await your message."

"We've got a long road ahead, but I have faith."

"So do I," Josephine said. She squeezed William's shoulder, then shut the car door behind her and went inside.

September 1941
Casablanca, Morocco

Josephine stood on the balcony of her hotel suite overlooking the city. Its white buildings fronted a cornflower blue sky that blended with the sea's horizon in the distance. A cacophony of men's voices yelling as they loaded and unloaded ships carried on the breeze, along with the salty scent of ocean water and the fragrance of spices. As a pilot, she deemed it perfect flying weather.

Never in a million years had she thought she would end up in this place, but the winds of war often blew souls to the most remote regions, and World War Two had blown hers to the Moroccan coast. Hitler had invaded Poland, and Britain and France had declared war. Poland, at least, had been warned, and their spies had informed Britain and France of German artillery and troop movements. Still, the country had fallen to Hitler within three months…and William had been right. The same month that Poland had fallen, the French approached her to spy for them, the pitch presented by a dashing—and married—captain named Jacques Abtey who worked for the Deuxième Bureau. After her acceptance, he had become her mentor, her protector, and then her lover. She and her husband Jean had long-since separated; their lives had taken different routes.

She continued her espionage career doing what she had done for William—attend embassy parties, foist alcohol on high-ranking diplomats and officials, and get them talking about troop movements, which countries might join the war, and other intelligence. But instead of coding it, she would write notes on the palms of her hands and on her arms under her sleeves. Jacques would worry about forwarding the information to the necessary parties.

The Germans had occupied Paris in June 1940, causing her to flee to a chateau 300 miles south, where she continued to work for the Resistance. She also hid refugees in the basement and helped get them papers to neutral Portugal. She and Abtey had even traveled to South America to smuggle intelligence documents to the exiled General Charles de Gaulle, head of the Free French government. Abtey had accompanied her as a manager and had been nervous about being discovered, but Josephine played her usual role of the eccentric star who brought her menagerie of animals along with her and no one looked twice at Abtey…or her sheet music with invisible ink. Mission: Accomplished.

They were eventually given orders to go to Morocco to set up a liaison and transmission center, working with the French Resistance, British Intelligence, and American spies working undercover as diplomats. The latter were known as the 12 Apostles and had been sent to set up mercy shipments. At least that was the cover story. America had not entered the war, but Josephine was confident they soon would.

Given the speed at which Rommel was making his way through North Africa, hope in anyone who could stop him seemed a distant dream, and the Nazis took advantage of their gains to disseminate propaganda, which declared they had already all but won the war. Britain and America countered this campaign by releasing the Atlantic Charter, which stated both countries' desire not for expanded territories, but the expansion of international trade, the restoration of self-governance for all occupied countries during the war, and the allowance of all peoples to decide their own forms of government. The Arabs and Berbers of North Africa knew the Nazis disdained them as much as they did the Jews, and had looked favorably on the concepts in the Atlantic Charter. But it seemed a small victory in the face of the German onslaught.

The door to the suite slammed shut and Josephine turned to look through the billowing white linen curtains. "Jacques?" In the back of her mind, she looked for a weapon at hand, anything that could be used to fend off an attacker. Spying the water pitcher on the patio table, she edged toward it.

J'ai Deux Amours

"Yes! I have great news, ma chère." He stalked to the balcony and picked her up with both arms, then whirled them around. Josephine squealed like a teenager, relieved.

"What's put you in such a good mood?" she asked. He set her down and they both sat at the patio table. He leaned over the table and spoke in a hushed tone.

"You won't believe who I met."

"Who?" she said, quickly.

"A member of the Costello Mafia gang."

"From Chicago?"

"The very same."

"What on earth are they doing here?"

"Mostly smuggling. Cigarettes. His name's Sydney, but he thinks I'm FBI sent to spy on his operation. He wanted to put me on his payroll to secure my loyalty. So I put it to him that if the Germans rolled in, his operations would surely be shut down. And if the Americans joined the war, his operations could be construed at aiding and abetting the Germans. Well, he got agitated at the thought. So we decided on a mutually beneficial agreement."

"Don't tell me. We get to use his boats to send intel and arms?"

"Exactement, ma petite chou."

Josephine beamed. It was excellent news indeed. "We can supply guerilla fighters all across North Africa. But first…"

"Yes?"

"We'll need the approval of the local chieftains," she said. "There may be centralized power in the heart of the city, but on the outskirts, it's tribal law. Hmmm." She thought for a moment, then slammed her hand on the table. Jacques started. "I know. I'll arrange dinner tonight with the Sultan's cousin, Moulay Larbi el-Alaoui, and the Pasha, el-Glaoui."

"Do you think they'll join our cause?"

"Of course. They have no choice. We're going to win this war, Jacques. I know it. And they'd better know it, too."

Jacques came around the table and scooped her up in his arms, then planted a kiss on her lips. "I love your optimism. Some days, it's the only thing that keeps me going." He went inside and tossed her on the bed, then unbuttoned his shirt and kicked off his shoes.

"Jacques, if you're going to ravish me, at least close the patio door." He grinned.

Moulay Larbi el-Alaoui Residence
9 p.m.

After a few cups of sweet mint tea—for Muslims did not partake of alcohol—and an exchange of introductions and assorted pleasantries, the group sat down to dinner. A cluster of low round tables sat in the middle of the dining room area, with colorful cushions gathered around. Mosaic tiles decorated the walls and a collection of patterned rugs adorned the floors. Communal bowls lay on the tables, filled with couscous and stewed meat; mechoui—slow-roasted lamb; tagine—meat and vegetable stew with dried fruits and nuts; and b'stillah—a sweet and savory pie with chicken, onions, and warm spices in a pastry, topped with cinnamon and powdered sugar. Josephine had become intimately acquainted with Moroccan cuisine since her time in Casablanca; she found it delicious.

"My, what a sumptuous spread you've laid before us, my dear Larbi," she exclaimed.

"It is my pleasure, Madame Baker. My house is your house." Larbi bowed to his guests as they took their seats. The dinner party included Moulay and two of his wives; Jacques; Thami el-Glaoui, the Pasha—a title of high rank—of Marrakesh and one of his wives; and Josephine.

Josephine followed custom and ate from the communal bowl with her right hand, and only from the section facing her. The group made more small talk about family, Josephine's shows, local dishes, and the like. They skirted around the subject of war. After they finished their meal, servants brought out dessert, which was kaab el ghazal, or gazelle horns, along with more mint tea and some spiced coffee. The gazelle horns consisted of almond paste scented with orange flower water and cinnamon, enclosed in pastry. Josephine had to stop herself from eating half the platter, especially with Larbi's encouragement. It was times like these she could forget the cares of the world and enjoy the company of others, taking in the familial ambiance. It was a time to relish, as these moments were far too few.

After the dessert was cleared, the wives left the table. Josephine felt both privileged and frustrated with the lack of women's rights in the Arab world. But there was a whole religion built around women's roles. Any change to that would have to come from within, she thought.

It was Larbi who brought up the subject first as he lowered his voice. "So, how goes the war? My sources tell me Rommel is poised to take Tobruk from the Australians."

Jacques looked at Josephine and she nodded, permitting him to tell them all they had learned so far, and to ask for the favor. They would take the news better from a man. Jacques returned the nod and spoke in equally hushed tones.

"The German Africa Corps is proving more formidable than the Italians. But I'm about to close on a deal—and this goes no farther than this table—with American mobsters for the use of their boats to transport arms and other goods. Their sponsor is the high chief El Hadj. Now, I know you have a network of lookouts along the docks and other areas of the coast, as well as inland. The French Resistance is also working with British intelligence and American diplomats. I would like to ask a favor. Would you agree to allow your people to move our guns and men in support of the Allied cause?"

A pause ensued as Moulay's brow creased and he fell silent. Then he slowly nodded. "I believe in the Allied cause."

Josephine sighed, realizing she had been holding her breath.

Larbi continued. "Having El Hadj on our side will be very good indeed. He is well connected with the Berber Rif chieftains. I would like for my men to be armed, and, in return, I will send you any information we gather from our travels and our work. You and your men may also use my many homes as safehouses. I also have homesteads in the Atlas Mountains, which can be used as radio houses to send messages to Britain via Gibraltar."

Jacques beamed. "I think you may have just saved the day."

A din arose in the kitchen, with both moans and cheers, causing those at the table to look up from their huddle. Larbi shouted.

"What is going on?"

After a few moments, a servant rushed in, a smile on his face. "The Japanese have attacked Pearl Harbor in America. They have to enter the war now."

Josephine slammed her hand on the table. "I knew it! I think the war's won now, gentlemen."

Larbi regarded her with amusement, then turned to Jacques. "She is quite dramatic, no?"

Jacques nodded his head. "With certainty."

Still beaming, Josephine finally spoke up. "But there's still a lot of work to do. Larbi and Thami, what if Jacques visited the chieftains in the main cities…Rabat, Fez, Agadir, Safi, Casablanca, Marrakesh, to get them to help?"

"Face-to-face is important. It's how we do business," Thami said. "If you can arrange it through El Hadj, it would be even better."

"I'll meet with my contact and get started as soon as possible," Jacques said.

"Then let us toast to an Allied victory." Larbi raised his cup of spiced coffee and they all followed suit.

Days later, with Jacques on a tour of the major cities after having received approval from El Hadj, Josephine met with one of the 12 Apostles, James Everett, in her dressing room at a local theater. She had agreed to put on a few shows to keep up her cover. Josephine told him of Jacques' meeting with the mysterious Sydney, and their dinner with Larbi. James seemed genuinely pleased with their progress so far, but both knew dark days lay ahead.

"It's an abrupt feeling, this war. America was isolated, in its own world, letting Europe work out its own problems. And now…we've

J'ai Deux Amours

been dragged into the chaos. I knew it would eventually happen, but…" he trailed off.

"But it's different once it actually does." Josephine finished the thought. He met her gaze and nodded.

"What will America do now?"

James leaned back in his chair, which was covered in feather boas, and looked toward the top of her closet, brimming over with costumes and fake jewelry. "It's a multiple-front war, from Germany, to Japan, to North Africa…We're going to need time to assess the situation, appoint generals, draw up battle plans, and start manufacturing arms, tanks, planes, rations. Even we spies are going to be spread thin. We've received orders already to start gathering information."

"Such as?"

"The depth of the main ports, the force of the tides and their times, how wide the roads are and their state of repair, the maximum weight roads and bridges can take."

"I can get some of that for you." She blew a smoke circle from her filtered cigarette. "And don't worry, I'll do the research myself. There are listening ears about."

"Then you understand."

"Even in this lawless backwater town, where we can use lawlessness to our advantage, it's good to stick to at least a few basic principles."

October 1941

Josephine and Jacques sat on a bench near the beach, enjoying a cool night, eating ice cream cones. It was a clear night, and the stars twinkled in their heavenly expanse. Josephine had delivered her intel to James, who passed it on to his superiors. It was obvious the Allies planned to invade, but exactly when and precisely where was anyone's guess. A faint droning filled the air, which grew to a deafening roar as a squadron of U.S. planes approached the city. Suddenly, the sky was awash with leaflets. Josephine picked one up and read it. Each leaflet had a picture of President Roosevelt next to an American flag, with a message from

General Eisenhower telling the reader that American forces were soon landing to liberate the citizens from Nazi and fascist rule. Josephine jumped up, barely able to contain herself as she shouted with glee.

"Jacques! What did I say? You don't know the power of America."

She left Jacques on the bench as she headed for the city square, running as fast as she could, along with others who had been taking an evening stroll. The noise overwhelmed—airplane engines, explosions from bombs, people shouting. Josephine thought it glorious, until a fighter dove toward the crowd, firing machineguns. People began running every which way. Josephine felt a pair of strong arms pull her up and away from the melee.

"Come on! We need to take cover," Jacques said.

They ran toward a hospital, which were usually spared during raids, and ducked inside. Doctors and nurses filled the lobby, surrounding a man who was shouting orders. They knew there would soon be an onslaught of the wounded and dying, and they were making ready. Josephine vowed to offer whatever assistance she could.

It would be three days until she and Jacques would finally leave the hospital, doubled over with exhaustion. A kindly doctor had ordered them to leave before he consigned them to a bed, and so they reluctantly made their exit and headed back to the hotel. They both fell into bed and awoke 18 hours later.

The Allied invasion had been successful, toppling the Vichy French government. More than 500 Americans had died, along with more than a thousand Frenchmen, but the Allies had control of hundreds of miles of North African coastline, along with their strategic ports. The tide had turned against the Axis powers.

May 1944

Paris, France

The war had been won in Europe, with Hitler and Mussolini vanquished. Jacques had rejoined his wife, whom he had sent away to be protected from the war. He had confided in a friend that he could not

J'ai Deux Amours

be "Monsieur Baker," living in her shadow. Male pride, she thought. How many happy couplings had foundered on those perilous shores?

The Nazis had plundered her chateau, but she pledged to rebuild and restore it to its former glory…and beyond. She was making her way through the shops to look for home goods such as curtains, furniture, and rugs, when the cry of a woman in distress rang out. Josephine followed the sound, and spied two men wrestling with a woman. One man had a pair of scissors and was cutting the woman's hair, while the other man spat in her face. They were yelling, "Traitor!" On the ground were a dozen eggs, all broken, with the yolk running down the slight slope toward the street.

"Stop that!" Josephine said. At her voice, the two men turned. The menacing looks on their faces turned to abject shock when they realized who she was. "Get away from her." Josephine walked toward the woman and gathered her up, ignoring the two men, who stood stock still. The woman was about 40, with short—and shorter—brown hair, wearing a worn-out dress that had seen better days.

"My car is just there." Josephine waved at Yves. He pulled up into the alleyway and got out, at which point the two men sprinted away. After piling the woman into the back seat, Josephine climbed in after her. The women, who had appeared angry earlier, now broke down in tears, shaking.

"There, there. You're safe now. I can't believe men would take to molesting women in the street in broad daylight," Josephine said. She handed the woman her handkerchief, and she took it.

"What is your name?"

After the woman blew her nose and wiped her tears, she composed herself and sat up in the seat. "Catherine Michaud. And it's happening all over."

"What is?"

"Men molesting women in the street. They're calling us traitors, "horizontal collaborators," even innocent women. A woman the other day was stripped half-naked and smeared with tar and paraded through the street. People yelled at her and threw rocks. She almost died. Yes, some of us had to sleep with Germans. It was the only way to get food for our starving children. My husband died in the war and I have three children and a sick mother. I had no one to care for them if I went to work in a factory. What was I supposed to do?" Catherine's chest heaved in silent sobs. Tears ran down Josephine's face, too, even as white-hot anger welled up within her. French women had just gotten the right to vote, but American women had fought for—and won—that right in 1920. France was more than 20 years behind. Josephine wrapped her arm around the women's shoulders.

"Let's see if we can do something about it."

November 1944
Women's March
Eiffel Tower

Women had come from all over France to attend the Women's March Josephine had helped organize. Catherine had been her stalwart aid the whole time, introducing her to local women, women who had been attacked, and women interested in contributing to furthering women's rights. Josephine was not sure it would come together, but it did, and now, she looked out over a sea of women who had gathered at the Eiffel Tower to make speeches, sign a declaration, and support one another. Many had tried to dissuade her, citing the war's aftermath as an excuse. 'Your efforts should be put toward telling women to go home and have children to help rebuild France,' they would say. And she would reply, "Without the women of France feeling safe, secure, and valued, you won't get healthy children anyway."

Josephine was the first scheduled speaker at the march, and she stepped up to a makeshift podium. She had supplied the microphone herself, and she adjusted it as she had so many times before. It was a cloudy day, with rain threatening, but she said a silent prayer to ward off any downpour.

J'ai Deux Amours

"My fellow comrades in arms!"

The crowd cheered and she waited for the applause to die down.

"As Mahatma Gandhi marched 240 miles to protest the taxation of salt by the British, so we have marched from the L'Arc de Triomphe to here to protest the treatment of women by men. We may not have marched as long, but we have long been oppressed. We may not have marched as hard, but the hardness of our determination is unequaled. Women are not to blame for the machinations of men, for their thirst for power, for their lust for war. The women of France have raised its children, cared for its sick, served in its military, and struggled to survive. We have helped secure a victory for France. And yet…" She paused for effect. "And yet…we get the blame, and the shame, and the scorn for doing what we had to do to get food, clothing, and heating for our children. Without the sacrifices and compromises we had to make, many of us would not be here today. For where were our men? Why couldn't they protect us? They were on the battlefield. They were minding the war. But we had to mind the home front. To make sure the crops were picked, the cows were milked, the bread was made, and the children had something to eat and to wear.

"If you suspect someone collaborated during the war, take it to the courts. Men in the street are not the judge or the jury. Who are they to decide what punishment to mete out? As Jesus said, 'Let he who is without sin cast the first stone'.

"I believe in our cause, and in the righteousness of our defense. If we stand firm, we can accomplish anything. Vive la France!" More cheers swelled, and it was music to Josephine's ears. She waved to the crowd, then descended the podium, as another speaker walked up. The organizers had invited a host of feminists, everyday women, actresses, and entertainers to speak, and the vast majority had been only too willing to participate. As the day wore on, Josephine found herself ecstatic but exhausted. She could feel her age with each passing day, but the movement was making progress.

They had argued to the government that if they wanted children to thrive, mothers without husbands would have to be able to work to feed them, since the government was hardly able to do so itself, and there was a shortage of men. She knew women would have to keep up the pressure on both the government and employers, even in the face of opposition.

June 1948
Château des Milandes

The government had just passed the Right to Work Act for women, who now did not need their husbands' permission to vote or open a bank account in their own name, and Josephine cheered when she heard it on the radio. She yelled to her new husband, Jo Bouillon, to come to the living room. They kissed and hugged, and he opened a bottle of champagne to celebrate.

"You see, ma chère? You can do anything you put your mind to. So what is next on your list?" He swept her up in an embrace as they swayed to his humming of "Get Happy."

"Oh, Jo. I want children. Lots of them. I want to share all the love I have to give."

"Well, we do have to replenish France, so…" He planted a kiss on her neck. "How about we get started?"

Epilogue

In this story, the intelligence that Josephine Baker gathered prior to the invasion of Poland allowed them to fight Hitler for 3 months (instead of the one in reality), in which time, France and Britain were better able to prepare for war. Josephine's contributions shortened the war by a year, which ended in 1944 (1945 in reality), saving countless lives. Her fight for women's rights in the aftermath of French suffrage helped secure women's ability to earn money and maintain access to it via bank accounts without needing their husband's permission. In reality, these rights were not bestowed on French women until 1965.

In reality, Josephine Baker converted to Catholicism in her later years and adopted 12 children of different ethnicities and faiths, calling them "The Rainbow Tribe." She and Jo Bouillon divorced in 1961, after 14 years of marriage. She lost her home due to unpaid debts, and she began to perform again. After starring in a revue at the Bobino in Paris on April 8, 1975, she received rave reviews. However, four days later, she was found in a coma in her bed and was taken to a hospital, where she later died, on April 12, 1975. Her funeral attracted more than 20,000 mourners and she was the only American woman to receive full French military honors. On November 30, 2021, a symbolic casket was interred in the Panthéon, a mausoleum for the remains of distinguished French citizens.

Our Lady of the Gatling Gun

Marsheila Rockwell

January 30, 1885

CHARLOTTE ADAM LAFOUNTAIN LOOKED UP FROM WHERE SHE and the other Métis wives were busy making bannock and fashioning *les boulettes* for the men's dinner. Her son Antoine had just stormed through the kitchen door and strode angrily into the parlor where Gabriel Dumont and several of his loyal captains—including Antoine and his brother, Calixte Jr.—had gathered to plan their next steps.

In July, their leader, Louis Riel, had been fetched from exile across the southern border in the Montana Territory. Riel had been instrumental in getting the Canadian government to grant the Métis their rights in the Red River Settlement fifteen years ago, having forced the Crown into a treaty to bring Manitoba into the Confederation. Now the Métis in Saskatchewan had summoned him back to do the same for them here, after years of the government refusing to address their grievances. But even the silver-tongued resistance leader had been unable to move the cold heart of the Governor, whose silence in response to Riel's last petition sent in December had been the final affront. The Métis and their Indian allies had been pushed right up to the brink, as evidenced by the shouting that erupted when Antoine delivered his news.

Charlotte didn't need to hear what her son said to the men in a rapid-fire blend of French and Michif before the yelling began. She already knew. All of the women there did, even if not all of them were willing to comment on it.

Madeleine Wilkie Dumont, Gabriel's wife and the aunt of two of Charlotte's daughters-in-law, was not one of the reticent ones.

"It didn't work."

It being, of course, the foolish plan hatched out of Turtle Mountain to smuggle a Gatling gun over the border to them here in Batoche, hidden in a coffin supposedly carrying the body of a tribal chief being returned to his people for burial. As if the white governments on either side of the imaginary boundary they mockingly called the Medicine Line cared anything about Indians trying to honor their dead. Quite the opposite—the idea of disrupting a funereal procession and desecrating the remains of a great warrior had drawn the American soldiers like buffalo to the jump.

"We tried to warn them," Antoine's wife, Madeleine Ross LaFountain—"Maddy" to her family—replied, clucking her tongue and shaking her head as she flipped the bannock in the skillet with practiced fingers. Many Métis preferred to bake the flour and lard staple in an oven when they had access to one, but the LaFountains came from a long line of renowned buffalo hunters, and even if there were no buffalo left, they still clung to many of the ways of the hunt, including cooking bannock quickly over an open flame. "But they are *men*."

Maddy didn't elaborate aside from rolling her eyes heavenward, but the words she left unsaid were nonetheless conveyed by her rebuking tone. Métis were the children of Indian women and French and Scottish fur traders. Most of those who'd settled and become farmers had converted—willingly or *non*—to the religion of their fathers, which taught that men were the undisputed heads of the family unit. This teaching was at direct odds with what many of their mothers and grandmothers had passed down to them from their own tribes, which were often matriarchal in nature and valued their women for more than the number of offspring they could bear or the orderliness of their households.

"You should not say such things," Marguerite Riel, Louis's wife, chided. Of all the wives, she did not assist with the cooking, sitting off to the side as if her hands were too precious to sully with such menial labor. Many of the Métis women revered her, as the beautiful spouse of their great resistance leader and the mother of his cherubic children. They fussed about her and wouldn't let her lift a hand, taking on work which should rightfully be hers and leaving her to do little but stew in her own worries. But Charlotte knew the other woman was sickly, though Marguerite did her best to hide it. Trying to keep that firmly in mind, she spoke less sharply than she might otherwise have done when she replied.

"If one sees a split in the wood of his brother's spear, does he let his brother go off to the hunt without showing him the fault? Of course not. He is obliged to tell his brother of the flaw. Should his brother, thus warned, go off to the hunt without fixing the spear and then be injured, or even killed, because the flawed spear failed him, he creates work and hardship for his kin that need not have been."

Madeleine Dumont snorted.

"You should be giving the homilies at *Saint-Antoine de Padoue*, instead of Father Moulin," she said. "Perhaps the men would stay awake then."

Marguerite gasped in shock while Maddy laughed.

"You should show more respect to the Church!" Marguerite insisted, half-rising in her seat before slumping back down in a swish of black skirts. The woman was pale, Charlotte saw, and sweating. She pushed her own chair back from the kitchen table and stood, dusting floury hands off on her apron. The white powder was stark against the aged fabric of the apron, and Charlotte felt a sudden bolt of red-hot shame lance through her at the poverty it displayed, that she, the mother of two of Dumont's captains, did not even have a decent apron while Riel's wife lounged in relative finery, with her starched lace collar and beribboned skirts. Here on the prairie, ribbons were scarce, worn only on the most joyous or solemn of occasions. Certainly not for watching others make bannock and the round meat *boulettes* that were less and less meat and more and more flour these days.

But Charlotte's embarrassment was quickly followed by chagrin at her own pettiness, then anger at the Canadians—the cause of her family's poverty, and indeed, that of all the Métis people. And that emotion, though hurriedly banked, did not fade, or cool. Nor was it ever likely to.

As she crossed over to Marguerite to help her up and into her coat and then assist her outside, into the chill evening air, Charlotte pondered the other woman's words.

Even most Métis now held more respect for the Church than they did for the traditional ways their mothers and grandmothers had passed down to them, though many families had merged the two sets of beliefs, so that the women traveled with infants in cradleboards strung with both rosaries and dreamcatchers, and the men offered tobacco and prayers to St. Francis before going off to hunt.

If the Church had such a strong hold over a people that also revered the earth and her ways, the power it wielded over the Europeans who had no such connection to the lands they had stolen must be even stronger.

And if they revered the Church that much, even soldiers would be unlikely to stop the transport of cargo that clearly belonged to it....

"Madeleine!" Charlotte called over her shoulder after she'd gotten Marguerite several feet away from the farmhouse, where the night breeze could cool the sweat on her brow and bring color back to her cheeks. Both Maddy and Madeleine Dumont appeared in the doorway in answer to her summons. A curt jerk of her chin brought them shivering to her side.

"Meet me tonight in the barn, after the moon has set. It's time to take matters into our own hands."

Later that night, after the men had eaten their fill and were asleep—save for those who patrolled the area, much as they had done when making camp while following the herds—the four women met in the barn.

Our Lady of the Gatling Gun

Including Marguerite, whom Charlotte hadn't truly meant to invite, but whom she hadn't tried to keep the meeting a secret from, either.

It wasn't that Charlotte didn't trust Marguerite, exactly. But Louis Riel had gone into exile across the white man's border alone and come back with a wife and two children, and even if that wife were distantly related to most of the Red River families, it only meant that Charlotte had to feed, clothe, and give her shelter. It didn't mean she had to place the safety of their entire community on a bond of blood that had yet to be tested.

It didn't help that the woman was also far too religious for Charlotte's liking. Charlotte was hardly a heretic; she took the Sacraments like any good Catholic. But she was also a pragmatist, and she understood the primary appeal of the Church to the men who had once been lords of the plains. For hunters and warriors who felt the extermination of the buffalo not only as a loss of their livelihood, but as a blow to their pride and very identity, Church doctrine provided a lifeline, an alternate source of validation, teaching that man ruled over all and that the animals, plants, and Mother Earth herself were subject to him—that man was above them, instead of equal to and dependent on them, as the Indians believed. Submission was transformed into a virtue: Man to God, wives and their children to husbands, Indians and Métis half-breeds to white Europeans. Bending the knee to their occupation thus became an act of godliness, not of rank cowardice. It didn't take the wisdom of the dam builder *amik* or *migizi's* eagle eye to see that the Church was at the very least complicit in the oppression of the Métis, if not an active accomplice of the government in controlling them.

All the more reason to believe the women's plan would work where the men's had failed.

"Do you have it?" she asked Maddy in hushed tones, her breath puffing out in front of her like a cloud. She was trying not to breathe too deeply; the air was close here, smelling of old hay and fresh dung.

Maddy nodded, pulling out a folded piece of paper from beneath her coat and handing it over to her mother-in-law. Charlotte unfolded it carefully.

Dumont had shown his captains a sketch of a Gatling gun when first explaining the plan to smuggle one over the border. He'd given the drawing to Antoine for safekeeping, and Charlotte had caught a glimpse of it while bringing food into the men's meeting. Doubting it would be of any use to them now that their plan had failed, she'd had Maddy find it among Antoine's things and bring it to her.

The sketch was not terribly detailed, as far as Charlotte could tell, though she had little experience with guns that were used explicitly for hunting men and not game. But the artist had done them the favor of including a soldier standing beside the gun for scale, giving Charlotte a rough idea of the thing's dimensions. It had ten gun barrels mounted around a central shaft that looked to be in length perhaps two-thirds the height of the soldier. There were other parts of the contraption as well, but the only one Charlotte could readily identify was a hand crank.

She turned to Madeleine Dumont, who was a Wilkie, the same family Charlotte's sons Octave and Bernard had married into, and passed the sketch over to her. "I need you to get this to the Wilkies and the Bergers in the Montana Territory. I think one of these would fit in a two-man canoe. Tell them to get two canoes, their best painters, and be ready to do some modifications."

Then she turned back to her daughter-in-law.

"Maddy, your grandfather Hugh made many friendships while trading for the Hudson's Bay Company, on both sides of the border. He was a shrewd trader and a generous man, and there are many outstanding favors still owed to him, and hence to his heirs—to your father Roderick, and to you. You need to send word to his friends, and their families, and start calling in some of those favors.

"This is what I have in mind...."

As she spoke, both Maddy's and Madeleine's mouths dropped open, and their eyes went wide first with astonishment, then with excitement. Meanwhile, Marguerite's eyes grew large as the full Great Spirit Moon, but they held far less fire than the other women's, and far more fear.

Our Lady of the Gatling Gun

February 1, 1885 – April 18, 1885

The days that followed that first meeting moved as swiftly as a hungry wolf chasing down a rabbit. Madeleine Dumont left for the Montana Territory herself in early February, unwilling to leave such an important task to a messenger who might, if cornered, turn out to be less loyal to her husband than she was. Maddy made a whirlwind tour of her nearer siblings' homes, reminiscing with them about their grandfather while she skillfully pumped them for any information they might have regarding his HBC contacts. Once she had a list of names, it didn't take long before she was riding out herself on the pretext of visiting an ill cousin—not much of a deceit, truly, since so many of their Métis relatives were in the same situation as those in Batoche and the surrounding areas, battling both starvation and the diseases that inevitably accompanied it. At Antoine's insistence, Maddy took their second eldest boy, Elzear, along; he'd been taught by his father how to use a rifle almost before he'd learned how to sit a horse, and he was a crack shot. Maddy was in good hands.

But if the days before the departures of the two Madeleines had passed swiftly, the weeks after moved as slowly as cold maple oozing from a tree. Charlotte spent her time eavesdropping on the men's plans whenever she could, trying to understand what was happening with their machinations so she could determine how to best adjust her own. From what she had gleaned, the Canadian government had not yet roused itself to send the full might of its army, but it would not be long now before Prime Minister John Macdonald did just that; Riel had proclaimed a Métis Provisional Government in response to rumors that the police were coming to arrest both him and Dumont. Charlotte had no real confidence that her plans would come together before that happened, or before troops arrived in Batoche—the snow had finally begun to thaw in early April, making it that much easier for the Canadian army to mobilize. Fighting had already broken out at Duck Lake, where one of Dumont's brothers had been shot and killed and he himself had been wounded. There'd been fighting at Frog Lake as well. Many men had already died, or deserted.

But she had to try. She was Métis, and the Red River flowed in her veins.

More than that, she was the matriarch of a Métis family, and she had shepherded that family through famine, pestilence, and more death than any one woman should have to bear. If she had to lead them through war as well, then she would wear the mantle of the soldier as proudly as she'd worn that of mother, grandmother, and hunt wife.

Which was why, when Marguerite, whom Charlotte had been expending energy she could ill spare to keep from revealing her plans to Riel, Dumont, or any of the other men—including Charlotte's own sons—dared to question her, the older woman set aside her concerns for the health of their great leader's wife and responded with enough fire to scorch the prairie.

"Why are you doing this?" Marguerite demanded, her voice sounding high and plaintive in Charlotte's ears. "Acting like it is you who is Louis's general and not Gabriel? It's improper!"

Charlotte barked out an incredulous laugh.

"*Improper?*" She leaned close, not only to keep her words between them private, but so that the other woman would not miss the ire, or the fire, in her gaze. "I will tell you what's *improper*.

"The Canadian government starving the Indians to force them onto reserves, onto land that will never sustain their numbers. Trying to do much the same to the Métis, by taking our land and giving it to white settlers. All the pretty, pretty promises they make to us, but somehow never manage to keep.

"And the English Métis—the ones who forget that the 'half' in 'half-breed' means half-Indian as well as half European—they are no better! Taking the government's side against us—their kin, by both blood and marriage—because they wrongly believe that their European blood and lighter skin will save them, that what is done to us will not someday be done to them, when the Canadian government at last decides it wants what they have, too.

"*That,* my dear, is what's *improper.*"

Marguerite tried to move away, but Charlotte wasn't finished. Her hand shot out, clasping around the other woman's thin arm like a vise.

Our Lady of the Gatling Gun

"My husband Calixte's father fought with Cuthbert Grant at Seven Oaks when he was still a boy. My sons Calixte and Antoine fight with Gabriel now. The LaFountains have *always* fought for the Métis, and for our Indian brothers and sisters. And we always will. Because we know who we are, and where we come from.

"If you can't say the same, I'd suggest you figure it out well before the fighting starts, or you may find that lace collar on the wrong side of a hunting knife."

Marguerite's other hand flew to her neck as she let out a gasp, her eyes widening in alarm.

Charlotte hadn't meant the words as a personal threat against the wife of their revered resistance leader—she wasn't quite so sure of her or her family's position as that, despite her proud words to the contrary. But Marguerite's continued refusal to grasp what was at stake here, and her annoying tendency to mimic a startled deer whenever she heard something untoward, were almost enough to make the LaFountain woman change her mind, Riel's wife or not. The other woman could either pull her weight on the side of the Métis, as her husband was doing, or she could pile her children into a Red River cart and scurry back across the border to Sun River. At this point, Charlotte didn't much care which Marguerite chose, so long as she actually chose *something*. All the same, the older woman had to stop her own free hand from inching toward the skinning knife she kept in the pouch at her waist.

Just then, a ruckus swept through the village near where the two women stood. Charlotte released Marguerite and stepped away from her. As they turned in unison to see what the cause of the commotion was, the younger woman surreptitiously rubbed at her arm.

They watched as Dumont's men escorted the four Grey Nuns from St. Laurent into Batoche. Seeing the women's black and taupe habits and their swinging crucifixes glinting in the afternoon sun made the final pieces of Charlotte's plan fall into place.

"Of course I am on the side of the Métis!" Marguerite snapped suddenly, the brief respite afforded by the nuns' appearance having allowed her to locate her composure and, seemingly, a bit of backbone. Charlotte watched the nuns enter the home of Francois Xavier Letendre *dit* Batoche, which was the largest in Batoche and had been commandeered by the Provisional Government to serve as a residence for both Riel and Dumont. Then she turned to see Marguerite drawing herself up in righteous indignation. "I am the wife of the great Louis Riel! How *dare* you suggest otherwise?"

Charlotte was unimpressed. She had borne Calixte a dozen children and helped raise as many more of her own grandchildren. She knew that the louder the protestation, the surer the guilt.

"Then prove it," she replied.

Marguerite's eyes narrowed.

"How?"

"Make friends with our four new residents. Offer them every courtesy. Do your utmost to gain their trust." Charlotte leaned in close again. Marguerite flinched visibly, but to her credit, did not move away. "And when the time comes...."

"Yes?" Marguerite prompted when Charlotte trailed off meaningfully. The younger woman's voice was barely above a whisper, her face a study in dread.

"Be ready to betray it."

The two Madeleines and Elzear arrived by horseback later that same day, having beaten the messenger they had sent ahead of them with word of their coming. Charlotte lost no time in cornering them, shooing Elzear off to care for their tired horses, and demanding to know the status of her plan.

"Well?" Charlotte asked once she was sure no one could overhear.

Maddy couldn't contain a grin.

"One of Grandfather Hugh's contacts came through, and Madeleine's people were able to make two canoes into a casing, just as you directed, though they had to refashion the ends to do so. They used pitch to seal the halves together, but placed wooden pins in four spots to secure it for travel, and to make it easier to open when the time came.

Our Lady of the Gatling Gun

They showed us how to knock them out quickly with the butt of a hunting knife. And Grandfather's friend showed us how to assemble and use the—"

"But where *is* it?" Charlotte asked, frustrated by Maddy's chatter. Granted, everything her daughter-in-law was telling her was important, but she was apparently saving the best for last when Charlotte wanted that first and foremost.

"The cart's at least a week behind us," Madeleine Dumont replied. "Winter broke sooner in the south, and snowmelt has inundated the roads with mud. It's slow going."

Charlotte nodded, disappointed but not surprised.

"Why didn't you stay with the cart?" she asked Madeleine.

Madeleine shrugged.

"We passed many of Gabriel's messengers on the road as he sent for help from family and allies; we knew the fighting had already started." She met Charlotte's gaze levelly. "If my husband is going to die here in Batoche, I am going to die beside him. Not take the chance of arriving weeks too late just to mourn over his grave beside the thing that might have saved him."

Charlotte had no ready reply for that.

"Now, if you'll excuse me," Madeleine continued, "I understand Gabriel's been wounded and I'd like to go see him. I picked new spring herbs along the way that might help."

She didn't wait for Charlotte's permission, just nodded to her and Maddy before turning smartly on her heel and heading toward the Batoche residence.

Maddy watched her for a moment before turning back to Charlotte and continuing on as if the other woman had never spoken.

"It's really quite lovely. Before they painted it, they smoothed a layer of clay over the whole thing to help give it more dimension and to disguise the seams. Of course, it could only be dried in the sun, not fired, so it's not going to last much beyond the trip. It's wrapped in blankets now to protect it from cracking too much as the cart moves over rough roads." She paused, and for a moment, sadness seemed to wash over her features. "But then, it's not intended to, is it? Last, I mean. Sometimes I wonder if we are, either."

Before Charlotte could chide her, the sorrow was gone again—hidden almost as quickly as it appeared, as it always was by Métis wives—replaced by another emotion even less welcome.

Fear.

"Antoine?" Maddy finally asked, after a long moment of fraught silence. "There was word of Gabriel's wounding and Isidore's death, but none of the messengers spoke of Antoine."

"He's well," Charlotte replied, her own expression momentarily softening. "He's with Gabriel. You should go see him."

She understood Maddy's worry. How could she not? Life on the prairies was one punctuated by loss, but when a child lived to have their own children, it was easier for a mother to fool herself into believing that child might actually outlive her. But this war with the Canadians could well take all her children and grandchildren in Saskatchewan, if that Red River cart with its precious blanketed bundle didn't arrive soon.

At this point, she could only pray to both the Creator and the Christian God, and hope that one of them might actually answer.

April 19, 1885 – April 24, 1885

The next day, the nuns, though they had been fussed over by both Madeleine Dumont and Marguerite Riel and even slept in Louis Riel's bedroom (the resistance leader having given up his own bed without hesitation), nevertheless thought they would feel safer inside the confines of *Saint-Antoine de Padoue*'s rectory, so Riel had them escorted there. Marguerite, true to her word, went with them, insisting on ascertaining the comfort of their new lodgings before releasing them into the care of Father Moulin. Madeleine Dumont also went along to apprise Father Moulin of his impending delivery, ostensibly a gift from the Métis congregation of St. Peter's Mission in the Montana Territory to their Canadian relations. Afterward, they met with the LaFountain women.

Our Lady of the Gatling Gun

"The nuns did not bring much with them from St. Laurent," Marguerite replied when questioned. "But they do have extra veils, since those are what get dirty most quickly."

Charlotte nodded, pleased.

"That will be enough. Madeleine?"

"Father Moulin was quite pleased to have been thought of by the Jesuits at St. Peter's. He insists on believing it is a token of their regard to him personally, as opposed to a gift from one Métis community to another." The disdain that twisted her lips was gone as swiftly as it appeared.

"All the better," Charlotte said, chuckling. "If he thinks it's a gift meant for *his* glory rather than the Church's, he'll have to overlook any flaws it might have, as they would only reflect poorly on his vanity."

"What of the Canadians?" Marguerite asked. "Louis will tell me nothing, saying if I am afraid, I should pray for our deliverance."

"Antoine just grunts and waves me away," Maddy added. "I can tell he is worried."

It was Madeleine who answered. She and her husband had always been close; Charlotte thought it a wonder the woman had not yet divulged their plans to him.

"Gabriel says there are rumors of troops coming on a train from the east; maybe five hundred men, maybe more."

Even Charlotte gasped; without aid from their Indian allies, some of whom had not yet arrived and some of whom she feared never would, the Métis forces totaled less than half that number.

"And they say that the Canadian government is afraid because they believe the warriors who killed Custer stand with us. They do not want what happened to Custer to happen to them."

Charlotte quickly put her shock away, replacing it forcefully with a confidence she wasn't sure she felt.

"They should be afraid," she said grimly, "because once our 'gift' gets here, we will make what happened to Custer look like children merely playing at war."

A few days later, Charlotte was serving food to Riel's Exovedate, his Provisional Government council, as they argued over tactics. Dumont wanted to harry the troops that were now marching toward them, led by a General Middleton, but Riel was afraid that would expose them to attack from the police at nearby Prince Albert, whose forces the Métis had embarrassed at Duck Lake. Riel often remarked on the spirit leading him, and as Charlotte listened to him speak of it yet again, she wondered if it were truly a spirit of the Christian God, as he claimed, or something else. Perhaps something darker, one of the things that walked the cold, windswept prairies at night, looking for men to consume. Her thoughts flashed briefly to the *rougarou*, and she shivered, resisting the urge to cross herself.

In the end, though, Dumont's wisdom won out, and he and Riel left with a force of almost three hundred Métis and Indians the next night, riding south toward Tourond's Coulee, leaving about forty men behind. They had been gone scant hours, though, when messengers arrived at the village, warning of a force advancing toward Batoche from Qu'Appelle.

Dumont's brother Édouard and Emmanual Champagne rode out in all haste to fetch Gabriel back, and returned a few hours later with Riel and about a hundred and fifty of the better-armed men, the rest having continued on with Dumont's original plan. When it turned out that the "advancing force" was nothing but some horses, Dumont's wisdom was once again borne out.

Some time later, distant canon fire erupted and Métis women, many with sobbing children wrapped about in their skirts, began gathering near the rectory as they cast worried eyes toward the south. Some of the women prayed audibly and wrung their hands, but many were murmuring angrily.

Then a messenger galloped in on horseback, breathless, and Riel finally appeared to see what the commotion was. When the rider reported that Dumont had sent him for reinforcements, the angry murmuring grew louder.

"What are you doing here on your knees praying when your men are out there on their knees fighting?" Madame Caron demanded, her younger children trailing after her like a line of ducks.

"We need to pray to God—" Riel began, but to Charlotte's surprise, his wife cut him off.

"We *need* to help our men," Marguerite declared.

Madeleine Dumont moved to stand by her side.

"If you will not do it, *we* will."

Charlotte moved forward as well.

"Elzear, fetch our wagon!"

Other women began to clamor in kind.

"*Non, non*!" Riel replied, exasperated. "We will go. The *men* will go. You women stay here and prepare the rectory to receive our wounded, should there be any."

"Should there *be* an—?" Maddy began, outraged, but Charlotte grabbed her arm, cutting her off.

"Let him be," she said. "This will give us an excuse to get into the rectory, and up into the second story, where the nuns are staying. I want to know how much of the village you can see from there…."

April 25, 1885—May 8, 1885

The Métis men brought their fallen home from Tourond's Coulee the following Monday via horseback and Red River cart. By the grace of God, they had lost only six, whereas the Canadians had lost more than fifty. It was considered a great triumph by many, though in truth, had the Métis not been taken by surprise by Middleton's scouts, the bulk of the Canadian column would likely have perished in the ambush Dumont had laid for them in the deep ravine at Tourond's Crossing. So, while the victory was welcome, it was also seasoned with the sharp tang of disappointment.

Perhaps more important than the outcome of that skirmish was the fact that the men had used up the majority of their ammunition in the fighting. In the days that followed, while Middleton waited for reinforcements, too frightened to advance on Batoche with only the men now in his command, the Métis women melted down whatever lead they could find for bullets and the men dug rifle pits amongst the trees and bush all along the trail that led from the crossing to the village.

And then there was nothing to do but wait and see what reached them first—Middleton's reinforcements, or the Red River cart with its precious cargo.

Charlotte heard Dumont and Riel arguing more than once during that fraught, liminal time. Dumont was impatient and wanted to attack Middleton's camp before his reinforcements arrived; the Métis knew the land better than their enemies and it would be a simple matter to sneak a small group of men past the general's picket lines...set some fires, slit some throats. But, *non*, Riel would not hear of it. His spirit had told him the final battle must be fought here, in Batoche.

Charlotte wondered if Riel's spirit knew about her plan and that's why it was counseling patience. Or if the rumors she had heard about Riel having spent time in an asylum while in exile were true, and the spirit he claimed was guiding his decisions was just a figment of his troubled imagination. She hoped for the first, but very much feared the second.

And then scouts from the other side of the river arrived with reports of an empty cart found on the Carlton Trail with two dead Indians beside it.

Charlotte rushed to find Maddy and Madeleine when she heard the news.

"Only two?" Madeleine asked, growing pale. "There were six men with the cart. Two of them were my close cousins!"

"What happened to them? Where is the—?" Maddy began, but Charlotte cut her off.

"They don't know for sure. The scouts said footprints led off into the brush, sunk deep, as if the people who fled were heavily burdened."

"Middleton's men?" Maddy ventured.

"My cousins would not have abandoned the cart," Madeleine replied, shaking her head.

"And soldiers would have taken the cart and everything with it, and kept to the trail, where the going is easier," Charlotte opined. "The Wilkies must have come under fire and decided to travel the rest of the way on foot."

Our Lady of the Gatling Gun

"But how long ago?" Maddy asked. "Did the scouts say how long the Indians had been dead?"

It seemed a callous question, especially given that whoever they were, those dead Indians were likely relations of some sort. But war had come to the Métis women, and they had to harden their hearts and focus on the task at hand. There would be a lifetime for grieving, later. If any of them survived.

Charlotte shook her head.

"They could not say for certain. A few days, at least."

"A few days!" Madeleine exclaimed. "Then they should have been here by now!"

"If they had used the ferry to cross the river, we would have known," Maddy pointed out. "*Everyone* would have."

Charlotte knew that was true. The women's camp, where they had dug caves into the riverbank and camouflaged them with brush for the women and children to hide in during the fighting, was just north of the ferry landing. If the Wilkies had come that way with their burden, all of Batoche would have heard of it by now.

But if they hadn't used the ferry, they would have had to cross the river somehow....

When she realized, Charlotte almost laughed. Instead, she turned to Madeleine.

"Go find Gabriel and ask him to meet us on the riverbank just west of the cemetery. If I'm right, we should find our missing prize there, even if the Wilkie boys aren't with it."

Madeleine looked confused, but she didn't argue. As she left to track down her husband, Charlotte looked at Maddy.

"Come. We need to go wading."

Charlotte and Maddy's skirts were soaked several inches up from the hemline and Charlotte's feet were going numb in her boots by the time Madeleine returned with her husband. The two of them appeared to be arguing.

315

"…what is so important? I have to secure the village defenses before the Canadians advance again. I do not have time for…whatever this is!"

Madeleine snorted, even as she held out her hand for Gabriel to help her down the bank to where Charlotte and Maddy were probing through the reeds.

"We are *also* tending to the village defenses! Now, hush. We are here."

The couple came up alongside the two LaFountain women. Charlotte nodded in greeting, but Maddy did not lift her eyes from scanning the riverbank. After a moment, she gasped and pointed.

"There!" she shouted, breaking out in a run through the sucking mud toward something Charlotte could not at first make out.

"I see it!" Madeleine exclaimed excitedly, pulling her husband along behind her as she hurried to where Maddy stood.

It took Charlotte longer to reach the same spot; the cold had seeped into her joints, paradoxically making every step feel like treading on hot coals. She knew she would need to get out of the water and her wet boots soon, or risk permanent damage to her toes. But when she finally reached the others, she was gratified to see a slightly larger than life-sized Mary Immaculate bobbing calmly in the small pool formed by a deadfall of rotting logs, her blue robes blending in with icy water of the Saskatchewan River. The Virgin's painted hands were clasped before her in prayer, her face serene and miraculously free of cracks.

"What in the name of…?" Gabriel asked, his voice full of wonder as he crossed himself.

Madeleine turned to Charlotte.

"How did you know it would be here?" she asked.

"I didn't," Charlotte admitted. "But it's two canoes stuck together. And canoes *float*."

Maddy laughed at that, but Madeleine's face was still tight with worry, her eyes roving across the far bank, so Charlotte hastened to add, "I knew the Wilkie boys were smart enough to realize that the best way to get the statue across the river without risking further discovery was to send it over on its own. I'm sure they're halfway back to the Montana Territory by now. They'll send word when they can; don't fret."

Our Lady of the Gatling Gun

Madeleine frowned, clearly unconvinced, but Gabriel spoke before she could give voice to her skepticism.

"I'm sure you're right, Madame LaFountain. But perhaps you might now fill me in on *why* my wife's cousins made such a dangerous journey just to deliver a statue to us?"

As Maddy hurried off to collect Antoine, Calixte, and others of Gabriel's men to carry the statue from the river to *Saint-Antoine de Padoue*, Charlotte filled him in on the plan she and the other women had hatched, and on the statue's true purpose, and the treasure it held inside.

He was laughing heartily enough, by the time Maddy returned with Antoine and the other men, that he wound up grabbing at his head where he'd been wounded at Duck Lake, causing Madeleine to scold him roundly. Together, the men made short work of extricating the statue from the mud and carrying it up to the church. Once there, Charlotte took the lead, knowing that Father Moulin considered himself a prisoner of the Métis men rather than a refugee under their protection. As a result, he had refused to give them the Sacraments, a circumstance that bothered the wives far more than it did their husbands.

Well, some of the wives. Charlotte herself didn't have much use for Father Moulin; as far as she was concerned, he'd made his allegiance to Canada over the Métis who fed and sheltered him abundantly clear. But right now, she needed him, so she plastered on as sincere a smile as she could muster—it wasn't a facial expression she employed often—and began speaking in excited tones, her gaze flicking briefly to the other women to urge them to follow along.

"Father! Look what has come from our relations in the Montana Territory! A statue of Mary Immaculate! Isn't she beautiful?" They had washed off most of the river mud before bringing it up the embankment, so it was indeed a striking figure, and the late afternoon sunlight caught the Blessed Virgin's face, making it seem to glow. "What a great honor they bestow upon us, and upon *Saint-Antoine de Padoue*!"

The other women chimed in loudly in agreement, and more women began to gather to see what all the noise was about. As the crowd grew and the murmurs of acclaim spread, Marguerite appeared behind Father Moulin, accompanied by the Grey Nuns. Her eyes widened for a moment at the sight of Dumont and three of his captains holding the wooden statue, before moving to meet Charlotte's. Then she launched into her part of the plan.

"Oh, look, Sisters! It's here! Did I not tell you it was coming? What a comfort it will be to have Our Mother watching over you as you sleep!"

Father Moulin's head snapped around at that, but the nuns had already taken the bait.

"Oh, *oui*!" Mother Augustine said, both her English and her French flavored with a pinch of Irish brogue. "Do please move aside, Father, so that these men can bring the statue upstairs to our quarters. We will begin a rosary immediately! We will pray for peace to prevail in this conflict."

"But…*non*…wait…," the priest spluttered, but it was too late. He had been outmaneuvered by the Métis women before he'd even realized there was a battle being fought.

Charlotte dearly hoped that was a sign of things to come.

She and Maddy accompanied Gabriel and the men up the stairs, while Madeleine Dumont skillfully intercepted Father Moulin before he could follow along, insisting on telling him and the mass of onlookers the whole story of how the statue had come to them with the aid of her Wilkie cousins. The nuns' room was quickly crowded, and Charlotte and Maddy kept the four sisters occupied with contradicting opinions about the best placement for the statue, having the men move it first to one side of the room and then the other, then back again. Meanwhile, Marguerite used the cover provided by the press of too many bodies in too small a space to rummage through the nuns' belongings and find the extra veils she had told Charlotte about. She quickly found the long black mantles and secreted them beneath her skirt.

When she signaled Charlotte from the door, the older woman brought the men's suffering to an end, directing them to place the statue in the southeastern corner, which would provide easy access to both the single southern window and the most southerly eastern window, as that was the direction Middleton's troops would be coming from.

Then there was a pounding on the stairs, and Elzear ran into the nuns' room, followed quickly by Madeleine Dumont and Father Moulin.

Our Lady of the Gatling Gun

"*Imbaabaa!*" he shouted to Antoine. "The Canadians are coming! The Canadians are coming!"

The boy was carrying his rifle, and Father Moulin was yelling at him that weapons were not allowed in the rectory, which admonitions Elzear pointedly ignored.

Gabriel looked over to Charlotte, who nodded.

"We have this. Go do your part," she said.

"We'll drive them to the pound, *Madame*," he replied, referring to the Cree method of corralling buffalo in a small enclosure.

"What?" Father Moulin asked suspiciously. "What's that you're saying?"

Gabriel and his captains rushed past him without responding, while the nuns all took kneeling positions on the bare wooden floor before the statue, crossing themselves as they began to recite the words of the rosary in Latin.

"*In nómine Pátris, et Fílii, et Spíritus Sáncti....*"

When Elzear made as if to join his father and the other men, Maddy grabbed his shoulder and pulled him back.

"Give me your rifle, son, and go help your grandmother."

Elzear opened his mouth as if to protest, but took one look at his mother's suddenly grim face and quickly turned and obeyed her. Meanwhile, she pushed past Father Moulin and grabbed the handle of the door, pulling it closed.

Charlotte had stridden quickly over to Marguerite, who pulled the veils from beneath her skirt, much to the consternation of both the four nuns and Father Moulin.

"What in God's name—?" he began, but he stopped short when Maddy raised the rifle to her shoulder and pointed it at him.

"Don't take the Lord's name in vain, Father," she chided gently, a small smile budding on her lips as she gestured for him to move to the opposite corner of the room. She seemed to be enjoying herself.

"Now, you listen here, Madeleine LaFountain," he began in a huff, but he stopped once more when Maddy levered the rifle.

"With all due respect, Father, we're done listening," Charlotte replied. "Now it's our turn to talk." As she spoke, she placed one of the nuns' long back veils on her head, over her braided hair.

Marguerite followed suit, then handed a veil to Madeleine Dumont, who did the same.

The nuns had stopped praying, but they did not interfere, just watched with curiosity to see what the Métis women would do.

"I'm sorry, Sisters," Maddy said, taking her eyes off the priest for a moment to look over at the nuns, "but I will need you to join Father Moulin on the other side of the room, for your own safe—"

Father Moulin took the opportunity presented by her brief distraction to lunge at her, perhaps thinking to wrestle Elzear's rifle away. To Charlotte's amazement, Maddy calmly swung the rifle toward him, aimed, and quickly fired off a shot, hitting him in the leg. He fell to the floor with a scream, clutching at the wound. Maddy ignored him.

"As I was saying, Sisters," she began again, but the nuns needed no further prompting. They stood and quickly hurried over to the corner Maddy had indicated, pausing only long enough to collect Father Moulin and help him along, the priest limping and crying the whole short distance. Charlotte wasn't sure, but she thought she heard Mother Augustine tell him to stop being such a baby. Apparently even the nuns were tired of his antics.

Maddy handed the rifle back to Elzear with instructions to watch the religious—shooting Father Moulin again if necessary—and then hurried over to where the other women were working to break open the statue with the various knives they kept about their persons. Even Marguerite, whom Charlotte was somewhat surprised to discover owned a blade more fit for the prairie than the kitchen. As Riel's wife used the butt of the knife to pound on the spot Madeleine Dumont pointed out, pausing only to cover her mouth when a cough wracked her thin frame, Charlotte admitted to herself that she'd misjudged the other woman. When it mattered, Marguerite had made a choice, and she had chosen her people. Charlotte could ask for no more.

Maddy slipped her own veil on and then began pounding at the last pin with her knife, turning her face away from the chunks of painted clay that broke off with every strike. After a few blows, there was a loud *crack* and the women all instinctively jumped back, away from the statue.

Our Lady of the Gatling Gun

The façade of the Virgin Mary did not budge for long, agonizing moments—enough time that Charlotte began to worry that her plan was going to fail. Now, at the last, when all their resources had been committed to it and it was no longer just some clever idea she'd dreamt up and browbeat the other women into going along with.

Now, when it was the sole strategy that would either save or doom them all.

And then the front half of the statue fell forward and to one side with a thump, revealing the prize inside.

Rifle fire had begun in the distance, moving steadily closer as Gabriel and his men led the Canadians into their trap, using rifle pits to function as the "chute" to Charlotte's "pound" in front of the rectory. Charlotte moved over to the southern window to try and catch a glimpse of the advancing troops. She made sure to pull the veil around her shoulders, so anyone looking up at the rectory would assume she was one of the nuns and hopefully forebear to shoot. She had not been with the two Madeleines in the Montana Territory, so did not know how to assemble or use the surprise they had in store for Middleton's army. Nor was she as strong as she had once been. She knew she would be of little help to them as they maneuvered the heavy parts into their proper places.

But it wasn't lack of knowledge or even strength that kept the older woman rooted at the window in her self-appointed lookout position.

It was fear.

Fear that, in these final moments, she would turn around and see that it had all somehow gone wrong, that somebody somewhere along the way had made a mistake and what had arrived on the banks of the Saskatchewan was not the deliverance Charlotte had promised them all it would be.

That the Métis would be defeated here, today, in Batoche, and it would all be her fault.

"It's ready," came Maddy's excited voice from behind her. Charlotte closed her eyes for a heartbeat, sending up a prayer to the Creator.

Daga, Gichi-Manidoo.

Then she turned, and saw it.

A Gatling gun. Just like in the picture Gabriel had shown his captains.

Before Charlotte could say anything, the wooden sill of the window behind her exploded in a shower of glass and splinters as a bullet tore through it, narrowly missing her and lodging in the back half of the Virgin Mary statue. Even as she flinched away, she heard Gabriel's call from outside.

"That's it, men! Into the pound!"

"Now!" Charlotte cried. She hurried over to help the other three women push the gun in place in front of the window, its multiple barrels pointed outward at the troops they could all now plainly see, then held it steady with Marguerite as Maddy turned the hand crank and Madeleine began feeding bullets into the hopper.

And fire and hell rained down on Middleton's troops, tearing mercilessly into his men as Charlotte and Marguerite swung the gun back and forth, back and forth, with Maddy manning the crank and Madeleine keeping the voracious monster fed until there was nothing left to feed it, and no one left to shoot at.

The four women, half-deaf from the echoing sound of the Gatling gun's continuous fire, half-blind and choking from the acrid gunsmoke, moved away from the weapon to stare out in shock at the carnage they had wrought.

The flat area in front of the rectory was littered with the bodies of the dead and dying. Charlotte thought there must be hundreds of men; maybe all of Middleton's troops. Screams and sobs still punctured the air, even after the gunfire had begun to peter out. Métis men, identifiable by their capotes, walked through the sea of red-uniformed bodies, putting those that could not be saved out of their misery. Charlotte was the last to look away.

"What have we done?" Maddy whispered, her face drained of blood. The other two women wore similar looks of horror.

"Done?" Charlotte repeated, squaring her shoulders and lifting her chin as she looked at the women who would one day, along with her, come to be known as the Saviors of Batoche. "We have fought for our people, the Métis—for our rights and for our homes. Just as the LaFountains have *always* done.

"Just as we always will."

Our Lady of the Gatling Gun

How History Was Changed:

The decisive Métis victory over Prime Minister John Macdonald's forces at Batoche had a domino effect, not only in Canada and the United States, but across the world.

In Canada and the western United States, the Métis used the Gatling gun Charlotte and the other woman had successfully smuggled over the border to go on to win several more victories, ultimately reclaiming most of the traditional homelands of the Red River Métis: Saskatchewan, Manitoba, Alberta, the Montana Territory, and the northern half of the Dakota Territory. They called these lands *"Danakiiwin,"* or simply, "Home."

John Macdonald quickly lost favor in Canadian politics after his defeat, and his fall from grace meant that hundreds of residential schools across Canada were never built, nor were their counterparts in America. Generations of Indigenous trauma due to the forced assimilation, abuse, and murder that were the hallmarks of these schools never happened. The infamous Sixties Scoop never happened.

The Métis returned to their matriarchal roots when *Danakiiwin* was established, ensuring that women's bodies and voices would always be respected in their society. As a result, the Missing and Murdered Indigenous Women, Girls, Trans, and Two-Spirit (also known as Missing and Murdered Indigenous Relatives or People) epidemic never happened.

Worldwide, without the examples of the residential school system and unchecked settler-colonialism in America and Canada to follow, Hitler never rose to power. The Holocaust never happened.

And because Indigenous ways of knowing, culture, and traditions were never lost, *Danakiiwin* became a respected voice across the globe in conservation ecology. Under their purview, many pipelines, mines, and dams were never built, preventing a long list of environmental disasters. Ancient stewardship was respected and emulated, and climate change was halted and reversed before it could destroy the planet and the humans who live on it.

So many of the most awful things we've experienced in this timeline simply never happen with a Métis victory at Batoche. Kinda makes you wish we'd actually won, huh?

Shifting, Swirling HERitage

Author's Note:

Charlotte Adam and her husband Calixte LaFontaine/LaFountain, their son Antoine and his wife Madeleine Ross LaFontaine/LaFountain, and Elzear LaFountain are my direct ancestors (Elzear was my great-grandfather). However, while many of the events related herein are historically accurate (for instance, Antoine and his brother Calixte did indeed fight at Tourond's Coulee and the Battle of Batoche with Gabriel Dumont, and Father Moulin *was* shot in the leg—though it was by the Canadians, not the Métis), many others are fictionalized. This is simply the story of one way the Battle of Batoche *could* have played out. I invite anyone interested in learning more to check out the Gabriel Dumont Institute Virtual Museum of Métis History and Culture at ttp://www.metismuseum.ca/.

Also, the language used by Charlotte and the other Métis is Ojibwe; historically, while they probably would have known Ojibwe, they would most likely have spoken Cree or Michif. However, since Ojibwe is the language I am most familiar with, that is the language I chose to incorporate here.

Playing the Long Game

Susan Shwartz

15 August 1118

Anna Komnene, born in the Purple, labored like a servant. She wore silk, but she sweated as she ground medicines, mixed potions, mashed food, wiped her father's face, and leaned over far too often to check in terror whether he still breathed. The clerical drone of *kyrie eleison, christe eleison* made her want to scream for silence. That would have won her only outrage.

Because she had been schooled to acknowledge facts, she had to admit that her father, Alexius the Basileus, Emperor of the Romans, was dying. But, until the breath was out of him, she would serve as his physician, servant, and loving dutiful daughter to her father while trying to comfort her distraught mother Irene Dukaina.

Her father had never betrayed her mother as he had betrayed her. Anna wanted to be her father's heir again. She was furious at him, but her love was greater than her anger.

No one would ever hint that Anna had not done her best to save her father. Early in his illness, she had taken charge, ordering Alexius moved so tenderly from the Grand Palace to the Mangana for its greater quiet so he could breathe more easily. She tended and fed him with a devotion she had never shown her four children. She could not imagine life without him, although she knew that, very soon, she must face it.

Anna watched the Emperor fight for breath in the cool room with its shadowed high ceiling, stone floors, and mob of guards, priests, and nuns clustering far too near.

Anna's mother distracted the clergy with prayers and tears, but not all of her words were loving or pious. That too was to be expected in the Imperial family.

While Alexius was still able to speak, Irene had attempted time and again to persuade him to name Anna heir again instead of her younger brother John. It was only fair, she argued. Anna had been declared heir at her birth, when she was destined to rule beside her cousin Constantine like a second Justinian and Theodora (although Anna was born in the purple and Theodora had been a common entertainer). But, Constantine, like the Alexander whom courtiers said he resembled, died young.

Anna's brother John's had been a very ugly baby, but he was vigorous. And a son. Alexius had turned away from his daughter. Her life and worth dwindled from heir to daughter and wife. Even her studies had been circumscribed to subjects suitable for a marriageable princess.

Anna fought being diminished. She had been fostered by her late betrothed's formidable mother Maria Alania. Her grandmother, the even more formidable Anna Dalassene, had prescribed reading for her as if it were the medicine she must take to be fit to rule.

The princess had never been able to resolve the paradox in her father's relationship with his mother. Alexius and Anna Dalassene had worked and lived practically as one being. The story was he had served her like a slave. But he had always balked her in one thing. She had never been able to convince him to restore Anna as heir.

Even at age fourteen, after Constantine's death, Anna had known enough to play the long game for Imperial rule. She had married the talented general Nikephorus Bryennius. Older than she and profoundly able, he had fought Godfrey of Bouillon off the walls of Constantinople before the Westerner raved throughout the Middle

Playing the Long Game

East and seized Jerusalem. Nikephorus had also won a battle against the Seljuk ruler Malikshah. His bloodline was good, and he should make a capable co-Emperor for her. In their years together, they had four children and built a marriage of respect, study, and collaboration. Now, however, when she needed him most, Nikephorus had been absent for days.

They had two daughters, who reminded Anna of herself, and two sons. She loved and tended them too, but would have rejoiced if they had entered religious life so that her girls' path to power would be smoother.

Throughout her marriage, Anna was deemed virtuous, when she really spent her life in subtle rebellion. In between infants, audiences, and interviews with the men who worked most closely with her father, she had secretly hired Michael of Ephesus to tutor her. She learned to understand the armies. She knew the Domestikos of the Scholae and could even speak to the Varangian Guards, who towered head and shoulders over her, in their own barbarous tongue.

Now, Anna glided over to stand by her father with a new potion. Amethysts studded the cup, protection in the Imperial Byzantine color against poison. Considered a woman's weapon, a traitor's weapon, Anna would not stoop to it even against the brother she detested worse than the Bogomil heretics. Certainly not against the father she loved more than anyone else in the world. And not before she was declared heir again.

"Try to drink," she urged the Basileus. Her father's lips were cracked, his breath foul, his breathing labored. She tipped the glistening cup to his mouth. Streams of medication ran down the wrinkles leading from his lips. They were very pale, almost blue, but at least, he swallowed some of the potion, and he had not coughed. That might have been fatal.

She eased Alexius down onto the bed again. His breathing grew stertorous as the crowd in the room sucked out all the air.

"All of you, get back!" she snapped. She wanted to order then out, but knew that would not be allowed. She could not take her eyes off her father's beloved face. Perhaps it had been years since she had been his special princess. Perhaps John had replaced her as heir, but in these moments, probably her father's last, Anna's sense of injury vanished. In these last moments, she saw only the father she had always adored. Such a good man, such a wise man, such a fine father. How would they live without him?

Her eyes blurred, and she wavered, drooping toward the floor. How cool it would feel. That might ease her. She had not slept for what felt like days.

Hands drew her up and urged her away.

"Even you must rest, princess," said one of the physicians, who had had little left to do but tend the Empress.

Her father had drunk the potion. Now, he might sleep. So Anna obeyed. She allowed Irene to help the physician guide her. On the floor by a window was a pallet, a very humble bed, but it was draped with the purple.

Fretful with exhaustion, Anna looked for her husband. Nikephorus should have been here, attending his father-in-law, supporting his wife, comforting Irene and allying with her to preserve their interests. Still absent.

She muttered a command that he be found and fetched, then staggered, bumping into a table. Someone—probably one of the monks—had removed the circular Byzantine chessboard that she had used to distract herself before her father's case grew so much worse. *Shatranj*, the Iranian chess game, they proclaimed, was gambling, and that was improper in the Presence. Ironic, seeing who had taught her to play. They had not, however, removed the Varangians' *hnefetafl* board and pieces. Spaces gaped in the center of the game. The heavy ivory king's position was exposed in what was decidedly a poor move.

Anna paused, trying to study the game. Her guardsmen played it while off-watch. She brushed her fingers over the cool, weathered ivory of the Basilissa figure. It was unusual to have a queen in a game of war and strategy. That might be why she liked it so much.

"Not now," she was told and guided away from the game. Maids pushed her down, down, all the way down onto the pallet. One woman tugged off her soft slippers, another covered her warmly, her mother smoothed her hair, and then Anna plunged into darkness.

Mutters, whispers, a few raised voices, and the sounds of boots on the tiled floor woke her. She thought she even heard her father speak.

"Drink," a nun ordered her. Usually, that was the order Anna gave her father.

Playing the Long Game

A cool rim pressed against her lip. Anna sipped rather than spill whatever it was the cup held. She heard her mother's voice raised, hoarse and agitated that the fragrance of the bread brought for Anna would make the Emperor sick. Did she need to know what was happening? She drank again, then yawned. The voices went away, and darkness returned.

When she woke, sun flooded the porphyry room, so like the chamber in which she was born and from which she took the title *Porphyrygenita*, born in the purple. She blinked herself awake, set bare feet down on the cold floor, and stumbled over to her father's bed. Reaching for his hand, she gasped. The imperial signet he had worn even in this last illness was missing.

"Who took it?" Anna's voice lowered to a hiss. She cast an angry, reproachful glance not at the physicians but at her own mother. No one even bothered to ask "took what?"

"Your brother John," Irene said. "He brought his guards and Sebastokrator Isaac." Anna had never trusted him. "And his friend, that Turk, John Axuch."

Anna grimaced. The Turk might always have spoken courteously to her, but he had been her brother's creature since they were boys.

"Isaac and the Turk drew me away while your brother knelt in prayer at your father's bedside. The priests escorted them. I could not see through their backs."

Anna flinched and grimaced. Of course the priests would block them! Donation after donation, foundation after foundation she and her mother had created. But John made his gifts to the church too, and no priest would ever support a woman over a male for anything, least of all the title Anna hoped to win.

"You *let* them," she accused Irene.

"I could not stop him! He brought his guards. Would you have bloodshed in the Basileus's room?"

It would not have been the first time in a city where assassination was a weapon in rulers' hands. But...this was her father. He should pass in greater dignity.

"So my brother stole my father's ring," Anna concluded. Without the signet, it would be harder for her and her husband Nikephorus to claim the throne.

Anna patted her father's now-ringless hand.

"The Basileus is due for the next dose." His personal physician, an older man from Pera with the dark hair and rich robes of his people, presented it on a tray.

Anna sniffed at the cup. She bent over her father, but he turned his head aside.

Over and over again as the day waned, Anna struggled to get medicine and sustenance into her father. He refused. Finally, he let his eyes flutter open.

He recognized her! He was actually smiling at her. Anna's eyes filled with tears.

But her father's smile took on a slightly ironic cast as if, while Anna slept, Alexius had played his own move in the long game of Byzantine power. His hand was cold in hers and, as the sun set over the Bosphorus, it grew colder and colder. The priests could no longer be denied. They crowded around the bed, touching Alexius's lips with the Eucharist, anointing him with holy oil, and chanting, always chanting in their deep voices. The Master of Ceremonies hovered to make certain that every act was performed according to time-honored ritual.

Irene flung herself forward, onto her knees. She and her husband had often disagreed, but there had been love between them.

Alexius, Basileus of the Romans, stopped breathing. The priests' chants rose.

The death chamber erupted. Women wept, screamed, beat their breasts, and tore their clothes. Servants ventured forward, tiptoeing around the Imperial ladies and their maids.

The Master of Ceremonies approached to try to rouse the emperor, just as he had done during Alexius's life. Servants washed and dressed the dead man as if for his normal round of ceremonies and duties. The gems on the Emperor's robes and *tablion* shimmered as his body was forced into them.

Irene screamed in grief. She grabbed up a knife, but even as guards and servants hurled themselves toward her, the widowed Basilissa hacked not at her throat, but at her long, beautiful hair, shearing off great chunks, leaving ragged edges. She slashed at her garments, rich, even though soiled

Playing the Long Game

with long wear, and demanded a black gown, a mourning gown, not fit for an Empress, but only for a serving maid. Her women circled her, concealing her thin, bared body from the guards and priests until she was dressed in the humble clothes she had demanded.

Anna's maids huddled around her in cold comfort as, one by one, the guards came up to her to say, in accented Greek, just how sorry they were, what a good ring giver her father was, how generous and eager for fame. She replied in their own language, drawing smiles from underneath their facial hair. She had always been a favorite of the Varangians. They had enjoyed explaining axes and battles to the tiny princess she had been and laughed when she understood every word. They understood that one day, she would become their Basilissa and their personal charge.

She waved them away as politely as she might. Then, she tried to take her mother's knife and shear off her own hair. Irene Dukaina, now as humbly dressed as the lowest servant, forestalled her.

"Not you," she gasped. "Bathe. Eat. There is fresh bread. Dress properly. Look like the Basilissa you are. No matter what befalls, keep your head up. You are *porphyrygenita*. And you are my chosen heir."

Had grief dazed her mother? Did she think that all Anna had to think of right now was dressing up? The incense Anna had forbidden in the death chamber so that her father could breathe swirled up into the high ceiling. Now that he was no longer breathing, prayer and mourning required it.

Irene gestured. Anna's own maids snatched her away, into a private chamber to bathe her and array her in the Purple, a very dark shade to signify mourning. She wished she could have worn black. They brought her the headdress with its heavy jeweled pendants that dangled almost to her slender shoulders. They thrust cold ornaments onto fingers and wrists. The imperial robes weighed her down, a constant reminder of what she and her mother had long plotted.

She emerged, saw her mother huddled in a corner with a priest and a nun, and went over to bow. Her mother eyed her and nodded. "Now, it is in your hands," her mother whispered.

Play the long game, Anna.

Shifting, Swirling HERitage

The first thing: she needed information. She knew who had stolen her father's signet. She knew why. What she needed to know was how much progress her wretched brother had made in claiming their father's throne.

She gestured at one of the priests who had entered while she was being forcibly groomed. Perhaps his information would be more recent.

"Tell me what is going on," she snapped. And when he paused, she snarled "Now!"

The man narrowed his eyes at the imperious tone. Even a mourning *Porphyrygenita* must not speak that way to a man of God. And if she did not know that, he was just the man to tell her. Repeatedly.

Anna's command brought over one of the Varangians, who watched her with the blend of curiosity, affection, and respect that the crimson-clad guardsmen had always afforded her. They would, she decided, be like the Praetorians of the Western Empire to her when she ascended the throne.

"You will tell me what is going on," she repeated her command.

The priest glared at the small, angry woman. Seeing the tall guardsman waiting behind her, he bent his head complied in a much more conciliatory voice.

"After your brother the Caesar John left your father's side, he went to Hagia Sophia. The clergy acclaimed him."

He backed away slightly from the look on his questioners' faces.

"Go on," Anna forced the words from between gritted teeth.

"From there, the Basil… he went to the Magnaura, the Great Palace. The palace guard wasn't going to let him in without proof of his identity"— as if the stolen signet ring was not enough!—"but the crowd recognized him."

The crowds of Constantinople had torn down the previous Hagia Sophia and caused the deaths of tens of thousands. They could make or break an Emperor. Or an Empress.

"He entered the Palace," cut in one of the crimson-tunicked guards. "He has been clinging in there like an octopus on the rocks."

It would not have been suitable at all to laugh at that description, so Anna refrained.

Irene brought over a message on which the seal was broken. The *Imperial* seal.

Playing the Long Game

"I have received a message," Irene said. "My son will not join the funeral procession. I begged him to see his father properly interred, but he refused."

So Irene had been working while Anna slept. Apparently, John's hold on the City was not yet as strong as he wished. Did he fear assassination? Wasn't one dead family member enough, at least for now?

Hours passed. Prayers droned on. Anna and Irene wept. In between bouts of tears and oppressive insistence that they eat or pray or rest, preferably all of them at once, they received and sent more messages.

Just when Anna was ready to erupt, servants flung open the door and brought in the bier that would carry Alexius to the monastery of Christ Philanthropos, as Alexius had planned long ago. The bier was shockingly plain. Not suitable for an Emperor at all, let alone one as great as her father.

Irene shook her head. "It is not what he deserves but he asked to be taken to the monastery, so that is what we will do. They are trying to clean the catafalque there even now, but the funeral will be very, very bare. A merchant might be carried to his tomb in greater splendor."

That set her weeping again. It was a ritual performance, and Irene was a fine actor. It helped, though, that her mourning was real. So was Anna's, but she needed to stand like an icon.

From the City below erupted shouts of acclamation. The people, the volatile, violent mob of Constantinople, had acclaimed her brother John as the next Emperor!

"Where is my husband?" Anna demanded of anyone who might know. A terrible thought chilled her. Nikephorus had not been present at Alexius's death. Did he now serve John?

"He stands near the Basileus," said the priest, and backed away further, not in reverence but in fear of the new Emperor's turbulent sister.

"I have to see him."

The guard began to lose control of his face beneath its golden beard. Despite the mourning in the room, he grinned at her. The guard had not yet been withdrawn to attend John. That was interesting. Fascinating, in fact. Anna's eyes fell on the *hnafetafal* board. Now, she saw a blockade taking shape in one corner of the board.

Time to shut in Brother John. Time to trap him.

335

The weight of her robes suddenly reassured her that she had a right to make demands. "Take me to my husband," she commanded. "Now!"

She commanded her women to straighten her garments. Her mother was right. She must look the part. Thinking better of it, she demanded a new robe of Persian brocade with a more glittering *tablion*. The splendor was highly unsuitable for a mourning daughter, but very suitable for a Basilissa. Irene approached.

"I will know your plans." Her mother too understood command, even delivered with reddened eyes, shorn hair, and a scratched face.

"My Varangians—"that sounded good. *My* Varangians—"will escort me to my husband and my brother," Anna told her. "If this is my Empire, I will fight for it."

"Daughter, no. Whatever you intend, whatever you think of, let me take responsibility. My life is over, with only repose and prayers at my monastery at Theotokos Kecharitomene to look ahead to."

The shouting increased as the mob grew closer. John was riding in arms back to the Great Palace. He was surrounded by cheering subjects who acclaimed him Emperor, who would destroy the plans Anna and her mother had spent their lives making.

"I want my husband," Anna said. "I need to know what he is doing to stop this."

She strode toward the door. On her way, she passed by the Varangians' chess set. One of the maids, or perhaps a disapproving priest, had jostled it. Heavy stained ivory figures lay scattered on the board. The King's guards and those that had begun a barricade in one of the board's corners had fallen. So had the king. It was not a particularly mobile piece, but the heavy ivory carving with its crown covering half its head could have escaped the board at any moment.

As indeed John had.

A Guardsman came up behind her. To Anna's shock, he pressed something into her hand. Her small fingers closed about the hilt of a dagger. It was not the sort a warrior might use. Instead, it was shorter, with the jeweled hilt and the watered steel that a patrician might prize.

Was she to use this on her brother or to defend herself? That would, she realized, depend. She tucked the dagger away beneath her heavy robe.

Playing the Long Game

Surrounded by a robust splendor of Varangians in full crimson uniform, Anna marched out of her father's death chamber. Yes, her procession was highly irregular, but it might be the closest she would ever come to battle. Since her marriage at age fourteen, she had always offered to accompany her husband, to tend him, to act as his secretary, to consult on tactics, if he wished.

Nikephorus always laughed at her. He would not, he said, have her act like the hoydens of the West, who rode with their husbands on Crusade and, at times, died with them or, worse yet, wound up in some warlord's harem. Anna must remain decently at home in the Palace with her children and her studies. Not that he knew much about them except when she could help him with the occasional chronicle or a spare digamma in Homer.

Why had Nikephorus not attended her father's death? Why had he not come to console her mother and, for that matter, herself?

Anna practically crashed into the Guardsman ahead of her. What dared to halt her procession to the Throne?

Richly but somberly clad, her brother's toady John Axuch stood before Anna and her people. Their lines opened, so that he could see her and salute her properly as his master's sister. Lickspittle.

The Turkish convert bowed deeply, expressing sorrow in beautifully measured phrases that attested to the education that he and her brother—and she herself—had shared. He eyed her attire, judged it appropriate, and offered to escort her to her brother and husband.

A quick glance told Anna that the Turk had not come unaccompanied. But it was to her advantage to get in close. She inclined her head in assent and followed him. A commotion behind her indicated that her guards had been barred from entering with her. That was not good. Nevertheless, she persisted.

Past the golden tree with its fluttering leaves on which equally glistening mechanical birds twittered, rose the Throne of Solomon flanked by its gilded lions, their tales thumping the stone floor. The lions' mouths opened, and roars came out of them.

John sat there, on the throne that had been her father's and should be hers. She heard him doling out offices as gifts, just as their father had done. Brother Isaac, that thief of her father's signet, stood nearest the imperial throne, standing almost as an equal. Cousins were rewarded with resounding titles, while John Axuch himself was named grand domestic and commander of the armies.

What was the nothing with which her husband—once destined to be Co-Emperor—had been bribed?

Anna broke free of her guards to take up a regal stance in front of the throne. John's hand rested on its arm. A trick of fine Byzantine craft would enable him to raise the throne in the air so that she would find herself looking at his feet like a suppliant.

"Don't even think of it, *brother*," she hissed.

"Anna, Anna," came the voice that she had heard during her adolescence and throughout her entire life: scolding, encouraging her, exhorting her to be fair, to be reasonable when she felt anything but. "What is the meaning of this?"

And just like that, her husband of so many years, the father of their four children, betrayed her.

"You know perfectly well!" she hissed at Nikephorus. "I hear honors named, but none for you."

"I am a royal kinsman, the Emperor's brother in law."

"You should have been Basileus. Remember? We were to rule like Justinian and Theodora!"

"That was your mother's plan and, I think, to a lesser degree, a dream in which she indulged you. You were always spoiled, Anna. The Basileus Alexius supported his true-born son…"

"Once my mother gave him one. But I was to be heir!"

"I cannot violate your father's last wishes, Anna," Nikephorus said. "I wanted to please you and serve your mother. But I never wanted this. It is criminal…almost treason. Perhaps even heretical!"

Heresy, even more than treason, was fatal in Constantinople.

Rage erupted from deep behind her eyes and burst from her mouth. "You should have had the womb and I, the …." she chose a word for the male genitalia that she had picked up while spying on the Varangians practicing with their great axes. It was explicit, it was coarse, and it precisely expressed how she felt. "You are weaker than a woman. My mother, my father's mother...Even I myself... and we all have been betrayed by *men*."

All these years of preparation, self-restraint, and listening, constantly listening...it was too much! She had not realized just how angry she was, or how her grief brought it to the surface.

A light like Greek fire exploded behind Anna's eyes. She felt her hand reach, as if by instinct, inside her robe and draw out the dagger the Guardsman had given her.

Arms grabbed her—Nikephorus on one side, John Axuch on the other—and pulled her back from the throne. John rose, but soldiers from elite regiments interposed themselves and started toward her.

"She is not right in her head!" Axuch set himself between Anna and the Imperial guards. "She has been tending your father, mourning, suffering, and she is frail, feeble..."

Only a woman, Anna thought. That what they pleased to call her weakness might save her made her laugh. The laughter turned to tears. And when Nikephorus pulled her against his shoulder (taking pains to remove the knife she held in shaking fingers), she hated herself for having to lean against him rather than faint.

"It is hard for her to lose everything," John Axuch told Anna's brother. "Of your mercy, send her on retreat, let her rest, and heal. She is not herself."

"What do you say, brother in law?" John asked.

"I am at fault," Nikephorus's voice was grave. "I knew her and her mother's ambition. I should have stopped them. I vow that she will never enter the Palace again, and she will conform herself to proper behavior. My life on it. My wife is not without resources. She can read. She can write. She tends our children. She prays. And I will watch her until we go off on campaign. Thereafter, I will guard and serve you as Emperor."

This early in his reign, such as it was, John needed a grand gesture. Anna was shocked to find out that *she* was to be the official act of mercy. "Then take her home, brother. But, there is one thing more I want from you, *elder* sister."

With the hand that wore their father's signet, the new Emperor pointed at the cold floor at his feet.

Nikephorus's hand against Anna's back pressed her down, and down, and down. He was stronger than she. So the ritual humiliation was inevitable. Better to assent than to be forced.

Anna Komnene bent, knelt, and hunched herself forward, her heavy robes falling against her, into the full *proskynesis*, the prostration due an Emperor of the Romans. The gemmed ornaments on her headgear clicked on the stone floor. It was cold against her brow, and tears of sheer fury fell upon it.

No one helped her rise when her humiliation was deemed complete. She pushed upward, managing to keep her back straight. Then she surrendered to the escort. With the Magnaura barred to her, she must have a new home. Her spineless husband remained behind with her brother, who would remain, she told herself, Basileus until she could develop the strategy that would win her the throne.

One good point. Her guards were still Varangians. John did not command them all.

And their loyalty was to her.

At least, she had not been compelled to join her mother at Theotokos Kecharitomene, after the excruciating rites of Alexius's funeral finally ended. Although the convent might be a fine place to finish up her life, especially if her dreams continued to fall short of her ambitions, Anna still had fight left in her.

Servants brought over her possessions from both palaces to her new hermitage. She still lacked the round chessboard confiscated by monks. But the Rus board and heavy pieces, large heads hunched over disproportionately small bodies, stood on a marble table. They knew she had a taste for barbarian art and indulged her in that much. *Spoiled*, Nikephorus had called her. He would pay for that.

Anna picked up the ivory statue of the Queen and balanced it in her hand as she set up the rest of the board.

Playing the Long Game

Hours later, she sent for the leader of her guard. Her husband, now and forevermore in name only, and John Axuch were right. It was not a good idea to kill kin or an anointed sovereign who was *isaposteles*, equivalent to the Apostles.

She would learn from the chessboard. She would play the long game. It was the best game for artists. For historians. And for rulers.

To win, she must lock in her enemy, bar the king all means of escape to the sides of the board, and finally pick off his defenders, leaving him isolated. Vulnerable—a lovely word. The strategy had worked for her father in Aleppo and Nicaea. Alexius had snatched it from Bohemond's grasping hands. It had worked for that treacherous swine Bohemond, who won the siege at Antioch. The Treaty of Devol should have made Antioch a Byzantine fief—but that Bohemond and his heir Tancred had repudiated it.

No surprise there. Alexius had taught Anna that failures sometimes happened, but it was best to regard them only as setbacks. Like her current situation.

To play the long game, Anna would start by playing the roles deemed acceptable: dutiful daughter, studious woman. Even obedient wife. Bryennius had even had his notes for a biography of her father brought to her before he went off campaigning with her brother. He thought they would keep her occupied. He would go over them with her, he said, when he returned from the campaign. She thanked him and kept the irony out of her voice.

So, she must play the role of devoted wife again for however long her chess game took to play out. Thank the Holy Mother that Nikephorus was away and getting too old for it, or she might have had to birth another child to distract the court—assuming a Byzantine court could ever be distracted. It might even have been another boy. Everyone would have liked that. But both of them were getting old for the old game. Besides, if her husband had tried to touch her again, she might have killed him.

John and his followers only thought she was sulking in her tents like Achilles, or permanently broken. As a scholar of her father's reign, she could call on all manner of resources from the Bureau of Barbarian

Affairs to the network of spies that Alexius himself had created. John would be using those spies for his armies. Anna had other uses for them. And she could write to her mother in a code different from the Caesar cipher encryption technique she had learned when she was still her father's heir: Irene and she had devised a new code to use between them.

Like the Empire's strategies themselves, Anna's new long game required not knives but diplomacy. For it to work, she required information. Simple enough: known as a scholar, Anna would be expected to deploy merchants and monks to inform her about the nations they visited. Soldiers, too, though it would be much harder for her to contact them. John might have been an ugly child, but he was far from stupid and her husband knew her far too well.

To distract them, Anna spent several months progressing on her husband's notes, hoping that the spies who watched her thought she had resigned herself to the consolation of philosophy.

Gradually, as the scandal, if not the memories, subsided, she began to send out her own agents. Fortunately, the merchants with whom a noble lady might be expected to deal were her best tool in conducting her operations. They knew the languages of the Muslims, the Jews, the Rus, and the Franks as well as their habits. As much as any of those barbarians trusted outsiders, they trusted merchants and allowed them to roam.

For Anna's purposes, merchants were far more useful than the Imperial couriers and logothetes. She must reserve the officials for the most important missions, once she determined them, and deploy them carefully, if at all. At least, if John caught her using them, they would be immune from civil and critical prosecution. She had gold for gifts and bribes, which amounted to the same thing. A good thing: her father had left Byzantine's *solidus*, its gold currency that was a watchword throughout the East, in excellent condition. If Anna could not draw directly on the empire's resources, she had her own—including the heavy, intricate jewelry, more regalia than ornament, that might prove even more valuable as gifts than as legal tender.

Given merchants, agents, and monks—although the Westerners, Muslims, and Jews were as stubborn as heretics—she thought she need not regret an inability to use the empire's beacons or relays. Her game

Playing the Long Game

required more time, and more subtlety if she were to win not just the Throne of Solomon, but the East.

As merchants returned to the Golden Horn and craved audience with the Princess or her women under the guise of showing them their wares, Anna received their reports too. When the men and women of the West had first come to Constantinople, she had observed them. Now she remembered and combined her memories and the notes she had taken then with her informants' words.

The men who had accompanied Godfrey of Bouillon, Bohemond, and the other crusading paladins to the East at Alexius's plea to the heretics' Pope tended to enjoy war for its own sake. They spent years away from home, leaving their estates in the charge of their wives. The men themselves tended to die young. That left power and wealth in the hands of their women, who gained control over their own property, the ability to preside in their husbands' stead over courts and to provide soldiers when needed. So it was noble women, actually, who controlled Frankish property in the West as well as in the Kingdom of Jerusalem and the Muslim cities in the East.

So who were these women? What were they?

There were the nuns, the women all tagged Anonyma, sisters whose names had never been recorded because they were unimportant. That was not humility. That was annihilation. It was a terrible thing to take away a woman's name. As bad as taking away her future.

Seven of the eight greatest Western crusaders, however, had brought their wives with them. They all had names. Some like Godehild, one of Baldwin I's many wives, died along the way whereupon her husband Baldwin had married two more women—Arete from Armenia, now locked up in a particularly unpleasant convent—followed by Adelaide, also sent packing.

Some of the other noblewomen, such as they were, like Elvira, bastard daughter of Alfonso of Leon and Castile, consort of Raymond of St. Gilles of Toulouse, returned to Europe after their lords died, as had the noble widows Hadvide and Dodo. It would take longer than Anna had patience for, even in the long game, to send messages to them. But they had correspondents in the East, and those she could uncover and have her agents approach.

Mary of Scotland, Talesa of Aragon...the women's names were a roll call of banners and trumpets. Then, there were women like Emeline, less strictly protected, who had been taken captive. Like the women called Anonyma, they were probably imprisoned in some Seljuk harem, probably even less content than Anna herself.

At least, she slept alone. Blessed Mother, what a relief!

There were even women in the East who reigned like lords, like Morphia of powerful Edessa, now Queen Consort in Jerusalem, and her heiresses apparent, Melisende, Alice, and Hodierna. The Queen Consort must be concerned with her daughters' education. Anna, celebrated for her learning, could make herself of use there.

Other women of the West became warriors. Even the great lady Ermengarde led a crusade of her own. Anna might deplore Amazons among the heretics, but, little as she thought of women who were not of her bloodline, none of these ladies could have survived for a moment if they had been total fools.

That was a lesson Anna did well to heed. She had indeed been hasty and prideful. *Spoiled.* Nikephorus's rebuke rankled. She would learn better. It would make her a better ruler. And a better ally and overlady to the women to whom she now reached out in the longest game of all. Anna no longer sought just the Throne of Solomon. She wanted peace in the East by uniting the smaller kingdoms there within an empire ruled by a Basilissa who negotiated rather than fought.

Analyzing her spies' reports, Anna realized that women who administered lands, like the husbands who wielded it, needed heirs. Heirs needed peace in which to grow up. Their sons would accompany their fathers as soon as they could wield weapons creditably. But they would also have daughters, nieces, granddaughters, who might be as precious to them as Anna had been to the grandmother for whom she was named and her own mother Irene. And the daughters, the nieces, the granddaughters, were likely to outlast their brothers.

So Anna concluded that her allies might indeed comprise a powerful regiment of ladies. With the reports in, the gifts went out. She sent imperial gifts to these ladies: gold, jewels, romances like *Fierebras* and the *Song of Antioch*, translated from the Frankish; Latin chronicles like that of

Playing the Long Game

William of Tyre for more learned women. She even dispatched richly caparisoned horses and grooms to their sons, lest their menfolk suspect Anna of a women's plot.

So much for the women of the West. What about the next generation of Muslim ladies such as young Zumurrad Khatun and Shajar al-Durr in North Africa? Anna's father had allied with Muslims against the Franks when he needed to. What would stop her from making such alliances? Young girls—herself a conspicuous exception—could be pliable when plied with gifts. She would send not just jewels but tutors, urbane and erudite monks who might be able to convert them. That would strengthen any alliance she could make, now and in the hereafter.

Kyrie eleison. Anna crossed herself. She only hoped it would be so.

Day after day, month after month, Anna's dreams and schemes came to greater light. She began to dream dreams as bright as those she had known when she was a child and when Constantine lived. Why could she not lead her own army? Why could she not, if she wished, ride at its head all the way to Jerusalem?

Why? Because her ambitions would be reported, and then she would be permanently immured, probably far away from the capital. Besides, the allies she hoped for would not permit a Byzantine incursion led by a woman with imperial aspirations. To play the long game, to rule, Anna must consent to become as immobile as the king on the chessboard.

John, however, had to campaign. So much the worse for him, for her husband who accompanied him, and for all the other officers, soldiers, and men.

Eliminate the king's defenders. That was the name of the long game.

Campaigns came and went. Armies came and went. The Varangian offficers' long braids turned silver. Generals retired or died. Her own husband Nikephorus, returning with his Emperor after various campaigns and visiting her in her house away from the Palace, looked gray and sickly. She should have felt regret, but his betrayal had cut too deeply. Nevertheless, as if to indulge her, he reviewed her progress on his biography of her father and pronounced it well done. At least, she did not compulsively imitate Xenophon. Then, he returned the manuscript with all his so-called corrections, certain that she would make his changes, and rode off on the next campaign.

They were competent, these men and generals. She had better ideas. So did the ladies whose spies clearly told them that Anna was making progress. Thus far, she had made no converts, but established cordial relationships and frequent correspondence among the ladies of the East. Conversion might come if the ladies sent their daughters to Constantinople. As guests, never as hostages, nothing so crude.

As time passed, this cordiality turned into agreements, agreements into treaties. There would be men and weapons covered by those treaties. When Anna called for aid, it would be given. She might ride to Jerusalem yet, as queen over Outremer, Edessa, and the other cities of Eastern Christendom. As for the *dar al-Islam*, as she had learned to call it, she had yet to understand what she might do with it. It could even be that Anna would unite the entire East and proceed, as Alexander had, into Persia and India—if she and her allies lived so long. But that was hubris: she must concentrate on the work at hand.

As months and years passed, John's armies grew. His reign and his dynasty flourished, as their father had hoped. She could not wish him failure, but still…

The Tagmata regiments remained strong, but the men closest to him—with the exception of John Axuch and Nikephorus—fell away into death.

Once again the armies returned to camp outside the city walls at Philopatium. It was a site that John seemed to favor. Repetitive pattern—that was a tactical error. Anna studied the maps. After that, it was a matter of promises and bribes to hire agents who would infiltrate the camp.

She was older now, wiser and wary with the years. She knew she would have this one chance to strike and strike fast. Bribes took out more and more of the soldiers, especially the mercenaries. Byzantium had the best-paid mercenaries in the world, but gold was as much an addiction as hashish and shone more brightly. She trusted the Rus. She did not trust the mercenaries from Normandy, their remote cousins. They reminded her too much of Bohemond and his nephew, and, as she recalled, they had turned against the Emperor at Manzikert.

John was the center, the king. But Anna had gained control of the center of the world.

And finally, one evening, as he and his armies lay encamped at Philopatium, she commanded her men to strike. They struck once, and they struck hard. She could see the fires in the camp spread. "*Nike!*" she whispered to herself. *Victory.*

At last.

Anna would have liked to have joined her strike force to witness the battle herself, perhaps even participate. But she knew better than to attempt it. She suspected that the Varangians would have locked her in her quarters, if they did not presume to sit on her themselves.

They brought her her father's signet, and she slipped it on. She had her victory now. It was time to consolidate it.

Anna commanded that her brother, her husband, and their allies be marched in before her as prisoners into the Magnaura. She received them—ambassadors from the Empire of Betrayal—from her hard-won seat on the Throne of Solomon. Its hydraulics raised her high above her traitors into the air. Nikephorus eyed her reproachfully. John had at least spared her that. After these years of quiet planning, Anna found that she didn't care for the throne's height. It made her feel more conspicuous than she was, and conspicuousness could be deadly. Anna made the throne descend. Standing, she gestured to her estranged menfolk, to tell them the circumstances under which they must live the rest of their lives.

But two things first: Nikephorus was injured. She might be estranged from him, but he would be tended even if she had to do it herself. Her husband recoiled from her as if she were the she-demon Lilith herself.

"The Emperor's own physician has treated me," Nikephorus told her. "No need to trouble yourself."

Anna knew that physician. Another of the clever men from the Jewish quarter in the Pera district. She could not do better herself. After what medicine had preserved her father to do to her, she might as well be done with it. Hereafter, ruling would suit her better than nursing.

"Where is your friend?" she asked her brother. John Axuch had probably preserved her freedom, if not her life, even if she had despised him as her brother's creature. Even by her standards, she owed him.

John looked down. "Died, defending me. He joined the Guardsmen, the ones whom you did not suborn, and took an ax in the gut."

Anna crossed herself in the Turk's memory. "He will be buried with great honor," she promised. "You will oversee it yourself. And I do mean 'see'. I—or We—see no reason to rob you of your eyes to render you unfit to rule. Instead, we take away only your freedom. You have begun a foundation of pious men dedicated to Christ Pantokrator, the ruler of all men. *And* all women. You shall complete it, and your friend can be buried in its church. Before the high altar, if it pleases you. I will however, have your dealings with merchants and the secular authorities overseen."

John's eyes shot to Nikephorus Bryennius. Her husband was older. As a man grew older, campaigning weighed hard on him. Nikephorus looked sick and in pain. But Anna knew just how formidable he still was. Best to get him out of the way. Far out of the way.

"No, I will not permit contact between the two of you. You, *husband*, shall go to the Holy Mountain, Mount Athos, to oversee the hermits and the monks and to preside over their councils. I shall send a deputy with you to administer the annual stipends to the monks and see that they are not diverted. There are no women on Athos: this is good because you have never respected any of us. Besides, Athos is isolated. At least, you can exercise your prowess as an officer in protecting the monasteries from Muslim invaders."

She would not tell him that if she had her way, those invasions would cease, and that, speedily. The ladies of the Middle East should have little patience with that type of adventurism. The Christians would not stand the blasphemy. The Muslims would not waste resources they could use to rebuild. Either way: both were useful to Anna and her dream of Empire.

Playing the Long Game

"The rest of you," Anna decreed, "will be consigned among various monasteries throughout the Empire. You might say your farewells now because you will not be permitted to communicate with one another ever again."

"Anna, who will serve you with all of us gone?" Nikephorus asked in that concerned tone that he had always used to remind her how much older and more experienced he was. How relieved she would be to be rid of the condescension.

"My father's advisers, the ones who are loyal to me. Your own strategies. My father's policies, which I understand even better than all you wise, wise men." Yes, the bitterness seeped into her voice. They would just have to bear with it. Without judgment. Judgment was now *hers*.

She turned back to John. They called him Kaloioannes, or John the Good. Well, then, she would be Anna the Better. Anna the Bettor, for that matter, as her gamble paid off.

"There is one more thing I want of you, brother," she told him. "Return the honor that you forced from me."

Wearing her father's signet, she pointed at the floor. Her guards approached the former Emperor, determined to enforce her command. She did that for herself. "*Now.*"

John had always been pious, skilled in humbling himself. He would have the rest of his life to do so in his religious foundation. But the "honor," the drastic humiliation that he had imposed upon Anna and that she now demanded of him, would sting as much as she remembered. She met her brother's dark eyes until he looked down and dropped into the full *proskynesis* due the Empress of the Romans.

Anna took a deep breath. Exhilaration washed over her. *Caution, Anna*, she warned herself.

She had been destined for co-rule first with Constantine, who had died, then with Nikephorus, who had faltered. And it had been taken from her. She must not let this opportunity slip from her grip and from the capable hands of the ladies with whom she sought to deal.

She would send her notes and histories with her husband into his exile, where he could occupy himself with writing as well as prayers. No doubt people would be more willing to read what he had written than any history a mere woman might have written.

Anna vowed that she would no longer write history: she would create a history in which women could appeal to other women for help and support and peace, but always with Anna, the Empire, and her successors in command. From now on, Anna would share the Throne of Solomon with no one except her memories of the father who had turned against her. And, of course, the triune God.

Brother, husband, and their loyal officers were marched off in separate directions. Anna returned to the throne and sat down in it. Her men, monks, and ministers with their polysyllabic titles must silently wait until she spoke first. And she could speak for as long as she cared to. What a pleasure it would be never to be interrupted again or told what she really meant to say.

That is a throne, *not an armchair*, she could imagine her formidable grandmother Anna Dalassene rebuking her. *Do not be petty.*

No, Grandmother, it is a curule chair, such as the ancient Romans had. You taught me about them. From this seat, I rule. From it, I make judgments. In it, I think.

The Basilissa had not won the long game, merely this phase of it. From now on, she would play it with people and across generations, starting with her own children: Alexius, John, Eirene, and Maria.

Which of Anna's children would rule after her? Her sons would have the advantages of their birth and gender. She need not worry about them. Of her daughters, Eirene, her mother's namesake, might be the younger, but Anna thought she might be more clever, more apt to be taught the long game, the game of Empire. She hoped that they would be friends. They could even rule together, a more capable pair than Zoe and Theodora.

Anna had learned she could not command the succession after her death. Her father, a better ruler than she would ever be, had tried, but she herself was lasting proof that the plans of even the strongest ruler—the best *man*—could be overset.

A thought about her heirs struck her. She smiled the close-mouthed smile she had long ago learned to use to conceal her thoughts. *To kratistos.* To the strongest.

Playing the Long Game

After a fashion, Alexander's last words to his generals had worked. Anna's political adversaries would test the strength of the claimants—which was good for the Empire, if not their peace of mind. After all, if they wanted peace of mind, they could always enter the religious life, at a suitable distance from the heart of empire. She hoped they would all enjoy it as much as her brother and husband.

The sun was setting over the Golden Horn when Anna dismissed the last of the logothetes whom she was sending out as emissaries to the ladies of Jerusalem, Cairo, Damascus, and the other cities in which she had built her influence. They had suitable missives and even more suitable gifts: elegant presents too subtle to be bribes. The women's letters and the evidence of her own spies made Anna moderately certain of favorable replies.

Responses first. Then meetings. Then action. If success did not come within her life, it might come within the reigns of her daughters.

She had issued her commands. Her emissaries would have left the City immediately.

Anna rose from the throne to return to her private quarters and sit back in a chair that was neither a throne nor a relic of *Senatus Populusque Romanus,* if she remembered her Latin correctly. It was merely comfortable. *Her* chair. Just as it was now *her* throne and *her* Empire.

She had worked hard, but even a Basilissa need not work all the time. Sinking into the purple comfort of her own chair, she felt in her bones that she was no longer as young as she had been.

She brushed her beringed hand over the red-stained ivory queen of the chess set taken so long ago from her father's death chamber. Moving it into its strongest position, she gazed out over the water. Her logothetes had long journeys to gain and return with the treaties that would reshape her Empire.

This time, her smile was as eager as it had been when she was a young girl and Empire seemed within her youthful grasp. Her father, for all his wisdom, had been wrong. What was the good of a holy war if you could instead create a holy *peace* across the nations? Faith could come later. She *believed* that. The priests would object. Too bad, she thought with a mild shock of horror, if they did. They had never supported her.

She might have words with the various nuns, she though, in their convents too. Beginning with her mother's own foundation. Maybe men had ruled the church for too long too.

Anna Komnene, Empress of the Romans, stared out over the Golden Horn. The sunset had never glowed as brightly as the evening in which she set in motion her dream of an empire—*her* empire—at peace.

The Shield Maidens

Carrie Harris

Hibernia, 1014

JOHN AND RICHARD WERE WRESTLING WHEN THEIR MOTHER ARRIVED at the encampment of Limerick warriors near the Tolka River. They shoved each other across the muddy ground outside the impromptu camp, laughing and exchanging good-natured taunts. As Rusla rode closer, her mare's breath steaming in the early morning air, John flipped Richard over his shoulder. John stood over his fallen opponent, crowing, until Richard grabbed one foot and yanked it out from beneath him, sending him sprawling. Then two young men lay on their backs in the mud, roaring in amusement.

Rusla rode up to their impromptu fighting pit, looking down at them, braids and beards clotted with mud. Sometimes it astounded her to see them so grown. It seemed like only yesterday that they were always underfoot, begging for her to watch them practice swordplay or archery or paddle around the lake in their little boat. They had come of age on her longships, never blinking an eye at sharing a rowing bench or fighting alongside any of her crew regardless of their sex. After all, she had taught them everything. She had kept them alive and fed and safe after their father died.

Now they were grown, and they were inseparable. Maybe a little on the small side—an inheritance from their Hibernian father. But she of all people knew how to use small stature as an advantage on the battlefield, and she had taught them every trick she knew, both on the field and off. They could hunt wild boar without getting gored and catch fish with their hands, lying on patient bellies while the unsuspecting creatures swam right into their waiting palms. They fought with overwhelming ferocity, working together instinctively to overwhelm their opponents. They treated women and women's work with respect. She had raised them well, and if they wanted to indulge in a bit of play to blunt the pre-battle nerves, she couldn't begrudge them that.

They beamed at her, tunics and trews plastered to their bodies with swathes of thick mud. The rain had stopped for the moment, but she'd been in Hibernia long enough to know that it was only a matter of time before the skies opened up again, turning the ground to boggy mush. It would be difficult territory for troops to move through, especially at large scale, but that wasn't her problem.

She returned their eager grins with a fierce one of her own, her teeth flashing in a face no less dirty than theirs. For the night's work, she would have to pass through neutral territory undetected. When it was her time, she would die in battle as befitting a warrior, not taken unaware by an arrow through the trees. So she'd streaked her face and smothered the blazing hair that had earned her nickname among the locals. Inghen Ruadh, they called her. The Red Woman, due to the hair on her head and the blood on her hands.

"Móðir," said John, panting. "Care to join us?"

Richard gathered a big handful of mud in one hand, taking advantage of John's distraction and preparing his next attack. Rusla almost regretted having to interrupt their fun, but she had no choice.

"We are needed," she said, stopping Richard in his tracks. He looked up at her for a moment, brow arched, before dropping the clod to the ground. It had been a long time since she'd needed to tell them anything twice. They trusted her, just as she did them. "Weapons and armor. Quickly. I shall leave the horse here, and we will set off on foot."

The Shield Maidens

They didn't argue or ask questions, although they might have wanted to. She was stealing them away on the verge of a great battle, robbing them of the chance to once again prove their mettle. It would have been within their right to question that, but instead they scrambled to their feet and hurried toward the encampment at the top of the hill.

Halfway up, Richard paused to look over his shoulder.

"Will we still get to fight?" he asked hopefully.

"The Ard Rí knows what he has in us, and he's not the sort of man to waste a resource," she responded.

"Right."

"Come on, ye dunga!" yelled John from the top of the slope. "Or do I have to do all the work again?"

With a sheepish grin, Richard charged the rest of the way up the hill. Rusla shook her head as she led her mare up the hill where she could be safely housed until Rusla's eventual return or given away in the event of her death. Some folk feared such an event, but she'd gotten long past that. When her end came, the Valkyries would choose her to walk the halls of Valhalla. After all, they of all people could not deny her bravery simply on the basis of what was between her legs.

The three warriors moved silently through the old growth of the forest, their light footfalls barely making a sound. The rain had started again, pattering gently on the ground and making the mud run down their faces. Still, enough of it remained to help them avoid detection, and that was what counted.

Rusla had relayed their orders in brief, simple terms, pitching her voice low. A silence fell over the small group as her sons digested the task that lay before them, broken only by the snap of a twig beneath John's foot and Richard's amused snort in response.

Finally, John said, "It's an insult, aye? A fighter of your caliber ought to be out on the field with Murrough, leading the charge, not hiding in some backwoods camp."

Rusla just smiled.

"She's not angry, sheep-for-brains," murmured Richard, ducking under a low branch. "Do you really think that Inghen Ruadh would take such an insult lying down?"

He held the branch off to the side for Rusla, who passed beneath it without a word. They would figure it out on their own. Her eyes roamed the thick trees, alert for any sign of humanity while her sons puzzled out the problem before them.

"They're sending us to sit on our thumbs with the noncombatants, and she's not insulted..." said Richard.

"Which means we'll be busier than it sounds?" John asked, finishing the thought.

"I believe so," she said, nodding. "This whole battle is about the Ard Rí. The rebels seek to remove him from power, and the old man is wily enough that they can't afford to leave him alive. There's always some chance that he might rally enough support to retaliate. Murrough is deluding himself if he thinks that keeping his father off the battlefield will ensure his safety. If I were on the other side? I'd dispatch some small teams to search the surrounding countryside for him. If they kill the high king, they win."

"Well, why doesn't the old man just leave then?" demanded Richard. "He's..." He trailed off, thinking. "But he can't, can he?"

"Not hardly," said John. "One sign of weakness like that, and his support will dissolve like a fart in the wind. He's got to stay."

"I don't think he has it in him to run anyway. He'll watch the battle from up high. If it goes badly, he'll send runners down with new orders. He won't turn his back on his warriors when his skill at strategy could mean the difference between life and death. The other side will spot one of the runners or the camp itself, and they'll come for him," added Rusla. "Some of them must have brains in their heads. It'll happen."

"When they figure it out, they'll come with as much force as they can manage to scrape up," said John.

"Let them come," she replied, yawning. "I'm bored."

The Shield Maidens

Rusla could hear the flapping of the leather and linen that made up the high king's shelter before she could see it. The Ard Rí had selected his position well; the swell of the ground and a steep slope hid the structure from view until the last possible moment. Dense forest surrounded the plateau, thinning out to a stand of saplings immediately around the pavilion. She squinted up at it as she rounded the rocks. Richard and John stopped a few paces behind her, awaiting her orders.

"We may need to erect a few screens," she said thoughtfully. "We're entirely too visible from the south. Head down to the bottom and figure out where they'll do the most good. How many do we have, Stikla?"

Grinning, Stikla stepped out from behind the trunk of a thick elm, the naked blade of her sword resting on her shoulder. She and Rusla had always been evenly matched; they had the same lean build, the same wiry muscles, the same height and weight. If not for her red hair and Stikla's blond, people would have confused them. But ever since their first longboat, she had led and Stikla had followed, and neither of them had ever questioned it.

"What gave me away?" asked Stikla.

"I'll always know where you are," Rusla teased. "That's simply the way of things."

"Móðirsystir," said Richard, holding his arms open. "It's good to see you."

Rusla waited while Stikla and the boys exchanged embraces. She knew the importance of maintaining bonds in a warrior band; sometimes in the thick of the blood and the fear, the only thing that kept one's feet moving forward was the knowledge that their brother or sister in battle would not let them fall, and that they had an obligation to do the same.

"Four," said Stikla, tugging on John's beard and making him yelp.

"Hm?" asked Rusla.

"Four screens. The king had his largest cows slaughtered for the purpose, and their leather is of high quality. We've just finished cutting the poles. Just tell us where to put them."

"I'll head down and signal up to you," offered John. "If only to get you to stop tugging on my face."

"I'll cut down some brush to disguise them with, unless you have anything else for me to do, Móðir?" asked Richard.

"No, get on with you. I had best go talk to the king before the fighting starts," replied Rusla. "Make haste. The latest intelligence suggests they will be here much sooner than expected."

As she spoke, a flock of ravens took flight overhead, cawing raucously. They all turned their heads to the sky, tracking the birds without comment. Nothing needed to be said. It didn't matter which gods one prayed to; the meaning of this omen could not be denied. Woden and the Morrigan both hovered close, watching and waiting. Blood would be spilled, and soon.

The high king was still an imposing figure despite his advanced age. When they'd first met on the shores of Limerick some years earlier, his hair had still shown traces of its original red fire, but now it had all gone white. Wrinkles creased his face. But his body was still hale, and his hands sported calluses from the grip of his enormous sword. This was no figurehead who sat on silken cushions while others fought his battles for him. His willingness to get down into the dirt with his people was one of the many reasons Rusla respected him.

As she entered the pavilion, he rose from his prayer bench, picking up his sword and scabbarding it. Like the rest of his people, Brian Boru wore no armor, and his survival through so many battles testified to his skill with the blade. Now, worry creased his face, but he still summoned a smile when he saw her.

"Inghen Ruadh," he said. "You honor me with your presence."

He took her face into his hands and kissed her on both cheeks before pulling back to look her in the eyes, abandoning the niceties for frankness as was their wont.

"Well, Rusla?" he asked, amusement trickling into his voice. "What complaints do you have this time?"

"There's no sense in arguing with a man who refuses to see sense, Brian," she replied, not unkindly. "You've made your choice. I intend to see you survive it. We will be ready when the fighting starts."

"I consider myself lucky to have inspired such loyalty."

"Luck has nothing to do with it," she said. "You judge me on the strength of my skills. That is more of a rarity than you might realize."

"I'm afraid I can't take credit for that, my dear. Brehon Law clearly establishes the rights of women, and I'm simply a steward of it."

"What the law says and what men do aren't always the same. Besides, there's a difference between letting a woman own her own sheep and standing back to back with her on the battlefield."

He put his hand on the hilt of his sword and nodded at her.

"I've fought beside many a warrior in my long life," he said, "and you are the one I've picked to stand back-to-back with here, when the end of all things looms. Let the historians put that in their pipes and smoke it."

The battle began at dawn. The proud banners of the commanders flapped in the wind as thousands of warriors took their places in long lines that seemed to go on forever. The high king watched from behind one of the carefully placed screens as the blue banner of his son stepped out of line, bellowing a challenge to the assembled enemy. It was a foolish gesture, the kind likely to get him killed. If Rusla had been on the field, she would have beat some sense into him.

The high king sent off the first of his bodyguards to tell Murrough to stop playing around and lead his troops. It was as Rusla had assumed. He would send off all but his personal bodyguard, trusting that she would keep him safe. She'd planned for it. Her raiders hid in the trees around the base of the plateau, in perfect positions to pick off anyone who strayed too close. Richard, John, and Stikla were each stationed halfway up the slope, guarding the approach. She would hear anyone approaching long before they reached the top.

The battle raged on. The sharp tang of smoke filtered through the trees. Birds wheeled through the air, crying in alarm and hunger. Although the fighting was too far away, Rusla kept thinking she heard the metallic clang of clashing swords and the low moans of the wounded. But her keen eyes spotted nothing, and her sentries sounded no alarm. As time ticked by, the wind carried with it new scents: the sharp metallic tang of blood, the bitter scent of dead and dying warriors.

The king stood at his viewing post for a long time, the white knuckles of his hand on his sword the only sign of his growing agitation. He dispatched another of his bodyguards to correct the position of some of his Northmen and resumed his watching. While the remaining men rearranged themselves to close the gap, he leaned down to murmur in Rusla's ear.

"Does my son's banner still fly?" he asked.

With a pang, she realized that he could not see it, that he had been straining to make out the battlefield. He would not admit this weakness aloud, but he had entrusted her with it.

"It does, but he is badly surrounded by enemy forces and has been pinned in place for some time. You might consider redirecting some of your warriors to help him. They're rather scattered at the moment. Consolidating them would help protect your son."

"Have any of the runners I've dispatched so far returned?"

"Only one, sir."

He considered for a moment, presumably making the same calculations Rusla had already made in her head. He only had a few runners left. His personal bodyguard, Niall Ua Cuinn, would never leave his side, although he stood back a respectful distance to allow his king private conversation with Rusla. She respected Niall. As the Ard Rí had progressively taken her into his confidence, she and the guardsman had taken each other's measure. They had sparred. She respected his skills, and he had offered her the same honor. When the battle came to them, she would go where her blade was needed most, trusting that Niall would guard the king with his life.

"Murrough must not fall. The throne goes to him when I am gone. See it done," said Brian heavily. "I cannot watch any longer. I will take to my bench and pray. Fetch me if there are any developments I should be aware of."

The Shield Maidens

Rusla clasped him by the arm, and the two exchanged a wordless glance of support. Then he returned to the pavilion, looking older than ever.

The attack came suddenly. The king had resumed his vigil at the screens, his shoulders slumped at the revelation that Murrough's banner had fallen despite his efforts to bolster his son's forces. Rusla strained to catch sight of it again in the distance, but it failed to reappear. She had tried to tell Murrough that his plan was foolhardy. He ought to have listened, and now he had likely paid the ultimate price. A smart opponent would make sure the high king's son was truly dead before moving on.

A whistle from the back side of the plateau caught her attention. Aslaug had been stationed there in the hopes that her keen eyes would buy them plenty of warning time. The choice appeared to have paid off. Surprised shouts filtered up to the top of the plateau. From the sounds of it, Aslaug was pelting them with arrows. A thin lipped smile spread across Rusla's face. Everyone knew how the Northmen fought. They screamed to the heavens as they charged full tilt at their enemy, trusting in a combination of intimidation, size, momentum, and superior armor to win every battle. Often, the tactic worked. But she was no North*man*, and her people took a smarter approach. She did not even need to look to know what was happening at this very moment. Aslaug's signal would have triggered the rest of her hidden raiders to collapse in on the intruders, cutting off their retreat and pelting them with arrows from every side to cut down their numbers. If they attempted to break through, they would be met hand-to-hand by Stikla, Richard, and John from a superior position on higher ground. If enough numbers managed to break through, they would signal to Rusla. Otherwise, it was her job to keep a lookout for additional attackers while the bulk of her people were occupied in battle.

Neither Brian nor Niall needed instruction. The high king squeezed her arm briefly before hurrying into the pavilion, where the stiff leather would protect him from any stray projectiles. Niall loomed over him like a mother hen until the two of them disappeared into relative safety.

Rusla waited and watched. The sound of battle reached her ears, and she itched to join in, but she knew her place and trusted her people. So she waited and listened as the clang of metal and the shouts of the injured grew louder and louder. But she remained in position, scanning the unguarded slope until she finally spotted them: a group of three marauders, chain mail splattered with blood and other unidentifiable fluids, crept up the hill toward the pavilion with murder in their eyes. They had not spotted her yet. She ducked behind a tree to wait for them to pass her by.

Despite their best efforts at stealth, the trio made more noise than a full herd of cattle. She had no problem tracking them with her ears. She sank down to a crouch as they grew close, mentally planning her attack. The armor would present a bit of a problem, but she knew from experience how to work around it.

A footfall. Another. They came into view, passing her without sensing her presence. Few folk ever thought to look down. She waited a single breath and struck the closest man, slashing the backs of his knees. He pitched forward, letting out a yelp of surprise at legs that would no longer hold him, but she did not so much as pause. She lunged, striking up and underneath the mail shirt of the second man, the sharp point of her sword puncturing the soft meat of the lower belly and driving up into the chest. His eyes went wide as his lifeblood gushed over her hands. She tugged at the blade, but it had driven deep, and her wet hands slipped. There was no time to work it free. She released the weapon and rolled away just in time to avoid the strike of the only remaining marauder.

She found herself next to the man whose legs she'd cut, who was busy gasping out the last of his life onto the ground. He wouldn't be needing his sword, so she helped herself. She brought the weapon up just in time to block the final marauder's next strike. They exchanged blows for only a few moments which stretched out into eternity. Rusla's muscles screamed and sang as she fell into the rhythm of battle. It was impossible to deny that this was her calling. She had earned her place here, and no man who faced her could deny it.

Her opponent was skilled with a blade, but he was used to muscling his way through a fight, and she was too quick for him. Besides, he had fought his way here, and she was fresh and well-rested. He was panting before long, the tip of his sword drooping between his strikes, his chest heaving beneath the mail shirt. It was her opportunity, and she took it, diving beneath a block that was just a bit too high and driving her sword deep into the meat of his thigh. Once he was hobbled, the rest of the battle didn't take long. She finished him off and turned to see chaos behind her.

The high king and Niall stood back to back, encircled by a group of Northmen. A few bodies on the ground testified to the skill of the two men, but the numbers were not in their favor. Where were the rest of Rusla's people? She whistled for them but knew that it was likely futile. They would have come if they could. She could only hope that they were engaged in battle and not bleeding out their last moments alone under this indifferent sky.

She joined the fray, cutting down two men from behind before they realized she was there. One of the marauders turned, his eyes going wide as he saw who they faced.

"Inghen Ruadh!" he spat. "She-devil!"

She saluted him with her sword and attacked. The battle raged on. To her immense relief, her sons fought their way to her. Stikla appeared and then disappeared again as the battle took her up and down the hillside. Her heart sang at the sight of them. The enemy kept coming in wave after wave as word spread of the Ard Rí's presence, but they would not falter. The ground was littered with the bodies of their enemies, and there was plenty of room for more.

They were facing down a particularly large group of men in Leinster colors when Niall gave a shout of alarm. On the opposite side of the plateau, past the shattered remains of the pavilion, emerged a figure out of the hazy air. He was tall and dark, with a braided beard so long he had tucked it into his belt. It dripped with gore.

Brodir of Mann had come for the high king, and he had not come alone. At least ten men followed him, roaring for blood. He charged, sword held high, and they followed on his heels. For all their skill, Brian and Niall could not stand against this onslaught alone. Rusla was facing two Gael warriors at once; there was no way she could get there in time. But her sons could.

John and Richard launched themselves across the clearing, bellowing their challenge, and took two of the Northmen off their feet. One of Rusla's attackers took advantage of her distraction and managed to bloody her forearm, and she wrenched her attention back to her own fight before she lost her life. She cut one man down, but she was winded and hurting. She needed just a moment to catch her breath, and then she would be fine.

"Richard!"

John's agonized shout wrenched Rusla's attention across the plateau once again, just in time to see her son's body crumple off the end of Brodir's sword. John's horrified shock at the sight cost him his life. Another of the marauders struck his head from his shoulders with one mighty swing of a war axe.

Rusla saw red.

An enormous wailing built up inside her. She threw back her head and vented her grief and fury at the clouds, howling so loud that the very gates of Valhalla must have shaken. Her boys! Her precious sons! She would make these animals pay for stealing them from her. She would show them the wrath of a mother wronged. Her blade became a whirlwind, and she cut them down one by one, maddened with loss. The blows came: a kick to the side, a clout to the head that made her ears ring. She did not care. She would kill them all.

She cut her way through the attackers to Brodir, just as he swung his mighty sword at an off-balance Brian. She wanted to run him through, but the possibility of failing in her mission could not be abided. Her boys had died to protect the Ard Rí. She would see it done, no matter how much she hurt. She would abandon her need for vengeance in their names alone.

She blocked Brodir's strike, metal clanging against metal. His eyes widened as he turned toward her. The high king struck with a surprising

The Shield Maidens

swiftness, taking advantage of his opponent's distraction. With a swift stroke, Brian Boru cut Brodir's throat.

It was over. The plateau was quiet except for the groans of the dying. Stikla staggered up the edge of the hill, supporting a bloody and staggering Aslaug. Rusla was grateful for their survival, but her heart remained empty. There would be no joy in this victory. She fell to her knees next to the bodies of her sons and wept. Such loss could not be borne, and for what? She could only hope that Brian proved worthy of this sacrifice. It had to make some difference, or she would storm the home of the gods and make them pay.

After a moment, the high king knelt beside her, taking her hand in his bloodstained one as she cried.

"I will see to it that they are always remembered, that I promise you. Everyone will know the names of Inghen Ruadh and her sons Richard and John. Their lives and your sacrifice will matter in the days and years to come. That I pledge you," he said.

It was not enough. It would never be enough. But it would have to do.

Ireland, 2025

Years later, in the 2025 Women's World Cup, the US Women's Soccer Team met Germany in the finals. Fans called the US team "the Shield Maidens," after generations of brave fighting women. After all, their captain, Rory O'Neill, was a direct descendant of famous Viking shield maiden Inghen Ruadh, who had saved the high king of Ireland in the early 11th century, and the new striker, Brianna Brady, was a distant relation of Brian Boru himself. Their games—and all US women's soccer—had been sold out ever since the power duo had first taken the pitch together. Little girls in horned Viking helmets beat plastic swords against plastic shields, practicing their war cries as the team took the field. When they won, it seemed inevitable.

Shifting, Swirling HERitage

The clock ticked down. Thirty seconds left. The US team charged down the field as one, passing the ball back and forth between them and looking for an opening. O'Neill received the ball at center mid, tapping it between the legs of one of the German defenders to Brady, who buried it top left corner just as the buzzer sounded. The Shield Maidens had scored another victory in a long line of successes, and the crowd loved them for it.

Interviewers descended down on the field, crowding O'Neill and Brady as they hugged it out, knocking fists with their teammates and congratulating their opponents on a well-fought battle. But once the impatient interviewers got her to slow down long enough to talk, Rory O'Neill gave this speech:

"It astounds me that there are still places in this world where women are considered weak. More than a thousand years ago, my ancestress, Inghen Ruadh, fought by the side of High King Brian Boru, and her strength and sacrifice inspired generations of women since then. Without Inghen Ruadh and her fellow women warriors, think of what we would have missed. There would have been no Shield Maidens protecting the Underground Railroad or working hand-in-hand with the Night Witches to defeat the Nazis on those dangerous night raids. Throughout our history, we have seen time and time again that women are strong, and that our strength is worthy of respect.

"Some places still live in the dark ages. They don't realize this. They think that women's work is something to be embarrassed of, that women's sport is somehow less than because we play differently than the men. But different does not mean lesser. Inghen Ruadh wasn't picked to protect the king because she fought like a man. She was selected because she fought like a woman. And Brian Boru, in his infinite wisdom, saw her mettle. They fought and sacrificed together, each of them losing their children at the Battle of Clontarf. They were forever bonded by this experience, and I shudder to think of what the world would have been like if their partnership had been forgotten.

"We dedicate this victory to Inghen Ruadh, to Brian Boru, to all of the Shield Maidens who have come before us, and those who will come after."

The Shield Maidens

With that, both Rory O'Neill and Brianna Brady threw their hands in the air and shouted their battle cry, and hundreds of thousands of women old and young joined them.

Historical Context:

Over the years, scholars have debated whether or not Viking shield maidens are fact or fiction. Mentions of these female warriors from Lagertha to Brynhildr were made in multiple Norse sagas and stories, but were those tales actually based on real people? It's impossible to say for certain. Part of the problem comes from the fact that early Vikings were illiterate, so there are few direct accounts to help solve this mystery. Instead, our sources are largely limited to transcriptions of Viking stories passed down to later generations who eventually recorded them, potentially mixing fact with fiction, as well as records from literate societies who interacted with the Vikings.

As a result, the predominant belief has been that the shield maidens (as well as similar groups like the Valkyries) were nothing but legend. However, recent bio-archaeological findings indicate that at least one woman was buried with the trappings of a Viking warrior in what is known as the Birka grave. Before this revelation, Birka was believed to be the resting place of a great war leader buried with a full complement of weapons and the pieces of a game (possibly tafl), which has been interpreted as indicating a particular gift for strategy. Once DNA analysis indicated that the skeletal remains were female, this story shifted. Perhaps this was the wife of a great general. Perhaps there had been some mistake, and the bones had been swapped. This great warrior couldn't possibly be… female?

But the findings are clear. They suggest the possibility that female Viking warriors did exist—or at least one of them did—and their stories have been lost or buried. It's impossible to know for certain, but there is evidence to support the argument.

For the purposes of this story, I decided to write about the Battle of Clontarf, which was fought between mixed groups of Vikings and Irish. I picked Clontarf for a reason—the high king Brian Boru died there, and for years, many scholars argued that Brian the Great was a myth just like the shield maidens. But thanks to the tireless work of researchers like Morgan Llewelyn (who wrote both fiction and non-fiction about the mighty king), the tides have arguably changed, and sufficient evidence gathered to prove that Brian is no mere legend.

If Brian and the Battle of Clontarf both existed, that gives credence to a statement in the Cogad Gáedel re Gallaib, a medieval Irish text, that the sons of a woman called Inghen Ruadh (or the "Red Woman") died in the battle. Inghen Ruadh is also mentioned in the Gesta Danorum, or the History of the Danes. The stories said she was a successful and bloodthirsty Viking raider who was always accompanied by her deputy, Stikla.

Unfortunately, the timeline of these stories is muddled. It's highly unlikely that one woman would have lived long enough to have done all of these things. It's possible that the stories of Inghen Ruadh got jumbled up with tales about a similar woman called Rusla, when in reality they weren't the same person. Since "Inghen Ruadh" is a nickname, it's possible that there were multiple warrior women who used it, whether intentionally or unintentionally. After all, a red haired female warrior would stand out on the battlefield, and especially one of her supposed skill. If shield maidens existed, it's probable that there would have been more than one to fit that description. Onlookers could have gotten them confused. Of course, it's also possible that the whole thing is a myth. But again, if the Battle of Clontarf is taken as reality, it's likely that the sons of someone called Inghen Ruadh met their ends that day. Combined with the stories from the Gesta Danorum, it's possible that she was a warrior, although she almost definitely wouldn't have been called a "shield maiden," since that term is a modern one.

Details about the Battle of Clontarf are rather muddled, since nearly all of the key players died, and no one was left to summarize exactly what happened or what each individual force intended to do. It was a large scale battle with multiple forces under individual command, and it resulted up to an estimated 10,000 casualties. Interestingly, Brian Boru

The Shield Maidens

did not take to the battlefield. By this point, he was in his late 60s or early 70s, and his son Murrough or Murchad led the battle in his stead. But Brian's skill in strategy was one of his strong points, and after giving his orders, he set up camp on a high plateau from which he might observe the battle from a safe distance. There, he was accompanied by his bodyguards and an attendant.

It's safe to say that the battle did not go well for anyone. On one side was Boru and those who remained loyal to him, including some Viking troops. On the other was the Viking King of Dublin, the Irish King of Leinster, and a Viking army led by Sigurd of Orkney and Brodir of Mann. As the leaders fell one by one, the rank and file warriors beneath them carried on. The story says that Brian was such a spectacular tactician that the orders he gave before the battle carried his troops through despite the decimation of nearly their entire leadership, leading them to victory by using the high tide to their advantage.

However, Boru didn't survive to celebrate. Towards the end of the battle, Brodir discovered Boru's hideaway, and the two engaged in fierce battle. Brodir slew the aged king with a mighty blow to the head, but not before the king inflicted what would be a killing knife wound to his opponent's side. The two both died from their wounds, and in the aftermath, leadership of Ireland became fractured once again, and the tale of Inghen Ruadh, if she ever truly existed, was buried along with the tales of the other warrior women who fought and lived as Viking raiders.

One might argue that the survival of Brian Boru might not have been enough to keep the stories of shield maidens such as Inghen Ruadh alive. However, if anyone was in a good position to do so, he was. Under Brehon Law, the high king kept an official poet who might have written about the woman who saved his life, and in a more stable Ireland, those records would have been more likely to survive, teaching women through the ages that they too can be warriors.

The Way of Water: Jeanne's Resurrection

Donna J. W. Munro

May 21, 1431

M*y Dear Sisters of the Beguines,*
   It's all true.
The voices. The inspiration. The winning.
She led the army I paid for against the English claims and saw my sweet boy, Charles, raised to King.
Jeanne d'Arc, they call her. La Pucelle—the maiden.
She'd have them call her warrior as well.
She lies in Rouen awaiting her sentence after the farce of a trial from the Burgandians, English tits that they are.
We can save her, sisters. As sure as our honor oath to Marguerite Porete, we will save the exceptions and raise them up. We will be a haven and in turn, our sisters will rise. It is the way of water to wash away the wrongs in a flood of love. It shall be done.
I swear to use all that you've invested in me to free her. We cannot allow them to pass her from man to man, or worse destroy her with their fears and superstitions.

Shifting, Swirling HERitage

I leave for Rouen tonight with a bribe from the throne and my own stores. Expect us at the Brussel's motherhouse by three nights hence.

Your sister in Marguerite's heart,
Yolande de Aragon

Chapter 1

The snow-crusted cobbles of Saint Ouen Abbey crunched under the rude carriage wheels carrying Yolande the final few feet of the journey. Sabine drove the carriage with such skill none of the friars or English guards would question her disguise as a man. Square shoulders and deepened voice with a face hidden by a false beard and dirty hood completed the fiction. They'd let them pass through gate after gate as merchant suppliers without question.

Yolande herself took the robe of an ascetic, hair hidden, face misshapen by gum paste and paint. In her belts, she held small purses of gold to pay for her target's rescue. She'd have her and be gone by first light.

"Ho driver, what do you bring?" The stable friar rubbed his sleepy eyes and held steady the rein of the first horse.

"Ale, Master Friar," Sabine said in perfect baritone. "Salt, woven wool, and inks from Venice. And a case of fine parchment as well."

Those treasures were sure to distract the entire abbey long enough to get Jeanne out. Yolande slid out through the shadows making her way through the courtyard toward the monk's dormitory turned prison for a 19-year-old peasant girl who'd changed the entire world. Yolande remembered meeting the girl for the first time not two years before. Back then, she'd been full of fire and shining bright with the surety of a loving God, demanding that the king give her troops and give credence to her voices so she could make him king of all France.

"Check her, sweet mother," Charles had whispered as the girl knelt before him. "Check that she's a maid and not some cracked bit of tart raving."

Yolande led the girl back into a private room past leering courtiers and men with more balls than sense. The maid's tension reverberated in her terse steps and her clenched fists, but her gaze brimmed full of

The Way of Water: Jeanne's Resurrection

determination. Yolande was reminded of herself, a strong woman often at the mercy of lesser men. God touched or not, this child's spine was steel. She'd need Yolande's help and in those moments when Jeanne held her head high in the company of her supposed betters, Yolande decided she would be the benefactor Jeanne needed.

Yolande shut the door of the private chamber and said, "I'm to check your lady bits to see that you're a maid."

Jeanne had reddened at the thought of such violation. It was a normal procedure for royal maids, but for a peasant girl like her, it was an outrage.

"You don't intend to—"

"No, Jeanne. True strength needs no test. I admire you. The strength it took to put on men's clothes and walk away from all you know…I care not if you are a maid. I can see the fire in you."

Jeanne stared with the intense belief that only the young or the insane have and nodded. "They say you are sent to help me."

"They?"

"My angels. They say they help you, too." Jeanne took Yolande's hands in hers and squeezed lightly. "Lady, between us we will see the Dauphin crowned and all the provinces united."

"That's what they say?" Yolande watched Jeanne's eyes as they seemed to latch on some visage floating high above in the vaulted ceiling. This girl had some gift, though Yolande wasn't sure how divine it was. She'd seen things in her years as a Beguine sister that the wisest scholar among the sisterhood couldn't explain. As the sisters liked to say, this girl walked in the footsteps of Marguerite. "I will support you, Jeanne. With money and supplies. Your angels' goals align with mine. My purse and good word will open the doors you need opened."

In that moment, the two became friends, sure. And in that moment, they both recognized they were of the same cloth. Women out of time with a purpose higher than any man-made institution, crown or church.

Sneaking past the gossiping guards in Jeanne's prison, Yolande couldn't help but wonder what Jeanne could have done if she'd been born a boy with money and power. In two years, the girl had remade the war, crowned a king, and changed the boundaries of a kingdom.

"I told her, if you don't put those gal clothes back on, I'm going to piss in your food," a soldier old enough to have served the Black Prince rattled out in gutter English. An assault on Yolande's ear, but she understood him just the same.

A younger guard threw down his dice, wincing at his lack of luck. "Damn you, Liam. You have the luck of the Devil himself. Instead of wasting my pay on you, I ought to spend my efforts on the bitch of Orleans. Skip the piss and beatings and go straight on into making her squeal like the pig she is?"

The other soldiers roared with laughter when the boy grabbed at his loins and flapped his codpiece, a right vulgar gesture that left Yolande sure that these animals couldn't be trusted with anything as delicate as a faked disappearance. Money would not be enough to buy the silence of such men. She hugged the wall and inched past them as their lusty, drunken laughter filled the outer cell. Once past the doorway, she found herself in a close, arched hallway that stretched the length of the small building. At the front and the rear, two sleeping guards perched on stools using their short pikes as balance to prop up their lolling heads.

Above the cell door a hanging brassier cast a flicker of light that spilled across the gray stone floor. Yolande took a deep breath to steady her heart, then let herself sink into the character she'd crafted along with her disguise. Her back stooped and she shuffled forward in a measured, meditative way affecting the manner of an old friar tending the condemned.

Yolande paused outside the closed cell door to measure the metal of the sleeping guards. The first had a brutish look as peasant soldiers often did. A poor boy from the north as sure as she was from the south. From the looks of him, it might not take much to sway him. A gold piece and a bruise, a promise that after the war he'd be pardoned by the French king, or maybe she'd have to kiss him with the thin-bladed misericord dagger strapped to her thigh. She'd regret killing him, but she would if she had to. The other soldier looked older. A rugged man with scars crossing on his exposed hand and cheek. He'd not be easy to deal with if he woke.

One way or another, she'd have Jeanne out and on the way to the motherhouse before dawn.

The Way of Water: Jeanne's Resurrection

She slid open the lock and slipped into the cell, pulling the door nearly closed behind her, and gasped like she'd been struck with the butt of a staff when she saw Jeanne framed in the moonlight spilling in from the cell's small window. The child she'd met just two years before had been hardy, peasant stock. Thick from good bread and fieldwork. Full of the bright love of God and shining in her belief. What a glory she'd been!

Not the wretch she found here–a bundle of sticks and sickly flesh, rummy eyes with parched, cracked lips and shorn hair. The women's clothes she'd promised to wear lay bundled beside her and boy's clothes were tied on her with a rough cord and knots she couldn't have tied herself. The damned guards knew she'd be blamed for it. Jeanne kneeled against her rough cot, her skeletal fingers knotted in prayer, looking for all the world like a wraith risen. The stench of Jeanne's overfull piss bucket and the rotted food dumped in the corner bit Yolande's nose with miasmic foulness.

"Oh, Jeanne!" Her voice's quaver no longer reflected that of the disguise she'd donned. It was true horror at the state of France's maiden hero.

At her name, the girl, just a girl even after the battles and the horrid, lengthy trial, looked up at her with confusion.

"Father, have you come to give me confession or will you still deny me that comfort because of the clothes your guards make me wear? Do you have no shame? No divine understanding of this horror inflicted on me?" Jeanne's poor voice rasped painfully.

Yolande realized the girl still thought she was a friar. If she were of her former strength, she'd have known from the first.

"Jeanne, I come to save you and we must hurry."

The girl turned fully to look at Yolande with a critical eye.

"My queen?"

"Yes, yes. I think we've gone past that haven't we? You're a saint. I'm a queen. Can we just be sisters with names? Jeanne, I can't let them do what I know they must."

Jeanne looked confused. "I am to live here in penance. I don't mind. It gives me time to pray, but the soldiers want…"

The girl grimaced and turned back to her prayer as if Yolande wasn't standing with her. As if Yolande was another voice or temptation. She had to get Jeanne to understand and fast. Before the guards woke up and called hell down on their heads.

"The guards will take your pride and strength. Your maidenhood is but a token to them. It's nothing compared to what's coming. Sister...Jeanne... I come to take you away because tomorrow they mean to burn you as a heretic for wearing men's clothing. It's unfair, but it's the only way they can be rid of you."

She glanced back, confused as an infant on its first day. "Won't King Charles—"

"I love that boy like my own, but now that he's the crowned king you aren't his asset, you understand? Alive you are a hurdle. A roadblock that can be used against him in the name of God. But dead you are a symbol to rally France, a symbol he can use as he will."

A look of horror washed across Jeanne's face and she sat on the cot, looking for all the world like she'd been betrayed by her dearest. Why wouldn't she feel that way? She'd put the Dauphin on the throne. But she'd never understood the burden of being a powerful woman. If you became an asset dead, you'd be dead soon enough. Women were, after all, expendable.

"They come to burn you tomorrow, Jeanne. You could die for France—"

"If that's what God wants."

"But does God want that? I think it's men who find you inconvenient."

Jeanne shook her head, clasped her hands, and glanced skyward anxiously. "If it is what God wishes—"

"I'm here, sister. If God wanted you dead, I wouldn't have made it this far. I wouldn't have a carriage outside waiting to carry you to new purpose. Do you see that?"

The grim acceptance on her young features melted. Hope bloomed in her cheeks. Yolande pulled the girl in for a hug, something she'd never do as queen, but as sister—

"Father?" The voices of the guards outside the cell door rose together in surprise. There was a clattering, probably the sleeping watch rousing with the sudden appearance of a man of the cloth come to check on Jeanne. Murmured excuses and deflections sounded through the cracked door.

The Way of Water: Jeanne's Resurrection

"She's in men's clothes."

"Raving all night–"

"Swearing in some other–"

Yolande turned to Jeanne and handed her a dagger from her sleeve. She hiked up her skirt and pulled her misericord from the sheath on her thigh.

"For you, Jeanne," she whispered to the girl. "For Jeanne and Marguerite. Defend yourself, child."

The four guards from the passageway came in, followed by a robed friar. None had weapons drawn. None were prepared for the fury of a Beguine-trained warrior.

The first soldier, the young one from the north, didn't see the flash of her thin blade as Yolande spun low, slashing beneath the chainmail into the woolen britches at the top of the man's thigh, opening a deep gash in his artery. A strike to his nose dropped him into the spreading pool of his own blood.

It was enough time for the guards to draw their own infantry swords. Longer than her weapon, those swords had smashed the bones of many French warriors, deadly even in the close quarters of the monastic cell prison. Yolande had to be clever and quick with her blade. One wrong step and she'd find out if Jeanne's faith would carry them both to their reward.

The closest of them swung his blade, missing her shoulder by inches as she spun away. Yolande crouched and swept the feet from under another of the men as the first recovered from her feint.

"Jeanne!" Yolande warned.

The last of the men rushed Jeanne, shoulder down and his teeth grit. His sword grip revealed him as a veteran of a higher order of training. Would he kill Jeanne? Yolande couldn't be distracted as the other two came at her. Thankfully, her two attackers weren't as well trained. Dipping between their clumsy swinging swords, she slid her thin blade into the chainmail's gap at the arm and chest, felling the closest of the soldiers. The second attacker stooped to aid the first, foolish boy. Yolande hated to do it, but she plunged her blade into his throat's soft spot above the right collar of his mail, severing the artery with a quick twist.

"Murder!" screamed the friar from behind the knot of fighting figures as the second soldier fell at the friar's feet. The dying man gasped for breath as his blood streamed from the jagged wound in his throat. "Murder!"

The fool would bring every soldier in the abbey down upon them.

Next to Yolande, Jeanne and the soldier traded blows with the edges of their swords. She wouldn't hold up against his strength, not with the thin gruel and lack of exercise she'd had for months.

Another of the guards crowded into the fray and grabbed Yolande's wrist in her distraction, wrenching it back in a spiral that made her yelp in pain. The lightning of her ripping shoulder joint loosened the grip she had on her blade and his weight drove her down onto her knees. The triumph in his eyes was as crushing as the fist he smashed into her ear. Even with the two she'd bested, more soldiers, the card players, crowded into the fray.

Lost, Yolande thought as she collapsed beneath the brute, head ringing with bright pain. She lay panting on the bloody cobbled-floor, the stench of blood and shit in her nose, and her head spinning. She had to get up. She couldn't make her limbs lift her. She watched through the veil of the blows she'd taken as the soldier, her attacker, turned on Jeanne.

Jeanne had been backed into a corner of the cell. Both remaining soldiers ringed her, entrapping her and laughing at her weakness.

"Another crazy woman," Yolande's attacker said to the friar.

The friar didn't answer.

Sabine had snuck in behind. From the floor, Yolande grinned through the pain as Sabine opened a ragged smile in the friar's throat then turned the still wet tip of her blade in a quick arc, plunging it deep into Yolande's attacker's temple.

Only Jeanne's attacker remained, still closing in with wicked intent. Jeanne collapsed to one knee but held her dagger in front of her with the determination of a true knight. Of a sister.

Yolande's arm lay useless at her side, but she pulled herself up as the remaining soldier raised his sword for a crushing blow. She didn't know if God watched every creature closely as the Franciscans often said or if He only had time for watching the mechanizations of men, but she called to Him anyway in her moment of pain and need. Somehow, she found the power to push herself up and leap on the final guard's back.

The Way of Water: Jeanne's Resurrection

She grabbed his chin and throat and yanked as his arm's arc began to fall toward Jeanne's upturned face. She pulled him off balance, locking her embrace into a strangling hold as he fell back onto her. Yolande cried out as her injured shoulder caught fire with new, ripping pain, but she bit her lip and pulled the hold tighter, grunting with the effort.

Jeanne watched with astonished eyes as the delicate queen she'd revered strangled a man to death. Once the struggling ceased and the men were still, Yolande got up, straightened her robe, and with her good arm offered a hand up to Jeanne. The girl didn't trust her after watching a queen fight like a seasoned soldier. It wasn't done. Yolande knew it was hard to understand.

"You are frightened of what we've done here, dear girl, and I don't blame you. But their work was the work of men, not God." Yolande tied her arm tight with a sling torn from the dirty bedding, then led Jeanne out of the blood-soaked cell with Sabine flanking them, a stolen sword drawn and ready for a fight. There was no time to strip off the bloody garments or to wash gore from their hands. They had to flee before the other soldiers at the abbey came to switch the watch. Time was short if they wanted cover their escape. "Let us help you. Didn't Jesus say, 'Come to me, all of you who are weary and carry heavy burdens, and I will give you rest? Let us live his words, sister."

The girl nodded, linking with Yolande's good arm as the three made their way out of the dormitory, into the coach. Sabine tucked them in and pulled a bundle from the top of the coach. She slung the long sack over her shoulder, then trotted back into the building. Jeanne had seen dead soldiers wrapped for burial before, Yolande knew. The shape shouldn't have been a surprise other than it being small and thin. Shaped like a girl.

"That long dead girl will burn with those soldiers tonight. A diversion, Jeanne. They will think you paid your debt to their false court, at least for a while. It will give us enough time to escape."

Orange tongues of flame licked out of the windows, screaming and cracking with the power of the bright fire Sabine had set. They'd only find bones and melted metal in the morning.

Sabine climbed back up on the coach, whipping the horses into a trot away from the chaos she'd left. Between the distraction of the abbey on fire and Sabine's gruff manner and disguise, they disappeared through the city gates heading north into the quiet dark.

Year of our Lord 1431. May 24

Most holy Father, Eugene IV,

Though I am aware of your present struggles to tame the pretenders and heretics close to Rome's heart, I'm afraid I must add to the weight of your burden as the shepherd of this deranged world.

Saint-Ouen's dormitory burned this last eve, taking with it the souls of five Englishmen guards, a holy friar, and the girl known as Jeanne the Maid. They burned together in her cell as if the adversary himself opened a door to hell. Ashes and bones are all that remained.

Papa, this war is near done and the girl can stoke no more rebellions. Perhaps her death, not in the hands of the church or man, is best. Perhaps now, your peace may be realized as I endeavor to raise up the true king of France, Henry VI.

Your loyal servant,
Bishop Pierre Cauchon

Year of our Lord 1431, May 30

My Lords of the true kind,

This missive must be destroyed once you've digested the horror within. Should the news scratched on this parchment find responsive ears, the scales may tip in favor of the pretender king.

Here's the meat of this stew.

For all the trust you put in God, his servant has failed to end the Maid. Before we were able to transfer her from the Inquisitor court to Rouen's court for execution, agents unknown made off with her using an elaborate and deadly fire to cover their

The Way of Water: Jeanne's Resurrection

ruse. It took days of digging through the ash of her prison to find the proof of her escape. The burned corpse of a girl we believed to be the maid was determined to have been long dead.

This treachery cost the lives of six soldiers and one of our friars at St.-Ouen Abbey.

To quell possible questions, we burned a mute peasant girl we dressed in boys clothes in her place and tossed the ashes into the Seine and read public condemnation of the Maid written by scholars from the University of Paris to the assembled crowd. A neat solution for a nasty problem. But even with the visiting soldiers of Normandy and a long tradition of support for the English king, the local people mourned her death. Shouts of 'Jeanne' and 'La Pucelle' filled the sodden morning air along the stinking Seine.

I fear that we have not heard the last of Jeanne and her infernal voices. I charge you, in the name of God and his holiness the Pope, catch the heretic and send her to her just punishment at the foot of God before she sows more strife among the laity, so impressionable. She must be found and silenced.

Bishop Pierre Cauchon

Chapter 2

In the Beguinage estate outside of Brussels morning light brightened the white-washed cell and filled the window glass with rose-filtered light. Jeanne was tucked up into a bed, layered with woolen blankets, and snoring with a contentment Yolande understood.

How close the girl had come to her end at only nineteen.

"Yolande, the other sisters want a word. I can watch over the maid." Sabine wore her favored soft britches and simple woolen tunic that fell higher than most, but within the Beguinage's walls, she could live in her own comfort.

"Bring her when she wakes."

Sabine nodded as she took the stool. She took a small book from the folds of her tunic and began to read, one of the great joys of the sisterhood.

Yolande pulled the train of her dress up over her immobilized arm with a wince and made her way down the hall toward the grand library that lay beneath the chapel doing her best to hide the blows she'd taken in her adventures. Hidden from the uninitiated, the entrance was at the back of a wardrobe, a sliding door with a knothole release led to a long set of stairs, and then another false stone door on an igneous pivot. With a push on the right stone, the wall swung open lightly under her fingertips.

An encased flame in a channel winding along the wall's bottom edge of the spiral stairwell's narrow side gave off enough illumination to find the steps without fail. Twelve circles round and Yolande stepped into the cavernous great room at the center of a web of stone catacomb passageways completely lined with full bookshelves as far as the flickering overhead chandelier light reached. Yolande breathed in the smell of burning oil sweetened with fragrant herbs that reminded her of growing up here, learning languages and fighting, engineering and maths. To her the subtle bite of the cleansing smoke felt like coming home. In the central stone chamber, walls that weren't filled with shelves for tools and materials were painted white and hung with bright maps of the whole known world. Around the room, women sat at tables tinkering with objects and clockworks, painting on velum sheets, carving and sculpting lovely likenesses of all God's creatures, and discussing or debating ideas in small, animated groups—doing the things they'd chosen to do to enrich themselves.

"Welcome home, Yolande!" One of the nearest sisters threw down her work and ran over, giggling like a girl though she was clearly in her middle years.

"Ah, Suzane! How goes your writing, my friend?"

The lady smiled and pulled Yolande to her spot at the table. "Well, and how goes politics for you?"

"I've lived to see France uniting under a good French king. The people know who they are. It is what I hoped for when I left the Beguinages for my marriage."

The other sisters around them seemed to grow quiet, so Yolande put her hand in Suzane's and focused in on the head table. The post of Mother rotated between the sisters and was purely a role of

The Way of Water: Jeanne's Resurrection

management among equals, this time being Madeline's rotation. Beside her sat Lucina, the fastest scribe among them.

"Sisters, this council is called to discuss our newest recruit arrived with Sisters Yolande and Sabine from Rouen." Madeline's voice bounced around the room reaching all the sisters.

The other sisters applauded having already heard the details of their escape and Sabine's neat clean-up work at the abbey. It wasn't the first time a bit of subterfuge had been used to rescue a promising woman and it certainly wouldn't be the last, but few of the women they had ever liberated were as notorious as Jeanne.

"There are many questions we must answer in the coming days. Can we shelter Jeanne here, so close to the English forces? Will she wish to learn from us or return to the fray? These things are questions for Jeanne when she can tell us her wishes."

"If they find her here, we too will be put to the question."

Another sister who Yolande knew had been sore abused by the men of the English, shouted back, "Let them come. I'd be burned to ash before I let another maid suffer at the rough hands of the occupiers."

Yolande knew the pressure of Jeanne's presence left the sisters in a terrible position. This act put their tenuous safety and jealously guarded autonomy at risk all for one very volatile girl. A stand against the Church and offices of man in support of Jeanne put the whole web of sisters spread across Christendom in jeopardy of forced dissolution, or worse at the hands of the Inquisition, should their quiet work against tyranny be discovered.

"We Beguine sisters don't fear men clashing their swords against the stone of our resolve," Sabine's deep voice rasped out over the mutterings of the gathered sisters. "Marguerite Porete died for our path. What are we if we turn away one like Jeanne? We might as well put on the wimples and take orders as nuns beneath the thumbs of greedy abbots and behind walled convents away from the good we could do for the world. It isn't what we are, sisters!"

Sisters devolved into whispers as all looked back at the entrance Yolande had used herself moments before. There stood Sabine and at her side Jeanne, thin and pale, but her wide brown eyes were full of the strange wonder every woman's held when she first found the hidden sisterhood of the Beguines.

Yolande had been a Beguine sister her whole life, as had her mother, but she understood how any girl, noble or not, might be overwhelmed.

"Come in, Jeanne." Yolande waved her in and patted the table beside her. Suzane jumped up to get her a seat, not because she had to, but because she was, like all the sisters, always glad to invite a new sister in.

Sabine nudged the girl and murmured something, then strode off to her seat at the other side of the room. Jeanne made her way over with efficient steps. The movements of a strategist. Not fearful. Her gaze didn't dart about with fear, though she did sweep the room, taking in each entry point and every sister.

She folded into the chair Suzane had arranged between hers and Yolande.

"They are talking about me," Jeanne said. "About…my life?"

"That's right," Suzane said. "You're an amazing woman, Jeanne. A woman worth saving from a wrathful world."

Yolande reached over and squeezed Jeanne's hand, then stood. "Sisters, now that Jeanne is awake, would you allow Suzane and me to teach her our ways? Give us a few days to show her the life of a Beguine Sister. Once she understands Marguerite and the Way of Water—"

"Then she can decide things for herself, eh?" Madeline turned to the others, allowing for debate. There was none. "Seems that the sisters agree to this path. Let's call this council closed for now. Sisters, please lend aid where you can as Jeanne learns our traditions."

The others sat silently, though as one they tapped their acceptance three times on the tabletop.

"Settled then. We will meet again in seven days. Send word to the sisters in Paris, Amsterdam, Zurich, and the forest sisters of the East. By now, the deception in Rouen has been uncovered. Lay distractions for the Inquisition. Sow sightings in the south to lead them away."

The challenge seemed to energize the sisters. In small groups, they began their work, writing falsities to mislead any pursuers. Jeanne would be safe so close to the site of her trial and condemnation, at least for a while. Yolande sighed with relief. The sisters' courage always bolstered her own. She hoped the same for Jeanne.

The Way of Water: Jeanne's Resurrection

"Come, Jeanne, I think you should meet our Marguerite." Together, Yolande and Suzane led her away from the great room down a catacomb of books, lit from above by recessed flames fed by gas from the ground that lit as the three walked across the alternating metal tile panels set in the floor, a strange system mechanically minded sisters had explained to Yolande a time or two. She didn't have a head for such things. It wasn't her gift. Like Jeanne, she had gifts meant to move men and armies.

She watched the girl as she marched between, taking in every sight, including more books than she'd likely seen in her whole life. Soon she'd know that this place housed twenty more halls of books like these, hand-copied and preserved, stolen from the best castles and monasteries in all of Europe. Even into the Saracen kingdoms in the East.

The three entered a darkened chapel tucked away between bookcases. Suzane pressed a switch to light an overhead lantern that cast its glow on a simple desk with writing implements and blotters, chair pulled away slightly as if the owner would return in a moment. Next to that desk, a marble statue of a lovely, plain-dressed woman raised her face toward heaven. Above her, etched into a delicate wooden archway were simple French words deepened by the play of light across the cavities of each carved letter.

"What does it say," Jeanne asked.

"It says, 'A soul annihilated in the love of the Creator could, and should, grant to nature all that it desires without reprehension.' Our dear martyred sister Marguerite Porete burned nearly a hundred years ago for ideas like this one. Her ideas, you understand?"

"What does it mean?" Jeanne asked, brows furrowing.

Suzane moved forward into the chapel and touched the hand of Marguerite. "She was a mystic burned at the stake for believing that a relationship with God is more important than the institutional rules of the Church. She believed a soul united with God is united with divine purpose that like a gentle stream that cuts through forests and stone banks alike makes the world over in the image of the divine, that the soul becomes divine in such work. The Church's restrictions and moral gatekeepers can't stop the flow of God's grace to all things that seek redemption through mystical annihilation, the way a boulder is worn away into shining sand."

Jeanne turned to Yolande, grabbing her arm. "That's blasphemy."

Yolande nodded. "A church that can be bought and sold, a church so split there were three popes, Jeanne. You were at the whim of the Bishop of Reims, an English puppet. The papacy is too much business for someone like Marguerite or you. Spiritual awakening and the love of God is pushed aside in the tangle of man's political posturing."

Suzane retrieved a book from the shelf bound in plain leather with pages thumbed to softness. Yolande knew the tome and was glad that Jeanne's would begin her education with Marguerite's *The Mirror of Simple Souls*. Reading the gentle wisdom in it had opened Yolande's mind to the potential of a new kind of world. One where everyone truly was equal before God and country. One that she and the sisters worked to achieve even though the ideas had cost Marguerite her life a hundred years before.

"Some ideas are so true that corruption seeks to bury them. Your ideas and your voices, for example. A united France without an absent English king. Your calling was fulfilled, Mademoiselle, and the men in power deemed your usefulness over. Do you not think that the Pope himself wasn't aware of your works and your ultimate martyrdom? He too would profit from raising you as a saint. And a dead saint is so much more useful than a live pain in the arse."

Yolande covered her laugh with an artful hand. Suzane was a simple soul, full of sharp words of truth for any who'd hear. Jeanne surely would appreciate that lack of guile once she understood it.

But the humor didn't strike Jeanne the same. She seemed to stagger under the weight of the Pope's betrayal. The poor child still believed in the goodness of Rome. Of course she did. She'd come to think that the English were the only thing to fear. She hugged Marguerite's book to her chest, no longer the strong maiden, servant to angels of God, but a betrayed girl suddenly finding that the world didn't love her as she'd assumed for so long.

"Jeanne, your future is yours. There are so many things you can do with that fire in your heart. Things that we Beguines can help with. We are in every royal court and every church in Christendom. We have ears that hear the heartless orders of men with no care for their souls. Read

The Way of Water: Jeanne's Resurrection

her book. Pray and reflect on your future in this foul world. If we can help, we will. If you want, you can join our order."

Jeanne held the book in her hand tightly, as if it would get away.

"I can't read."

Suzane said, "I'll teach you."

"I'd like that," Jeanne said and looked up at the desk once more. As simple as it was, she might have feared the yearning in her heart to learn and know things, to be able to read things herself. That it might lead to sin. Jeanne would have to find a way to accept her freedom if she could. Yolande pulled Jeanne away and out of the room, showing her the stairs that Suzane would use to lead her back to the quiet of her cell.

"Rest well, Maid. God's work through you may not be done. Jeanne's life, your life, is finally, your own to live."

Year of our Lord 1434

Jesus, Mary.

Hussites and rebels of Bohemia, I write you a second time with a contrite heart. Brothers in blood and faith, I've long preached against your desecration of our beloved sacraments, our holy statues and churches, and those who deliver salvation to Christians. Wrongly, I've been led to judge the teachings of your leader Jan Huss. Wrongly, I've believed in the rightness of the agents of the church against the truth I knew in my own heart.

Yes, la Pucelle has survived the stake and the wrong interpretations of the English-influenced churches of France. But la Pucelle's belief in the purity of the church has not survived.

The call of God's justice echoed louder than the bloodthirsty cries of witch and heretic of Rouen's traitorous churchmen. Their foul acts against my life weren't all I experienced. They sold salvation and aligned with kings, not based on God's will, but on money and power. It taught me much.

Since my escape, my heart has softened to your cause, followers of Huss. The study of scripture with my own eyes and heart has made me over. I do not agree with your destruction of cathedrals or monuments, all gifts to God. Your violence is misapplied. Leave off the destruction of saints' bones and baptismal fonts. Join me in remaking the church in the image of our great spiritual teachers, truth seekers of God. Jan and his communion for all, bread and wine, body and blood. Marguerite with her personal experience of God's love. These are scriptures brought to the people instead of the people brought to the heel of whichever king pays best.

When I can, I will find you in Prague. Bring your hearts and devotions. Swords will come later. I will send word.

We can, we will change Christendom.

La Pucelle
Servant of God

Chapter Three

During the hard day of travel from Paris to Brussels, Yolande's mind measured all that had happened since they'd pulled Jeanne from that stinking cell in Rouen. At first, when Yolande visited the Brussels house, Jeanne had been moody, a despondent spirit struggling with the freedom she'd been granted, unsure what to do without her army and the pursuit of a united France. In the five years since, that had been achieved. Even in the absence of Jeanne's guiding hand, the people and the King used her memory as a unifying symbol to come together and win back the lost northern French so misled by the English-led soldiers.

So many of the sisters tried to befriend Jeanne but it was Sabine and Suzane who became Jeanne's saviors as she'd learned the Way of Water, Marguerite's annihilation of ego, and how to be Jeanne without being a martyr.

Five peaceful years and now, the Church knew where she was.

Five years later and they still wanted her to burn.

Yolande rode straight through, only stopping in Brussels to gather information as she could, then she wound through secret tunnels into the Beguinage's grounds.

The Way of Water: Jeanne's Resurrection

Suzane met her and took her to where Jeanne did her daily exercise in the open air.

"Her training is beyond even my level," Sabine said as Yolande watched Jeanne practice close-quarter short sword combat movements in the courtyard between the Beguinages' dormitory halls. Ten other sisters practiced sword play, combat holds, and defensive throws in the wide green space, though none seemed to dance through the exercise the way Jeanne did. "She is a gifted fighter. If she was a man—"

"She'd be a king or a lord leading an army," Yolande finished, knowing the talent when she saw it. "She still could be. Please, Suzane, get the others out of harm's way, give the alert to lock down against intruders, and meet us upstairs in the attic. We still have a few minutes."

"Just you then?" Suzane asked.

"That's what the Mothers think is best."

Suzane hurried off, leaving Yolande to her mission.

Jeanne turned into a parry and smiled when she caught sight of Yolande. She put her practice blade away in a storage cavity in the nearest bench because like so many of the tools of pursuits and callings shared by the sisters a sword in a woman's hands wasn't acceptable to those outside of the Beguine sisterhood.

"My lady—" Jeanne started to bow.

"I've told you, call me Sister or Yolande. There is no better or no worse before God." Yolande embraced Jeanne, enjoying the breathless exhilaration finally back in Jeanne's voice.

"As Marguerite wrote," Jeanne said with a sharp nod, leaning back and standing straight, sword arm relaxed but always ready. A soldier's stance. Then she glanced around, a sweet innocence creeping through the mask of stern reserve, almost like she was afraid of being caught. "I'm changed by this place, Sister. The voices in my head and the warmth of God's hand in my life left me in the jail cell. Here…I still don't hear them, but I feel my feet on the path I'm meant for."

"Walk with me, Jeanne, and tell me how you like the sisterhood. You've become quite the scholar, I hear. Reading so fast the librarians struggle to keep up." Yolande drew Jeanne inside where her surprise waited, coming ever closer to steal the quiet life Jeanne had made for herself.

"I scratch out my letters, too, though never as perfect as Suzane or as fast as Sister Lucina. Reading the scripture for myself, saying the words that Marguerite left, Wycliffe and Huss and the others... I am changed."

Yolande knew it. There's a freedom in not being bound to the Church's stifling traditions. Lifting the right words in one's mind was intoxicating, especially for the faithful like Jeanne. But in the world outside the walls of the Brussels house they still hunted for Jeanne in the manors and villages of France. Her family had fled to the south under Yolande's protection, their lands confiscated, and holdings burned under orders from Pope Eugene himself.

"Jeanne, you've made yourself a target again with your letters to the Hussites," Yolande said drawing Jeanne up the stairs into the tallest eaves of the motherhouse. The window peeked out to where fallow fields backed up into forest. Yolande pointed out to the edge of the parkland that lay between the Beguinage and the city. "Do you see the troops hidden there?"

The girl's gaze hardened as she stared out into the blinding afternoon's light at the pools of dark seething with movement between the trees.

"They've pinned you here. I only found out because my dolt of a son-in-law let it slip in front of a courtier in my employ. He and the damned Bishop you faced in Rouen want to finish what they started. The troops think you a pretender."

Jeanne gritted her teeth in anger for a moment, then nearly shouted. "Let them see me. If they see me, they'll know me."

Yolande knew this would be the first reaction. Though she'd trained and grown, Jeanne still had the heart of a revolutionary.

"They'll burn this house to the ground if they find you here."

Horror dawned on Jeanne's features.

"They can't!" She squeezed her eyes shut and pressed the heels of her palms against them. "They can't take this from my sisters. What about the books and all the things we've done here."

It was home to Jeanne. How Yolande wished she could just leave her here to her peace.

"They will. They'll find you and when they do, they'll not leave a stone standing upon another stone."

The Way of Water: Jeanne's Resurrection

Jeanne dropped her fisted hands to her side. "I'll run through the tunnels into town. I'll lead them away, let them catch me in Brussels, and then the sisters will be safe."

"No. You're as much a sister as any. We all want to survive to help others. You are worth saving." She grabbed Jeanne's fisted hands, brought them to her lips, and pressed them there in a gesture of sisterhood. "You're worthy."

"You're so worthy," Suzane said from behind them, deeper in the attic.

Tears broke from the Maid's eyes and she nodded. "I want to do what's right. I'll break like water on this stone. Please, help me escape so my sisters will be safe."

A pounding and shuffling rose through the floor as metal clad men forced entry into the motherhouse. Yolande hoped the sisters had been able to hide all the things that would get them killed if they were found.

"Hurry! We'll use a different route." Yolande tugged Jeanne toward Suzane who led them through the attic rooms to a hidden door built into a stone-fronted chimney. She beaconed them to dark stairs that led down to a tunnel. She wrapped Jeanne in a hooded cloak as Yolande donned the same. After a hug for Jeanne and a whispered prayer, Suzane left them to hurry down the long—and long-deserted—tunnel.

Plain coffins lay in chiseled cubbies. Dry white bones and skulls pressed into the walls with patterns that looked like mosaics of any great cathedral. As they ran, Yolande hummed hymns between ragged breaths to fortify herself. Eventually, as they rounded the catacomb tunnel that paced the Seine, Jeanne joined in, her singing stronger and full of steady, youthful breath. Her voice filled the tunnel with a sweetness that lifted them above the fear and the panting sweat of escape.

It wasn't the first time Yolande heard Jeanne sing, but this time it filled her with the strength to run past the exhaustion creeping into her muscles. Though the sisters would slow the combined soldiers sent to extract Jeanne, they couldn't hold them forever.

"Light ahead," Jeanne said.

Dim as it was, Yolande knew the tunnel was ending, dumping them in a sewage runoff leading into the Seine. If they could get to the river and run downstream, Yolande had a boat waiting for them. They were so close.

"Halt!" The dim light of the sewer tunnel clotted up with deeper shadows, clinking and thick as a risen wall.

"At least five," Jeanne whispered, skidding to a stop. "I didn't bring a sword."

Their desperate exit had left them nearly defenseless.

"I have my blade," Yolande pulled the thin misericore from a holster hidden in her left sleeve. "But against five?"

Jeanne tensed up, soldier stance, as if she held a lance and shield and could defend them with her own bare hands.

"Sister, let's grant nature all it desires, eh?" Yolande whispered, hiding her blade in her sleeve.

"The way of the water," Jeanne said with a sharp nod.

As the men made their clattering way down the cobbled path toward them, the sisters adopted a softer posture, a shaking and weak visage.

Water changes form.

When the soldiers set upon them, Yolande pretended to faint, going limp so that two had to catch her. She made her body heavy and wide so that they couldn't just throw her over a shoulder.

Jeanne began to weep in false hysterics as the others grabbed her shoulders and hands, dragging her back toward the entrance. It took all three to drag her as she struggled and sagged against them, making every step a fight.

Water creates resistance.

One of Yolande's hands stripped the knight near her head of his scabbard and sword as he struggled with her. She dropped the sword into her other hand. With a whipping motion, she brought the sword's pointed hilt up in a punch that crushed the soldier's cheekbone to splinters.

In the tumult, Yolande fell in a pile of limbs and wove them expertly through her remaining soldier's fumbling legs, bringing him down face first with a clattering thump. As he fell, she tossed the sword toward Jeanne and her stunned captors.

Even as she used her dagger to dispatch the two fumbling men at her feet, Yolande couldn't help but steal glances at Jeanne as she overcame her three attackers. With a sword in her hand, Jeanne was a poet. And with the way of water training, she'd become a dancer as well. How she

The Way of Water: Jeanne's Resurrection

spun like a starling in a sunbeam. Dipping, cutting, striking with her elbow then knee, flipping above clumsy attacks, catching the men at the joins in their armor.

Water overwhelms.

Once the men were down, Jeanne stripped them of their gear, dressing herself and Yolande in their grieves, tunics, and mail, then tucking Yolande's braid up into the helmet. This disguise would serve them as long as they hurried.

Charging into the stinking slurry of city runoff, Jeanne led the way, following the downslope. A natural leader full of the strength of her youth. She was no spy in waiting. She'd never serve as Yolande had, a political queen running the movements of a nation through silent manipulations. Jeanne wasn't meant to contemplate, read, and copy like Suzane had done her life through.

Suzane. Yolande's heart panged at the thought of her. Some of the sisters had to be left in the motherhouse and would be tortured by the soldiers and Inquisitors to find Jeanne. Suzane had volunteered as many of the others fled to the underground to wait for the soldiers to leave. It might well mean her death. The others would mourn and rebuild no matter what damnable actions the soldiers enacted on the motherhouse, but how she hoped Suzane would be there to help.

Yolande said a little prayer as Jeanne led her out of the sewer and into the park at the north gate where the wall sat atop the sewer. They were out of the wall and as far from the motherhouse as they could be. There were no soldiers in their view, but they couldn't see the wall behind them.

"Should we run for it?"

Jeanne shook her head. "I've made my way in life by being sure and steady. People respect it. Even Marguerite said, 'she that walks in the way of illumination, that she might be taught the divine work of God.' So, let's walk in the cool path of illumination." Jeanne marched out with the precision of a soldier on patrol.

Yolande fell in step behind, straightening her back and walking with the same sharp staccato as Jeanne. She longed to look at the wall, to see if they were being watched by their hunters. She wished to see if there was a plume of smoke rising from the spot where the motherhouse she loved might be burning.

She couldn't.

Jeanne's life depended on the sisters' protection and Yolande's connections.

The wide green field stretched out before them in a long swath. The shadow of the wall fell across the wildflowers framing the path they marched on. Yolande shook inside the heavy chainmail, her body still thrumming from the excitement and blows of the fight. This exposed flight with her back to the wall that could be full of archers ready to rain down death wasn't her normal role in the Beguines' net of work, but Jeanne's measured steps steeled her against the fear twisting in her belly.

Jeanne was a natural leader with a purpose-filled heart that the world needed, no matter what she decided her role would be. She deserved to be more than a martyr trotted out by powerful men. She'd earned her path to salvation. Yolande and the sisters would deliver her to it.

They marched in the bright sun, the sounds of screams coming closer behind them, but they didn't pause. When the first arrows whistled through the sky, they ran.

Fire erupted in Yolande's shoulder, knocking her to the ground feet from the tree line. The arrows fell in a sputtering rain around her, outlining her. Her arm screamed and stomach turned into her throat as she struggled to her feet. Yolande of Aragon couldn't be caught aiding Jeanne's escape. A powerful queen in a network of women who operated independently and outside of the Church? She struggled to her feet and stumbled after Jeanne who was miraculously untouched by the long arrows. The girl didn't know Yolande was hit so she was in the trees, dodging between them as Yolande stumbled on, taking another of the bolts right through her back.

Her breath came out as wet, ragged gasps as she fell forward into the nearest tree, finally out of the field.

"Je...Jeanne!" She cried.

The girl heard and turned, face crumpling when she saw Yolande slipping down the tree trunk. She ran back, kneeling next to Yolande to

The Way of Water: Jeanne's Resurrection

check her wounds. From where she lay, Yolande saw the portcullis rising with a squad of men behind it ready to give chase.

"They are coming, my girl," Yolande mumbled, blood from her lungs bubbling hot on her lips. "Run to the river below the woods. Find the agent waiting with a boat…greet her with the words 'annihilation of the spirit' so…so she knows you. This code… opens the door of every motherhouse. Now, go Jeanne." The words hurt but she had to get them out.

"Can you walk?" Jeanne reached for her, tugging her up even as the soldiers clattered across the bridge and into the field just minutes from their position in the trees. The slight jostle of Jeanne trying to lift her made pain lance through Yolande's body. She coughed, spraying blood on Jeanne's cheek and hair.

"Leave…me! You must escape or it's all for nothing! God carry you and sisters protect you, Jeanne." Yolande grabbed the girl's hand and squeezed it. "Do good."

The men were getting closer when Yolande gave Jeanne a little shove.

The girl nodded and ran off in the cover of the forest for the peasant craft waiting with a disguised German sister at the helm. She'd run to the sisters who'd pass her from house to house and hand to hand, keeping her safe for the great things she'd do.

Yolande used her precious few seconds to pull the final gift she could give to her sisters and Jeanne from the purse around her throat. If she allowed the men to carry her body back to the English, the French, or the Church, she'd be recognized and they'd know the Beguines for what they were. They'd see how far the net of the sisters' influence was cast. She couldn't allow that.

Thinking back as she flicked the stopper out of the bottle and tipped the special poison out over her face, she remembered learning the teachings of Marguerite as a great joy. The most wonderful kindness of her life had been to learn of her own soul's destiny. And learning how to seek it, the way of water and the method of fire had given her the strength to do so many wonderful things. Things most women couldn't even afford to dream of.

The soldiers grabbed her hands, tugging her up just as the fire poison took root in her flesh, igniting in a bright, roaring explosion fed by the fuels within her, the accelerant she'd coated herself with and eaten for the last few nights. The explosion left only a moment for her to thank the creator for a life of meaning before she and the soldiers were gone.

Of Simple Souls, the Way of Water, and the Path of Fire
A Chronicle of Pope Jeanne's Ascent

Recorded by Sabine of Brussels, Beguine Sister

From simple peasant with God's message upon her tongue to warrior and prophet, Her Holiness Pope Jeanne I, followed the path of divine inspiration. Much has been written of her time with the King of France, her escape from the corruptions of the schismatic church leaders and their Inquisition, and her diplomatic work with the reforming brother Hussites and other seekers of a purer Church with a kind, servant's heart. With the material and military help of the Hussites and other groups who'd been victim of the Church in the past, Jeanne's election to the reformed Papacy in 1440 led to the redirection of the church as an institution walking in the footsteps of Christ.

She adopted the reforms of Wycliffe, allowing the scripture to be written and read in the languages of the people, and directed priests to be the teachers of language and writing as part of their pursuit as shepherd of God. She embraced the Hussite reform movement giving the sacraments, both blood and body, to all, poor and rich, laity and clergy. With the help of the united Germanic princes, she introduced reforms to the collection of tithes and eliminated the corrupt practice of selling salvation through indulgences.

She revealed the selling of orders and church station to be a sin.

She outlawed indulgences,

She distributed church lands in fair, parcels to freed peasants across Christendom.

And honoring the teachings and importance of the many lady saints, prophets, and sisters both of the cloth and the Beguines, she recognized that God created women with a longing to serve that is equal to men of the cloth, opening the taking of orders and ordination to any with the calling from God be they man or woman.

The Way of Water: Jeanne's Resurrection

As the kingdoms of Christendom ventured out into God's wider creation, her Holiness has written and preached extensively on the wisdom of those other peoples of the world and of how God comes to all people with the mystery and power that is God's nature, knowing that God's message to others is love and that love binds us across the differing perceptions of God's ineffable nature. To persecute them for their understanding of the loving creator goes against the simple exhortations that Christ gave in the Beatitudes, to all creatures and peoples of creation.

And finally, Pope Jeanne declared the burning of heretics, witches, and the formerly persecuted peoples outside of Christendom a mortal sin.

There have been threats and revolts from reactionary fundamentalists, but Pope Jeanne's support in Christendom has kept her safe and above the fray. Perhaps other Popes might have built palaces or commissioned great art for private chapels. Maybe another would have mined the newfound peoples and places for wealth to improve Christendom, leaving those others poor, angry, and confused about the nature of God's unending love.

These are not the ways of mirroring the Christ's simple soul.

As St. Marguerite taught, one must cut loose the baggage of the world and desires before being immersed in love and fit for heaven. It is the way of water and fire that Christ gave to Marguerite so long ago and the way taught to her holiness, Pope Jeanne when she bowed the knee in Orleans.

Blessed be the light and truth,
Sister Sabine
Acolyte of St. Marguerite, St. Suzane, and St. Yolande
Servant of Her Holiness Pope Jeanne, la Pucelle

Tellers of the Time-Twisting Tales

The author of twenty-five novels and more than ninety short stories, **Rigel Ailur** writes in almost every genre, but predominantly science fiction and fantasy. Her novels include the *Vagabonds' Adventures* action thrillers, the *Sorcery & Steel* fantasy series (with Laura Ware), the science fiction series *Tales of Mimion*, and the galaxies-spanning *A Little Piece of Home*. Her short stories appear in the long-running *Brave New Girls* anthology series and several other anthologies including the IAMTW's *Turning the Tied* and *Double Trouble: An Anthology of Two-Fisted Team-Ups*. She writes for adults, teens and middle grade. In nonfiction, she contributes television reviews to the *Outside In* series and to the *SciFi Bulletin* online. Most importantly, she dotes on her astronomically adorable feline kids. For more information visit BluetrixBooks.com.

Lorraine J. Anderson, bookkeeper by day and a creative person by night, only confuses the two on rare occasions. Her work has been in a number of anthologies, and her fiction ranges from pure fantasy to murder mystery. She lives in Michigan with three very naughty cats who redeem themselves with scritches and cuddles. Find her at lorrainejanderson.com, where you can find links to her fiction and one of her hobbies, a YouTube channel, which includes her singing in public in front of actual audiences.

Rasana Atreya, a former electrical engineer, crafts women's fiction rooted in the vibrant culture of India, challenging the notion that intellect and romance are mutually exclusive. Her narratives, woven with the threads of resilience and self-discovery, traverse the complex lives of women, and occasionally, men. Her works include *Tell A Thousand Lies*, shortlisted for the 2012 Tibor Jones South Asia Prize, and *Daughters Inherit Silence*, a finalist in the California Adult Fiction category of the 2023 Indie Author Project. Her achievements are acknowledged in the scholarly publication *Emerging South Asian Women Writers* by the University of New Mexico.

Author and screenwriter **Diana Dru Botsford** wrote the critically acclaimed *Stargate SG-1* novels *Four Dragons* and *The Drift* in addition to the Scribe Nominee short story "Perceptions". Her most recent short story contribution was "Everything and Nothing" for the 2023 IAMTW anthology, *Double Trouble*. She co-wrote the episode "Rascals" for *Star Trek: The Next Generation*. She created, wrote, and produced the multiple award-winning time travel web series, *Epilogue*. Her television and film production credits range from cult-favorite animated series such as *Spiral Zone* and *Heathcliff* and the feature film *Pound Puppies & The Legend of Big Paw* to CBS series *Harts of the West* and *Nightgames*. Her work in Visual FX includes films such as *Nightmare on Elm Street VI*, *Dusk 'Til Dawn*, and *Terminator 2*. She has also written and directed for the stage, her works folding in ASL performers as main characters for new interpretations of family-orientated stories such as *Alice in Wonderland* and *Stuart Little*.

Deborah Smith Daughetee has spent most of her career writing and producing such television shows as *Murder, She Wrote*; *Dr. Quinn, Medicine Woman*; and *Touched by an Angel*. She has published short stories in magazines and anthologies. In addition, she has also written audio dramas set in the world of the 60s classic television show *Dark Shadows*, including her Scribe award nominated, "The Lost Girl". She is the CEO of Kymera Press, a comic book publishing company that supports women in comics. She writes the comic series *Gates of Midnight*, which was the winner of the 2019 Irwin Award, and publishes the Bram Stoker Award-Winning *Mary Shelley Presents Tales of the Supernatural*.

Dana Fredsti is a former B-movie actress with a background in theatrical combat (a skill she utilized in *Army of Darkness* as a sword-fighting Deadite and fight captain). Through 15 plus years of volunteering at EFBC/FCC (Exotic Feline Breeding Facility/Feline Conservation Center). She's been kissed by tigers and had her thumb sucked by an ocelot with nursing issues. She's addicted to bad movies and any book or film, good or bad, which include zombies. She's the author of the cozy noir mystery *Murder for Hire: The Peruvian Pigeon*; the *Ashley Parker* series (touted as *Buffy* meets *The Walking Dead*); the dark fantasy series *Spawn of Lilith*; and co-author of the science fiction adventure trilogy *Time Shards*, an exciting time travel/post-apocalyptic mashup co-written with her husband and fellow author David Fitzgerald. They also co-wrote "Maid of Steel," a dark fantasy story appearing in the Sword & Sorcery issue of *Weird Tales*, and they are currently collaborating on *Tarau: The Fall*, a grimdark fantasy novel, for Weird Tales Presents/Blackstone Publishing. She has also written short stories for anthologies including *Weird Tales: 100 Years of Weird*, *Joe Ledger: Unstoppable*, *Joe Ledger: Unbreakable*, *Mondo Zombie*, and *Hard-Boiled Horror*, as well as several optioned screenplays. She was the co-writer/associate producer on *Urban Rescuers*, a documentary on feral cats that won Best Documentary at the 2003 Valley Film Festival in Los Angeles. She lives with her husband, their dog Pogeen, and a horde of cats in Eureka, California.

Carrie Harris is the author of over thirty-five novels, games, and comics. Her catalog includes original works such as *Bad Taste In Boys* and *Elder God Dance Squad* as well as licensed books for franchises including *Marvel*, *Warhammer 40k*, *Arkham Horror*, and the *World of Darkness*. She is a three-time Scribe award finalist, a former coordinator of WriteOnCon, and a writing instructor for ELVTR. She lives in New York with her husband, teenagers, and a very anxious dog named Slartibartfast.

Rosemary Jones reads a story or two every day. To never be without reading material, she lives with 3000+ books in all genres. A significant number of early 20th century fiction and poetry includes such early advocates for the vote as Jean Webster (just check the young ladies' comments in *Daddy-Long-Legs* and *Dear Enemy*) and Alice Duer Miller (read her poem "Why We Oppose Votes for Men" for a giggle and a growl). She also collects Nellie Bly memorabilia. When she isn't reading, she writes, and her short stories have appeared in numerous anthologies. She has written two novels for the *Forgotten Realms* franchise, three for

Arkham Horror, and will have a collection of stories and novella reissued for *Cobalt City's* 20th anniversary in 2024. Find her online at rosemaryjones.com.

Shabana Kayum was born in post-colonial Guyana and raised in Jersey City, New Jersey. She enjoys writing speculative and magical realist fiction and poetry, and her passion project is a collection of interrelated short stories set in a ghostly jungle in the heart of Guyana. Currently she is pursuing a Master of Liberal Arts in Creative Writing and Literature at the Harvard Extension School. She resides in the deep woods of the Pocono Mountains.

Donna J. W. Munro teaches high schoolers the slippery truths of government and history at her day job. Her students are her greatest inspiration. She lives with five cats, a fur covered husband, and an encyclopedia son. Her daughter is off saving the world. Her pieces are published in *Corvid Queen*, *Enter the Apocalypse*, *It Calls from the Forest*, *Apparition Lit*, *Pseudopod 752*, *Shakespeare Unleashed*, *Novus Monstrum*, *ParABnormal*, and many more. Check out her young adult novels, *Revelation: Poppet Cycle Book 1* and *Runaway: Poppet Cycle Book 2*, and her website for a complete list of works at donnajwmunro.net.

Marsheila (Marcy) Rockwell (Chippewa/Red River Métis) is an award-winning tie-in author and poet. Her work includes novels set in the *Marvel Universe* and in the world of *Dungeons & Dragons Online*, as well as numerous short stories, poems, and comic book scripts. She lives in the desert with her family, buried under books; you can find out more here:.marsheilarockwell.com.

Mariah Southworth writes horror, fantasy, and science fiction and hales from the northwestern United States. She deeply loves mythology and history and incorporates this into her writing. Her short stories have appeared in a wide range of anthologies, and her self-published children's book series *I Am A…* is available on Amazon.com. For more information, visit her website at mariahsouthworth.com.

Tellers of the Time-Twisting Tales

Susan Shwartz wandered for forty years in the desert of financial services marketing before returning to her first love, writing fantasy and science fiction. A five-time nominee for the Nebula, a two-time nominee for the Hugo, with nominations for the World Fantasy Award and the Edgar, she has published around thirty books, including anthologies, science fiction, historical fantasy, and *Star Trek*. She has also published about 90 short stories, novelettes and novellas and published nonfiction in *The New York Times*, *Vogue*, *The Wall Street Journal*, *The Washington Post*, and *Analog*. She holds a Ph.D. in English (medieval) from Harvard University, collects SF art, and loves the opera, the theatre, and travel. She now lives in exurban Connecticut with her partner.

Laura Ware's column "Laura's Look" appears weekly in the *Highland's News-Sun* and covers news items or ideas she can talk about for six hundred words. She recently published a collection of one hundred of her favorite columns from the past twenty-five years. She is the author of a number of short stories and several novels including *The Silent Witness*, *Seek and Ye Shall Find*, and *Death on the Air*. Her essay "Touched by an Angel" appeared in *Chicken Soup for the Soul: Random Acts of Kindness*. Laura lives in Central Florida. Check out her website and sign up for her newsletter at laurahware.com.

K. Ceres Wright received her master's degree in Writing Popular Fiction from Seton Hill University and her published cyberpunk novel, Cog, was her thesis for the program. Her short stories, poems, and articles have appeared on the *Strange Horizons* and *Amazing Stories* websites, and in the *FIYAH Magazine of Black Speculative Fiction*; *Luminescent Threads: Connections to Octavia Butler* (Locus Award winner; Hugo Award nominee); and *Sycorax's Daughters* (Bram Stoker Award nominee); among others. She is the founder and president of Diverse Writers and Artists of Speculative Fiction, an educational group for creatives.

Acknowledgements

With huge thanks and deepest appreciation to everyone who contributed. We're grateful that you helped make this anthology a reality. Thank you!

Anonymous Reader
Julie Andrews
James Aquilone
Stephanie L. Bannon
Chad Bowden
Amanda Bridgeman
Lois Athena Buhalis
Michael A. Burstein
Pat Cadigan
Christopher Paul Carey
Lis Carey
Malissa Close
Matthew Cole
Rob Cole
Alexandra Corrsin
Carol Elaine Cyr
DrLight
Lisa Eckert
Christine and Ron Edison
Mary Fan
Colleen Feeney
Iva B. Ferris
Karen Fonville
Renee Carter Hall
Kevin Halstead
Russell J. Handelman
Nova Hansen
Patrick Hay
Madeleine Holly-Rosing
Brad Jurn
Jason D. C. Kim
Bill Kohn
Lexy Kokoros

Kymera Press
LaFountain Family
Pat Laemmle
Daniel Lapikas
Matthew Lathrom
Chun Hyon Lee
Jessica Maison
Andrew Marshall
Suzanne Mattaboni
R. Hugo McIntyre
Sirrah Medeiros
Pam Menz
George W. Minor
Lee Mitchell
Stuart Moore
Gail Morse
Tao Neuendorffer
Richard Novak
Heidi B. Pilewski
PJK
Mary Jo Rabe
Sam Reid
Kim Rios
Carolyn Rowland
Paul Simpson
Judith Stevenson
Denise & Raphael Sutton
Katrina Tipton
Liz Tuckwell
Dayton Ward
Estelle Wardrip
Amanda Ware
Samaire Wynne

Bluetrix Books

www.BluetrixBooks.com

Fantasy, *Science Fiction*, ADVENTURE, Mystery, Romance, Action, *Suspense*

Made in United States
Troutdale, OR
08/05/2024